A Suitable Marriage

Muriel Bolger is an Irish journalist and award-winning travel writer. In addition to her works of fiction she has also written four books on her native city, including *Dublin – City of Literature* (O'Brien Press), which won the Travel Extra Travel Guide Book of the Year 2012.

Previously by Muriel Bolger (fiction)

A Degree of Truth
Family Business
Out of Focus
The Pink Pepper Tree
The Captain's Table
Intentions
Consequences

A Suitable Marriage

MURIEL BOLGER

HACHETTE
BOOKS
IRELAND

First published in Ireland in 2020 by
HACHETTE BOOKS IRELAND
First published in paperback in 2021

1

Cataloguing in Publication Data is available from the British Library

ISBN 9781473691506

Typeset in Garamond by Westchester Publishing Services

Printed and bound in Great Britain by
Clays Ltd, Elcograf S.p.A.

Hachette Books Ireland policy is to use papers that are natural, renewable and
recyclable products and made from wood grown in sustainable forests.
The logging and manufacturing processes are expected to conform to the
environmental regulations of the country of origin.

Hachette Books Ireland
8 Castlecourt Centre
Castleknock
Dublin 15, Ireland

A division of Hachette UK Ltd
Carmelite House, 50 Victoria Embankment, London EC4Y 0DZ

www.hachettebooksireland.ie

For my good friend and very special person,
Kathryn Farrington, who introduced me to the decadently
opulent mansions of Rhode Island several years ago.

Part I

Chapter I

'*Il neigeait, nei-ge-ait* – it's soft,' corrected Mademoiselle Corneille. '*Nei-ge-ait*, like the sound of the snow itself falling. There's nothing sharp about it. Try it again, Delia.'

'*Il neigeait*,' Delia began and the governess nodded her approval.

'*Bon. Continuez.*'

Outside it was snowing. Not anything on the scale of the blizzards that confounded Napoleon in Hugo's poem that the sisters were studying, but enough to change the landscape that had greeted them that morning. They had woken up to a strangely silent and white world. From the upstairs windows all the sharp edges had been obliterated. An alien yet strangely familiar vista of muted shapes and curious curves spread out before them.

The schoolroom was warm, if they positioned themselves between the heavy tapestry screen and the fire. When they sat too close to it, Mademoiselle warned them about getting their faces burned and ruining their complexions forever. But despite the fire blazing in the hearth, the rest of the room was arctic and the tall sash windows let in draughts that whistled and groaned when the winds blew in from the Atlantic. And they were doing that with some force this morning.

'Now it's your turn, Mona. *Continuez, s'il vous plait,*' Mademoiselle said, pulling her shawl tighter around her.

The older sister began. '*Il neigeait. L'âpre hiver fondait en avalanche. Après la plaine blanche une autre plaine blanche.*'

'*Non.* Soft, I said, soft, Mona,' Mademoiselle repeated. '*Blanche* – let it just fade off your tongue, *b-l-a-n-c-h-e*, the way Delia did it.'

'I don't see why I have to learn this.'

'Because French is the language of the court and of educated young ladies, that's why,' their tutor answered.

'I accept that, but sordid poetry about battles, and horses dying in the snow, and soldiers hiding in their dead bellies. They're hardly topics I'll be discussing at soirées and dinner parties in society drawing rooms,' Mona protested.

'You never know, sister dear. You might marry a military man and, if you do, then you'll be able to impress his generals and superiors with such gems,' Delia said, enjoying the chance to tease her sibling.

'That's easy for you to say,' Mona snapped, 'and I certainly hope that my future holds a bit more excitement than those prospects.'

'Miss Mona, should you end up being married to a general, you'll thank me for making you persevere. If you applied yourself more, you would find it a little easier. Your sister is no brighter. She just gives her studies a little more attention. I can see your mind is wandering again, so let us finish this lesson by reading through "l'Expiation" from the beginning,' Mademoiselle said. 'And remember, we'll revise the subjunctive clauses tomorrow morning.'

'Oh joy!' laughed Delia looking at her sister's pained expression. A few seconds later the lunch gong sounded and she sighed. She would rather be hacking or hunting out of doors any day than being cooped up inside. She enjoyed nothing more than being free to go riding every morning with Mona.

When he was in Ireland, their brother, Clement, often joined them. Delia envied him. He was currently serving in India with his cavalry regiment, and his letters home, infrequent as they were, made her envious. He painted images of unimaginable pageantry and colour, of exotic foods and strange customs, of animals whose names she had only read. The letters he sent to her and her sister didn't dwell on the military operations or the brutality of the Burmese conflict. Instead, they focused on the society in which he mixed when not on duty. And it certainly seemed to be glittering.

His latest correspondence had assured them that he was still alive and uninjured, but it also contained some news that had sent them into a tizzy of speculation. He announced that he'd recently become engaged – to Lady Elizabeth Stokes, whose father was a high-ranking official, an advisor to the viceroy of India.

They'd have to wait until he returned on leave in a few months to meet the young lady, whom he described as 'charming and cultured and very affable'. She would be accompanied by her mother and a distant cousin, who would chaperone Lady Elizabeth on the journey back to England.

'And she has two unmarried older brothers, both serving in India too,' their mother had informed them gleefully, when they first heard of the betrothal.

'Perhaps I could marry one of those instead of doing the season as a debutante,' Mona had said. 'I'm nervous at the thought of all those balls and parties and the beaux! What if they don't like me or take no notice of me?'

'That won't happen. You'll turn heads anywhere you go,' her mother said.

'I wouldn't worry about things like that,' Delia told her.

'Well, I do. I'm apprehensive at the thoughts of someone I don't even know yet wanting to marry me before the year is out. He might turn out to be horrible, and I mightn't even love him.'

'Oh, Mona,' her mother said. 'Marriage is about more than a romantic ideal of love. You'll see as you go through life. Love is a bonus – it's not always guaranteed in marriage.'

'But you love Papa, don't you?' Delia said.

'Indeed I do. But that doesn't solve everything. You have to work at relationships. Life isn't always easy.'

'Well, I hope you find somebody nice, Mona,' Delia told her sister. 'Somebody that I'll like too.'

'So do I,' she had replied.

The Kensley-Balfe sisters were very beautiful. They had taken after their mother in stature – on the tall side, but not tall enough to look awkward or unfeminine. Mona was fair with grey eyes and a dusting of freckles on her nose. Delia's auburn hair gleamed with highlights when caught by the sun. Her eyes were hazel, the sort that changed colour, appearing to be green at times, at others soft brown.

The girls lunched together in the morning room with Mademoiselle. They would join their parents for dinner in the evenings. When it was just the immediate family it was cosier to eat in there too, rather than in the cavernous dining room, which needed the warmth of more than the countless candles reflecting in the cut glass and silver to make it welcoming.

'I was told to remind you that you have a fitting this afternoon, Miss Mona,' Annie said when the soup had been served.

'I'm not allowed to ride in case I get a chill, and now you've reminded me that the dressmaker is expected this afternoon and I'll have to stand shivering for hours while she fits me.'

'Sure, your mother had it all organised before the snow. She's sending the carriage for her,' Annie replied.

'You know Mama,' said Delia, 'she's only making sure your frocks and frills will be the envy of the other debutantes.'

'

Don't I know it,' Mona said. 'And there's no need to gloat – you'll be doing all this when it's your turn next year. We'll see how you like it then.'

Mona's coming out was getting close – she'd turn eighteen in the spring, with Delia following just a year and a half behind. Lady Leonora Kensley-Balfe was already in a flurry. She had been making lists for months now. She knew her girls were handsome and engaging, and that they were growing up. She had ensured they were schooled and groomed to the standards required for them to be accepted in society as well-finished young ladies.

And now there was the added stress of making sure they'd create a good impression on their future daughter-in-law's family when they arrived. The Stokes were high born, as were they.

She'd already engaged the services of dressmakers, one in Ireland, the other in London, who were both busy sewing gowns. When Delia had asked if she could have some new dresses too, she was told, 'You'll have your chance next year.'

Making sure her daughter would be properly attired to impress was only one element. Attracting a suitor for her, one who would be deemed suitable to all, was the other. It was a mission she undertook with the precision of planning a military operation. Her husband had teased that she'd have made a good army officer.

'You've no idea what's involved,' she'd told him.

'Perhaps not, but I have a feeling you're going to tell me.'

'Mona will need a wardrobe for every eventuality – for day wear and evening wear, for the theatre and for horse riding, for carriage rides in the park and for the endless round of afternoon teas and tennis parties, where she'll be vetted by prospective mothers-in-law as to her suitability to snare one of their sons.'

'Did we do all that?'

'Oh, Peter, you are impossible. Of course we did.'

And he just laughed.

Lord and Lady Kensley-Balfe didn't keep a house in London any more. They rented one for the season each year, but because they had two girls to launch into society in the coming two years, they had taken a five-year lease on an elegant townhouse overlooking a park in one of London's most fashionable neighbourhoods. One where they could be seen as they went about their pursuits of riding, strolling and driving, while allowing them to keep an eye on others doing the very same things.

Later, the girls were summoned to the study by Annie.

'The study?' asked Mona.

'Yes, the study. It was the housekeeper's idea. Mrs Murphy suggested to Her Ladyship that it would be warmer to do the fittings in there. Sure, you'd get your end from the cold standing in your chemise up here while Lizzie Coveney pins and tucks.'

'Good old Mrs Murphy. She has the right idea.'

'You don't have to come,' Mona told her sister.

'But I want to,' Delia said.

'Please yourself,' she replied.

Delia always enjoyed watching the process and marvelled at the speed with which a dress could be sewn. Odd-shaped pieces of fabric seemed to magically join together to create clothes designed to flatter or be functional as the need arose. From a very early age she had persevered with the needle. Mrs Murphy delighted in having such a willing helper, and she showed Delia how she meticulously darned snags and candle burns in the linen wear, making them disappear altogether. She also showed her how to sew on buttons and make clothes for her rag doll from scraps of material, while Mona concentrated on embroidering samplers.

'Aren't you even the tiniest bit excited about being presented to the queen?' Delia asked. 'Having the chance to wear all that fancy finery and to go dancing all night, and to be back in London again. Imagine having men fighting over you, maybe even having a duel for your hand. Wouldn't that be romantic?'

'Of course I am. And I am looking forward to being back in London. But I doubt if anyone would want to duel over me. I think that's illegal now anyway. I just hate having to stand for hours while I'm being told to hold still or hold up my arm or turn around while the hem is pinned,' she said. 'But I suppose we couldn't have gone riding in the snow anyway.'

'Come on, let's see what Lizzie Coveney has brought for you to try on today.'

Before they had come back to Ireland for Christmas the girls had accompanied their mother to the haberdasher's in London. Lady Kensley-Balfe kept a keen eye on the latest fashions to arrive from Paris and had these copied or modified to suit her taste. And they were always accessorised with hats from a Parisian milliner and the softest kid or velvet gloves from Milan. Her shoes were bespoke too, crafted in London.

Usually she made these trips on her own, but on this occasion she had told her daughters, 'It's time you learned about these things too. I won't always be around to advise you.'

An acquaintance of Lady Kensley-Balfe's had recommended they visit a newly opened emporium that was causing a sensation among the ladies in the city. It was called Liberty. Apart from its intriguing array of luxury goods from India and Japan, it offered bundles and bolts of muslins from the Orient and luxurious fabrics with exotic-sounding names like Nagpur and tussore silk. Delia loved the distinctive smell of the newly milled fabrics. Her mother had chosen several to take back to Ireland with them. The others were left with the dressmaker in London. Now they were about to see how they looked and fitted.

The women crowded in to the study. When Mona tried on the turquoise silk that Lizzie Coveney had been working on, they all exclaimed at the way it draped and held the gathers, making it both demure and alluring at the same time.

'You've turned that into a beautiful gown, Mrs Coveney.'

'Sure, it was a dream to work on. It's much heavier than the silk from China,' the dressmaker replied.

'It does feel good and the colour's perfect on you, with your grey eyes and blond tresses,' her mother said, as Mona stood on a chair for the dressmaker to pin the hem.

Lizzie Coveney sighed with relief. Fittings didn't always go so well and Lady Leonora was a demanding client when it came to detail.

'Now let's see the bronze-coloured one on you. It's raw silk and if it sits as well as this one, I can have them both finished by Friday – if the snow doesn't get any worse.'

Lady Kensley-Balfe said, 'Let's hope it doesn't. We were hoping to go across to London early next week. There's so much to be done.'

'Will you be wanting me to come over with you this time?' the housekeeper asked.

'No, Mrs Murphy. You can stay here with Delia. We'll only be gone for a week or so.'

'Thank goodness for that. I really hate the mail-boat crossing, especially in weather like this,' Delia said, remembering all the times she'd been seasick.

'You can come with us at Easter,' her mother promised.

There was a knock on door and, before Lady Kensley-Balfe could answer, Mrs Murphy shouted, 'Wait a minute. Don't come in. That'll be Tommy,' she explained. 'He'll not be expecting to see Miss Mona half-dressed like that.' She shooed Mona out into the freezing adjoining room, thrusting the clothes she had been wearing into her arms. 'And you, Lizzie, you'd better be going with Tommy or you'll never make it back in this weather. And he won't want to be late meeting the train with His Lordship on it.'

The icy winds blew and the snow stayed for the best part of a week before melting. By then everyone was suffering from cabin fever, as Lady Kensley-Balfe was determined that they would not fall victim to colds and chills and only sanctioned a short walk each day 'to change the air' in their lungs.

Nothing was going to get in the way of her elder girl's coming out.

Chapter 2

The house seemed very quiet when the family had decamped for London. Delia continued her routine of lessons each day with Mademoiselle Corneille and took her meals in the big kitchen with Cook, Mrs Murphy, Annie, Tommy and other members of the household.

She loved times like this, listening to the local gossip and the banter between the staff, some of whose families had lived on the land for generations. They knew everything that everyone was doing and they all seemed to be related to each other. This inevitably led to conversations about what had happened to people who had lived thereabouts.

'Sure, if we didn't lose our folk to hunger or famine fever, we lost them to America and Canada. Once those unfortunates left these shores, if they were lucky enough to survive the journey, they never came back again. And for so many there wasn't anything to come back to. They were evicted to the side of the road, to be taken into the workhouses or to eat grass like common animals,' Mrs Murphy told them.

'I don't understand why no one helped them?'

'Many tried, but it was too much,' Mrs Murphy explained. 'As I often told you, there were some people, like your grandfather, set up soup kitchens and gave them work. Some imported cheap India meal to help feed them. But there were others, unscrupulous ones, who looked on the disaster as a way of clearing their lands of peasants.'

'That's shocking,' Delia said.

'You shouldn't be filling the girl's head with horror stories like that,' Tommy told Mrs Murphy.

'It's life, and she's old enough now to hear it.'

'I'm not sure Her Ladyship would agree with you.'

'Ignoring it won't make it go away,' Mrs Murphy answered. 'It might be forty years, but the horror is still fresh in the memories of many.' She sat staring at her plate, as though her mind was elsewhere. No one said anything for a bit.

Delia knew that Mrs Murphy's whole family had perished in the local workhouse. She also knew that it was thanks to a Church of Ireland curate that she had survived and come to work at Kensley Park. Whenever she told this story to Mona and Delia, Mrs Murphy prefixed his name with 'that sainted man'. And she'd add, 'it didn't matter to him whether we were Protestant or Catholic, we were all people who needed help.'

'How old were you then?' Delia asked.

'I

can't be sure, nine or ten. Birthdays didn't mean much to us and there was no one to tell me. I'm not even sure what month I was born in.'

'That's terrible.'

'No, Miss Delia, I'll tell you what was terrible. What was terrible was the way some landlords treated their workers and tenants. You might have heard of Major Dennis Mahon,' she said, not stopping for any comment. Tommy and Annie nodded in agreement. 'He was a bad one, even though I shouldn't be speaking ill of the dead. His estate was in Strokestown, in Roscommon, and it's said he evicted about one thousand five hundred families off it, burning their cabins after them so that neither they, nor anyone else, could live there again.'

'What happened to him?' Delia asked.

'His tenants revolted and, may God forgive me for saying it, and far be it from me to condone murder, but it was what he deserved. He got his comeuppance if you ask me.'

Delia was thinking of the derelict cottages just outside the boundary walls of Kensley Park. She and Mona had often played in them, pretending they were peasants and using twigs and their rag dolls to represent the large families they believed had once lived there. When their mother had found out where they had been, she chastised the governess and forbade them to go there again.

Now Delia wondered what had become of the cottages' occupants.

The snow had melted completely, and the following morning she went riding alone, despite promising her mother that she wouldn't do so. The grooms were busy and there was no sign of Tommy. Riding since she was about eight, she was very comfortable around horses and saddled the mount herself. She missed Mona and realised she'd have to get used to being on her own when her sister was launched into society.

She kept to the bridle paths and along the back road. It led by the ruins where she and Mona had played. This deserted cluster was one of several dotted at the edges of fields outside the family estate. What remained of the thatch was a sorry sight, sagging and sodden. The roofs had collapsed completely. The stone and lime walls had disintegrated in parts and fallen inwards too. The half-door and the timber from the tiny window frames had long been stripped and used for firewood. As she approached, two rocks came flying out of one of the window apertures, startling her and her horse. He whinnied loudly and reared up, unseating her and throwing her to the ground. A young man rushed out from the ruins.

'Oh my God, are you hurt? I'm so sorry. I had no idea anyone would be using the path. Here, let me help you up.'

She was unsure of the man, but she knew she couldn't do it on her own. She had felt something stretch as she fell and she could feel pain in her ankle.

'Sit down here on the grass and I'll get some help. You can't get back on your horse like that.'

'I could if you would help me back in the saddle. I live in the estate just behind that wall.'

'I'm not sure about getting back on your horse. You could do yourself more harm.'

She went to loosen her riding boot but he stopped her. 'Don't do that. It'll lend support until I get help.' Kneeling down beside her, he said, 'May I?' before running his hand over her booted foot. 'It feels swollen already. I think you'll need the doctor to examine it – let me go and fetch him.'

'Or you could ride my horse up to the house and ask the housekeeper or the groom to send the carriage down for me?'

'That's a much better idea. I'm Hugh Dunne,' he said, extending his hand to her, 'and I really am sorry for frightening you. It was never my intention.'

'Miss Kensley-Balfe,' she replied. 'And just what do you think you were doing hurtling rocks about like that?'

'I was having a look around the ruins to see if they could be restored,' he said, in an accent that wasn't familiar to her. It sounded Irish, yet there was something else there too. 'My family used to live somewhere around here a long time ago. They're gone now, but I grew up hearing about this place, and

I made a promise to them that I'd come back one day and see it for myself.'

'It looks pretty much past its best to me.'

'I was thinking the same thing myself. Look, you're shaking.' He took off his greatcoat and put it over her knees. 'I'm going to ride up to the house right away and get help. Will you be all right on your own here for a bit?'

'Yes, I'll be fine. Thank you. It's not far – there's a disused gate and once you reach that you'll see the back entrance to the estate further on.'

'I don't deserve thanks for causing your injury. I'll be as quick as I can.'

She looked after him as he rode away. Who was he and where had he came from?

It was a little while before she heard the sound of hooves returning and saw him leading the posse. He was followed by one of the stable boys on horseback, with Tommy driving the carriage and Mrs Murphy's head sticking out of the window.

A few hours later, after the family physician, Doctor Canavan, had come from the village and confirmed that her ankle was not broken but badly sprained, she was sitting in the warmth of the kitchen with her bandaged foot elevated on a stool. She hadn't noticed Mr Dunne disappear in all the fuss.

Mrs Murphy had reigned supreme over the kitchen, and

when the copper pots and large joints became too heavy for her to lift, Cook had been engaged. She still made jams and bread and cooked when the family was away, and to everyone this space remained 'Mrs Murphy's kitchen'.

'Your mother will kill me when she hears about this,' she said, putting a cup of tea down beside Delia, 'and you out there on your own with a total stranger. God knows what could have happened.'

'Oh, Mrs Murphy, no harm came to me, and he was really kind and considerate.'

'He was, but you shouldn't have been out riding in the first place. Just imagine what might have occurred had he not been there.'

Delia didn't tell her that if he hadn't been there her horse wouldn't have bolted.

He'd said he'd made a promise that he'd come back – but back from where? Was he an American? She hadn't asked. And who did he promise? The chance to ask the stranger with the kind eyes and the gentle touch any questions had gone. And the more she pondered these things, the more she regretted not finding out more.

'He said his family were from hereabouts once. Their name is Dunne. Would you have known them?' She asked Mrs Murphy.

'Sure child, every second family is Dunne around here and that's a long time ago.' She replied. Normally she'd have

have been the one ferreting all that information from the unsuspecting man, without his even being aware of it, but she had been in such a state over allowing her charge to go off on her own, never mind possibly having a broken ankle, that it hadn't occurred to her to be curious about him.

Chapter 3

In London, Lord and Lady Kensley-Balfe were in demand, attending race meetings, balls and theatre events. Although the season began in January, the debutantes usually made their first appearance 'out' in society around Easter or at Queen Charlotte's birthday ball, a tradition that had gone on for years. Mona was becoming more excited at the thoughts of being presented to Queen Victoria and other members of society.

It was commonly acknowledged that this was the golden moment to make an impression. Anxious mamas would look on, hoping their girls would attract the right sort of suitor. That usually meant one with adequate means, enough to support a sizeable estate and keep a decent stable. A title was considered an added advantage, as was being the first-born male, as he'd inherit the family fortune.

Lady Kensley-Balfe was well versed in who fitted into each and all of these categories. She had done her own investigations and, secure in the knowledge that Mona was going to make a favourable impression, had earmarked a few 'possibles' to head the guest list when they gave their own ball. Calling and At Home cards had been printed with their London address, and the wording for their invitations to various events decided upon, before she and her husband returned to Kensley Park with their daughter.

No one had informed them of Delia's mishap, and when they returned the ankle was much improved, although Delia was still ordered to keep it up and strapped.

'I needn't have fretted so much,' she told Mrs Murphy that evening. 'I don't think Mama realised I had broken my promise and that I had gone out alone. She's too focused on the business of Mona's season to think of anything else. She just asked if it was still sore and told me to rest it. Papa was more concerned and said he was going to instruct Tommy that one of the grooms will have to go along with me in future.'

'You were lucky then, missy. But let's not have any repeat performances, or you'll have me to deal with,' Mrs Murphy said, wagging her finger at her.

'I promise.'

That night Delia told Mona what had happened, mentioning the mysterious Mr Hugh Dunne.

'You are such a dreamer,' Mona replied. 'Only you could make a chance encounter like that sound romantic. It's like something in the penny dreadfuls that Annie reads, where you have to wait for a week to find out what happens next. "And then he vanished, never to be seen again. To be continued ..." And don't tell Mama I've been reading those. You know how she feels about that sort of thing.'

Delia laughed. Mona was right. It was like something that would happen in a story. If she hadn't seen the evidence with her own eyes, she could think she'd imagined the whole episode.

A letter came the next morning from Clement. It had taken several weeks to reach Ireland and its contents sent his mother into an even deeper frenzy of organisation. In it he announced that he'd be arriving the following week, with his wife-to-be, Lady Elizabeth Stokes, his future mother-in-law, Lady Constance, and her lady's maid. Lady Constance's sister, and the distant cousin who had accompanied them on the voyage, were going to stay with relatives in the south of England and wouldn't be joining them.

'Everything must be perfect,' Lady Kensley-Balfe told the staff, who had been assembled once she had read the letter. 'These are by far the most important guests we've ever had at Kensley Hall.'

'Mrs Murphy, I'm relying on you to make sure that every-thing runs smoothly in all matters of the household. We'll need fires in the guest bedrooms and the best linens on the beds. You can get some girls in from the village to help with the extra work and, Tommy, we'll have to keep the carriage and horses on call at all hours. My husband will talk to you about the hunt and, Cook, we'll need to discuss menus and supplies. And the flowers – I'll have to see what's in bloom in the hothouses.'

When she had dismissed the staff, she told her daughters, 'I expect you to behave like the ladies I had hoped you would become. And I hope you'll have that bandage off your foot by then, Delia.'

'It seems strange to think of having another sister of sorts. I wonder what age she is and what she looks like,' said Mona.

'What if we don't like her?' Delia said.

'Then you'll keep your counsel and hide those feelings. But I see no reason why you would not like her. She is Clement's choice, which I am certain will be impeccable,' their mother said.

Clement was ten years older than Mona and, during those early years, his parents were convinced he would remain their only child. Then Mona came along, followed quickly by Delia. As part of the Kensley-Balfe tradition, from childhood he was destined for the military. And with his posting to India came the knowledge that he wouldn't take a wife until he was thirty. Although it was not strictly forbidden to marry earlier, the accepted practice among the officers and the Indian civil service was that these men would remain bachelors until then.

He was a little off that age, but rules were often bent and dispensations given.

'I asked around in London, and I'm glad to say that she's not one of the "fishing fleet",' Lady Kensley-Balfe said. 'Her family have lived in India for years and she was educated by English governesses. Her brothers were sent back to England to be educated.'

Delia was about to ask her mother to explain, but she stopped her. 'Please try to think before you talk, Delia, and do try not to ask so many questions. It's indelicate and not very ladylike.'

Lord Peter Kensley-Balfe was excited at the prospect of having his son and heir back on the estate for a while. Clement had followed him into his old regiment and in all probability would follow him into politics too. It was two years since he'd been home and for a while now, Lord Peter had been thinking of handing over the reins. Kensley Park had been in the family for several generations, and with a bride on the horizon, another generation would probably follow shortly after.

He had always enjoyed an easy relationship with his tenants, and hoped his son would too, although he did have some misgivings on that score. He had always had a special bond with Clement, and he felt great pride in how well he was distinguishing himself with his regiment in Calcutta. It was Clement's manner that bothered him. He could be aggressive, especially when he had been drinking, and he carried his position with an air of entitlement that his father found disturbing.

Running the considerable estates meant that when Lord Peter was in residence he spent a lot of time with his steward, attending to land, tenant and stock-related matters. And although his official business took him to the city most weeks, his womenfolk could not have told anyone what he did there, except that he spent a lot of that time in his office in Dublin Castle. All they knew was that when Tommy drove him to Ballina he took the train to Dublin and back again, usually a day or two later.

It would be a relief to have some male company at the dinner table for a change, for much as he loved his wife and daughters, there were other topics of conversation besides coming out and playing social tag.

He did appreciate how much effort Leonora had put into their girls and recognised that Mona had reached maturity with the same confidence and elegance as her mother. Delia still needed more taming, though. She was too intelligent for her own good, strong-willed and determined – as he told her often, she ought to have been a boy.

Home Rule and the Home Rule Bill were exercising his mind, but he didn't take talk of such matters to his womenfolk.

And now, with the prospect of his son's wedding, there were things that needed to be put in place should anything happen to him before his son's commission ended.

The next afternoon the Kensley-Balfe women called on a neighbour. When they returned home, Mrs Murphy beckoned to Delia.

'The young man who came to fetch help when you twisted your ankle was here earlier. He called to enquire of your progress. Wasn't that nice of him? He's very polite. He said to tell you how guilty he's been feeling for causing the injury and how sorry he is. His Lordship came in from the stables when we were talking. I thought he'd have a conniption when he heard it was Mr Dunne who'd come to get help after your fall, but instead he thanked him and then insisted I give the young man some tea, and he sat down and joined him. There they were, the two of them, at my table, chatting like old friends. And he was asking His Lordship all about the ruined cottages on the back road. They had some rough maps spread out before them and I saw them shaking hands before they left. A gentleman's agreement, I head His Lordship say.'

'What sort of agreement is that?'

'Sure, I wouldn't be a party to that sort of information,' Mrs Murphy replied. 'But I can tell you that your young man is from America. I heard him tell His Lordship that.'

'My young man, Mrs Murphy?' Delia laughed, remembering his kindness and the concern on his face and the way his hair fell over his forehead when he bent down to cover her with his coat. She didn't know what to say. She was sorry she'd missed him. She would have liked to thank him for the help he'd given her, even though it was all his fault. She'd probably never see him again. And he'd most likely be going back home to America.

Doctor Canavan came by again and rewrapped the bandage on Delia's ankle. 'The swelling has gone down nicely, but you still need to rest it as much as possible,' he advised.

'I'll see that she does,' her mother told him.

'I'm tired of doing that, Doctor Canavan. When can I go riding again?' Delia asked.

'You may go on a gentle walk on horseback, but only if you mount and dismount from a stand and then only if you promise not to canter or gallop. I know it's frustrating, but believe me, Miss Delia, when I tell you that if you sprain it again or jolt it suddenly it will take much longer to heal and it may cause you problems all your life. A little patience will pay long dividends, I assure you. And I'll be back next week to check up on you.'

She had to content herself with that. It was better than nothing.

After their lessons had concluded the following after-noon, the sisters went to the stables together, where Delia, as instructed, mounted from a stand she had used as a child. It was a crisp day. The vapour from the horses' nostrils was clearly visible as they walked along. Vestiges of frost still clung to the bare branches. Occasionally, some wildlife they disturbed could be heard scurrying or flying away in the undergrowth.

'We'll not be doing this much longer,' Mona said as they meandered around the boundary walk and out into the countryside to the little wood.

'Why not?' asked Delia.

'Don't you ever think anything through? We'll have guests to entertain for the next few weeks, then I'll be going to London for my presentation at court. If things don't work out I'll be back after July. If they do, and I'm a social success, I won't be back for the rest of the summer because I'll be too busy going to house parties and country weekends with all my new acquaintances.'

'Perhaps Mama will allow me to come over to London. We could go riding in the park together. Do you think she might?'

'I doubt it. She'll be too busy chaperoning me to take care of you.'

'I don't need taking care of,' Delia protested.

'Yes, you do.'

'Ask her for me, please,' Delia pleaded as she reined in

behind her sister's horse, following it back along one of the narrow pathways.

'I will, but I don't think it will do any good.'

'Then I shall ask Papa.'

Mona just laughed.

As they neared the spot where she had had her accident, Delia heard banging and hammering coming from the end cottage. It grew louder as they approached and she could see some newly cut timber stacked outside it on the overgrown verge.

'Someone's working in there,' said Mona as they came level with the ruins.

'Yes, someone is,' came a disembodied voice from inside. 'Will I frighten the horses if I come out?' it asked.

Delia recognised the unusual accent. 'Mr Dunne, you may come out,' she said, laughing, and he appeared in the empty doorway, smiling. He had a nice smile. She didn't remember that, but then he'd been too concerned on the previous occasion to smile at all. He looked different somehow. Instead of the greatcoat he'd put over Delia to keep her warm, he was now attired in a tweed jacket and was not wearing a necktie. Sweat glistened on his brow as he pushed his hair back off his forehead.

'Forgive my unkempt appearance, but I'm working.' He looked at Delia and then at Mona and said, 'Hugh Dunne, at your service.'

'This is my sister,' Delia said, feeling awkward. She wasn't used to making introductions with tradespeople and wasn't sure if she should give her sister's first name. Was that too familiar? Or would using the surname only be too dismissive? She did neither.

'I'm glad to see you're back in the saddle, Miss Delia, and I hope you'll have no long-lasting effects from your fall.'

'I hope I won't either,' she replied. 'And thank you for calling to enquire.'

Mona stopped her from saying anything else. 'It looks like the rain is moving this way. We'd better walk on. Mama will have a fit if we get soaked. Good day, Mr Dunne.'

'Mona's right. I'm not allowed to gallop or canter yet, so we'll be off. Good luck with the work, Mr Dunne,' Delia said. As her mount began to move, she asked, 'Why are you working on a broken-down cottage that no one owns?'

'Ah, you're wrong there. It belongs to me now. Good day, ladies,' he replied with a smile, raising his forefinger to his forehead in a salute. 'No doubt, I'll be seeing you this way again.'

When they had gone through the gates of Kensley Park, Mona said, 'So that's the knight who came to your rescue. He seems nice, and well-mannered too, but you mustn't encourage him. Mama would not approve of you becoming friendly with someone like him.'

'She doesn't have to worry. I won't be inviting him to dine

with us, but it would have been rude to ignore him. He was being kind. Papa has met him. He was in the house the other day and Mrs Murphy served them tea in the kitchen. She was as proud as a peacock telling me about it. It made her feel very important.'

'That's strange. It's not like Papa to see people downstairs.'

'I know. That's why she was so excited. I wonder if he's going to live there, in the cottages?'

'Does it really matter?'

'Of course not. I'm just curious.'

'And you ask too many questions,' Mona told her as Tommy came out with the stand for her to dismount and the first heavy drops of rain began to fall.

Chapter 4

It rained solidly for four days. It was the sort of rain that soaked everything, leaving puddles and mud everywhere. It was the sort of rain that held no promise of blue skies. It was the sort of rain that turned what could be seen of the landscape into a grey misty vista that almost matched the greyness of the clouds. It was the sort of rain that dampened everyone's spirits.

Lady Leonora forbade the girls to go outside lest they take a chill. They were all getting on each other's nerves. The staff were diligently dusting, polishing and shining everything within touching distance. The grates had been blackened, the fire dogs gleamed. Vases were dwarfed by the arrangements of foliage and spring flowers they contained.

'Do you have to keep playing that? It's going around and around in my head,' Mona exploded. 'Don't you know anything else?'

'I'll have you know that *Liebestraum* is a very complex piece, and difficult to play, and if you had kept up your practice you'd be able to master it too,' Delia told her.

'I don't like Lizst. He's too flamboyant,' Mona said.

'Well, I do. And Mama wants me to play it for our visitors when they're here,' Delia said.

Her sister took her book and flounced out of the room.

Shortly afterwards, as the sound of hooves and carriage wheels came up the driveway, Lady Leonora called, 'He's here! They're here. Tell your father and ring for Mrs Murphy to open the door. Come, girls, we must be outside to meet them, despite the rain .'

Clement, who had been riding alongside the carriage, dismounted and helped the ladies out in turn. They held their skirts up and out of the puddles. Clement kissed his mother on both cheeks and shook hands with his father before they embraced.

'Where are my little sisters?' he asked, looking around. 'They can't have turned into these beauties since I left.' He hugged Mona first. 'You're all grown up, and Delia, look at you – the plaits are gone and you're as tall as your sister! May I present Lady Constance and her daughter, my future wife, Lady Elizabeth.'

'We're honoured and delighted to welcome you to our humble home,' Lord Peter said. 'You must have had a horrible journey in this weather.'

'Truthfully, it has been miserable,' Lady Constance

answered. 'But we are so pleased to meet you at last, and to be here.'

'I'm sure you'd like a little time to freshen up. Let's show you to your rooms, and when you're ready, come down and we'll have something to eat and get to know each other,' Lady Leonora said.

When they were out of earshot she whispered to her husband, 'The mother's quite tall and awkward looking, isn't she?'

He nodded.

'Elizabeth is pretty, in a china doll sort of way, but they seem nice, don't they? Girls, what do you think?'

'Mama, you're always telling me not to be so pass-remarkable,' Delia said.

'She's right there, my dear. Give us a chance to say more than hello to our guests before we have to make our minds up about them.' He laughed just as Clement came in, looking all around the room, as though checking that nothing had changed.

'God, it's so good to be home again. I can't believe I'm really here. And as for you two,' he said to his sisters, 'I'd hardly have recognised you had I met you anywhere but here. You've changed so much. You're really are all grown up and quite beautiful. But what did you do to yourself, Delia?'

She told him about her fall and he sympathised.

'I've seen that happen more than once on the polo pitch. It's a nasty injury. It's just as well it's not you who is going to be presented – all that dancing and gadding about wouldn't do it any good.'

'Tell us how you met Elizabeth,' Delia asked.

'Now, child, give your brother a chance to rest himself, and remember about asking so many direct questions,' her mother cautioned. 'But, of course, Clement, we all want to know. Oh, there's so much we all want to know.' She smiled indulgently at her son.

Once the guests came down and had been served tea by the fireside, conversation flowed. It didn't go unnoticed that Lady Stokes liked to mention their close association with the viceroy, Lord Frederick Temple Hamilton-Temple-Blackwood. She laughed and qualified this with, 'Yes, I know it's quite a mouthful, with Temple in there twice, and it's a nightmare when it comes to addressing an envelope.'

'Don't you find it frightfully hot over there?' Lady Leonora asked. 'I'm not sure I'd be able for it.'

'Yes, it is and one never really gets used to it. The humidity is stifling, and no matter how much one washes and bathes, five minutes later one is glowing again. But India has a charm of its own, and we usually decamp to Simla in the mountains for the worst of the heat. That's where Elizabeth met your Clement. At the Viceroy's Ball, wasn't it, dear?'

Elizabeth had hardly said a word up to now – perhaps because her mother didn't stop talking for long enough to let anyone in. Now she just beamed at her fiancé and nodded.

'I knew the minute I set eyes on her that she was meant for me,' Clement said. 'And I'm so glad that she feels the same way and has agreed to marry me.'

'So am I,' Elizabeth said.

'Are you going to marry here or in India?' Mona asked her, but it was Lady Constance who answered.

'Oh, in India, dear, of course, with her father to give her away,' she told them. Then, addressing Lord Peter, she divulged, 'He was in Eton with the viceroy, who, by the way, insists on being at the wedding, as he says he feels responsible for them meeting each other. We'll hold it at Christmas. By then our boys, Nicholas and Richard, will be out of Eton and have returned home.'

'Then we'll have to have a ball to celebrate your engagement before you set sail again,' said Lady Leonora. 'Once Mona is out. It'll be a double celebration.'

'Will we have it here?' Mona asked.

'That's doubtful,' her mother said. 'We'll be at the height of the season so it will have to be in London.'

'Then I have to be there,' Delia said. 'Oh, I know it wouldn't be proper for me to attend, but I want to be there to see the style and to celebrate a little with you both.' She turned to appeal to her brother.

'We'll see,' he told her, and she knew she'd probably be allowed if he wanted it. After all, he was only going to be home for a few months and then they wouldn't see each other again for a few years.

Clement excused himself to go downstairs to say hello to the staff who hadn't been at the door when he'd arrived.

Meanwhile, Lady Leonora suggested that perhaps the ladies might like a rest before changing for dinner. Lady Constance said she would and the hostess accompanied her upstairs. This was the first chance the three young women had to be alone together.

'I'm sorry,' Elizabeth said. 'Mama talks a lot, especially when she's nervous.'

'Why would she be nervous?' asked Delia.

'Meeting the parents – and daughters, of course – of her daughter's betrothed.' She smiled. 'That's not something she's ever done before. I told her she was worrying over nothing, that if they were like Clement they were sure to be nice people, but she couldn't relax in case she didn't make the right impression.'

'Mama was the very same,' said Mona, 'but don't let her know I said that.' They laughed.

'I'm so happy to meet you at last,' Elizabeth said. 'Despite everything Clement has said about you, it's not the same as actually being here, face to face.'

'We were curious about you, too,' Mona said. 'And there's so much to talk about. We want to hear all about India and your life there.'

'Perhaps you will come out there sometime and see it for yourself?'

'It's a lovely thought, but I don't know if that will ever happen – unless I'm a complete failure as a debutante.'

'That's highly unlikely,' Elizabeth said, 'with your looks and pedigree. I don't see you becoming one of the fishing fleet.'

'I've heard of that before, but what does it actually mean?' Delia asked.

'It's a term used for the girls who don't succeed in their season. They head off for India in search of a husband,' Elizabeth explained.

'And do they really all meet husbands when they make the journey?' Delia asked.

'I know a lot who do. You have to realise that there's a dearth of eligible women in the Raj, and, because mixed-race marriages are forbidden, these are often the only eligible women the men will have the chance to meet while serving overseas, which could be for many years.'

'I suppose that makes sense,' Mona replied.

'It's nothing new, you know. The East India Company started shipping potential wives from England for their officers way back at the end of the seventeenth century,' Elizabeth told them.

'We'll be in trouble with Mama if we don't get changed soon,' Delia said as the clock chimed the hour.

'It's so lovely to meet you both. Having sisters is quite a

novelty for me – I've only two brothers. You'll meet them in London, soon.'

They went upstairs to get ready for dinner.

Before the first course was served, Lord Kensley-Balfe stood up. 'I'd like to propose a toast to our guests, our future daughter-in-law and her mother, and to having our son back in our midst, no matter how briefly. It's wonderful to have you all around the table together. Good health.'

They all replied, 'Good health.'

As the meal progressed, Delia could tell that her mother was delighted with everything so far. Lady Constance's chatter dominated the conversation.

After dinner, Clement produced a small package of photographs, which were passed around and scrutinised. There were a few of the happy couple together, at a tennis club, a regimental polo match and at their engagement party. There was one of Clement with his foot on the head of a tiger, his rifle held triumphantly in the air. Delia stared at it. 'You went tiger hunting?' she said to her brother.

'Of course,' he answered.

Lady Constance interjected. 'Everyone does it in the Raj, even the viceroy. It's a colonial sport. The royals have been doing it for centuries.'

'And did you go too, Elizabeth?' asked Delia

'Yes, I did. Just once, although the women don't carry guns. They just follow and watch.'

Elizabeth explained, 'The tradition is that the men must finish off their own animal. That's when that photograph was taken. I thought it very cruel. Tigers are beautiful when you see them close up and watch the way they move so gracefully and silently. But there is something awful seeing them lying there, their eyes lifeless, just being a trophy for someone. I didn't enjoy it at all. It's different if a tiger's attacking. Sometimes one comes down from the hills and that can be a real threat, but apart from that I think we should leave the others alone.'

'Perhaps they need to do it to control the population,' Sir Peter said. 'I'm sure Clement told you that we hunt foxes here. But they're vermin and do a lot of damage to our livestock. It's our way of culling them.'

'Yes, he did, and that doesn't sound as gruesome. I wouldn't like to hunt, but I'm looking forward to horse riding while I'm here,' Elizabeth said. 'It will be so nice to do it in the cool, instead of having to set off at six in the morning to avoid the heat of the day.'

'You've really killed a tiger?' Delia said to Clement, still dwelling on the information.

'Of course,' he replied proudly. 'Several.'

'I know you have to shoot people when you're a soldier, but that's different, isn't it?' she said, almost in tears.

'Oh, Delia, it's time to grow up and stop being such a

baby. You always were too soft, rescuing birds with broken wings and adopting kittens and newborn chicks. This is life and life can sometimes be cruel. Now don't go getting upset, especially on my first day home.'

He made to put his arm around her and give her a hug, but she moved away. It didn't offer any comfort. She never imagined her brother could do something like that. She knew Mona would scoff and tell her to grow up too if she told her how she was feeling. But there was something different about Clement, something hard, and she didn't like the way he had ridiculed her in front of everybody.

She went to bed that night thinking if he could be that heartless, what else was her beloved brother capable of? She tried to put the thoughts out of her head, but they kept coming back.

Chapter 5

Clement and Lord Peter went for an early morning ride around the estate. The rain had stopped, and the sky was brighter than it had been for days. The earth was sodden and there was flooding in parts, where little streams had broken their banks and the fields could absorb no more.

They encountered several farmhands on the way, many offering their congratulations when they stopped to pass the time of day with them. The head gardener exclaimed, 'Good Lord, sir, it seems no time since you were a mischievous little boy, climbing the trees in the orchard, and now you're going to be wed. That makes me feel very old, that does.'

'You can't imagine how it makes me feel,' his father said, and they rode on. 'I've arranged a meeting with the land steward later and he can talk you though developments.'

'He seems to be handling everything very well,' Clement said.

'He's a good man, and trustworthy too,' said Lord Peter. 'Not like that fellow before him.'

'You weren't to know he'd swindle you. I'd have been taken in by him too.'

'Well, I'm wiser now, even though it means keeping a closer eye on income and expenditures myself. Excessive drink is a curse. It destroyed that man and turned him into a common thief. It still angers me to think that if Tommy hadn't been overheard complaining about the rent increases, I might never have found out what he'd done.'

'That's true, and that blackguard could have added another rent hike the following year and siphoned that off too,' said Clement.

'Probably.' They rode on in silence for a bit then his father said, 'Let's go out the west gate and I'll show you the parcel of land I wrote to you about, the one I bought in December.'

'Is that what you were sorting out with the Land Commission last week?'

'Yes, they wanted the new maps of where it borders Kensley Park's south boundary and runs right down to the Moy.'

'So you eventually got your wish to own your own stretch of fishing waters.' Clement laughed. 'You always said it was the only thing missing in your world.'

'You remember that?' His father grinned. 'And you're right. It was the only thing missing. It was the Crosbies' land, but with the bad reputation the old man had around here, the heirs wanted to cut ties with Ireland and decided to sell up.'

'Was the big house by the river included in the sale?'

'It was, and it's a fine one, although it hasn't been lived in for a while. It has a fine walled garden too. I've been approached by an agent who says there's some interest in it as a small hotel. I wasn't sure at first, but I'm coming around to the idea. I don't need another property on my hands and the town would benefit from a new enterprise. It would mean redrawing those boundaries too. And I'd like to have your opinion on it.'

'I'd be delighted to give it,' Clement replied.

His father suggested they should ride down there with their steward to take a look.

As the clutch of derelict cottages close to the rear entrance of the estate came into view, Clement caught sight of two men working on one of the roofs. They appeared to be dismantling the remnants of the dilapidated thatch.

'What's going on here?' Clement asked his father. 'Who are these men? Do they have permission to be here?'

'Yes, they do. I recently sold the tenure on that strip of land. It's never been used for anything in my memory and those ruins are a bit of an eyesore. I always intended having them demolished, but never got around to it.'

'Who owns it now?'

'A Mr Dunne. He's an Irish American. A pleasant enough chap. It was the oddest thing. I recently came home and found this stranger in the kitchen with Mrs Murphy. He's the fellow who rescued your sister when her horse threw her, so I felt I owed him something.'

'So you just sold the tenure to a stranger? Wasn't that a bit impulsive?'

'Perhaps, but after he'd gone I did a bit of digging. His family were famine evictees from around these parts, and I think they were actually tenants hereabouts. You know, several of ours had fled when my father returned from parliament in London, terrorised by reports and rumours that they'd be next to be evicted and burned out. That was untrue, of course, but he always felt guilty about it. This chap had some rough drawings, made from talking to relatives of his who'd left about that time too. There's a strong possibility that these ruins could have been where they had lived before disaster befell them.'

'And you just handed over the land like that?' Clement asked. 'Is he genuine?'

'We came to a financial arrangement. It's only a worthless strip, cut off from the main part by the right of way from the back road,' his father said. 'It's been lying there fallow for several decades.'

'But he's a stranger. How do you know he's not trying to

take advantage of your generous reputation? I mean, what do you know about him? He could have fabricated a story like that.'

'To what end?' Lord Peter asked, looking over at Clement, who didn't reply. 'My son, India and the military are obviously rubbing off on you, and not in the best way, it seems. I felt it was the right thing to do. You have to follow your instincts sometimes. Mine seldom let me down.'

'You were wrong about the last steward,' Clement said self-righteously.

'I wasn't. He was an honourable man when I engaged him, before he started drinking to excess and took up gambling. It was desperation that drove him to do what he did.'

At that point they were almost level with the cottages. Hugh emerged from inside. Lord Kensley-Balfe stopped, nodded to the two workmen and said to Hugh, 'I see you're making headway already, Mr Dunne. I like a man who is decisive.'

'Good day, Your Lordship. I'm trying to secure the original walls before starting to extend this one.'

'This is my son,' Lord Kensley-Balfe said. 'I was just telling him about you.'

The two men acknowledged each other and Clement asked, 'You're going to extend it?'

'Yes, sir, I'm going to add a new section to the rear.'

'And you're doing some of the work yourself?' Clement said. 'What is your trade?'

'You could say I'm the proverbial Jack of all, yet master of none.'

'I don't understand,' Clement said.

'I'm a draughtsman and I've been working around enough projects to think I know what I'm doing.'

'Do you intend living here when it's finished?' Clement said.

'That's a moot point, sir, and one I can't give a definitive answer to right now. I was engaged to work on a significant project in Newport, Rhode Island, but because of a family bereavement, that was postponed for a year. I am not sure yet if I still have to honour that commitment, or even if the project will go ahead. Meanwhile, I'm here and will concentrate on this.'

'Then let us not detain you any longer, Mr Dunne. Good day to you,' Lord Kensley-Balfe said, nodding to the two workers before they rode off.

When out of earshot, Clement said. 'That's an ambitious undertaking, isn't it?'

'I agree, but the young man impressed me, and I feel he'll make a success of it. He's certainly enthusiastic.'

'And he seems to have taken you in completely. I don't think I'd have been so gullible.'

'Then I think we'll have to agree to differ.' They rode in silence for a bit before Lord Peter coughed and said, 'By the way, may I commend you on your choice of Lady Elizabeth. She reminds me a little of your mother when I met her. I think she'll make you an excellent wife.'

'Thank you, Papa. That means a lot to me.'

Back in the drawing room, the women were talking – or rather, Lady Constance was talking and the others were listening.

'I am frightfully aware of social mores. If you think there are society rules in London, Dublin and this part of the world, you should try living in India.'

'Really?' Lady Leonora said.

'Oh, yes. There, the pecking order is unbelievable, with titles, royal and otherwise, ranks and other tiers of hierarchy – there are something like sixty-six categories – and woe betide you, if you put someone sitting next to the wrong person, meaning someone who is below them on the scale.'

'Who decides things like that?' asked Delia and she saw her mother frown at her with a frown that said *don't ask so many questions*. So she added, 'It's fascinating hearing about life over there.' Her mother's face relaxed.

'Well, child, tradition is part of it, but there's an actual official government list that one can consult, so that people can follow the correct protocol. Then there are ceremonial customs and rituals that one must observe, too.' Without drawing breath, she continued, 'Elizabeth, of course, has been brought up with these, so she should be an asset to her husband and help his rise through the ranks.'

Mona could see her mother didn't like the implication that the only reason her son would rise through the ranks was because his wife could seat people properly at her soirées. But she knew her mother was too much of a lady to let that show.

'Of course, being close associates with the viceroy, Lord Frederick, will be a big help too. You know, he and my husband were at Eton together. His wife is the most incredible woman. She was asked by Queen Victoria herself to try to make better the plight of women in India, and last year she raised a fortune to supply medical aid to those who are suffering. Can you believe that?'

Again, there was no pause before she continued. 'She managed to get the support of many of the Indian princes, like the maharajahs of Durbunga and Kashmir, and to extract very generous donations from them towards a fund she was setting up. I don't know how she does that and all her other duties. And she's the most generous and gracious of hostesses. Of course, Elizabeth and I help on some of her committees too. Only the inner circle is invited to do that.'

'It seems as though you all lead very busy lives. I hope you don't find us too dull, Lady Constance,' Lady Leonora said.

'On the contrary. This is bliss, being away from all my duties and not having to solve problems. And it's lovely to have these few weeks together, to get to know your family and friends. It's so difficult to get a real impression of someone from a distance, and you know how little information men give you, despite how much you press them. They are no good for detail. No matter what I'd ask Clement, he'd just say, "Wait until you meet them and you can draw your own conclusions." Isn't that just typical?'

'I hope we're living up to expectations,' Mona said to Elizabeth.

'Of course you are,' said Lady Constance, answering for her daughter. She smiled at Lady Leonora, who was fully aware that she would have made enquiries into the good name of their family, ensuring that it wasn't besmirched by any whiff of scandal. 'And we'll be keeping a close eye on how your coming out will go and who you may snare. Someone with a large fortune, I trust. And preferably an eldest son.'

Lady Leonora excused herself on the pretext of needing to talk to Cook.

She told Sir Peter later that 'it took more will power than I ever knew I possessed not to tell her what I thought of her. The woman is a nightmare. She's vulgar and rude and she lets her tongue run away with her. I don't know how I'll remain civil for the next few weeks.'

'My dear, just be yourself,' he told her. 'You have nothing

to prove and you can be grateful she lives on a different continent. She'll be on the high seas before you know it, and you may never have to see her again.'

'It can't come soon enough, Peter. I'm hoping that as Elizabeth looks nothing like her, she won't turn out like her. You know what they say – an apple never falls far from the tree. I just hope that in Elizabeth's case it has rolled far, far away.'

'Elizabeth seems much more reserved than her mother, and well-read too, Leonora. I had a good conversation with her in the library. I like her a lot. She has a good mind,' he said. 'And when you cut through all the ridiculous over-emphasis on keeping their place in society, I think she'll be good for Clement.'

'I like her too,' his wife agreed. 'And the girls have been really well-behaved, although I keep expecting Delia to come out with something embarrassing.'

'She's growing up. She asked me to see if I could get around you to allow her to come back to London with us next time.'

'I'd prefer to leave her here until after Mona has been presented. Tell her she can join us after that, and be there for Clement's engagement ball.'

'She may not be delighted to hear that, dear.' He sighed.

'I have other things on my mind right now. You know, Peter, I'd decided to fill my diary with carefully chosen engagements to keep us busy for Lady Constance's stay. Now

I'm not so sure I want to inflict her on our friends. "The viceroy" this and "the viceroy" that, and his bountiful wife and her committees. "Did you know my husband was at Eton with him?"' she mimicked.

Sir Peter just laughed and gave her a kiss on the cheek. 'Come, dear, best foot forward. Let's go down and we'll face her together.'

Delia's ankle was much better when the doctor next called to check it. Her first question was, 'May I now go riding, properly, again?' She had missed out over the previous few days and felt Mona was getting to know Elizabeth much better because they had gone off galloping together, while Delia had stayed behind.

'Yes, but only if you promise to use the mounting stand for at least another month and rest as much as possible in between. A sudden jarring before it's properly healed could leave you with a weak ankle for life,' he cautioned again. 'And I'd advise that you refrain from galloping for a few weeks.'

She promised she would. He was scarcely out the door before she went to find Elizabeth and Mona to tell them she'd be joining them when they rode out that afternoon.

They took their usual route, and Delia listened as the two girls discussed the sister of someone they both knew in London, Letitia Fairleigh. Letitia had spent several years in India before her father retired from the army. She was in disgrace and had fallen foul of her family when it was discovered that she was secretly meeting her music teacher and had been for some time.

'They kept her locked in for months, but as soon as she was allowed out of her room, she bolted to be with him.'

'Never!' said Mona.

'Yes, she did. They ran off together,' said Elizabeth.

'Where is she now?' asked Delia

'Who knows or cares? They're probably living in rented rooms somewhere, trying to live off whatever he makes from giving piano lessons.'

'Unimaginable. She ought to have had more sense,' said Mona. 'No wonder she's been disinherited.'

'It's what she should have expected for bringing disgrace on her family and its good name,' said Elizabeth. 'She ruined her sister's prospects too. Everyone thought she'd marry that chinless earl from Beddington.'

They had come to a place where they normally began a gallop though the fields to a small wood. It was so familiar to the horses that they instinctively gathered momentum as they reached it.

'You can't do this,' Mona said to Delia. 'You'll damage your ankle even more.'

'I know. You go on ahead,' Delia told them. 'I'll go the short way and I'll just canter. I promise. You'll have caught up on me in no time at all.'

Delia was never happier than when she was out riding. She loved feeling the wind in her face and the sense of freedom it gave her. She would have loved to have taken off at pace through the fields, but the odd twinge reminded her of what the doctor had said.

She cantered gently for a bit, then slowed down. 'Oh, I've missed this. Have you?' she said, leaning forward to pat her horse on the neck. When she straightened up she heard the sound of hooves coming behind her. They slowed up, and when she turned to look, it wasn't the girls but Mr Dunne who was in the saddle.

'I hope I didn't startle you, Miss Delia,' he said. 'May I call you Miss Delia, or is that that being too familiar? I never know in this country.'

She wasn't sure what to say. If she agreed, was she letting him be too familiar? But if she said no, wouldn't that make her sound pompous and unfriendly? She knew she didn't want him to think that.

'You may,' she said, as his mount fell into step beside hers.

'I'm glad to see you're out and about again. But should you be on your own?'

'I'm not,' she said. 'Here come my sister and my brother's fiancée.'

Mona looked surprised at seeing Delia and Mr Dunne together.

'Mr Dunne rescued me when I hurt my ankle,' Delia explained to Elizabeth.

'And meeting Miss Delia turned out to be a serendipitous happening for me,' he said.

'In what way?' Mona asked.

'If that hadn't occurred, I would probably never have met Lord Kensley-Balfe, and if I hadn't met him, I'd never have been absolutely sure which was my ancestral home, much less own it.'

'And do you know now?' Delia asked.

His reply, 'I sure do,' sounded very American to her. 'He came by himself yesterday and told me. He had papers to prove it. It's hard to fathom, isn't it?'

They agreed. Elizabeth started walking on in silence. Mona nodded and followed. Delia told him, 'I'm happy you got that news. Good day, Mr Dunne.'

'Good day, Miss Delia.'

When they were out of earshot, Elizabeth said, 'That would never happen in India.'

Confused, Delia asked, 'What would never happen?'

'Girls talking to men, unchaperoned. Do your mama and papa condone such behaviour?'

The sisters looked at each other, sensing disapproval, and Delia said, 'We just happened to meet on the path and were both going in the same direction. It's not as though we had an assignation. It would have been rude to ignore him.'

'You could have just passed the time of day and walked on. And his calling you "Miss Delia". What familiarity! In India the lower classes know their place and don't ever overstep the boundaries,' Elizabeth said.

'I don't think boundaries are an excuse for bad manners,' Delia came back at her. She looked at Mona, who was a few paces ahead and said nothing. Not another word was spoken until they reached the stables.

Delia followed her sister in to her bedroom and closed the door before confronting her.

'Mona, you could have rescued me out there. Elizabeth was being horrible, just like her mother. What right has she to criticise me like that? I did nothing wrong.'

'I didn't say anything because I happen to agree with her, but I didn't want to side with her against you. That young man shouldn't have stopped to talk, as if we were all old friends. We're not. We have a position to uphold. We've been given privilege and with that comes certain standards that we have to set.'

'I can't believe my ears, Mona. What has happened to you? You're letting those women influence you, and it's not for your good either.'

'I'm not, Delia, honestly I'm not. But you have to think of your reputation. He was very familiar and you were alone with him. How do you think that looked to Elizabeth, who is chaperoned everywhere? I think you should avoid that bridle path to the back road completely, and if you happen to meet him again anywhere, just nod and walk on.'

'Are you seriously saying I'm not to ride where I always do?'

'Yes, Delia, I am, and let's hope Elizabeth doesn't tell her mother or Clement about this or we'll never hear the end of it.'

'Clement would understand. He stops and talks to everyone and no one accuses him of impropriety,' she told Mona.

'Clement is a man and their future master. That's the difference. As women we only have our reputation and we have to keep that from being compromised. That's why there are rules and conventions, to protect us.'

'That's so unfair.'

'Perhaps, but it's the way it is. Now, be nice to Elizabeth for everyone's sake, but especially for Clement's.'

'I'll try,' she said grudgingly. She was still fuming when she went back to her room to change out of her riding clothes. Nothing further was said about the incident.

That evening the Kensley-Balfes had invited several friends for a musical soirée. Their guests had been chosen for their ability to hold a tune or command an instrument.

'Do you play?' Sir Peter asked Lady Constance, who replied, 'But of course. Music was a very important part of my education, and Elizabeth's too. In fact, we've both played for the viceroy and vicereine.'

'Of course you have.' He smiled graciously at her and said, 'I'm sure our guests would never have expected us to entertain them so royally.'

She smiled back with satisfaction. 'It will be an honour to play for them.'

After supper, everyone retired to the music room, and once they were all seated, Sir Peter left his place beside Lady Leonora in the front row to make an announcement. 'We are going to open the evening with an offering from our esteemed guest, Lady Constance Stokes,' and looking straight at his wife, he continued, 'who has played for none other than the viceroy and governor general of India and his wife, Lady Dufferin, who, as many of you know is an Irish woman, born in Killyleagh Castle in County Down. Their husbands were in Eton together.'

Lady Leonora almost spluttered. What a trickster he was! How he kept a straight face she'd never know. She was finding it impossible to do so.

He finished by saying, 'Lady Constance will be followed by her daughter, soon to be our daughter-in-law, Lady Elizabeth.'

He returned to his seat and Lady Leonora nudged him in his ribs with her elbow.

If anyone had been expecting to hear Chopin, they'd have been disappointed when she launched forth with a medley of Strauss waltzes, which got some feet tapping. Elizabeth sang a German song, which truthfully didn't have much melody, but she had a sweet voice. Delia played Lizst's challenging *Liebestraum* faultlessly. She glanced up and saw the pride on her parents' faces.

Lady Leonora had wanted to introduce an Irish flavour, so there were pieces from William Vincent Wallace's *Maritana* and from Michael William Balfe. Lord Kensley-Balfe himself sang a few of Moore's melodies, and Clement, who seemed to have been imbibing a little more than was prudent, was persuaded to close the evening by giving them the sanitised and not-so-sanitised parodies of some regimental songs, which went down very well with everyone.

'What you did to Lady Constance was very wicked,' Lady Leonora told her husband when they were in bed that night. 'I thought I'd disgrace myself.'

'I know. I could see that. I couldn't help it. When I saw her sitting there, all I could think of was her telling everyone about being close associates –'

'– of the viceroy,' they said in unison and dissolved in laughter.

When they stopped, he added, 'And you know, Leonora, she was really flattered by the introduction and thanked me for it later.'

'Such airs and graces. I'm so glad we're not leaving for London with them. I need a break – I don't think I could stay good humoured through the train journeys and the crossing if I had to hear her drone on and on about her relatives, who they know and who they've entertained.'

'They'll be gone soon. A few weeks in London will give her a new audience and you a bit of respite.'

'That woman acts as though she had not been brought up to privilege and class. Poor Clement. I hope his manoeuvres take him far away from her when he returns to India,' she said.

'Oh, I wouldn't worry about Clement. He doesn't let that sort of thing bother him.'

'Do you think he seems to be drinking quite a lot?'

'It goes with the military lifestyle, living in male company, facing danger and that heat. Most chaps go through a phase like that. It'll pass.'

'I hope so, I don't like what it does to him.'

The awkwardness that had been there for a few days between Elizabeth and Delia seemed to have blown over, but it had tinged the budding relationship somewhat. Delia was annoyed when Mona insisted they now take an alternative route for their daily ride, thus eliminating any chance of meeting Mr Dunne again. Had that been Mona's decision, it probably would never have become an issue, but the fact that it was because of Elizabeth's interference really rankled with her.

It made Delia wonder about Mr Dunne. She became more curious about who he was and where he had come from.

Chapter 6

Lady Leonora waved from the doorstep and heaved a huge sigh of relief when the carriage pulled away with Lady Constance, Lady Elizabeth and the lady's maid, Jayne, on board. She felt her shoulders relax for the first time since they'd arrived. Tommy was taking them to Ballina to catch the train to Dublin. From there they would take the mail boat to Holyhead, before continuing their journey to Kent, where they were expected at the manor of their relatives.

Clement remained at Kensley Hall and would follow in a few weeks, when he'd accompany Mona and his parents to the house in London. Delia would stay at home, in the care of Mrs Murphy and Mademoiselle Corneille, and travel over to be in London for all the excitement of his engagement ball

'That might be the last time I'll ever see you,' she told Clement.

'What a ridiculous thing to say. I'm not going to disappear out of your life, Delia. I know India is far away, but it's manageable. I'll be out of the army in two years and probably back here soon after.'

'But you're a soldier. You might get killed,' she said.

'Well, thank you for that vote of confidence! That's why we train so hard, to avoid being killed, and let me assure you, little sister, I have no intentions of letting anyone get me. So you can put those thoughts out of your head.'

'I will try,' she told him.

Trunks were packed, lists made and amended, accessories checked off, jewels wrapped. Eventually, everything was ready for the grand departure. Cook and Lady Kensley-Balfe's maid went ahead in the pony and trap. Now it was Delia's turn to wave from the doorstep as the carriage with her brother, sister and parents pulled away. She waited until it turned the bend at the bottom of the driveway then went back inside.

The house felt eerily quiet. Delia always hated when the family decamped, leaving her behind. She tried reading, but the silence seemed to enfold her in an oppressive way. She took out her sketchbook and pencil case and decided to go outside, where the birdsong filled the air and where she'd feel more alive. She went to tell Mrs Murphy what her intention was and found her with her coat and hat on, ready to go out.

'I'm going to take some eggs, bread and plum jam to

Mrs McCormack,' she told Delia. 'There's a new baby due there any day now, and she's been poorly of late. I may visit Mrs Lynch too. Your mother knows. I told her we'd have a surplus of some things with everyone away and, sure, it'd be a sin to let good food go to waste – and, of course, she agreed. Do you want to walk with me? I could do with some help carrying that basket.'

'It weighs a ton.' Delia laughed as she lifted it. 'I was going to sketch, but I can do that later.' It was a distraction on a day that stretched out with no prospects of diversion.

'We'll have to find something for you to do, apart from your lessons,' Mrs Murphy said as they headed for the back road. 'You could watch me cook and learn a few things. That way you'll know what's what when you have your own house-hold, which you probably will have some day. I've a bit of mending to do too, and you're a dab hand at the sewing. My eyesight is not what it used to be and it takes me ages to get the thread through the needle.'

Delia transferred the basket to her other hand as they walked. 'Mrs Murphy, can I ask you something?'

'You know you can, child.' She nodded. 'I'll have to stop calling you that – you're nearly a woman.'

'You never married or had children, Mrs Murphy. Do you ever wish you had?'

'What sort of question is that?'

'I'm curious.'

'I noticed. No, I never regretted it. Your family is my family. There was nothing outside these gates for me, and after the famine and the workhouse, they gave me all the security I ever needed – a home and enough to eat. Someone told me once that when there are too many children in the world, things like famines are sent to cull them.'

'You don't believe that, do you?'

'I don't want to, but it's the only thing that makes sense of what happened when I was small.'

Delia digested this for a bit before asking, 'Didn't you ever want more for yourself?'

'No. Money is not the most important thing. Being warm, having a full belly and having a place to put your head down at night and call home are. Remember, it's a rich man whose wants are few. Don't go chasing rainbows, Miss Delia. Be happy with what you have, and that's an awful lot more than most. But I think you know that.'

'I think I do.'

After a while, she asked, 'If you never married, why are you called Mrs Murphy?'

'I declare, how do you come up with the questions? Once I became housekeeper they started calling me Mrs. It's the done thing. The housekeeper is always Mrs.'

They turned right when they came through the gates.

'I have one stop to make before Mrs McCormack's,' Mrs

Murphy said, and Delia realised they were heading by the derelict cottages. 'I promised to bring Mr Dunne a square of my soda bread when I was passing. He's very partial to it.'

'He's had it before?'

'Yes, he has, a few times.'

Delia thought of Elizabeth and dismissed her immediately. Delia hadn't planned or orchestrated this meeting. She had a chaperone in Mrs Murphy, so there was nothing to damage her reputation by seeing him again. Was there?

She was astonished at the difference in the cottage from the outside. It had a bright new straw thatch that seemed to glisten in the sun. This sat like a sumptuous, plump eiderdown on the roof. The walls had been rendered and were already drying out in places. A small curl of smoke rose from the chimney. It was almost invisible in the brightness of the day. There were now new wooden frames in the apertures that had once held the windows, but they appeared to be much larger than the older ones they were replacing.

'Mr Dunne, are you there?' Mrs Murphy called as they approached. 'It's Mrs Murphy, Mrs Murphy from the big house.'

'I thought I heard voices,' Mr Dunne said, running his hand through his floppy hair. 'And Miss Delia. What a lovely surprise. How nice to see you, and fully recovered, it seems.'

'Yes, thank you.' She smiled back. There was something about him that made her feel different to the way anyone else ever had. When she saw him she wanted to smile. And she wanted to hear him speak in his funny accent.

'Ladies, would you like to be my first visitors? You can see what's going on inside. The cottage is still a workshop, but it's quite clean.'

From the way she looked at her, Delia could see that Mrs Murphy wanted to, so she agreed. 'I'm sure we'd both love to see what you're doing.'

'Then, please, come in, and let me take that. It looks heavy,' he told Delia, taking the basket from her. Once inside, he made space on a makeshift table for it. 'That's a ton weight. Have you rocks in it?' he asked Mrs Murphy.

'No, I've a few things for the neighbours, and I brought you some pots of my plum jam and a square of my soda bread.'

'What an angel you are. You spoil me. I'd marry you in the morning for your bread alone,' he told Mrs Murphy.

'You do talk a lot of blather,' she said and laughed coyly.

He turned to look at Delia and said, 'This woman has ruined me forever. No one will ever match this degree of excellence.'

They both laughed at him.

'I see the roof is finished,' Mrs Murphy said. 'It must be the smartest looking one for miles.'

'It does look well, doesn't it? A few men from the village fixed it up. Thatch is something I know very little about. We don't have much call for it in New York. But I'm in awe of the skills they have, especially when putting those comb-scallops on the ridge. I'd never have managed those.'

'It's much brighter in here than in my little cottage,' said Mrs Murphy. She lived in one the previous housekeeper had occupied when she was alive. It was the smallest of several in a little row inside the boundary walls. She had Tommy and his family and some of the farmhands as her neighbours.

'I knocked out some of the walls and made bigger window spaces to allow more light in,' he told her.

'I could never understand why they were always so small,' Delia said.

'That was to avoid paying glass tax,' he replied. 'The bigger the window, the more tax that had to be paid.'

'I never knew that,' said Delia, feeling she knew nothing of the world, while this virtual stranger, whose family had come from a home like this tiny one, seemed to know more about everything.

'It's a great sight to see new life coming back into the cottages. Watching them crumble and fall to pieces is a constant reminder of the poor souls who perished or had to flee from them during the dark days of the famine.'

'My people were among those,' he said. 'That's why I want to do this, in their memory. I showed His Lordship some sketches I'd made from things my grandfather told me when he was alive. My father had only hazy memories of living in Ireland, but he was able to confirm most of what my grandfather had told me. His Lordship discovered that my forefathers may have actually lived in one of these three.'

'The Lord save us,' Mrs Murphy said. 'Isn't that a wonder?'

'It is indeed. We aren't sure which, but he's promised to try and find out for me. Their landlords were called Crosbie.'

'And this was always called Crosbie's field and Crosbie's wood over there,' said Mrs Murphy. 'Do you know, I never met anyone before who came back from America.'

'American Irish, we like to think of ourselves. We've one foot over there while we hanker to come back. We still think of here as home. Not too many have returned, though.'

Delia wanted to hear his story and had to stop herself asking questions. It seemed inappropriate, and she had so many. Perhaps she'd learn more about Mr Dunne by listening.

'I could make a fresh pot of tea if you'd care to join me. The cups are clean – they're not bone china, I'm afraid, though.' He grinned at Delia. 'But we could turn it into a feast with a slice of this manna from heaven. Would that be taking liberties with you, ladies?' he asked.

Mrs Murphy looked at her again. 'What do you think, Miss Delia?'

'I think that sounds like a great idea.'

Moving the tools aside, he swept the sawdust and wood shavings from the rough table, and Mrs Murphy set out his cups on the cloth she had used to cover the basket. She cut a few slices off the bread and spread them thickly with jam, and the three of them stood in the little house, eating bread and drinking black tea.

Delia was remembering playing in the same ruins with Mona, speculating on who had lived there, and now here she was, socialising with one of the descendants and feeling totally at home. What would her mother say? Or her father? Or Lady Elizabeth? She'd probably have a strong weakness. Would Mona think she was compromising her reputation? Delia didn't know, but nothing felt wrong about it. She felt ridiculously happy and wanted to spend the rest of the afternoon there. She wished Mrs Murphy could go on to Mrs McCormack and Mrs Lynch to deliver her provisions and leave her behind, but she knew that was impossible.

Mr Dunne took the basket to the door, saying, 'That's a bit lighter now.'

Reluctantly she took it from him. 'Thank you, I hope we haven't taken up too much of your day.'

'You could never do that, Miss Delia,' he said, looking into her eyes and holding her gaze. She blushed and felt an awakening like nothing she had ever experienced. Confused, she turned away and followed Mrs Murphy out onto the back road.

Mrs Murphy talked about him all the way to the McCormacks', and about the chances of finding his ancestral home, and Delia was delighted to listen because Mrs Murphy knew more about him than she did, and she wanted to hear and absorb it all.

The McCormack children ran to meet Mrs Murphy. Their mother was standing in the doorway, her hand on her back, watching them. She was heavy with child. If it survived it would be her sixth living one in twelve years, and she looked weary. Like her, all the children had manes of red hair, pale blue eye and noses covered with big freckles. They danced around with delight at seeing the basket, knowing there'd be something for them in it. In their little world, Mrs Murphy and treats were synonymous.

'I've brought a visitor with me, Mary – Miss Delia from the big house.'

'Gooday, miss,' the woman said, looking flustered. 'Will you come in?'

Sensing her discomfort at her unexpected arrival, Delia declined. 'Thank you. Another time. You have your hands full with this lot, and we have another call to make, but Mrs Murphy wanted to drop a few things off for you.'

'Thank you for your kindness, miss, and may God be good to you,' the woman said.

'Have you everything you need for the baby?' Delia asked.

'Yes, I have indeed, thank you.'

When they left for the Lynches', Mrs Murphy said, 'You're just like your mother, do you know that? You understand people. I don't think Miss Mona would have asked Mary McCormack if she had everything for the baby, but your mother would.'

'Which is Mrs Lynch's cottage?'

'She's in the cabin behind the old blacksmith's forge, at the next bend. She's been widowed for nigh on thirty years. Her husband used to work on the farm. She doesn't have anyone now, poor soul. Her sons, all six of them, fine strapping lads, took the boat to get work in America. She finds it hard to stand these days. I usually try and get to see her at least once a week.'

It transpired that Mrs Murphy also usually filled Mrs Lynch's bucket with water and brought in some pieces of turf from the stack outside the back door and set them on the hearth for the woman to burn later.

'You're very kind, Mrs Murphy. Today has been a real pleasure,' Delia told the housekeeper as they returned home after leaving the remaining contents of the basket on Mrs Lynch's table.

'A pleasure. How could it have been a pleasure?'

'I've learned so much and I've met real people, people who say what they mean, not what they think you want to hear.'

'You are a strange one, Miss Delia.' She laughed. 'Real people indeed.'

'What did you think of Lady Constance and Lady Elizabeth, Mrs Murphy? Did you like them?' She knew she shouldn't ask, but she wanted to know.

'I never spoke to them outside my duties, so it's difficult to give my opinion,' Mrs Murphy answered tactfully. 'I don't think they would have too much to say to the likes of me, if they noticed me at all.'

'How could they not?' said Delia.

'Oh, child, you have a lot to learn about folk. There's them and there's us, and never the twain shall meet. Sometimes we're invisible to them until they need to see us. Anyway, there's no use fretting over such things. That's the way it is. I'll probably be too old to still be working here when Lady Elizabeth becomes mistress of Kensley Hall, and you and Miss Mona will be married with homes and families of your own, I suspect.'

'I never thought of her being mistress of Kensley Hall,' Delia said, reflecting. 'I don't want to think about things like that.'

'No one likes change,' Mrs Murphy said as they went in the kitchen door. 'And I need a cup of tea. Will you have one with me, Miss Delia, or would you like me to bring it upstairs to you?'

'I'll have it down here,' she replied and sat down at the long table, going over in her mind the afternoon and the people she'd met. And remembering Mr Dunne, and his smile, and the way he had looked at her when she told him she hoped she hadn't taken up too much of his time. And he'd said, 'You could never do that, Miss Delia.' She remembered his long fingers as he lifted the basket and handed it to her, and his smile. She couldn't get his smile out of her mind.

'I enjoyed today,' the housekeeper said.

'May I come out with you again?' Delia asked her.

'I'm not too sure, Miss Delia. I asked you to come today because I could see how you were feeling down when everyone had left. I didn't think we'd end up in Mr Dunne's cottage. I'm not sure your Mama or Papa would be too happy if they heard about that.'

'They don't need to know. I won't tell them if you don't.'

'I won't, but I don't like to be deceitful and they left you in my charge.'

'And what is it you think we did that was wrong, Mrs Murphy? We brought food to a few neighbours. They are not very likely to ask you if we took tea with Mr Dunne, are they? Anyway, he is a neighbour, of sorts, now."

'You're right, Miss Delia, and when you say it like that, sure, it is harmless.'

'So I can come with you again?' she pushed.

'Yes, you can, but I think it's best if we don't tell Miss Corneille either. She might let it slip.'

'Don't worry. It'll be our secret.'

Life settled into a pattern of sorts. The annual spring clean began, and those who were left in the house literally turned everything upside down. Rugs were taken into the gardens and beaten, curtains taken down and hung out in the breeze to air, alongside eiderdowns and pillows. Chandeliers were dismantled and washed prism by prism, ornaments rinsed and furniture polished until you could see your face in the table tops. The stable boys were redeployed to wash the countless panes of glass in the tall sash windows. Everything in the linen room was inspected, and anything in need of a stitch was put aside to be mended in the coming days. Amid this frenzy of activity, Delia continued her lessons with Mademoiselle Corneille. She practised her piano daily, apart from the day the tuner arrived from Dublin to work on it.

She only rode out with Tommy or one of the grooms, mounted and dismounted from the stand and didn't gallop or ride anywhere near Mr Dunne's cottage either.

That didn't mean she didn't see him, but then she had never made that promise to anyone. She accompanied Mrs Murphy whenever she could, and they always stopped to talk to him, sometimes for a few minutes, at other times for longer, usually taking some freshly baked bread for him, and for the workers when they were there. Delia looked forward to seeing what progress had been made each time she passed by.

Mary McCormack was delivered of another daughter, her fourth, and Mrs Murphy made sure she added poultry, extra eggs and butter to her basket for her. On wet days, Delia often came downstairs and sat with Mrs Murphy while she mended and chatted about anything and everything, reminiscing about people she had known who had departed.

'It wasn't only death that separated families. Look at Annie Lynch and her sons all in America. She'll never cast eyes on any one of them again in this world. They might as well be dead to her.'

'Don't they write to her?'

'I don't think so. She's never said anything about getting letters. I'm not sure that any of that family could ever read or write.'

Delia couldn't imagine a world without letters. That was how she knew what was happening with her family in London. She devoured each missive when it arrived, living through accounts of the fittings, rides in the park, soirées, high teas and visits to the theatre. She couldn't wait to join them and to see Mona again. As regards Lady Elizabeth, she still had reservations about her, but she kept those to herself. After all, Clement had chosen her as his bride-to-be, and because she loved her brother dearly, she'd try to love her sister-in-law for his sake, but there was just something she didn't like or trust about her.

Chapter 7

Mona's coming out had finally arrived. All the necessary preparations and protocols had been followed, and the application to be included among that year's debutantes had been filled. This had to be made by a lady who, herself, had already been presented to a sovereign or by someone from the aristocracy known to the family of the girl in question, a sponsor who would vouch for her breeding and good character. Lady Leonora had been presented to both Queen Victoria and her consort, Prince Albert, before he died.

With the unasked-for help of Lady Constance, who had come up to London with Lady Elizabeth to lend their support, several hopeful mothers had compiled lists of the most titled, highly ranked and eligible bachelors, along with their fortunes and expectations. Over-eager mamas had already invited some of these to their own social engagements, trying to get to them first. If the Kensley-Balfe daughters did not marry within three years of their debut, they'd be considered to have missed 'their opportunity' and could be faced with the prospect of a life as an old maid or, heaven forbid, living as a grace-and-favour maiden aunt with a brother or sister.

Lady Leonora was sure that was not going to happen to her girls. They were going to come out finished young ladies, well-read, accomplished in language, needlework, etiquette, painting and sketching, music and geography. Yes, her girls would be properly 'finished' and able to take their place in any social sphere, as she herself had done.

The house in London's elegant Grosvenor square was buzzing with excitement. Inside everyone was waiting expectantly for a glimpse of Mona, dressed and ready for her big moment.

'I can't believe it's finally arrived, your big day, your presentation at court,' Lord Kensley-Balfe said as he watched his daughter come down the stairs looking like a princess, a vision in white from head to toe, her veil held over her arm as she'd been taught. She was wearing the same pearls her mother and her grandmother had worn to court on just such an occasion.

'My dear, you look wonderful. So grown up, you make me feel quite old.'

'Thank you, Papa.'

'Me too,' said Clement, standing beside Lady Elizabeth and his future mother-in-law, who cooed and oohed when she saw Mona. 'Are you really my young sister? You seem to have grown up even more since we arrived here.'

'Oh my, you do look beautiful, Mona. Doesn't she, Elizabeth? That dress, and the lace. Beautiful, absolutely beautiful,' Lady Constance said. 'You'll be fighting off the suitors. And as for you, Lady Leonora, what a proud day for you all.'

Lady Leonora smiled and nodded at Lady Constance, too happy to let her dampen the day. Lady Leonora wore a beaded peacock silk dress, accessorised with peacock feathers arranged and entwined in her auburn hair. Both parents were to accompany Mona to the palace, and she felt thrilled to be seen with her father in his tailored long coat and top hat. Her mother made a final tweak to Mona's veil and she was ready. Lord Kensley-Balfe escorted his daughter out to the carriage, with two maids holding up her dress to prevent it trailing on the ground. Then he went back for his wife. All the staff peeped from behind doors and over the bannisters to watch them depart.

'Your mother was the toast of high-society drawing rooms following her court presentation,' Lord Peter told Mona a short time later, as they sat in a queue of carriages, waiting to be admitted to the palace. They had been warned it could be a long day and had taken some food along just in case.

'Can that really have been thirty, no, thirty-one years ago? I can't believe it.' Lady Leonora laughed, remembering. By the end of the London season, and the start of the grouse shooting one, she'd already had several proposals of marriage, the first at the Chelsea Flower Show.

'There was no shortage of eager suitors trying to fill her dance cards,' Lord Peter said. 'She was always in demand – invited to all the best balls and house parties. That's how we were introduced, at one of those, but she wasn't that easy to pin down – were you, dear? She made me wait.'

'The girls kept talking about this Lord Kensley-Balfe, a distinguished-looking gentleman who, by all accounts, the mothers had given up hoping to catch for their daughters. A bachelor gay, he showed no signs of settling down, and that made him a bit of a challenge.'

'But you got him, Mama,' Mona said. 'And I'm glad you did.'

'So am I,' her father agreed.

He had wooed her tirelessly, and she had finally agreed to marry him a year later. She was nineteen and he was twenty-nine. Lady Leonora considered herself fortunate. He'd been a good husband and father, and had given her a son who filled her with pride. She hoped her daughters would be as lucky.

'You do look especially lovely today, Mona,' she said, looking at her with fresh eyes. She had turned into a poised debutante, elegant in white, her embroidered dress fitting her perfectly. It had been worth all the effort to see her like this. Her long above-the-elbow gloves and hand-crafted court shoes could have been moulded on to her, her glossy fair hair gleaming beneath the lace veil.

'I hope I don't trip when I'm curtseying,' said Mona, trying to keep her hands still. 'I'm so nervous.'

'You won't, Mona,' her mother said. 'You've had lots of practice and you never tripped then.'

The carriage inched forward and Mona said, 'I wish Delia was here today.'

'Perhaps we were a little harsh not letting her come. But I'll not have any time to chaperone her,' her mother answered.

'Elizabeth and her mama could help while they're here, couldn't they?'

'Perhaps they could,' Lady Leonora said.

'Or Mademoiselle Corneille and Mrs Murphy could come with her?'

'I doubt if Mrs Murphy is robust enough for all the travelling, but Mademoiselle Corneille ... now why didn't I think of her? I'll send her a note tomorrow,' her mother conceded. 'I miss her not being with us too.'

The carriage that had been moving slowly down the Mall in a long procession towards Buckingham Palace finally came to a halt, and a liveried footman approached, holding the door open for Mona to step out on to the red carpet that led through the doors into the palace.

'Here we go, best foot forward,' said Sir Peter as he handed his wife down.

They followed the ushers, smiled at other debutantes and parents, ascended the marble staircase and joined another queue. The young ladies in white waited to be allowed into the anteroom, where they were seated on uncomfortably narrow gilt chairs before being admitted to the ballroom. The presentation would take place there. Mona's heart was beating faster as her turn came nearer and nearer, then she heard the Lord Chamberlain announce Lady Leonora Kensley-Balfe and Lady Mona Kensley-Balfe.

The moment had arrived.

Remembering everything she'd been told, Mona walked demurely to the top of the ballroom, to where Her Majesty was seated on a throne with a canopy above it. Mona took her time, curtseyed deeply and faultlessly, turned and exited without looking left or right. She was then marshalled to the Green Drawing Room to join the debutantes who had already been through the ritual. The atmosphere was very different to that in the anteroom, Now, relieved of all stress, the girls chatted and laughed, discussed their plans, arranged to call on each other and, remembering their manners, ate the chocolate cake that was offered to them.

Dinner that night was a jolly occasion, with Mona being allowed to have champagne.

'I'm so excited,' she told Elizabeth. 'I've already received some invitations and I'm looking forward to my first ball on Saturday. I hope I am asked to dance and that I can!'

'Of course you will be, and of course you can. This time next month you'll be a natural at it all, and you'll wonder why you were worried. At my first tea dance a friend of my father's asked me to dance, a waltz. I stood on his foot – twice. He was very gracious, but I saw him wince – twice.' They laughed.

'Honestly?' said Mona

'Honestly!' Elizabeth replied. 'And it must have hurt.'

'What are you two ladies hatching?' Clement asked.

'I was telling your fiancée that I'm apprehensive about my first ball.'

'There's no need to be. We all get it wrong in the beginning and tread on our partner's toes. That's a rite of passage, and I speak from experience.'

She felt much better after that.

For a change, the viceroy and vicereine were given a rest from Lady Constance's conversation, as she seemed genuinely interested in all the pomp and ceremony, and wanted all the details about the palace and what they saw there.

Later, Lady Leonora said to her husband, 'She'll probably dine off Mona's debutante experience when she goes back to India, and tell everyone about how her "future son-in-law's sister, the Kensley-Balfes, you know, was recently presented to Her Majesty Queen Victoria in Buckingham Palace ..."'

'Oh, you are wicked,' he laughed, 'but I'll wager you're right too.'

Upstairs, Mona was too animated to sleep, so she wrote to her sister. She told her everything she could remember about the day and how tiny she thought Her Majesty looked, sitting there on her throne.

And severe too. She didn't look very happy. She probably hates having to sit there for hours just to keep the gentry satisfied. There were over a hundred of us there today, and she has to face the same twice more at Buckingham Palace and then again at Queen Charlotte's birthday ball. Can you just imagine having to sit though all those curtseys? And at the birthday ball the debutantes have to not only curtsey to Her Majesty, but they also have to do a second one – to a birthday cake! I think I would feel very foolish doing that.

I wish you had been here, Delia, and I can't wait for you to come for Clement and Elizabeth's engagement ball. There'll be a supper first and you're to be included in that. I know that will make you happy! And we should have some photographs of today by then to show you. I can't wait to see them too.

It's very late, and as I now have a social diary and engagements booked in, and a wardrobe of new clothes to wear to them, I must try to get some sleep.

Try not to be too bored on your own. Love from your now-all-grown-up sister,
Mona

She eventually fell asleep.

Chapter 8

Delia had mixed feelings reading Mona's letter.

She was excited at the prospects of going to London and of being with her family again, but doing so would mean she'd miss out on chances to see and sometimes talk to Mr Dunne. She was confused at how she felt about him. He kept coming in to her thoughts, no matter what she was doing. It was something inside her that made her feel energised, excited and euphorically happy. She had never felt like this before. She looked out the window each morning hoping the sky was clear, because Mrs Murphy didn't like to walk in the rain and she couldn't go along the back road alone if she was to keep her promise to Mona.

'Try not to be too bored,' Mona had written.

Bored? She wasn't bored. She had never been less bored in her life. Nor had she ever worked as hard at her schoolwork, nor practised her piano with such determination. She took her meals downstairs with Mrs Murphy and the staff who had remained.

On one of the wet days she found Mrs Murphy at the table, her sewing box and scissors in front of her.

'What are you doing?' she enquired.

'Keeping busy. The devil finds work for idle hands.'

'But what are you doing to keep busy?' Delia asked.

'Making use of these odds and ends. There's always a bit of material that can be used again and it's a shame to let it go to waste.' She delved into a tall wicker basket on the floor beside her and pulled out a garment. 'See that frayed petticoat, that would make grand little pinafores or shirts for Mary McCormack's little ones. And the discoloured table linens, they can all be cut down and sewn into something useful.'

'The sewing would be no problem for me, but I wouldn't know where to begin making anything fit.'

'I can show you if you'd like. Pinafores are very easy to make – we'll need a back and a front the same size – but first we'll make a pattern,' Mrs Murphy said, finding some folded brown paper in a drawer and spreading it out on the table. She made a few pencil marks on it, explaining as she did. 'Those curves are for the armholes and we'll need pieces the same shape to use as facings.'

'It seems very complicated,' Delia said. 'Maybe I should just do the sewing?'

'It isn't. You'll see. Check the material so you're not using any that's damaged. Put the pattern pieces on it, pin them down and cut around them. That's all there is to it,' she said.

'That used to be mine,' said Delia, recognising the broderie anglaise border on the old petticoat. It was badly frayed at the back and along the hemline. 'Couldn't we put some of that on the pinafores?'

'Indeed we could, Miss Delia. You've got the right idea.'

Delia became so engrossed in her new pursuits over the next several days that she scarcely went riding at all. Tommy came to enquire if she was all right one morning and found the two of them in the kitchen, baking bread together. Delia was enveloped in one of Mrs Murphy's large aprons, flour all over her hands.

'Now there's a sight I never thought I'd see.' He laughed. 'Is it trying to poison us all you are?' he asked.

Indignantly, Delia told him, 'Definitely not. I'm learning from an expert!'

Mademoiselle Corneille arrived on the scene just then. 'You are late for your lessons, Miss Delia.'

'I am sorry, Mademoiselle. I forgot about the time. I'll make it up, but can I wait until my soda squares come out of the oven? Please. I want to see what they look and taste like.'

'As you have been working so hard, I'll agree, and for our next conversation class you can tell me in French how to make bread. That should extend your vocabulary.'

'It should, as I can already think of several words that I don't know.'

'Don't be too long. I'll be in the schoolroom,' she said as she turned to leave the kitchen.

'Wait a minute.' Mrs Murphy bent to the open oven. 'These are ready now, and Tommy, as you were so quick with your smart remarks about poisoning, can you tell me who made which batch? And you too, Miss Corneille.' Mrs Murphy could never quite get her tongue around 'mademoiselle'.

Delia thought they were very similar – the same colour, the same shape, and when Mrs Murphy tapped on the bottom of each loaf they made the same hollow sound, indicating that they were fully cooked.

'Now, Mrs Murphy, you have me there, for I can't see a bit of difference in them at all,' Tommy said, after studying them closely.

'Neither can I. They look exactly the same. May we taste them and compare?' Mademoiselle asked.

'Yes,' said Mrs Murphy, enjoying herself, 'take a seat.' She laid butter and jam out and took some plates from the big dresser. She then sliced through two loaves, one from each tray, and put a piece from the first on the four plates. Then she repeated the test with the second loaf. While they were deliberating, she wrapped some of the squares in clean cloths and put them aside for her baskets.

'Well? What's the verdict? Which one did Miss Delia make? Miss Corneille? Tommy? Can you tell?' she asked.

They couldn't.

'I think we need to try some more to be sure,' Tommy said. They laughed and Mrs Murphy made a pot of tea. As a result, the French lesson moved to the kitchen and the morning passed very unconventionally, with no clear winner in the baking stakes.

The heavens opened before Tommy went back to the stables. Delia felt the joy go out of the day, a day that had started so happily. 'Ye'll not be walking as far as the Widow Lynch's today. It gets very marshy down by the old forge on that bend,' he said, noticing that Mrs Murphy had prepared not one, but two baskets. 'I'll take those with me and ride down to the cottages when it eases off a bit and deliver them.'

'Oh, the blessings of God on you, Tommy. Sure the women will be depending on these vitals,' Mrs Murphy said. 'The small one on the top is for Mr Dunne, the man working on the cottage beside Crosbie's field. He's very partial to the soda bread.'

'Ah sure, isn't everyone?' replied Tommy. 'And don't I know who he is. We met when Miss Delia had her fall and we've exchanged pleasantries more than once since then.'

When he had gone, Mrs Murphy said, 'That served him right! Poison him, indeed. Even I had difficulty telling my own bread, Miss Delia. I was very impressed. It's just as well you're off to London next week. I'm not too sure if Her Ladyship would approve of the way we've been bending the rules in her absence.'

'I honestly don't think she'd mind. I'm learning so much, and it's been much more amusing than me staying upstairs all the time, trying to pass the hours. I love spending time down here with you.'

'And I love having you down here too, but it'll have to stop when the family returns.'

'I know. Do you think we could finish off the pinafores this afternoon, as we won't be going out? I'd like to do that before I go away.'

'That's exactly what I was thinking myself,' said Mrs Murphy.

A few hours later, they were almost done. Delia had unpicked the bands of broderie anglaise from the petticoat and was now using it to trim the bib fronts of the pinafores, while Mrs Murphy finished off the buttonholes. Then they spread the garments out on the table for a final inspection.

'This is very good work. You should be very proud of yourself, child. Oh, I promised myself that I wouldn't call you that again.' Mrs Murphy laughed. 'Although I don't suppose I'll ever see you any other way, even though you're not a child any more.'

'You can take all the credit for these, Mrs Murphy, for letting me pester you and for not chasing me away when you were doing the mending.'

'Sure, I can't wait to see the McCormack children wearing

these. They'll think all their birthdays have come together. If it's fine tomorrow, you could bring them down to them.'

Delia hoped it would be. It had been such an enjoyable day, and the only cloud, apart from those dripping rain on everything outside, was that she hadn't seen Mr Dunne and she only had three more days in which to do so.

The rain was relentless. It continued all day and dripped all night long, at times beating angrily against the window panes in Delia's bedroom. The sky was dark and leaden the next day, and it showed no signs of letting up. She was beginning to despair. There were things she wanted to tell him if only she could get to see him on his own. She wanted to tell him why she didn't ride by any more, and that, when she returned from London, she wouldn't be making her frequent visits with Mrs Murphy, not because she wouldn't want to, but because of what was expected of her and her position.

She didn't question whether he would be surprised by such revelations or why she felt compelled to tell him these things. She just knew that he'd understand. She felt there was a bond, something invisible yet very real, drawing them to each other.

The rain did stop eventually and the sun shone two days before she was due to travel. Mrs Murphy had prepared her baskets, and Delia took the heavier of the two and the brown-paper parcel, tied with string. Her senses were on high alert as they turned onto the back road, but her heart sank as the bright new thatch came into view. Several other men were building the walls alongside Mr Dunne. That meant that Mrs Murphy wouldn't stop longer than to hand over the bread and pass the time of day. That was what she usually did when he wasn't alone and Delia was with her.

Mr Dunne greeted them and said, 'I've missed this, Mrs Murphy – your bread just gets better and better. The last lot was the best yet.'

'Oh, that wasn't mine,' she said nonchalantly. 'Miss Delia made that. Now, we mustn't detain you.'

'Well, that's a surprise. What other talents are you hiding, Miss Delia?' he asked, and she felt herself blush to the roots of her hair.

'We have to keep going, Mr Dunne,' she said. 'We have things to deliver before I leave for London on Friday.'

'London?' he said, a look of disbelief on his face. 'You're going away?'

'Yes, London. Good luck with your building work. It'll probably be finished when I return.'

'I hope not, because that would mean I won't be here,' he said, as she followed Mrs Murphy down the road in the direction of Mary McCormack's. She was devastated. She couldn't believe that he'd be gone and she would never see him again. She couldn't bear the thought.

Only two red-headed, freckled children ran out to greet their visitors. Then their mother, who had obviously been feeding the baby, appeared at the door. 'Please don't think I'm being ungrateful, but I won't ask you to come in today,' she said to Delia and Mrs Murphy. 'Noreen, the eldest,' she reminded them, 'is feeling poorly.'

'Of course. Don't disturb her,' Mrs Murphy answered. 'We just wanted to drop off little things for the children.'

The woman smiled as Delia admired the little bundle.

'Here, let me hold the baby so you can see them properly,' Delia offered.

'I don't know what to say. I can never thank you for your generosity, Miss Delia,' Mary McCormack said. She took the garments out of the basket one by one and admired them. 'They've never had anything as grand as these before. They're so fine and beautiful. And they couldn't have come at a better time. Some of the children have been sick and listless all week. These will lift their spirits, I'm sure, as they have mine. May God be good to you, and to your family.'

But Delia's mind wasn't really on the conversation. The bombshell that Hugh had just dropped negated all the joy she should have felt in seeing the tears in the poor woman's eyes. Unbeknownst to Delia, Mrs Murphy had been busy in her spare time and had included shirts for the two boys so that they wouldn't feel left out. She'd even added some cast-offs of Clement's for Mr McCormack.

'I hope they're better soon, and you can thank Mrs Murphy, Mrs McCormack. These were all her idea, and she showed me how to cut the patterns. Maybe she could show you sometime too and you could have a go yourself.'

'Oh, I don't think I could do that,' the woman said shyly. 'But I'm sure Noreen could get a grasp on it. She has all the brains. She's even able to read and write. She's been teaching the younger ones, and me too, so we can keep in touch when she goes away to work. I'm not very good at it yet, but I won't give up.'

'It takes practice. I'm sure you'll master it,' Delia said.

Mrs Murphy added, 'You never know what you can do until you try.'

'I'm sure there are some books in the nursery from when we were learning that might be useful. I'll have a look when I get back and bring them the next time.' Delia smiled at her.

'You're very quiet,' Mrs Murphy said to Delia as they walked back home. 'I hope you're not coming down with something just before your travels or Her Ladyship will kill me.'

'I'm fine. I don't like leaving, yet I want to go to London.'

'Sure, that's only natural. And I've had a grand time these past few weeks. I'll miss you.'

'I'll write to you.'

'Now, as you know, Miss Delia, I may know how to sew and cook, but I'm not that great with the letter writing, but I do want to hear what's happening over there.'

'Promise me you'll try. I'll leave some envelopes already addressed and you can just put your letters inside. Get Annie to help you,' she said.

'All right, I'll do that. When we get home we'll do a final run through with Miss Corneille.'

Mademoiselle had received her instructions from Lady Kensley-Balfe. She was in charge of ensuring that everything they needed for their London visit would be in place by Thursday, as they'd have an early start the following morning. Tommy would accompany them to Ballina and on the trains for Dublin and Kingstown. He was to make sure they boarded the mail boat safely, stay in a boarding house overnight and return to Kensley Park the next day. All Mademoiselle Corneille had to do was see them from the boat to the boat train at Holyhead. From there it was a direct connection to London, where Clement would meet them.

'I'm sure she has thought of everything,' Delia answered absentmindedly, just as Mr Dunne's cottage came into view.

Chapter 9

Hugh Dunne was surprised by his reaction when Delia told him she was going away, and in a few days too. He hadn't been expecting that. He had to do something. Say something. But what? What could he say that would make any difference? She could have no time for the likes of him. She was completely out of his class. She was landed gentry – he was from peasant stock. But he sensed something between them that he had no words for. Still, she would probably end up marrying into another titled family, with all that entailed – swanky country houses, servants, horses and a huge sense of entitlement.

No, he might be wrong about the last bit. Delia didn't strike him as that sort of girl. She didn't display any signs of entitlement. She always acted as though she was at ease, no matter what situation she was in, whether chatting with the housekeeper, dealing with the doctor, or drinking black tea in his cottage. He never thought she'd do that, and when he'd asked her and Mrs Murphy to come in, he felt he had overstepped the boundaries, but she didn't act as though he had. He actually felt she'd enjoyed it.

He couldn't get her out of his mind. She had bewitched him from the moment he'd set eyes on her, after he'd pegged those rocks through the window space. From the instant he saw her on the ground, her hazel eyes looking up at him, he felt he was under a spell. He could conjure up the scent of her that day: lavender soap and frosty fresh air. It remained on his coat after Tommy had given it back to him, once they had got her home safely. She was brave. Another girl would have cried out in pain, but she had stayed calm, despite that.

Logic told him there was no question of them having a future together, no matter what his prospects were. Even if society allowed it, he couldn't visualise her in a thatched cottage, no matter how well restored it was. As for whisking her away to New York – that would never happen.

Having met and dealt with Lord Kensley-Balfe, he should not have been surprised to discover that his younger daughter had the same charm. He wondered what His Lordship would say, after his kindness to him, if he knew the thoughts Hugh was having about her. As for her brother, who had only shown disdain for him – why, he'd probably have him horsewhipped!

But despite that sure knowledge, Hugh dreamed and fantasised continually, often completing tasks without realising what he was doing. Every time he heard horses' hooves on the back road from Kensley Park, or coming along the bridle path from the little wood, his heart flipped as he waited in anticipation. A glimpse of her sitting on her mount as she rode into view was all he needed to satisfy the longing in him. He liked to watch her as she walked towards the cottages and when she was walking away from them, her auburn hair caught back in a ribbon and gleaming in the sunlight. When she spoke to him he couldn't take his eyes off her.

And now she was going away and he felt bereft. He had to do something, say something, but what? It was a hopeless situation.

Hugh Dunne had done well for himself, as the grandson of an Irish Catholic immigrant in the Bronx, New York. He knew his grandfather Jack Dunne's story by heart. Jack had told and retold it, as though he wanted it to be committed to memory and never lost. He urged Hugh never to forget it, in case the same thing could happen again. Hugh could still recall his sing-song voice telling him about it.

'Seeing land after weeks at sea was like we had made it to paradise. Sure, what fools we were. For many of us, we had just swapped the place we'd perish, one for another. We knew we'd never see our relatives again. Many of us never saw a green field after that either. Times were hard, very hard. Surviving the horrific sea crossing in the bowels of a creaking boat, in cramped, unsanitary and often unseaworthy vessels, without enough water or food, was far from the end of our troubles.'

Jack Dunne never told Hugh until he was much older that they had fled before they could be evicted from their cottage in Mayo and that three of his children had perished on the journey, victims of typhus, and that he and his wife, Nancy, watched their little bodies being thrown overboard, wrapped in old sail cloth, to sink into the cold inhospitable depths of the Atlantic. Hugh's grandmother never got over their loss.

He knew she had contracted a lung disease that would take her before her time, as it did so many of the Irish at the time. And, sure, they were refugees and they hadn't a farthing between them, but they helped each other, sharing whatever little they had. The Irish stuck together, but they had been ill-prepared for the winter's cold and had to take shelter anywhere it was to be found, several families together in damp basements, outhouses and the likes. His granda used to liken them to 'a flock of sheep, with no herdsman, following each other, not knowing where they'd end up'.

And so his story went, leaving Hugh with great admiration for this proud old man who had lived through these times and had survived, however scarred and wounded. He had instilled a yearning in his grandson to see where he had come from, perhaps even find the exact place from which he had emigrated.

Everything Hugh knew about his family he had learned from his grandfather. He knew that Jack had lived in a cottage close to a blacksmith's and, as a young boy, he had spent a lot of his time watching the smithy work. He often held a rich man's horse while the blacksmith fashioned and fitted a shoe. That sometimes got him half a penny.

He'd loved the smell of the furnace, and watching how it crackled and sent plumes of sparks into the air. He used to stand outside the doors for hours, feeling its heat and watching the smith as he picked up a piece of iron with tongs and held it in the glowing embers until it too glowed an orange-red. Then he'd remove it and begin hammering it into the required shape. Jack told him how he still remembered that sound – the sound of the hammer hitting the anvil as it beat out a tuneless rhythm. He'd watched gates, pipes, ploughs and all sorts of farm implements being made there. Hugh remembered his granda saying how no knowledge is ever wasted and that he never could have imagined how useful these lessons would be in his later life.

Many years and many thousands of miles later, within a few weeks of reaching the Bronx, word had gone around that J.L. Mott Iron Works was hiring. It was an enormous industrial sprawl, bigger than anything any of them had ever seen or could have imagined. They were looking for men with experience, not farmhands like him, but he urgently needed work and work he was going to get.

He went along and stood outside the works until the hooter sounded and the workers started to go home. He waited until he heard an Irish accent, then he stopped the man and asked what they made in the foundry. The following day, sporting his best cap and tweed jacket, he'd headed off and joined a long queue, snaking its way around the corner of the works. A foreman went down the line shouting, 'Experienced men only. If you've no training, then you're no good to us. Experienced men only.' Jack stood his ground as dozens of desperate and hungry-looking men fell from the line and sloped away dejectedly.

When Jack reached the desk, he was asked about his experience and he'd replied it had been in Ireland, mostly in farm machinery and implements. He was told to report the next day. He could read and write, and when they discovered that he could also measure and calculate, he was put on grade two, which meant he'd be paid more money.

'There's nothing in this whole world like the satisfaction of being able to provide for your family, Hugh. Remember that. I walked back to the tenement house that day feeling like a king, like I owned the world.' He'd promised his wife, Nancy, that they'd never have to live like they had in Ireland again, that the children would be schooled and that they'd make a good life for each other. Hugh knew that he'd kept his word, but he never got back to his homeland, nor had he ever got over leaving it.

It was during these chats that Hugh promised himself he'd go back some day, for his father and his granda.

And now Hugh had done just that. He'd made it back to Ireland and, following the scraps of information he had, he'd been able to pinpoint the very place from which his forefathers had fled. Could these be the fields they had planted and ploughed and where his father, his aunts and uncles had run and played before they had had to leave? He hadn't factored into his dream that the countryside around these parts would be pockmarked with so many ruins of cabins and stone cottages that it would almost be impossible to trace the exact one. If it hadn't been for Jack's yarns and his powers of recall, he would never have found its location with any degree of accuracy.

And, in a strange way, this was down to Delia too. Because of her he had met Lord Kensley-Balfe, and it was while showing him the rough maps he had made that His Lordship had identified where the old forge was and confirmed the cottages were on what had been Crosbie's land. That had been the last piece of the puzzle.

He thought he'd misheard when Lord Kensley-Balfe sat across the kitchen table in Kensley Park and told him, 'If we can agree on a price that parcel of land is yours.'

Hugh hadn't answered. Finding it was one thing – but he'd never imagined he'd actually end up owning the place.

'It's timely that you should show up right now. As it happens, we're in the throes of redrawing the boundaries for the Land Commission to include the Crosbie spread, which I recently acquired.'

'I don't know what to say, sir. I never expected that and I do remember my grandfather mentioning the name Crosbie.'

His Lordship suggested a figure. 'If you prefer we'll get an independent valuation, although in truth you'll be doing me a favour removing a reminder. There's hardly any land attached to the cottages, just the triangle they sit on, and losing that little patch is not going to make one whit of difference to the estate. Besides, it would be nice to see things turning a full circle. If you're happy we'll shake hands on it,' he said, extending his arm. 'A gentleman's agreement. And I'll get my agent to sort out the paperwork.'

'That asking price seems very fair to me.'

Lord Kensley-Balfe said, 'If we're both happy then let there be no more about it.'

Hugh Dunne had come to Kensley Park that afternoon as a nobody and was leaving as a landlord. He couldn't believe what had just happened – a landowner, and of his ancestral home too. No doubt the adjoining cottages had belonged to distant relatives. That was how it had been in those days. And it was all down to his grandfather's hard work. He rode back by the derelict ruins, already formulating plans for what he would do with them. He wished his father and grand-father were still alive. He would have loved to tell them of his discovery, that not everybody was exploitative and that there were still decent landlords in Ireland.

Lord Kensley-Balfe's treatment of him now played on his conscience and added even more weight to his sense of propriety. He couldn't take liberties with the daughter of a man who had shown him such consideration. He was well aware that he'd been playing with fire while the family was away. What would His Lordship say if he knew he'd invited Delia in to drink tea in his ramshackle cottage and that he regarded her as a – a friend? He recognised that she could never be that either. She'd always be the lady from the big house and he the son and grandson of peasants.

She hadn't given him any encouragement. But from their initial encounter, he had been totally obsessed with her. He could hardly breathe that first time when she'd looked up at him with her big amber eyes and asked him what exactly he thought he was doing hurling rocks about like that?

And now, just as randomly as she had come into his life, she was going to disappear out of it, and he couldn't bear the thought of the void that would leave. On impulse, he sat and scribbled a note on a page from his book of drawings and kept watch for the two women returning from the Widow Lynch's. He put the note in his pocket. As they passed, he came out of the cottage and addressed the housekeeper.

'Could I ask your advice on something, Mrs Murphy? As a woman who knows a lot, do you think I should put the fireplace on the back or the side wall in the room in the new part of the cottage? Paudie, here, thinks it should go in the middle, to keep the heat inside, whereas I think it might work on the end wall. Will you show her, Paudie?' he said. Mrs Murphy, delighted to be consulted, followed the workman.

'It's very muddy in there, Miss Delia,' Hugh said. He retrieved the note from his pocket and pressed it into her hand. 'Please take this and read it, and I think it's best if you don't let anyone know about it. I'm sorry about the scrappy bit of paper it's written on.' She pushed it up her sleeve when they heard Mrs Murphy's voice.

'Mr Dunne, far be it from me to be contrary,' she said, as she came back outside, 'but I'm inclined to side with Paudie. Sure, you're only heating the outdoors if you put it on the end wall. Putting it in the middle makes more sense. One lot of turf will nearly do the work of two.'

'I knew I could rely on you, Mrs Murphy. A rock of good sense. Thank you. I'll take your advice,' he said, hoping Paudie hadn't spotted the drawings he had already made with the fireplace and chimney in the centre of the house. He watched them walk away.

The sky was a wonderful pink that night and Hugh took that to be a good omen. His father always said, 'a red sky at night is the shepherds' delight'. If that was so, the morrow would be fine and sunny. If it was he wouldn't be able to blame the weather if she didn't turn up.

He couldn't sleep. He kept asking himself what had possessed him to do what he did. He'd exposed his feelings and, although he didn't regret doing so, he knew it could change everything. He hoped she wouldn't have found his note offensive. Had she tossed it into the fire as soon as she got back to Kensley Park?

He had risked everything by doing what he did. Now he kept questioning the wisdom of it, yet when he thought of her smile, her eyes, her slender waist, he knew he had no choice.

He couldn't let her walk out of his life without trying.

Chapter 10

In London, Mona's life was turning into a whirlwind of high-society events. There were so many invitations that refusals often had to be sent to avoid doubling up on engagements. The mamas were watching from their gilded chairs at the soirées and balls, speculating and making mental notes of who was dancing with whom, and who they ought to connect with to ensure the right introductions were made while the season was at its height.

Each morning Mona went riding through one of the nearby parks with Elizabeth and Clement. She was beginning to recognise some of the people they encountered on the way, and she had already noticed a tall dark-eyed rider on a few occasions. She had seen him at a tea dance, but she didn't know his name.

'My first theatre party in the West End, and at the Lyceum,' she told Clement. 'I can't wait to tell Delia all about it. Mademoiselle Corneille made us study the *Merchant of Venice*, but actually seeing Ellen Terry and Henry Irving perform it – it was mesmerising. You must take Elizabeth to it.'

'You really did like it.' Her brother laughed.

'I loved it,' she replied. 'Now I have seen for myself why they are the talk of London.'

He smiled indulgently at his sister and said, 'And I love your enthusiasm for everything. Don't ever lose that. It's infectious.'

That afternoon she and Lady Kensley-Balfe were at home to callers and the evening held the promise of another soirée, this one in the Savoy hotel.

'I'm told the Hattersley's ballroom in London is not large enough to fit all they wanted to invite,' Lady Constance told Lady Leonora. 'I've not met them before, but I believe their son, Desmond, is much in demand by the debutantes. Is Mona already acquainted with him?'

Lady Leonora was doing her best to be charming to this woman, but was finding it very wearisome. She never liked name-droppers, and Lady Constance was the worst she had ever encountered. She didn't bother telling her that the Hattersley and Kensley-Balfe families were long-term friends and related through marriage.

'I believe so.'

'Is he coming to our ball?' Lady Constance asked.

'He has already accepted. And Delia will be with us before that. I miss the child – she must be feeling a bit left out in Kensley Park on her own,' Lady Leonora said.

'Probably, but isn't it lovely to see my Elizabeth and your Mona get on so well together? It's as though they were already sisters.'

'They *have* become very close,' Lady Leonora agreed.

'Perhaps Mona will come to India some day, to stay with her and Clement after they're married. She'd enjoy the society there. Life is never dull because the viceroy is very fond of entertaining, but we can get a bit tired of the same faces. New ones are always a delightful distraction. And I'm not talking about the fishing fleet faces either,' she said conspiratorially. 'Not that I'm saying anything against those young women. Lord knows, there are enough young men in the regiments to go around, and the ladies' arrival docs prevent the men from making unsuitable liaisons with the native women.'

'She's going to miss Clement. They both are. They were quite young when he first left for India. But at least they'll have a few more months with him before he leaves again.'

Delia came back with Mrs Murphy and put the two empty baskets on a shelf in the storeroom. She could hardly wait to go upstairs and see what was on the piece of paper that Mr Dunne had pressed into her hand. She was about to excuse herself before Mrs Murphy made tea for the two of them, but was stopped in her tracks when she heard her say, 'This is likely the last time we'll do this, for it will all be different when you come back with the family. Her Ladyship won't want you spending all your time down here with me, now that you're almost grown up.'

'But I will still come down, Mrs Murphy. I'm not going to abandon you,' Delia said, sitting down at the table. She felt for the older woman, who until last year had always accompanied the family when they went to London.

'Sure, the house will be quare quiet with you gone,' she said.

'Enjoy the peace and quiet, Mrs Murphy. We'll be back before you know it and I'll write you all the news.'

She eventually escaped, went up to the drawing room and closed the door after her. She retrieved the note from her sleeve and smoothed it out. She didn't know what to expect. It simply read:

Miss Delia,
I can't stop thinking about you and I can't let you go out of my life without talking to you properly. Please meet me by the cherry wood tomorrow at eleven. In case you're worried, no one should see us there. I must talk to you, and unless I'm greatly mistaken, I think you want that too. If I'm wrong, forgive me.
Yours sincerely,
Hugh Dunne

She took a deep breath. If he was wrong? He wasn't.

He wasn't wrong at all. She wanted to see him. And he wanted to see her. But how could he have read her thoughts? There was no way he could have known that she felt the same. He must have sensed it, as she had done about him. A sort of telepathy. She had felt her heart drop when she had seen the workmen earlier because she knew there would be no chance for conversation with him. She didn't want to leave like this either, without getting to know him better. Without getting to know him at all, if he was to have gone back to America when she returned. She couldn't bear thinking about that.

She was confused and excited, but it was an adult confusion, something she hadn't experienced before. Her senses were on high alert, and she knew she would go to meet him, whatever the consequences. If Mademoiselle enquired, she'd tell her she was going to do a sketch for Mona.

She didn't know what he wanted to talk about, and she didn't know what difference it could make to their lives and situations, but she knew with every fibre of her being that she had to meet him and find out.

She took the note, folded it carefully, brought it up to her room and put it under her pillow. She reread it several times before finally going to sleep that night.

Hugh was at the cherry wood a long time before he needed to be. He paced anxiously up and down. Supposing she didn't turn up? Supposing she did? What was he going to say to her? What would she say to him? He hadn't an idea, yet instinctively he felt it would be the right thing, so long as he didn't get tongue-tied and make a fool of himself.

He checked the time every few minutes on his grandfather's gold watch. This nestled safely in his waistcoat pocket, secured by a gold chain. It had been a retirement present from J.L. Mott Iron Works, in recognition for an invention Jack had made to stop downdraughts in a line of anthracite stoves. He later patented it in Hugh's name and it proved to be a steady earner in royalties. Hugh never went out without the watch. It represented so much to him – his grandfather's work ethic and stoicism in the face of seemingly unsurmountable obstacles.

The hands edged their way slowly towards the hour. Then he heard a faint rustling. His heart started pounding as he turned towards it, and he saw Delia coming along the path. She was a vision, her smiling face, her eager gait as she walked towards him, the pink cherry blossom above her auburn hair and strewn beneath her feet. He had never seen anything as beautiful.

Holding out his hands to her, he smiled and said, 'You came. I wasn't sure you would.'

'Neither was I,' she replied, taking his hands in hers, 'but I'm here now.' They both laughed. Apart from pushing the note into her gloved hand, this was the first time they'd touched, and it was as though some current passed from one to the other and back again. He was aware that his hands were rough and hardened from the manual work he'd been doing. Hers were soft as gossamer. They stood like that, wordlessly, for a few seconds, looking at each other, and in those moments their worlds shifted.

'What did you want to talk to me about?' she asked when she felt she could speak.

They let go of each other and he said, 'I don't know where to begin, but Miss Delia, and forgive me for being so bold, you have taken over my world. Every thought I have is of you. I can't concentrate. I spend every hour of every day waiting to see you come along with Mrs Murphy. When you do, you turn a light on inside me. When you told me you were going away tomorrow, I panicked. I can't imagine what it will be like knowing you won't be coming along the boreen or the bridle path or that I mightn't see you again.'

Delia felt her cheeks flush, but she also felt elated. He liked her, as she liked him. 'You have had the same effect on my life. When you told me you'd probably be gone when I came home from London, I was devastated,' she told him timidly.

'I sensed that, but this is an impossible situation. We're from opposite ends of society. I know my place and I know yours and I shouldn't ever stray across the lines.'

'I know,' she said.

'We should never be more than nodding acquaintances, but

that's not ever going to be enough for me. I can't imagine – no, I don't *want* to imagine a life without you in it.'

She didn't say anything.

'Have I offended you?'

She shook her head.

'I feel I was fated to meet you. I had no intentions of being here so long, but when the opportunity arose for me to buy and renovate the cottages, I felt it was meant to be.'

'You really think that?'

'I do. It's as though fate threw us together. I think that happened for a reason, and whatever that is, there's a real cruelty in that, because it can never happen.'

'Why can't it?'

'You must know, Miss Delia, that's the way of the world. If your family knew you were meeting me like this, or that I'd held your hands, how do you think they'd react? Invite me to sit at their table and dine with them? I think not.'

'I know they wouldn't, and it's so unfair,' she said. He nodded and she continued, 'Do you remember the day we were talking on our horses when my sister and my brother's fiancée came along?'

'I remember it clearly.'

'They both chastised me after that for being so familiar with you, and allowing you to be so familiar with me. They told me I was compromising my reputation by being seen, never mind actually engaging in conversation, with anyone from your class. I had to promise them that I wouldn't go along by the cottages on my own again, or they'd tell Mama and Papa. That was when I started visiting with Mrs Murphy. It was the only way I could see you.'

He smiled sadly. 'That's what I mean. It's hopeless. I would have imagined your sister would be like you. The other lady I don't know about.'

'Mona is under her spell and thinks everything Lady Elizabeth says is gospel. Clement leaves his commission in a few years so she'll be the mistress here some day. You should hear her mother go on about rank and caste. They talk of little else. They're used to having servants who do everything, from cooling their glasses before they drink from them to standing behind them waving palms or whatever they use in India to keep cool. I doubt they even know any of their names either.'

'Unfortunately, that's not as uncommon as you might imagine,' he said, and she seemed to consider this.

'Is it like that in America?'

'In some places it's worse, but let's leave that for another time.'

'What will we do if there isn't another chance to meet?' she asked quietly.

'That's why I wanted to meet you today. I couldn't let you just disappear from my life without telling you how I felt about you. And I sensed you have feelings like mine,' he said, looking deeply into her eyes. She returned his gaze, and he felt he was looking right into her soul. He took her hands again. He loved this young woman as he had never loved anyone before. 'I am right. I'm not imagining it. Am I?' She shook her head. 'And there's nothing we can do, about it,' he said. 'But I promise you this won't be the last time we meet. I feel it in here,' he said, putting his hand on his chest.

'Are you going back to America?'

'I don't know yet. I can't think straight. It's probably for the best that I do.'

'I don't want you to.'

'And I don't want to either, but what if your parents found out we had met like this today, or the way we're talking to each other? How do you think would they take it? Your father would probably run me off the land, and he'd be justified too.'

'They can't stop us meeting,' she protested.

'But they can and they would. Think of your future, Miss Delia. Your parents will expect you to make a good match, and a marriage that is acceptable to everyone within your society, with someone from the gentry like yourself. They would never countenance having their daughter with a humble draughtsman. You know what I'm saying is the truth.'

'I do, but that's so unfair. What's wrong with us being friends?'

'That's the way life is. It's not always fair.'

'Will you write to me?' she asked. 'At least that way we can keep in touch.'

'Won't anyone get suspicious at strange letters arriving for you?'

'No, because I have a plan. I told Mrs Murphy I'd leave some envelopes with her, addressed to me at the London house. She doesn't think her handwriting is good enough for the postal service to cope with. What if I did the same with you? That way anyone in my family will think it's just another letter from her. I could put them inside a book and leave it with her to give to you when she brings her bread along next time. When you go to America, we'll have to come up with another way.'

'That's very devious, but very clever, Miss Delia.'

'I wish you'd just call me Delia when we're alone.'

'We haven't been alone before, except for when we met.' He laughed. 'Do you think you could call me Hugh?'

She smiled. 'I think I could, Hugh.' She liked the sound of that. 'I'd better be going back before I'm missed.'

'Thank you for coming to meet me,' he hesitated before adding, 'Delia. I don't know what I expected, but I'm glad you came.'

'So am I. Thank you for asking me ... Hugh.'

'There's something else I wanted to ask you. Did you really bake that bread the other day?'

'I did.' She laughed.

'I once told Mrs Murphy I'd marry her for that alone, but you, Delia, I'd marry you in the morning, even if you hadn't made it.'

'You have the Irish blather,' she teased, blushing again,

'I may have, but I'm not plámásing you, Delia, when I say I can't tell you how much I'm going to miss you. Life will be bleak without your smile to brighten it.'

'And so will mine without yours.'

He took her hands in his again and lifted them to his lips, kissing each in turn. He reached up and tucked a strand of hair behind her ear and, on impulse, they embraced and clung to each other, their bodies saying things they couldn't verbalise.

'Travel safely and hurry back.'

'I will, Hugh,' she promised, unspilled tears glistening in her eyes. 'I will.'

Chapter 11

Delia came back to the house to find Mademoiselle Corneille had been too busy to miss her. She had been occupied with making sure that their trunks had been taken downstairs in preparation for loading them for the journey. The governess had supervised the packing, and Delia felt sure that if she had not been so preoccupied with the last-minute preparations she would have detected a change in her young protégée. Mademoiselle never missed anything.

Delia did feel different, but she couldn't say exactly how. She felt strange, but not in a good way. As the morning progressed her stomach began to hurt and her head to ache. She took out her sketchbook and retrieved the note Hugh had given her and read it again and again. She lay down on her bed, her mind whirring. One minute excited, one minute dejected – she was in a heap. Had she really just embraced Mr Dunne – Hugh? Had they really said all those things to each other?

She didn't know how she was going to live without seeing him again. She'd love to have been able to share this secret with her sister, but that would never be possible. Mona would feel duty bound to tell their parents, and they'd make sure that Delia and Hugh's paths would never cross again. Her parents would disown her if they ever found out. Such a scandal would ruin not only her chances, but Mona's too. She couldn't begin to contemplate what her brother and his fiancée would have to say either. She mulled over these things until she thought her head would burst. She had a pain right across her forehead above her eyes.

Mrs Murphy came upstairs and knocked to tell her that lunch was ready. Hurriedly Delia shoved Hugh's note under her pillow, and she told the housekeeper she wasn't hungry.

'You've a few long days ahead of you, chi– Miss Delia. 'You need to eat something to keep your strength up.'

'Honestly, I don't feel like eating. I just want to rest.' Even as she uttered those words they struck her as being out of character. Would Mrs Murphy be suspicious? 'I have a bad headache, so I'll rest a while.'

'That's not a bit like you. You never rest in the middle of the day,' Mrs Murphy said, looking more closely at her. 'You don't get headaches either. You do look very flushed.'

'I don't feel well.'

'Are you hot?' the older woman asked, putting her hand on Delia's forehead. 'Holy mother of God, you're burning up, child. I'm going to send Tommy for Dr Canavan. We can't have you sick and you going away in the morning.'

'There's no need to fuss,' Delia said.

'I'm not fussing, but you're in my charge, and I'll not have anyone saying I neglected you. Loosen your bodice and I'll be back up with some cold water and some towels.'

She must have dozed, for when she opened her eyes again it was to see Mademoiselle Corneille, Mrs Murphy and Dr Canavan at the foot of her bed. They were talking in hushed tones. Her head still hurt and she could barely hear what they were saying.

'We're becoming good friends these days, Miss Delia,' the doctor said as he approached her. 'What have you been up to this time? Have you a headache? Hmm. Any pain anywhere else? Is your tongue sore?' He examined her, checking her neck for swelling before turning to the two women. 'I suspect we may be looking at a case of smallpox.'

She saw Mrs Murphy make the sign of the cross.

'Oh, sweet and merciful Jesus. She's been visiting some of the cottages with me recently – could she have picked it up there?'

'In all probability, yes. There have been several cases among the children in the neighbourhood recently. It's important that she gets all the rest she can.'

She watched him move to the foot of the bed and strained to hear what he was saying. It didn't make sense. Who were they talking about? '... serious illness ... a very high mortality rate ... well nourished ... no guarantees ...'

She heard Mrs Murphy saying, 'Her Ladyship will kill me.' Why, what had she done? Did she know about Hugh's note? The doctor was asking if she was feeling all right. Was Mrs Murphy sick? Nothing was making sense.

'I'm as fit as a flea. I've been exposed to worse over the years, but I should have known better than to take her with me.'

"There's no point in blaming yourself, Mrs Murphy. That's the way life is. It's not always fair.'

That's what Hugh had told her. Hadn't he? Had they been listening? Had they followed her to the cherry wood? She tried to concentrate but couldn't. She had to warn Hugh. She tried to get out of bed to go and find him but was restrained.

The room was candlelit when she opened her eyes again, and she recognised Doctor Canavan, sitting by the fire drinking tea. Mrs Murphy and Mademoiselle were standing by his chair.

'Tell me, Doctor, what we need to do to make her better.'

'I wish it was that simple,' Delia heard him say. 'We've a long way to go yet.'

A long way to go – was he going to America too, or London perhaps?

'I can tell you what to expect. There'll be more fever, the rash and the pustules. It will take some time to regain her strength and not be so susceptible to other illnesses. She'll need plenty of bed rest, although I doubt she'll feel like getting up. Give her plenty of fluids and no visitors. I'd send a telegram to her parents, too, to let them know the situation.'

They were

going to send a telegram to her parents to tell them what? That she had met Hugh in the cherry wood?

'I'll look after that,' Mademoiselle said. 'We were supposed to leave tomorrow to join them in London.'

'She'll not be going anywhere for the foreseeable future,' Dr Canavan replied. 'I'll come back in the morning and see how she's doing.'

When he returned the next day, Mademoiselle told him in a panic, 'The poor child is agitated and delirious. She keeps talking about a note that she thinks is under her pillow and she keeps trying to find it. I've looked, and there's nothing there, but I don't think she believes me.'

'That's not unusual in cases of high fever. The mind can fool us,' he assured her.

Delia's temperature continued to rise and she drifted in and out of consciousness. It was dark, it was brighter. She was hot, she was shivering, she vomited, her limbs ached. Dr Canavan was there, he was gone. Her mind played tricks on her and she imagined she'd hugged and even been embraced in return by Mr Dunne, and that she'd told him to call her Delia.

Her tongue and mouth became covered with red spots.

She found it hard to swallow. The spots turned to blisters and began breaking down. Either Mrs Murphy or Mademoiselle seemed to be permanently by her bedside, wiping her down with cold towels and encouraging her to take sips of water. It hurt to swallow.

She imagined her mother was sitting beside her, holding her hand and mopping her brow, telling her about Mona's conquests and how she'd taken the London season by storm. Then she was gone again, only to return later with more tales of the balls and beaux her sister was enjoying, and how enchanted Lady Elizabeth was by mingling in new high-society circles, showing off her fiancé, Clement, to her friends.

In lucid moments, Delia heard scraps of conversations. Mademoiselle said, 'Look at her lovely skin, God bless her, will she be left like that, with pockmarks all over her forever?'

'We'll have to make sure that doesn't happen,' the doctor replied. 'As those sores become pustules and scab over, they'll feel like peas under her skin. It's important to let them fall off naturally, although the urge will be there for her to scratch at them. If she does that's when permanent disfigurement can occur.'

Delia heard Mama suggesting, 'What if she was to wear some of my softer gloves, would that help?' and Dr Canavan answering, 'It can do no harm to try.'

When Delia opened her eyes to tell them she wouldn't scratch the scabs, the room was empty. Where had they vanished to? She must have imagined that, too, along with a meeting in the cherry wood and Mr Dunne giving her a note. She brushed her hair off her face and realised she was wearing cotton gloves. She tried to sit up, but sank back into the pillows, too weak to move.

The door opened gently and in came Mademoiselle, followed by Mrs Murphy, carrying a tray.

'You're awake, properly awake, Miss Delia. Thanks be to the good God and his blessed mother.' She put the tray on the table and came over to feel Delia's forehead.

'I declare to God, the fever's broken. The fever's gone at last. Oh, Miss Delia, you had us so worried. You've been so ill. We've never left your bedside for the last three weeks. I just went down to get a bite to eat and bring it back up with me to sit with you.'

'I'm so sorry.'

'Sure, you've nothing to be sorry for. It's meself that should be apologising to you, for putting you in mortal danger, visiting the McCormacks.'

'Are they sick?'

'Now, don't you be worrying about anything. I'll just go and fetch Her Ladyship.'

'Mama? Here? Isn't she in London? Or am I delirious again?'

'No you're not, chi– Miss Delia. She came home as soon as she got our telegram. She's been sleeping in the armchair beside you every night since she returned. You scared the daylights out of us all. I'll go and tell her the good news. I'll be back in a minute.'

Her mother came in, her eyes glistening with tears. She came to the bedside and took her daughter's gloved hand. 'Oh, thank God you've pulled through, Delia. There were days and nights when we thought you mightn't.'

'Mama, I thought I had been dreaming that you were here.'

'You were delirious, but, yes, I've been here. I came as soon as I heard you were unwell.'

'So I didn't imagine it all. And London, I never went to London, did I?' she said.

'No, you didn't,' her mother replied. 'But it'll still be there when you're better.'

'And the ball, Mama. Did you miss Clement and Elizabeth's ball?'

'I did, but that doesn't matter. Your getting better is more important than any ball.' She smiled at her youngest child. 'And get better you will. Mrs Murphy, Mademoiselle and a nurse that Doctor Canavan recommended have all been looking after you very well.'

'Oh, Mama, I am so sorry. I've spoiled Mona's season for her and for you too. She must be mad at me.'

'No, you haven't. And she's not mad with you at all. They've all been so worried, your father, brother and sister and, of course, Lady Constance and Elizabeth too. Who knows, they may even have told the viceroy about your plight by now,' she said mischievously and Delia laughed. 'Oh, it's wonderful to see that smile again – isn't it, Mrs Murphy?'

'It surely is, but we're going to leave you to get some sleep now.'

Her mother sat her forward, fluffed up her pillows, squeezed her gloved hand and said, 'Try not to scratch or else you may be left with permanent blemishes on your skin. The doctor is making up a potion for you, and when he arrives we'll put it on. It should help.'

Delia felt drained. Gratefully, she closed her eyes and sank back into the pillows and into a deep sleep.

Chapter 12

The next few days passed in a more lucid state. Cook prepared tasty morsels with which her mother and Mrs Murphy tried to tempt her, but her appetite was in no hurry to return. They sat her out in an armchair, a few minutes at a time, and her mother was concerned at how thin she had become. It was the end of the fourth week since becoming ill before she began to feel a bit more normal. The scabs were gradually drying up, and Doctor Canavan's potion had helped ease the itching as they healed over. He had also recommended that Lady Kensley-Balfe and the others nursing Delia should spend at least an hour out of doors every day in the fresh air 'to clear the lungs of infection'. Weather permitting, Lady Kensley-Balfe often did this on horseback, accompanied by Tommy or one of the grooms.

Still trying to unravel what had been real and what she had imagined, Delia relived her recollection of that meeting with Mr Dunne. But there was no sign of the note he had written, if indeed he had written one at all. She had almost convinced herself that that whole episode, too, had been a figment of her imagination, until Mrs Murphy crept furtively into her bedroom one morning after Her Ladyship had left for her ride.

'Miss Delia,' she said. 'May God and his blessed mother forgive me for what I'm about to do, but I can't bear the look of despair on that young man's face any longer. Mr Dunne asked me to give you this.' She took a folded envelope from her pocket and handed it to Delia. 'And when you've read it, I'll put it with the one you had under your pillow when you took ill.'

'Oh, Mrs Murphy, you've just saved my sanity. You've no idea how worried I've been wondering if that had really happened and, if it had, what had become of the note.'

'Well, you can stop your worrying now, because I have it well concealed. That young American is truly smitten, and it will all end bad, you mark my words. I told him this is not the way we behave here. I also told him that I'd give this to you, but that'll be the end of it. Now read it before your mother gets back or I'll find myself homeless at this stage in my life, and ending up back in the workhouse.' She walked over to the window behind where Delia was sitting and kept watch for Her Ladyship's return.

Delia tore open the envelope and read.

Dearest Delia,

I have been out of my mind worrying about you since I learned from Tommy that you hadn't travelled the day after we met.

When I heard that your mother had been sent for, I feared the worst. Because Mrs Murphy hasn't been doing any visitations, there was no one I could ask about you without arousing suspicion. They were dark, dark days, and after the McCormack children died from smallpox, I felt so helpless and afraid for you.

She let out a gasp. 'The McCormack children are dead? Oh, how shocking!' She started to cry. 'You didn't tell me. Why didn't you tell me that?'

'There would have been no point upsetting you. Poor Mary, may God have mercy on her, she's lost two of her brood.'

'The baby?'

'No. The baby survived, but the next two up died and the oldest lad is still poorly.'

'She must be heartbroken. Please tell her how sorry I am.'

'I will, when I get to see her again, but I don't know when that will be. Now have you finished that letter?'

'Not yet.' She dabbed her eyes and focused on the handwriting.

I prayed like I never did before that you wouldn't be the next to succumb. Please get well for me, Delia. Even if we

can never see each other again, that would make me happy.
I can't bear the thought of you being ill and suffering. I
miss your beautiful smile, and I miss you.

   With my tenderest love,
   Hugh.

She read it through again, before folding it and putting it back in the envelope. 'It would be rude not to answer this. I'll pen a reply after lunch, Mrs Murphy, and perhaps you can pass it on to Mr Dunne for me, without anyone knowing.'

'I'll do it this time, and only because you've been so sick, but I'll not be party to any clandestine dealings. Your parents trust me, and while I think very highly of Mr Dunne, he's not your sort, or their sort either, and a closer friendship would be unthinkable. And I told him that too,' she said firmly, moving away from the window. 'Your mama has just ridden back into the stables, so I think you should give that back to me for safekeeping.'

'Thank you. I'll give it back to you later, when I've replied to it – I promise,' she said, getting up to put the letter in between the pages of her sketchbook, which was on the bookshelf beside the fireplace.

When her mother came into her room a few minutes later and saw her standing there she said, 'My, my, you look so much better today, Delia. I declare the roses are coming back to your cheeks. Wouldn't you agree, Mrs Murphy?'

Mrs Murphy caught Delia's eye and said, 'I believe they are. Sure, isn't time a great healer? She'll be out and about before we know it.'

'I do feel a lot better, Mama. Perhaps you could go back and finish out the season with Papa and Mona now?' Delia said. 'I won't relapse. I'm feeling too well.'

'We can't be too careful, and you are kind to be thinking of me. Let me give that a little thought. Clement, Elizabeth and Lady Constance, of course, are coming to Dublin for the horse show in August, before they go back to India. I could go and join them then, although I'm reluctant to leave you on your own again. Perhaps you could come to Dublin with us,' she mused. 'I'll have to discuss this with the doctor and see what he thinks.'

Delia began to feel light-headed and Mrs Murphy, noticing, took her arm and guided her back to the bed.

'Remember what the doctor said – take things slowly. Now, don't you move from there while I go and fetch some tea.'

'I won't,' Delia promised.

Her mother said, 'She's right. I don't think you realise how ill you've been – it will take a while to get your strength back. It's been a bad outbreak and lots of families have been affected, so we can't be too careful.'

Delia wanted to say something about the McCormack children, but couldn't without implicating the old housekeeper.

Her mother would surely have forbidden her to mention such bad news to her daughter.

Hugh's letter was not the only one she received that day. She was lying down resting after lunch when her mother brought her two more, ones that Tommy had collected from Ballina. She sat in an armchair to read her own correspondence while Delia read hers.

One was from her father, enquiring how she was progressing and telling her how much she was missed. She read that before turning to the one from her sister. Mona updated Delia on her busy social life. A certain Desmond Hattersley was mentioned more than once, and reading between the lines, it appeared as though Mona was much infatuated by the attentions of said gentleman. Delia wished she had a face to go with his name, and faces to go with several of the other high-society belles and beaux that Mona mentioned in her correspondence. If only she had got to London for her brother's engagement ball ... Instead, she'd have to content herself with Mona's accounts.

Lord Hattersley's family held their ball at the Savoy hotel, and it was the best one I've been to so far. Such opulence and the latest gowns from Paris! You will love the fashion.

We, the Honourable Lord Hattersley and I, often pass each other while out riding in the park and he salutes us now when we do. Clement, Elizabeth and I have been invited to a weekend party at his country home in Kent in two weeks' time and I'm really looking forward to that. He claimed three dances on my card last Friday at the Moltens' ball, a bold move, which didn't go unnoticed by Lady Constance. She has eyes like a hawk, watches everything and, as she declared to us the next morning, 'If that young man does that again he'll have to make a declaration of his intent soon.' Can you imagine it, Delia, someone making a declaration for me?

I miss you terribly and wish you were here with us. Elizabeth sends her love.

Delia put the letter down on the counterpane and sighed in exasperation. Her mother looked up. 'Is something wrong?'

'No, It's just Mona. She keeps telling me about people I've never met and I find that very annoying.' She wanted to ask her mama what this Lord Desmond was like, but was afraid she might be breaking Mona's confidence, so she held her peace. Instead, she ventured, 'Do you think Mona will really meet someone during the season who'll want to marry her?'

'It's too soon to speculate, but she has made a very favourable impression on one or two young gentlemen. One in particular has Lady Constance's stamp of approval, and as you know, she doesn't grant that easily. She's so taken with him that, if Elizabeth were not already betrothed to your brother, I'd wager she'd have liked to have him in her own family.'

'He must be from the top drawer if she approves. Does he have a name?' Delia asked.

Her mother smiled. 'He does, but it's a bit previous to be talking like that.'

'Has he taken Mona's fancy, though? Could she love him so quickly?' she asked, thinking of how Hugh Dunne made her feel. Even the thought of him made her want to smile.

'There are many kinds of love, Delia, and it doesn't always happen the first time people see each other,' her mother told her. 'Respect, compatibility and kindness matter just as much, and love can grow from those things'

'Mama, I don't think I could ever marry someone I didn't love.'

'We all say that,' she answered indulgently.

'But you love, Papa. Don't you?'

'I do. Your papa and I have been very blessed – we found a soulmate in each other.'

'Then I won't settle for anything less,' she said firmly.

That made her mother laugh. 'Time will tell,' she said. 'But I think you've done enough talking for now. I'll leave you to rest a while.'

Delia was delighted when the door closed softly behind her

mother. She was itching to reply to Hugh. She sat at her desk and opened the ink well.

He'd started his letter with 'My dearest Delia'. Could she be so bold as to address him in the same manner? She'd never written a love letter before. She had no doubts whatsoever that that was what she was doing. She sounded out her options. My dear Hugh. Dear Hugh. Dearest Hugh. My dearest Hugh. She decided on 'Dearest Hugh'.

Dearest Hugh,

You have no idea how happy your letter made me feel.

I was devastated to learn that some of the McCormack children were not as lucky as me. That must be a very sad household now.

I am feeling a bit better each day and am trying hard to follow instructions and not scratch as I heal. That's not nearly as easy as it may sound. I'm beginning to look more normal again, and Dr Canavan says he may even permit me out of doors for short walks or carriage rides before the week is out. I can't wait.

I was quite delirious for a while and apparently talked and imagined a load of balderdash during the first two weeks of the fever. By the time I got your letter, I had actually convinced myself that our meeting in the cherry wood was a flight of fancy too! I am so glad it wasn't.

Having so much time to think made me realise that

I know nothing about your life in America, or your family, what you do over there, or what you intend to do with the cottages when you've finished restoring them. And I want to know it all.

I can't bear the thought of not seeing or talking to you again either, but we'll have to be creative about how this can be achieved. Mrs Murphy has given me dire warnings about the unthinkable consequences if our friendship was to be discovered, but I'm willing to take the chance if you are. She says she won't help us to keep in touch either, as she has her position to think about, and I do understand that.

I have to finish now, as she's going to be here any minute with afternoon tea, and I promised I'd have this reply written for her by then.

She paused again. He'd finished 'with tenderest love'. She agonised before writing 'with all my love, Delia'.

She blotted the ink, kissed the page, folded it and put it in an envelope. She also put the one Hugh had sent her in a separate one and sealed it, as a precaution in case anyone found it wherever Mrs Murphy would hide it for safekeeping. She tucked them under the coverlet until she could hand them over to her messenger.

She wondered when, if ever, she'd get a reply. She didn't know how this could be achieved without suspicion, but she knew that Hugh would find a way.

Chapter 13

'The weather is good and I think it's high time this young lady got back out into the big world,' Dr Canavan told Lady Leonora a few days later. 'A carriage ride will do her no end of good. She's been confined long enough. Just make sure she's well wrapped up. We don't want her getting chilled.'

Tommy was summoned by Mrs Murphy to get the horses ready. Delia was quite excited by the time the carriage drew up outside the front steps. She already felt tired from the effort of getting ready, but she wasn't going to admit that, not if there was the faintest chance that they might drive by the cottages and she might get a glimpse of Hugh.

Once they had settled her in, her mother tucked woollen rugs over Delia's knees, despite the warmth of the afternoon. When she tried to protest, she was told, 'You heard the doctor – no chills to set you back.'

Tommy asked, 'Where to, m'lady?' Delia had to stop herself from smiling when she heard her mother say, 'Just down the front drive and out around the perimeter. We can come home by the old Crosbie farm and along the back road. I think that should be ample for today.'

'Very good, Your Ladyship,' Tommy replied. Climbing up onto his seat, he took the reins and shook them twice. The horses took off at a slow, steady pace.

'It's so lovely to be outside, again,' Delia said, breathing deeply, as they trotted down the drive, the carriage gently swaying.

'There were days when I feared this might not happen,' her mother said.

'Was I really that sick?'

'You were. You've been very lucky. It was a severe outbreak across the neighbouring parishes. A lot of people have perished, especially the poor and badly nourished. Living in such overcrowded conditions makes it very hard to avoid contagion. Especially for those with very large families – there's little chance of escaping disease once it comes into those homes.'

'Why do they have so many children?' Delia asked.

'Because they believe that's what they're meant to do. Now, let's talk about something more uplifting,' her mother said uneasily.

'I'm so sorry – I know I spoiled everything for you and Mona and that you missed Clement's ball because of me, too.'

'I told you, you mustn't think that. There'll be other balls,

and we can do it all again next year when you come out.'
She smiled.

'I think I know how I caught the smallpox,' Delia said,
needing to ease her conscience. 'I went visiting some of the
cottages with Mrs Murphy when you were away.'

'I know. She told me. She also told me how good you were
with everyone, especially with old Mrs Lynch. In fact, I called
on her myself a few days ago and she couldn't stop praising
you. It's been very lonely for the poor old soul, but she's taken
in a young man who has business in the vicinity for a while,
and the difference in her is tangible. I suppose just having
someone to talk to helps. He's even helping to fix up her
cabin. She's had no one to do anything for her since the last
of her sons was forced to emigrate.'

'You're not disappointed with me for not asking your
permission?'

'No, Delia, I was quietly pleased that you took the initiative
and that you passed the time alone productively. We have a
duty to look out for our tenants – they are our neighbours
as well. Mrs Murphy told me about your dressmaking skills
too. I'd love to see them, but it won't be safe to call on the
McCormacks for a while yet. Their eldest girl, Noreen,
wrote me a letter on her mother's behalf thanking us for our
support and kindness. I should think they are still possibly
contaminated.'

'I know they've lost some of the children.'

'Who told you that?' Her mother sounded annoyed and Delia was afraid she'd get Mrs Murphy into trouble.

'I'm not sure. I must have overheard it when I was drifting in and out of the fever. Could I have imagined it?'

'Unfortunately not, but don't dwell on things you cannot change. Concentrate on enjoying your first outing in a while.'

The foliage on the trees and hedgerows was summer-rich with fresh greens, the meadows filled with poppies, dog daisies, wispy grasses, thistles, vetch, buttercups, knapweed and yellow rattle. As Hugh's cottages came into view, Delia saw that they had been seamlessly repaired and whitewashed, contrasting perfectly with their topping of golden thatch. There were windows where none had been before and the dry-stone walling at the roadside was being reinstated.

Tommy slowed the horses as they passed, for fear sudden noises might startle them, and, as he did, Hugh came through the front door. Delia's heart leapt when she saw him, his unruly hair flopping down on his forehead. He smiled his devastating smile as he greeted Tommy first, then bowed slightly and saluted the ladies respectfully. They acknowledged him with nods. She was so relieved to see he was still there, so near yet so out of her reach, and she out of his. Then he was gone, out of sight again. She sighed as they turned on to the back road, and she saw her mother look at her with concern. She knew she mustn't give herself away, so she said, 'Now that we're older, I don't suppose Mona and I will ever pick wildflowers in the meadow there together again.'

'Possibly not until you have children of your own,' her mother replied.

'I loved doing that, although I never liked the smell of dog daisies or the way the poppy petals wilted so quickly after we brought them home and put them in water.'

'That's probably because they hated being disturbed and being taken inside.' Her mother laughed.

They turned back in to the gates and around the side of the house to the front steps.

'The stables would have done, Tommy,' Her Ladyship said.

'No, m'lady. I collected you from the front door, and I'll deliver you back to the front door,' he said as he helped her down. 'Miss Delia.' He took her hand as she stepped out.

'That was wonderful, Tommy, thank you. I hope we can do it again tomorrow,' Delia said. 'Maybe go a little further.'

'Happy to be of service, I'm sure,' he replied, climbing back up on his seat and driving the carriage away.

Mrs Murphy opened the hall door and instructed, 'Now, back upstairs and lie down, Miss Delia, and I'll bring you some tea.'

'But I'm not tired, honestly I'm not. Can't I just go into the morning room for a little while, Mama? I promise I'll take a rest after that.'

Her mother acquiesced and they took tea together, before

Lady Leonora went to her room to reply to some letters. Delia sat staring out the morning-room window. She smiled as she thought about Hugh. She had to find a way of communicating with him, a way that would be safe. She tossed several ideas round her head, but was no closer to a solution when Mrs Murphy appeared.

'We passed by Mr Dunne's cottages and they look as though they're almost finished,' Delia said, thinking perhaps the housekeeper could be persuaded to act as a messenger again, but the look she got by way of response told her that was not going to happen.

'I'll say one thing for that young man, he's a hard worker. He's transformed the Widow Lynch's cabin since he moved in with her too, getting rid of rattles and draughts and fixing her roof where it was leaking.'

'Mr Dunne is living with Mrs Lynch? How did that happen?'

'I think I may unwittingly have had something to do with it. He needed somewhere to stay, and the good Lord knows that her cottage needed jobs done. She needed someone to talk to, too, as everyone was confined with the quarantine. It's not good for a soul to be on their own constantly. It can drive a person mad. I think I may have said I thought they could be good for each other, helping each other out, like. Tommy's allowing him use one of his horses too, when he needs to go into Ballina for supplies. I'm sure he would have cleared that with Her Ladyship.'

'I'm sure he would.' Delia laughed. 'You ought to be in the diplomatic services. You don't miss anything, do you?'

'I try not to,' she said meaningfully. 'There's a lot of guilt still around about what happened families like Mr Dunne's during the great famine. Young Noreen McCormack is staying at Mrs Lynch's too. She managed to escape the smallpox, even though she was one of the first to show any signs of it, so the doctor thought it would be good to get her away from that sick house for a while. Knowing now what we do, sure wasn't he right to do that?'

'Yes, but Noreen and Mr Dunne, both at Mrs Lynch's? I don't understand.'

'Aye, that's the way things are done around here. Family looks out for family. All I'll say is that it's made a difference to the Widow Lynch having young company about her. She's a different person.' Delia was digesting this as Mrs Murphy rambled on. 'Noreen's grandmother and the Widow Lynch's husband, God be good to them, were sister and brother. And they were related to my mother's people.'

'I never knew that.'

'And the family who had the forge for seventy years, the McGuinnesses, were on my mother's side too, but they perished in the famine, so I never knew any of them. I was told some of them were in the workhouse when I was there, but I was too young to remember them.'

'Is everyone related to everyone around here?' Delia asked.

'Probably, yes, if you go back far enough,' replied Mrs Murphy.

Just then, Mademoiselle came into the morning room to enquire how the outing had been. 'I was going to suggest we get back to doing a little French conversation, but looking at you it may still be too soon. You look flushed,' she said.

'I'm fine, really, but thank you both for being so kind.' Delia smiled at her tutor and at the older woman. She was flushed. She knew it and she knew why. She was flushed with excitement. The doctor had said she could take short walks in a few days' time, and the stables were just that, a short walk. She'd find a hiding place close by and get word to Hugh, somehow, that they could write to each other and find somewhere to conceal their letters. A seldom-used bridle path led from the stables to the cherry orchard at the east end of the grounds. Perhaps she and Hugh would be able to meet there some times. Her mother never rode or walked that way because it was too overgrown and the sun shone directly into her eyes at certain times of the year and she didn't like that.

Then Delia had another idea – now that Hugh and Noreen McCarthy were both residing at the Widow Lynch's, perhaps she could persuade Noreen to help.

Delia was happy. It didn't matter what the future held. Hugh was still in Ireland, and for now that was enough.

Chapter 14

News of Lord Kensley-Balfe's intention to return to Kensley Park the following week was greeted with delight, not only by his wife and daughter, but by the staff too. They were used to a busy household, and the past month and a half, what with Delia's illness and some of the family and staff being in London, it had been a strange and worrying time. Now everyone, above and below stairs, was looking forward to a bit of normality. The house had been scrubbed and scoured to within an inch of its life; the stables were immaculate and the trees and verges on the driveway pruned and clipped into obedience.

The sisters weren't to be united just yet, though, as Mona was to stay behind in London under Lady Constance's watch.

'I declare you look well, my child,' her father said, after enveloping Delia in a hug. 'I was so anxious and, to be truthful, worried you'd be left scarred by that wretched disease.'

'I had good nurses. They threatened me with a straitjacket

if I scratched.' She smiled up at him. 'Oh, Papa, I'm delighted you're home.'

'So am I,' he replied. 'It was time to check up on my favourite ladies.'

'How is Mona? I want to hear everything.'

'You should know your father better than that, Delia. Ask him anything about his bloodstock and he could tell you the seed, breed and generation.'

'Your mother is right. I'm certainly not your best source of information. You know how I am about frocks and colours – as for gossip, I never even recognise it as such.' He laughed.

Later, when they had a minute alone together, Lord Kensley-Balfe told his wife, 'I had to get away from that insufferable woman. If I heard the viceroy being quoted once more I'd have broken Clement's engagement off for him to spare him a future with a woman like that.. I can't help feeling sorry for Lady Constance's husband even though I've never met the chap. He must have been so relieved when she started planning to come to Europe for six months.'

Lady Leonora laughed. 'Oh, you are wicked, Peter, but I have to confess that I was almost pleased to have a legitimate excuse to leave early and escape, although I do feel sorry it all happened during Mona's season.'

'My dear, I can assure you she's making the most of it. I doubt she'll even notice I've gone.'

'I knew she'd be a success. I'm so happy she is enjoying herself.'

'She certainly is.'

Lord Peter took Delia out in the carriage a few times for her now daily morning dose of fresh air, and in the afternoons, if not tied up with affairs of the estate, he often accompanied Delia and her mother on a short constitutional walk. If her parents had other commitments, Mademoiselle tagged along and they conversed in French, causing Mademoiselle to tell her, 'You accent is very good – in fact, it's much better than your sister's, but don't tell her I said so. I think she may have been holding you back.'

'You know Mona hates grammar even more than foreign poetry.'

'If she spent less time complaining about it and more paying attention to it, she'd be better off,' came the retort, and Delia just smiled.

Her other lessons gradually recommenced and her walks got longer. She had even been told she could go riding again, but gently at first. 'We don't want you getting overheated,' Dr Canavan told her. 'And, charming a young lady as you've become, I don't want to see you for a long time again.'

'I'm so bored sitting around and taking things gently,' she told Mrs Murphy.

'Perhaps you could try sewing a few more things for the McCormack children while you convalesce. I'm sure Her Ladyship wouldn't mind, and it might give that poor family a much-needed lift after the tragedies they're suffered. I was going to ask Her Ladyship if she'd mind if I gave young Noreen a few lessons in housewifery. They'll stand to her when she takes the boat.'

'Takes the boat?'

'Aye. It seems like your young man has turned her head with his tales of fine houses and opportunities on the other side of the world. She's going to go over to some cousins of her mother's in America in a few months' time. They'll vouch for her and find her a place in service. There's no future for her here, and she can send money home to help the others. They'll probably join her in their own time.'

Delia didn't know how to react to this revelation. Mrs Murphy was a wily woman. Was she trying to imply that Hugh's interest was in Noreen, who was scarcely more than fifteen?

She answered, 'She's very young to go that way on her own.'

'To be sure, but no doubt there'll be lots of others around her age travelling and they'll look out for each other.'

'She'll miss her family. I never thought I'd miss Mona so much, and I know I'll see her soon again, but Noreen, all the way to America – will she ever return?'

'Probably not, the poor child, but for her it'll be an

adventure – for her mother a disaster. God knows I'm no expert on families, but I have eyes and I can see. They can drive you mad when they're around all the time, yet without them near there's always something missing.'

'You're a very wise woman,' Delia said.

'When you've been around as long as I have you'll be wise too.' She grinned. 'Now I must get on with my work.'

Delia was tempted to ask Mrs Murphy for one more favour, but decided against it. Instead, she hatched a plan. No one, apart from Mona, had actually forbidden her to associate with Hugh, and Mona was miles away and, by all accounts, far too preoccupied with the attentions of a certain Honourable Desmond Hattersley to be concerned with what her little sister was doing, apart from getting better. Her mother had never told her not to go by the cottage. She had simply made her promise not to go riding that way, or any way, alone. Mrs Murphy had told her in no uncertain terms that she wouldn't be complicit in passing on any further communication between the unsuitable two. She hadn't forbidden any communication, though.

Delia wouldn't talk to Hugh. She'd merely deliver a message to him.

Her chance came, thanks to her father deciding that Lady Leonora should accompany him to the city, to attend a dinner in Dublin Castle. Once they had turned out of the gates at the end of the main driveway, Tommy at the reins to take them to the station in Ballina, Delia changed into her riding attire, went to the stables and asked one of the grooms to prepare the horses.

'I'm sorry to put you to all this trouble. It's hardly worth your while saddling up, as I'm only allowed such a short ride, but I have to be accompanied,' she told the young lad.

'That's wise, miss,' he said as she settled her legs around the pommel and adjusted her riding skirt. He checked her stirrups and went to his mount his horse. He didn't notice her slipping the note she had written under the front of saddle. He was one of the farmhands who lived just outside the boundary wall, and she couldn't risk him getting suspicious.

'You lead,' she instructed. 'Let's just take a short stroll around the meadow and back by the old cottages. That'll be enough for today.'

'Right you are, miss.'

The sun dappled through the trees along the roadside as the animals walked at a leisurely pace. Delia had to resist the urge to take off in a wild gallop, to feel free and uninhibited. Instead, she concentrated on her thumping heart, which was playing a tattoo inside her chest as they came down the back lane. *Please, please, please, let him be there*, she prayed silently. If he wasn't, she wouldn't be able to complete her mission.

Hugh was lifting stones on to what had remained of the wall between the cottages and the overgrown road. She saw him the second he came into view. He straightened up immediately when he heard the hooves echoing in the laneway, and as he moved forward she shook her head. The groom called a greeting and Hugh answered him, before bowing slightly and raising his hand in a salute to her. She nodded in return. She retrieved the envelope and dropped it on the ground on the off-side of her mount and walked on. She looked back and saw Hugh pick it up. She sighed and looked ahead. She could sense him standing there, watching, until they were out of sight, and she had to stop herself from smiling all the way home.

Now all she had to do was wait. She had no doubt whatsoever that he'd respond. When she returned to the house she went straight to the morning room and started playing the piano.

'Now that's a sound I've missed,' Mademoiselle said, coming in to the room with her embroidery.

'And I've missed playing too.'

'Debussy's "Arabesque No. 1". You've chosen well. It's a very contemplative piece – not as frenzied as his second.'

'I like it,' said Delia. 'It's calming.'

'Calming?' Her tutor smiled. 'And what would you have to be anxious over that you'd need calming?'

If only you knew, Mademoiselle, she thought to herself. If only you knew.

The following morning, Tommy took Mrs Murphy and the kitchen maid into Ballina for provisions, and Delia forwent her ride in favour of a walk around the grounds. She took her sketchbook and pencil holder with her and headed straight to the overgrown pathway that ran beside the line of trees growing inside the boundary wall. She stood for a few seconds, listening to make sure no one else was about, before going over to the disused gate, which was almost halfway between Hugh's cottage and the back gates to the Kensley Park. The silence was broken only by some birds fleeing her intrusion into their territory.

She had spent a few days looking for the ideal hiding spot for their correspondence and had selected some stones to form a platform to keep the paper away from the damp ground. She'd completed the hidey-hole with a flat mossy stone.

She was fearful there would be nothing to find. She hadn't given him much time to respond. But – there it was – a letter, with a little flower drawn on the outside. She controlled the urge to tear open the envelope and read what Hugh had said, but the sooner she got back to the main walkways the better. Instead, she placed it into her sketchbook and continued her walk as normal, savouring the knowledge that he had replied and that she would read whatever he had to say in secret as soon as she reached the privacy of her room.

Thus began an almost daily exchange of news and ideas, thoughts and feelings. Over the next few weeks she learned much about Hugh's family in New York. Of his parents and grandparents and the struggles they had endured when they first arrived there from Ireland.

Delia painted pictures for him of what her life had been like. Sometimes she enclosed a pencil sketch for him. She knew nothing of factory floors or tenements, nor had she ever experienced being cold or hungry or what it was like having to go to work every day. She wrote of her childhood with Mona, of lessons with their governesses and music teachers, of their stays in London and the magical shops they had there. She told him of the excitement when Clement was around – her only brother who was so much older and more grown up than his sisters, more worldly-wise and sophisticated. She described the hunts and the hunt balls and the musical evenings her parents frequently hosted at both their Irish and English homes.

They contrived to meet while her parents were absent, but only managed it briefly on two occasions. When they did rendezvous, he took her hands in his and kissed them. These kisses ignited feelings she could never have imaged her body possible of producing. Once Lord and Lady Kensley-Balfe had returned from Dublin, they daren't risk meeting. Even delivering and fetching their letters became problematic by times. But there was no other option. They had to content themselves with these communiqués, which became longer and longer.

Each one peeled back and exposed a little more of themselves to each other.

Lady Kensley-Balfe was excited at the prospect of the upcoming Royal Dublin Horse Show Week, a centrepiece of the Irish social season. She arranged to have some of her gowns sent back from London for the occasion.

'I didn't get the chance to wear half of them, and they were the furthest thing from my mind when I left in such a hurry. Now I'll have the opportunity to show them off,' she told her husband.

'You'll be the belle of the ball, whatever you wear. You always are, even if I can't describe the shapes or shades.' He laughed. 'The young ones won't get a look in.'

Clement came back to Kensley Park ten days before they were due to leave for the city, and he and his father spent a lot of time in his office with their steward, sorting out estate affairs. At dinner on one of the evenings Delia felt him scrutinising her.

'You've grown up,' he told his sister. 'You seem to have matured in just a few months, almost as though you've blossomed.'

'I am grown up.' She laughed.

'No, you seem different somehow. I can't put my finger on it.'

'You've just forgotten what I'm like.' She felt herself blushing. Could he tell she was in love? Was it that obvious?

Her father unwittingly spared her when he changed the subject. 'I'm glad you'll have the opportunity of taking in the Royal Dublin Horse Show, Clement. There's never as much standing on ceremony here as in London.'

'That's very true,' his wife agreed. 'And this year we'll have the added fascination of seeing Mona mingle with her new set. The Hattersleys are coming over too, so I'll be able to see for myself how well the young ones are gelling. We don't want her to waste her time with the Honourable Desmond if there are no prospects of anything developing there.'

Clement surprised them by saying, 'I'd put my money on a betrothal announcement soon.'

His father said, 'And I'm inclined to agree with you.'

'Oh, Peter, you are impossible. If you really thought that then why didn't you say before now? And you too, Clement? You're just like your father.' She turned to her daughter for support. 'How can men be so blinkered? Don't they realise we are dying for such news?'

They all laughed and her husband said, 'I held my peace because you, my dear, might have meddled, and in matters of the heart I think it's better for young people to make their own decisions.' Delia was delighted to hear this reply. Perhaps he would understand that she liked Hugh and that all she wanted from life was to be with him. 'Don't you agree, Delia?

I'm sure you wouldn't like me to choose your spouse for you, would you?' he asked.

'Of course she would,' her mother interrupted. 'Who is more qualified to make a judgement as to the suitability and social standing of a prospective husband than her parents?'

Her father replied, 'Well, dear, let's wait and see who she picks when she comes out, for I'm certain she'll be in much demand.'

'What would you do if I wanted to marry someone you didn't consider "suitable", Mama? A working man, a groom or a farmer?' she asked casually, and again she felt her brother's scrutiny.

Her mother laughed at the absurdity of such a question. 'Why, we'd forbid it, of course, Delia,' she replied. 'We wouldn't stand by and watch you destroy your life, and your sister and brother's either, like the Fairleigh girl. She threw everything away – for her music teacher. Can you credit that? Disowned and disinherited for a piano player. I believe she's living in rented rooms in some unsavoury corner of London now.' She lowered her voice. 'And with a family on the way too.'

'Her brother's in my regiment. He's none too pleased at this course of events, I can tell you that,' said Clement. 'He came down very heavily on her.'

'And rightly so,' his mother agreed. 'I pity the family, so upright and respectable until this. She's also brought disgrace on her sisters and the families they married into – she's made them the laughing stock of the town. I believe they all have been shunned by society.'

'Well, dear, I'm quite sure we won't have worries of that sort with our girls,' her father said. There was silence for a few seconds, and then he surprised them by saying, 'You know, dear, I think we ought to take Delia with us to the Royal Dublin Horse Show. She's had a pretty miserable time of late. What do you think? Would you fancy that, Delia?'

'Oh, yes, I would, Papa. And it will be lovely to see Mona and Lady Elizabeth again. I may even have the chance to see this Lord Hattersley for myself.'

'I don't doubt it.' Clement laughed.

'He's very eligible,' Lady Leonora replied. 'And he cuts a fine dash in his riding clothes.'

Going to the horse show meant fittings and alterations to her wardrobe, as she had lost weight and developed a more womanly shape since her illness. When the seamstress came to the house, Mrs Murphy asked her if she could spare any off-cuts from the material she'd used. 'I want to make a coat for Noreen McCormack before she sets off on the cold sea voyage into the unknown.'

'I'll see what I can do,' Lizzie Coveney said, and when Tommy returned from driving her back to the town, he had two large brown-paper parcels tied with twine. Delia spotted him from the window and went below stairs to inspect the spoils with Mrs Murphy. Since she had spent those few pleasant episodes sewing real garments, she wanted to do more. She found it the perfect solution when she needed to retreat into her own world and think – and she'd been doing a lot of that lately.

'This one is beautiful,' she said, fingering a knobbly brown and oatmeal tweed, that jumped out at her from the mixture of odds and ends. 'It would look lovely with Noreen's colouring. And you could add a collar and trim in that chocolate velvet too,' she suggested. 'And maybe even a pork-pie hat?'

'Whoa! Hold your horses, young lady. I'm no milliner and I've no intentions of trying either, and since when, may I ask, did you develop such an eye for fashion?' laughed Mrs Murphy.

'I don't know, but I do enjoy sketching dresses and hats. Perhaps I could help.'

'You'll have to ask Her Ladyship. If she has no problem, then I'd be very happy. Young Noreen wants to watch and learn too.'

That brought her back to reality. Here was young Noreen, making plans to go off to the other side of the world to make a new life, and going with everyone's blessing. Could she not do the same?

Lady Kensley-Balfe wrote off to book rooms for the horse-show week for her and her husband and their party, which now consisted of Mona and Delia, who would share, Clement, Lady Constance and Lady Elizabeth and three lady's maids and a valet. They would stay at the fashionable Shelbourne Hotel, overlooking St Stephen's Green. Several of their friends and acquaintances had done the same. As a result, Lady Leonora had no worries about Delia being chaperoned or being kept amused while they were off attending hunt balls, dinners or soirées.

So stylish an event was horse-show week in Dublin that crowds gathered morning and evening on the pavements around the hotel doors to ogle the fashions of the gentry. To wonder at their incredibly tall and often feather-topped chapeaux and to envy their decadent lifestyle. By sharp contrast, children in ragged clothing and bare feet were often thrust to the front of the onlookers by their beleaguered mothers, before being sent on their way by the ever-vigilant doormen. These unfortunates begged for a ha'penny or two as the guests emerged from the brightly lit foyer holding up their elaborate dresses from trailing on the pavement as they made for the waiting carriages. These in themselves provided quite a spectacle. Varnished and lacquered to reflect any face, many sported coats of arms, and those in the know recognised the livery of the drivers. The horse brasses gleamed and the beasts were glossy and powerfully magnificent.

Delia had been excited at the idea of her impending visit, but not at the thoughts of being away from Hugh. She lived for his letters and they spoke frankly to each other about their prospects and their expectations. He kept insisting that he was not worthy of her and she persisted in denying this. The last letter she had before she was due to leave for Dublin had asked her to meet him – urgently. She didn't know how she'd manage it, with her parents both at home and her father constantly moving about the estate with Clement and his agent. She never knew where they'd appear.

Her mother noticed her agitation and said, 'You're very restless, Delia. I hope it's not too soon to be taking you away.'

'No, Mama, I'm just excited at the prospects of seeing Mona again, but I think I'll go outside and do some sketching.'

'The fresh air will do you good,' her mother agreed.

Once outside, Delia headed for the cherry grove, listening in case her father was close by.

She felt the colour rise in her cheeks as she saw Hugh step out from the thick undergrowth by the wall and walk towards her. He didn't take her hands in his as he usually did, instead he blurted out, 'I have to go back to America, Delia. I'll be gone when you return.'

'You're leaving? You can't.' She couldn't believe what she had just heard. Why now?

'I told you I had work commitments back home. They were only postponed because of a bereavement in the family and an already-planned visit to Europe. It appears, however, that they have returned early and want to get started on their project, so I have to go. It's very important for my career. If I perform on this and prove myself, I'll be a step closer to becoming a fully fledged architect, not just a draughtsman. After that, the opportunities will be endless.'

'You will be coming back, won't you?' she pleaded. He didn't answer immediately and she urged, 'Tell me you'll be back. You can't just go and leave me here.'

'I have to, and I won't promise you that I'll be back. There isn't any point. Trust me, Delia, it's for the best. We always knew this had to happen. You'll thank me for it in time to come.'

'I won't. I want to go with you, Hugh,' she said, tears springing to her eyes. 'You can't go. I love you, Hugh.'

'And I love you too, Delia, you know that, and I always will. I'll never forget you. I don't want to leave, God knows I don't, but I can't offer you the future you deserve or that your family plans for you. I can't rob you of those things. You'd grow to hate me for it.'

'I could never do that,' she insisted.

'Maybe not, but you'd grow to hate what it would cost you and what it would do to your family. Think of what your brother and sister would have to say. You'd be disowned by them too. You'd grow to resent the sacrifices you'd had to make and —' He stopped as they heard the sound of horses and male voices in the distance.

'Go, go! That's Papa and Clement. They're inspecting the

land with the agent. They can't find us together. Go over the wall, quick.' She ran back through the cherry wood towards the front of the house, praying that Hugh had got out of view before they caught him and quizzed him about why he was trespassing.

And, just as suddenly as Hugh Dunne had appeared into her life, he disappeared out of it. Where was he now? Had he gone to Cobh or to Dublin to take the boat to New York, or was he returning from Southampton? She only knew those ports from listening to Mrs Murphy's talk of families who had 'taken the boat' to America in the past. She hadn't an inkling which way he would travel. They had never discussed such things. There were so many things they had never discussed. She rode by his cottages every day after and they were empty and quiet. The day before they set off for Dublin, smoke was coming from one of the chimney stacks and she felt her heart somersault. Then she saw a small child talking to a donkey in the adjoining field and knew Hugh wasn't there.

That mystery was solved at dinner when she heard her brother say, 'I hear that fellow has gone back to America, and that he's let the blacksmith and his family take over one of the cabins. I still don't know what he's up to, but I don't trust him. I think he has ulterior motives, showing up here out of the blue like that. If you'd asked me, I would not have agreed to selling him that land. I think he's a gold-digger and he took advantage of you because of Delia's accident.'

'Well, son, it saddens me to see you turning into such a mistrusting creature. It was my decision to make, and I stand by it. There's plenty enough for you and your heirs, should there be any.'

'I'll not be taken in so easily when I'm in charge, I can tell you that,' Clement said, putting his glass down with more force than was necessary.

'That Dunne fellow showed initiative. And he did a remarkably good restoration job of those cottages. I'd wager that he has a bright future ahead of him,' her father said.

'That's not our concern.'

'Now, gentlemen, I don't think the dinner table is the place for such discussions,' her mother said.

'I apologise, my dear. You're right, as always.' Sir Peter smiled at his wife.

Clement ignored them both and continued. 'Did he say what he's going to do with the two smaller ones?'

'Enough, Clement. The topic is closed,' his father said

Delia knew the answer to that. Hugh had told her that he was going to see if any of his relatives in the States wanted to come back to live in Ireland. If not, he'd rent the cottages to some of the local workers. But she couldn't say anything. They'd want to know how she was privy to such information and she couldn't tell anyone that.

She was upset and bewildered by Clement's attitude. The more she was around him, the more she was beginning to see him in a different light, and it wasn't the way she remembered him. He seemed much harder and self-righteous than before. Perhaps being at war had made him like that. Or had she just been judging him through the eyes of a baby sister?

But she was heartened somewhat by her father's assessment of Hugh. A bright future ahead of him indeed. Just not with your daughter, she wanted to say, but she said nothing for fear of breaking down and crying.

She missed Hugh so much.

Did broken hearts ever mend?

She couldn't imagine the pain in her chest ever going away.

Chapter 15

Hugh's going back to America overshadowed Mona's return from London and the whole Dublin experience for Delia. The thoughts that she would probably never see him again filled her with a deep sadness and an ever deeper sense of loss. She had harboured a desperate hope that maybe she could talk this over with her sister, believing that if Mona had fallen in love with Desmond Hattersley then she'd surely understand how Delia felt about Hugh. But Mona had changed too. She seemed to be totally absorbed in the whirlwind of social engagements, and she was consumed by news of whom she had met, of her newly made friends and acquaintances, and with gossip about who had stolen a kiss in the orangery or who had tried to monopolise her dance cards.

She and Lady Elizabeth had grown very close, and when they shared secrets and talked in their own lingo, it made Delia feel more like an outsider, which only added to her loneliness. She also had a sense that Elizabeth, having become used to having Mona's friendship exclusively, resented having the younger sister around.

Mona hadn't given Hugh a chance. She'd hardly even exchanged pleasantries with him on the two occasions they had met. Delia knew that, in Mona's mind, it wasn't that he was unworthy of note – he was simply out of her line of vision. Her sister wouldn't have considered it being unkind. It was just the way she thought and had been taught.

Her parents and Lady Constance were swept up in their own bubble of socialising. The Hattersleys' arrival in Ireland was imminent, although they hadn't been able to secure rooms at the Shelbourne Hotel – it was fully booked and their party was too big to be accommodated. Instead, they would be staying on the other side of St Stephen's Green, at the St Stephen's Park Temperance Hotel.

After Delia's illness, Lord and Lady Kensley-Balfe wanted to take some of the focus away from her siblings and make her visit to the city a memorable one. Lady Leonora promised to take Elizabeth and her girls shopping, and she chose a morning when Lady Constance had other arrangements to do just that. After partaking of coffee and some French pastries in the ladies' lounge, the concierge announced their carriage.

Lady Leonora instructed the driver to take them to Sackville Street, to Clerys, a grand department store on the main boulevard. Right opposite, a new bookshop, Eason, had just opened, and Delia asked if she could purchase a book to take home to Mademoiselle.

'She loves reading and I know she intended visiting Hatchards when we got to London, but of course, because of me we never got there.'

'How thoughtful you are,' said Elizabeth.

'Not really.' She laughed, 'I have to admit that I have an ulterior motive, because when Mademoiselle finishes a book, I get to read it.'

'Mama, may we go up to the top of Nelson's Pillar first?'

'I was hoping you would not suggest that, Mona. I'm not particularly good at heights.'

'You needn't look down,' she said, laughing.

'I suppose I can't let you go unaccompanied.'

After the entrance fee was paid and they'd got their tickets, they lifted their hems and started to climb the spiral staircase, which seemed to go on forever. Delia started counting. Every so often there was a narrow slit in the thick wall, affording a glimpse of what was below. One hundred and sixty steps later they reached the viewing platform. Lord Nelson towered above them. Each side offered a different vista. They looked up Upper Sackville Street to Findlater's Church, and down towards the River Liffey, with Trinity College in the background.

'It feels as though it might topple over,' said Delia.

'Don't even mention that,' her mother said, keeping her eyes closed.

'You must look, Lady Kensley-Balfe,' said Elizabeth. 'You really must.'

She opened one eye and quickly closed it again. The girls laughed at her. Eventually she did look around and identified some landmarks for them, but she still stood well back from the railings and declared how very happy she was to be back on terra firma when they completed their descent.

'Your father will never believe I actually went to the top,' she told them. 'Let's get that book for Mademoiselle and then we'll walk back to the hotel. It's not too far and it's a fine day.'

Delia would have loved to have spent more time in the bookshop, and hoped she might get back there before their visit to the city was over. Looking along the shelves, she spotted *The Mayor of Casterbridge*. She had enjoyed *Far from the Madding Crowd* by the same author, perhaps because in many ways Delia had empathised with the heroine, Bathsheba Everdene, and her love for the highly unsuitable local shepherd. Why, oh why, did everything have to remind her of Hugh?

Lady Constance was waiting for them back at the Shelbourne, bursting with news that involved more name-dropping. After she had gushed forth for a few minutes, she eyed the small parcel in Delia's hand and said, 'I see you've been shopping.'

'It's just a book for Mademoiselle. It's Mr Hardy's new

title – he's a wonderful writer. Have you read him?' she replied, trying to be civil.

'I would have thought that was a bit adult for someone of her age,' Lady Constance said to Lady Leonora in that way of hers. It was neither benign nor accusative, but was laced with disapproval and the suggestion that she'd never permit such a thing in her household. It was clear to Delia that, no matter what she did, she would never quite reach this matriarch's standards of behaviour.

During the week they attended a matinée performance at Dan Lowrey's Music Hall, and on another evening they were present at a variety revue at the Gaiety Theatre.

'Don't you love the city by night, with all the gas lamps glowing and the busyness?' she asked her sister.

'Oh, yes, they're lovely,' Mona replied, and it was obvious that her attention was not on this topic at all. Delia sighed. The revue was lively and varied, but all through it she kept wondering what it would be like to go to something like this with a man she loved by her side. She went to bed and Hugh invaded her dreams once more.

Lord Kensley-Balfe had secured them good seats in the stand for the horse leaping events, and there they met anyone they considered worth knowing. If her family noticed the dampness in her mood, it wasn't mentioned, and she did enjoy herself.

She was pining, though, and kept going over things he

had written or told her. Hugh had opened her eyes to many new things. She wondered how Dublin would compare to New York. It didn't have an elevated railway, like the one Hugh had described. There were no buildings five storeys high, like the ones he told her he envisaged designing when he was qualified.

She'd told him he was a dreamer, and he'd refuted that. 'Wait and see. One day people will recognise buildings as my signature. But the competition is stiff. There are four of us who all started together and we're all hoping to secure a future with the firm, maybe go into partnership, who knows.'

'That sounds challenging.'

'It is.' He'd explained that New York and Boston were both growing cities, with property owners and railroad and steel barons virtually minting money – many with wives who were willing to help them spend it.

'I predict there'll be a thousand millionaires over there by the turn of the century.'

Despite knowing little of finance, that sounded impressive. The only dealing she'd had with money matters was one time when she and Mona were summoned to her father's study. Her father's smile had assured her there was no need to worry about this unusual event. Two men were with him that she didn't recognise, both solicitors, one acting for His Lordship, the other on behalf of their recently deceased grandmother.

'It's very irregular this, Your Lordship, girls inheriting and their brother getting nothing,' the younger one said.

Their father shot him a warning glance and said, 'Girls, I should explain, we need you to sign some documents and we'll witness these signatures. We have to do this because you are under age and we'll have power of attorney for you. Your grandmama has left you both a small inheritance, which, of course, you won't be able to access until you have reached twenty-one and are still unmarried, and as I doubt that will arise, I can't see what all the fuss is about, other than making it legal so that no one can ever get their hands on it.'

'But –'

'We've discussed this before, Mangan, and my mother discussed it with me before her demise. It was her wish and I'll see it through. My son has not been excluded. He will inherit plenty apart from my estates. He's my brother's only male heir, so his holdings will revert to Clement too.'

The matter was never mentioned again, and Papa and his agent continued to look after all financial matters.

The Kensley-Balfes hosted a soirée for thirty in a private room at the Shelbourne Hotel on the Friday of the horse-show week. The guests included Lady Constance, Lord and Lady Hattersley and their son Desmond, Lady Hattersley's sister and her husband, Clement and Elizabeth, and Mona. After much discussion, it was decided that Delia could be present too, and she had her first real opportunity to meet the man who was topping the list as prospective brother-in-law material.

'That would never happen in London, attending a formal function before she was out.' Delia could detect the disapproval heavy in the voice.

'Oh, but, my dear Lady Constance,' her mother replied, 'this is Dublin. Things tend to be a little more relaxed here on the edge of the empire.'

'Things are much stricter in India,' Lady Constance replied, 'what with the viceroy being present at so many of the functions we attend.'

'I'm sure they are, and perhaps our viceroy may honour us with his presence for a while this evening,' Delia heard her mama say, and she could tell from the tone that she was at breaking point with the other woman. 'I believe he's dining in another suite in the hotel tonight.'

From the reply she could tell their guest was miffed, but she had to have the last word.

'It's important not to let standards slip. We have our positions in society to uphold and we must never forget that.'

No one responded.

Delia liked Desmond the minute she met him. He wasn't much taller than Mona and had an open countenance and a devilish grin that revealed a dimple when he smiled. His first words to her were, 'So, you're the little sister that I have to charm. I hope I don't disappoint.'

Delia blushed. She didn't know how to answer that.

He included her in their conversation, making her feel more grown up than many

others did. He worked the room and was attentive to Mona, who seemed to be equally engaged with him. He singled Delia out at one point and whispered to her, 'I hope we can be friends. If I end up in this family, I'll need an ally. Don't look so shocked. That's what this is all about, isn't it?' He laughed. 'I'm here to be inspected. Do you think I'll pass? Do I measure up?'

'I have no doubts that you do.' She smiled. 'I'm getting the impression you're hoping that I'll put in a good word for you.'

'You know how the mothers are – untwisting the pedigrees and the prospects. I know they'll find no fault with those, but, *entre nous*, your brother's future mother-in-law's scrutiny and inquisitions reduce me to schoolboy status. I'm happy they'll be on a different continent most of the time.'

'Me too,' she said and laughed. 'Don't tell Mona I said that.'

'I won't,' he said, tapping the side of his nose to indicate a secret. 'Now, if you'll excuse me, I'm promised to dance this polka with your sister.'

'And I've been told I have to vanish at this point.'

Much to the delight of everyone, just before the hunt ball the following night in Dublin Castle, Desmond proposed to Mona, having sought father's permission earlier, and she accepted.

Mona's season was considered by everyone to be a success.

The family returned to Kensley Park, and the Hattersleys and Clement's soon-to-be family accompanied them for another round of celebrations, parties and equestrian pursuits.

Delia really liked her sister's fiancé and was genuinely delighted for her good fortune. Although included in some engagements, she was excluded from others, as the household adhered to strict society rules – those befitting the norms of friends of the viceroy of India.

When she was debarred, she ate with Mademoiselle, who had been delighted with her book and promised to lend it back when she'd finished reading it. At other times, Delia wandered down the service stairs to the kitchen and drank tea with Mrs Murphy. One day she found Noreen McCormack there, sewing with the housekeeper.

When Delia came into the room, she stood up to leave, but Delia stopped her and said, 'You're working very hard. Have you made any further plans for your big adventure?'

'Not yet, miss. But I will have very soon. I'm waiting to hear from Mr Dunne. He promised to get some addresses for me in New York so that I can apply for work. My mam has cousins in Boston and Cook has asked me to help out while the visitors are here. That way I'll have some experience when I get there. Sorry, miss, listen to me – I'm rabbiting on. Mam would kill me. She says I talk too much.' She laughed.

'And mine tells me I ask too many questions,' Delia said.

She couldn't get out of the kitchen quickly enough. Hugh was going to correspond with Noreen McCormack and not with her. Had she been blind? Noreen was younger than her, but could something have gone on between them at Mrs Lynch's cottage, as she was locked away, recovering from her illness? Perhaps that was what he had been trying to tell her when he said how far apart his and her worlds really were, and that it would be better for them to sever all connections. Had she been deluding herself?

She loved him with an all-consuming passion. And he loved her. Of that she had no doubt whatever. That he would be accepted as their equal by the gentry, or by any of their class, would never happen. That too was a certainty. He'd never be recognised or welcomed into the homes, society or families of her upper-class circle.

The Noreen McCormacks of the world may not have fine gowns and social accomplishments, but the need for survival seemed to infuse them with a driving ambition to make their way in the world, while Delia's horizons were set by tradition and convention. She was living in a gilded cage, but it was a cage nonetheless.

She fantasised about following Hugh to New York, wondering, should she ever manage to do so, would she be welcomed into Hugh's social sphere. Would they resent her, considering her to be hoity-toity and too grand?

She had confessed her feelings for him without holding anything back, and he his for her, yet he had been prepared to sail away, without even leaving an address. What did that say about him, or about her judgement? Perhaps she was just an immature child, as suggested by her sister, but that knowledge did nothing to make her feel any better. The hole Hugh Dunne had left was immense, and she couldn't see how she'd ever get him out of her mind.

All she knew was that she had to try.

Chapter 16

With so many guests in the house, activity in Kensley Park had been at a frenetic pace over the previous few weeks, causing Cook to grumble about being overworked, despite additional hands from the village being called upon to help in the kitchen and elsewhere.

In exasperation, Tommy told her, 'Try running the stables with this crowd. If it's not having mounts standing by for dawn rides and cross-country gallops at a whim, it's the carriage being ready at all hours for errands and visits, and keeping those stable boys on their toes ...'

'Would you listen to yourselves?' said Mrs Murphy. 'It's only a few months since you were complaining about not having enough to do. And, Cook, if I know you, next week you'll be sounding off about the glut of apples and blackberries that have to be preserved. And you, Tommy, you'll be trying to fill the hours in the day inspecting the martingales and harnesses. You don't know how easy you have it here, where we're treated with respect and well fed. Now, get on with the preparations. I need those supplies from Ballina and Her Ladyship needs the carriage after lunch. This will be the last time, until only God knows when, that this family will sit down together for a meal before going their separate ways, and I want everything to be perfect.'

Mona's fiancé and his parents were leaving the next day, returning to London before heading to their country estate in Scotland. At that last dinner together, Lady Hattersley told Lady Leonora, 'Autumn is my favourite time of year, with the trees changing colour, and my husband loves it for the grouse shooting. There's a long tradition in his family of giving an October ball to mark the opening of the season. I do hope we can persuade you and Lord Kensley-Balfe to come along with Mona to meet the Scottish side of the family.'

'And let her see for what she's letting herself in for,' said Desmond, winking across the table at Delia. 'There's Uncle Maurice, an eccentric, who insists on wearing a kilt at all times, even when the snow is thick on the ground and his knees have turned blue. He never trims his beard. It's so thick and unruly, he'd get away without a necktie and no one would ever notice. His wife, Aunt Clara, hand-feeds baby lambs and, on occasion, has brought one into the drawing room with a baby's bottle and suckled it by the fire. Interestingly enough, you'll always find lamb on her menus. And their butler, Murdo, he's as odd as two left feet, and his face is so long and thin that one eye would have been enough for him. He's been with them so long he thinks it's his house and tells them what to do.'

'Enough, Desmond,' his mother said when they'd finished laughing. 'You're creating an awful impression of our family. I wouldn't be surprised if Mona changed her mind about marrying into it.'

Her husband said, 'I hope not. We need fresh blood in the line, and you know what they say, Mona, to be forewarned is to be forearmed.'

'I can't wait', she replied. 'I just wish Clement and Elizabeth were coming along.'

'Duty calls, sister. I have to rejoin my regiment. Our passages are booked and I have to squire the ladies on the high seas and deliver them safely home. Just think, the next time we meet we'll both be married and Delia will probably be promised.'

Delia felt herself blush. If she had her way, she'd be heading in the other direction to get married too, but without all the fanfare and flourish she'd heard Mona and Elizabeth planning for their nuptials.

'I assume you'll wait until Delia has been presented before exchanging vows,' Lady Constance said to Mona.

'Of course. I'd like a summer wedding,' Mona said, 'and I'd like Delia by my side.'

'What a busy year you'll have,' Lady Hattersley said.

'Imagine, a presentation in court and a wedding to plan. It's all happening so quickly,' Lady Leonora replied and, addressing her son, she added, 'I can scarcely believe it. It seems like yesterday we were seeing you off into the army. Then you were but a boy, and now look at you, going back to your regiment so far away and about to be married. It's a shame we won't be there to witness that. You will take care of yourself, won't you? I worry about you.'

'You and every other soldier's mother and wife,' Lady Constance said. 'And that will never change. That's our role, to worry.'

'Enough of this talk. Let's not be gloomy,' Lord Kensley-Balfe said. 'This may be a farewell dinner, but it's not a wake! Let's charge our glasses and toast the young couples and the futures they are starting out on together, wherever they may lead.'

'To the future and the happiness of the young couples,' they echoed.

Later, in their bedroom, Lady Leonora sighed.

'Don't be upset, dear,' Sir Peter told her. 'We always knew this day would come. It's their turn now and we have to be happy for them.'

'That was not a sigh of regret, but one of anticipation. Just think that on Wednesday we'll have said farewell to "the great friend of the viceroy of India"!' She laughed. 'How is it that whatever she says sounds either like an edict or a censure?'

'Thank goodness they had their passages booked or they'd be heading off to Scotland to the Hattersleys' on the train with us, and I don't think I could have vouched for my patience for that length of time.'

'I certainly couldn't,' she said. 'Now, let's get some sleep. I'm exhausted and it's a busy week ahead with everyone leaving.'

'I long for a bit of peace and quiet,' he replied.

'So do I. Sleep well.'

Chapter 17

Tommy drove the Hattersleys to Ballina to catch the Dublin train. Mona was already moping and Delia suggested a walk, but she declined. She and Elizabeth had plans, as they only had a few more days together. Delia went on her own. She found it easier to think out in the open, where there were no distractions. She followed the path along the boundary wall, towards the spot where she and Hugh used to exchange letters. Something caught her eye as she approached the gate, a flash of brown, a skirt perhaps. She could have sworn someone was on the other side. She looked through the wrought iron but could neither see nor hear anything. Her mind must have been playing tricks. She even lifted the stone that had concealed their furtive line of communication, and, of course, there was nothing there.

She continued to the entrance, still convinced she had seen something. She went out onto the back road and looked up and down. Nothing. Her senses heightened – she felt sure she was being watched, yet she didn't feel frightened. From behind one of the giant oaks, out stepped Hugh. Her imagination was playing tricks. But then he called her name and she ran to him. They embraced passionately.

'I knew you'd come back,' she said, tears shining in her eyes.

'So did I. In fact, I never really left. In the few days I was waiting for the vessel to sail, I realised I couldn't go on without clearing things up. There are some questions that need answers.'

'Not here, Hugh. Anyone could come along and find us. Come back inside.'

He followed as she set off on the bridle path that she had come along. She stopped where the woodland thickened and they embraced again, then kissed. She felt safe in his arms and never wanted to release him.

'Delia,' he said, pulling away from her but still holding her hands, 'We haven't much time. I need to get a few things off my chest. Firstly, I love you and I want to spend my life with you. Secondly, I want you to come with me to America. We can make a new life there without disapproving eyes always on us.'

She looked at him, scarcely believing what she was hearing.

'Tell me what you are thinking,' He said softly.

'I want those things too, Hugh, so much.'

'I contemplated speaking to your father, but I think that may make him take you out of my range altogether.'

'It would. My parents would never agree and they'd probably marry me off to the first suitor, whether I cared for him or not.'

'I've been thinking about that too. In fact, I've thought of little else for the past few weeks. If you're willing to take a chance, I thought we could arrange for you to travel over with Noreen. That way you could take care of her and she of you. I promised to help her find work and I'll keep that promise.'

'But, Hugh, it's impossible. They'll cut me off with nothing and I have no money.'

'You won't need any money. I can't promise you riches and privilege like you enjoy here, or balls and soirées, but I can promise you my love and devotion forever. I have a bit put by from my granda's patent, and I have a good job with prospects. We won't want for anything normal folks have. I'll probably have to draw the line at a pony – initially, anyway.'

She smiled and looked into his blue eyes, which she felt boring into her soul, and said, 'I think swapping you for a pony is a fair exchange. I've been miserable since you left. And my sister got engaged. She and the family are all so happy that I couldn't let them see that I wasn't. It's been awful.'

'I'm so sorry to have put you through that. But do you honestly think you could bear to leave all this behind and spend your life with me?'

Without hesitation, she replied, 'Yes, Hugh. Oh, yes, please!'

He scooped her up and twirled her around. 'I knew I was right to come back and talk to you. I started so many letters but couldn't convey how I felt in them. I used to hold my granda's watch and talk to him, asking him what I should do. I just knew if I could see you face to face I'd know how you really felt. For days I've watched the comings and goings from the house but you were always surrounded by people. In desperation, I decided that, as a last resort, today I was going to leave this.' He pulled an envelope from his overcoat pocket and handed it to her. 'I didn't know if you'd ever look under our stone again, but I felt you would.'

'What is it?' she asked.

'Your passage and enough for contingencies for both you and Noreen. I've written detailed instructions in there. Unfortunately, I can't delay my departure any longer. I have to get back to New York or they'll get someone else to do my work. My address is in there. Wire me or write and let me know when you're coming, and I'll get to work on our marriage licence when I reach home. Please come as soon as possible.'

'I can't believe this is happening,' she said.

'Neither can I. You are sure, aren't you?'

'I've never been more sure of anything.'

'Nor have I, my darling girl.' He scooped her up again and twirled her around and around. She laughed out loud and he joined in. When he put her down again she looked over his shoulder into the disbelieving faces of Clement and her father.

No one said anything for what seemed like minutes, before Hugh stepped forward and said, 'Your Lordship, I'd like to marry your daughter.'

She pushed the envelope Hugh had given her up the sleeve of her coat.

Clement shouted, 'Take your filthy hands off my sister, you delusional rat. Who do you think you are, you little upstart? You're not worthy of talking to my sister, let alone keeping her company. Get off with you! If I see you anywhere near Kensley Park again, I'll have you horsewhipped. Do you hear me?'

Her father was speechless. He looked from one to another and put a restraining hand on his son's arm. 'Violence achieves nothing, Clement. You, young lady, go back to the house. I'll deal with you later.'

Her eyes locked with Hugh's and she reached out to him. Clement's crop cut the air as he struck out and she moved closer to protect the man she loved. Instead of hitting Hugh, it caught the edge of her cheek and blood spurted instantly from the wound. Incredulous, she looked at her brother, and the photo of him with the tiger he had hunted and killed came unbidden to mind.

'You scoundrel,' Hugh shouted as he went to help her. 'If that's how so-called gentlemen behave, I've had a lucky escape. Delia, are you all right?'

'That's none of your business,' Clement shouted at him. 'Get away from her and get out of my sight. I won't miss my target next time.'

Fearful of what might happen she said, 'Go, Hugh, go.'

Her father was visibly shocked at what had just happened. He turned to Hugh. 'Listen to her. Go and don't show your face around here again.' He took a handkerchief from his pocket and held it to her cheek. 'We'd better get you cleaned up.'

'I love you, Hugh,' she called out.

'And I'll always love you, Delia,' he said. He turned to Sir Peter and said, 'I'm truly sorry to be the cause of distress. You've treated me fairly, sir. We never saw this happening, but I do love your daughter, and nothing will ever change that. I'd go to the ends of the earth to make her happy.'

'That's enough. I won't tell you again, get off this property. *Now!* Clement roared at him, waving his crop menacingly, and Hugh turned to go.

The snowy white handkerchief had turned crimson and Delia's coat was splattered with blood. Her father picked her up and, half-running, half-walking, carried her to the house, taking a shortcut through the trees.

'Get her mother and Mrs Murphy, immediately,' he ordered his son.

Pandemonium ensued as they went into the drawing room where Lady Leonora, Lady Constance, Mona and Elizabeth were taking tea. They all jumped up to see what was wrong.

'She's had an accident,' her father said. 'Clement's gone for Mrs Murphy – she's good with things like this.'

'Let me take your coat off,' her mother said, but Delia had only one thought and that was to keep Hugh's letter safe.

'I'm cold. I'd like to keep it on for the moment.'

Her mother nodded.

'Oh, gracious. All that blood, I feel quite faint,' Lady Constance declared.

Delia said, 'Then be thankful it's not yours. Perhaps you should go to your room and you won't have to look at it.'

She could tell from her mother's reaction that she couldn't believe what she was hearing.

'Dear Lady Constance, you must excuse her. She's obviously not herself.'

'Mama, I am very much myself. In fact, I have never been more myself. I didn't have an accident – I was the accident. This cut was not intended for me, but Clement missed his target and I was in his way. Ask him about it.'

Everyone looked confused and awkward, and her mother turned to her husband. 'Peter, what happened?'

'It's complicated. I'll explain later.'

'Papa –'

He addressed the others and ignored her. 'Let's go into the morning room and make space for Mrs Murphy to see what she can do.'

Mona insisted on staying.

'You poor child, how this did happen?' Mrs Murphy asked her, bustling in and gently pushing Delia's hair out of the bloodied wound.

'Clement caught me with his riding crop.'

'Riding, but you're not in your riding clothes?' said Mona.

'I know. I wasn't riding. Oh, I'd love a drink of water – would you call for one.'

'I'll fetch it for you myself,' Mona offered and rushed out of the room.

Delia turned to Mrs Murphy. 'It was because of Hugh. I thought he was halfway back to America by now, but he wasn't. Before anyone comes back, I have a favour to ask, and no one can know.'

'What is it?'

'Promise me first.'

Mrs Murphy nodded.

'Take this and hide it for me.' Delia retrieved the bulky envelope from her sleeve and handed it to the housekeeper. 'It's vitally important that no one knows but us.'

Mrs Murphy took it, slipped it between the folds of a towel and put it at the bottom of the pile in the basket she had brought in with her potions and lotions.

'What does this mean – is Mr Dunne here?' she asked, as she dipped lint squares in warm water and gently swabbed the wound.

'He is, but I didn't know. It was while waiting for his vessel to depart, that he decided to turn back. He asked me to marry him. I agreed and that's when Papa and Clement came across us, embracing.'

'Oh, sweet Jesus, preserve us. I'd say that didn't make them happy.'

'He stood his ground and told Papa his intentions. I was so proud of him, but before Papa could say anything Clement went mad.'

'Holy mother of God. I told you it would end bad.'

Mona returned with a carafe and a glass. She poured some water for her sister and said, 'You didn't mean it when you said Clement did this, did you?'

'He did, he raised his crop to strike Hugh and I got in the way.'

'Who is Hugh?'

'The owner of the restored cottages outside the back gates. You met him one day.'

'The chap you were talking to on your horse? But what has he to do with this?'

'He told Papa he wanted to marry me.'

Mona laughed. 'He was joking ...?'

'No, he wasn't. Clement almost had apoplexy. He

frightened me. I never saw anyone so angry or with such malice on their face. He didn't look like the Clement I know. He looked – evil.'

'That boy always had a temper,' Mrs Murphy said.

'He was probably only trying to protect you,' said Mona.

'No, he had no reason to do so, and I'm sure that thought never entered his mind. He was trying to injure Hugh. You didn't see him, Mona. He looked like a crazed stranger.'

'Well, I'm not surprised. What were you thinking? What did Papa say?'

'That he'd deal with me later, whatever that means. I know he was shocked.'

'Thank goodness the Hattersleys had left before this happened,' Mona said. 'Though I can't imagine what Lady Constance and Elizabeth will have to say, and just as they are about to head back to India.'

'There would never have been a good time for them to find out. I know you didn't ask, Mona, but I said yes – I told Hugh I would marry him.'

'Have you lost your mind? You don't realise what you're saying. Look at the scandal Letitia Fairleigh caused to her family when she eloped with her piano teacher,' Mona said. 'And she ruined her sister's prospects with her selfishness. Everyone expected her sister's engagement to be announced imminently, but that didn't happen and the family has been shunned by society ever since. Do you think the Hattersleys would feel any differently? Is that what you want for us, to destroy us all?'

'That's not –'

'When did you become so secretive?' Mona asked.

'Maybe when you stopped being my friend and I had no one to talk to. I was lonely with you all away. I wanted to tell you, Mona, I really did, but you've been so preoccupied with your new friends and with Miss Who-Can-Do-No-Wrong Elizabeth to pay any attention to your little sister. We never spend time together like we used to. I thought when you fell in love with Desmond you'd understand how I was feeling, but you never gave me a chance to tell you.'

'That's childish talk. I haven't fallen in love with Desmond. He's very congenial and considerate. He's handsome. He's also very eligible and that pleases both families. I'm sorry you feel I've neglected you, but I'd never in a million years give my approval to such a match as you're proposing, nor would Elizabeth, so it's best you put those notions out of your head.'

'I'm not asking for Elizabeth's approval. It has nothing to with do with her.'

'That's where you're wrong. She'll be mistress of Kensley Park one day.'

Mrs Murphy had held her peace during this exchange, but she put a stop to it then by saying, 'Miss Mona, I need to get on with cleaning the wound, and I know you're squeamish about gory things, so perhaps you should leave for a little bit.'

'Don't worry. I have said all I need to say here.' She turned and flounced out.

'I'm afraid this gash may leave a scar, and you after getting away without any from the smallpox blisters. It's not as bad as all that blood suggested. I'll make up a paste and cover it, but I'm going to have put a bandage right around your head and under your chin to try and keep it closed until it starts healing.'

'You're very kind, Mrs Murphy, and thank you – for everything.' She took the older woman's hand and squeezed it.

'Has he gone now? For good?' she asked.

'Yes, he has,' Delia replied.

'Thank the sweet Lord for that. Maybe it's not too late to sort things out with your brother before he leaves.'

'Maybe,' she replied, knowing she'd never forgive him. She wanted to confide in Mrs Murphy, to tell her about the plans Hugh had made for them to be together. She, despite all her warnings, knew and liked Hugh, and it was clear to Delia that she understood how their feelings for each other were real. But to do so would be to put the woman in a vulnerable position. By knowing nothing she could be accused of nothing.

'Now, let's get you out of these soiled clothes and into bed. You need to rest, and if any of this gets out,' she said, pointing to the basket, 'I'll deny it. I can't afford to lose my place at this stage in my life.'

'It won't. I promise you. Please bring it to me later, whenever it's safe to do so.'

Chapter 18

Despite the throbbing in her sore face, Delia was happier than she'd been for weeks. She lay on top of the covers and closed her eyes. She knew the aftermath had yet to begin. She had hoped for a bit more support from her sister, but realised that she ought to have known better.

Since their arrival on the scene, Delia had seen her sister turn into a disciple of Lady Constance and Elizabeth, embracing their high-society mores and haughty attitudes. And she wasn't in love with Desmond? That had come as a shock. Was he in love with her, or was it to be a marriage of convenience for him too? She'd never settle for such an arrangement, no matter what the circumstances.

She pushed those thoughts away, remembering Hugh's scent, his hands holding hers, his embrace, his blue eyes and the feel of his lips on hers. With these thoughts to warm her, she knew she had the strength to withstand the fallout from that morning.

She sat up suddenly when her door was flung open, without a knock or warning, and in strode Clement, followed a few paces behind by their parents. She waited.

'I've been told I owe you an apology,' her brother said, holding out his hand to her. She could see he had been drinking, and as he approached she could smell the whiskey fumes on his breath. 'It was never my intention –'

'You don't owe it to me, but to Mr Dunne,' she replied.

'I never meant to hurt you,' he said.

'I know that, but you intended to hurt him.'

'What did you expect, when we found you cavorting with that peasant? What were you thinking? Throwing yourself at him like a loose woman. And this nonsensical talk of marriage to a penniless cottier? I'll see him ruined for this.'

'That's quite enough,' their father said to him as he went over and sat on the side of her bed. 'You know this is just infatuation, Delia. You're only a child, and once he has gone back to Boston or New York or wherever he came from, you'll forget all about him.'

'I'm not a child any more and I won't forget him, Papa. I don't want to forget anything about him. I love him.'

Her brother snorted. 'How long has this liaison been going on? You looked very free and easy with each other. I hope it didn't go any further than that?'

'You think you love him, but believe me, Delia, all young girls think their first attraction is true love,' her mother said, 'The roses smell sweeter, the colours look brighter and you seem to walk with a spring in your step. We've all been there, but this time next year you'll probably have difficulty remembering his name because you'll be so busy with your new society friends, as Mona is now. Who knows, like her, you may even be betrothed by then too, to somebody of our own kind.'

'I know that's your plan for me, but I'm not interested. I've met the man I want to marry, and I'll do whatever it takes, and wait however long is necessary, to be with him. I don't want to do a silly season in London. I don't want to be presented at court like something on a market stall, there for inspection or rejection, and possibly selected because you, dear brother, are married to someone close to the viceroy of India. Or, like Mona and Desmond, to be marrying for suitability's sake. There's no substance to any of that and it's not what I want for my life.'

'You may scorn, but it's "that" which has given you a lifetime of privileges,' her brother shouted. 'Do you know how lucky you are?'

Her father said quietly, 'We've been born into this, Delia. It's our way, but it comes with responsibilities. You may not realise it yet, but this lifestyle is not as vapid as you may think. It sustains the livelihoods of dozens of others. The entertaining, the gowns, the cooks, the servants, the house-keepers, the stables and farmhands – they need us as we need them. I want you to think about what you *do* want. What sort of future do you think you would have if you rejected all this?'

Her mother added, 'And you'd have no place in society ever again. You'd be a social outcast, you and your children, if there should be any.'

'They'd be disinherited too, because I'd make sure you were cut off completely, financially and physically,' said Clement.

'Just think, Delia,' her mother said, 'about how you'd bring dishonour and humiliation on all the family.'

'You couldn't expect to ever be received by any of us, or our families, in the future.' Clement added.

She wanted to say she didn't look on never having to meet his in-laws again as a hardship. She would have liked to have the opportunity of getting to know the Hattersleys better, though. She liked them and felt that she and Desmond had a genuine bond, but she kept her counsel on these matters. She was still coming to terms with Mona's revelation that she wasn't in love with Desmond, that their marriage had been brokered.

'Do you know where this – young man – is now?' her mother asked, her voice breaking. She was trying hard to hold back her tears.

'Don't worry, Mama, he's gone, and not because of Clement's attack. He's on his way back to America. He has responsibilities there. He only came today to say goodbye and to ask me to marry him. And I told him I would.'

'And you can put that stupid notion out of your head. That's not going to happen, ever,' her brother said.

'Of course it's not,' her mother agreed, 'but I'm curious to learn how you met this young man and became so intimate with him without any of us knowing. And how you had arranged your meeting today.'

'We hadn't arranged to meet. I saw him for the first time when I fell off the horse in spring, Mama, and he rescued me and got me home safely. We became friends. He's kind and good and would never do anything to harm me.'

'Except by dishonouring you and bringing shame to your doorstep. If he really cares about you, then he'll get out of your life and stay out of it,' her brother said.

'I thought he'd left weeks ago, when the blacksmith and his family moved in,' Lord Kensley-Balfe said.

'So did I, Papa. I didn't know he would be here today. We said our goodbyes before I went to Dublin with you, because of all the reasons you have against our relationship. He didn't want to compromise me or my reputation. But as soon as being apart became a reality, and we discovered how much we missed each other, he came back. It was by pure coincidence that I walked that way today and met him. Truthfully, I don't know what he would have done if I hadn't.'

'He'd probably have had the arrogance to knock on the front door and ask to see you, Papa. He must think you are an easy touch, selling him that land after hearing his sob story. He won't find me that gullible.'

'Don't disrespect your father like that,' Lady Leonora told him.

'Isn't it obvious? He's an opportunistic fortune-hunter, if you ask me,' Clement said and she could feel the anger rising again in his voice. 'If he thinks he'll get a penny from you, or us, he's sadly mistaken. You've brought shame on all of us by your conduct. You've compounded it by doing it in front of Elizabeth and her mother too. I don't know what they think of this state of affairs.'

'They so love high-society gossip – they'll have something juicy to tell their friends. Or maybe they'll sweep it under the carpet in case it reaches their delicate ears,' said Delia, feeling empowered by the bandage around her head. 'And you seem to have forgotten that if you had not been so free and easy with your crop, no one would have been any the wiser. It's thanks to you that everyone, including the staff, knows. And it's thanks to you that I've come to see you for what you are – a bully.'

He sneered. 'And what would you have done had we not come along just then? Tell us!'

Before she could reply, their father said, 'That's enough, Clement. This is getting us nowhere. Can you leave us alone? I'd like a private chat with Delia. I'll see you downstairs in my study. And stay away from the decanter.'

When the others had left the room, he waited a bit before

saying his carefully considered words. She always knew when Papa was choosing what to say. He joined the tips of his fingers and slowly drew his palms together as though in prayer, and then reversed the movement, several times, and he always had a certain expression when he did so.

'Forgive me, but I have to ask you this. Are you sure nothing untoward happened between this man and you? He hasn't dishonoured you in any way?'

She laughed. 'Oh, Papa, you need have no worries on that score. Hugh is a gentleman, and my virtue is intact. You met him, Papa. You trusted him. You even said he was a decent and hardworking chap. I do love him. I truly do.'

'I don't doubt that he's decent, and he did have the gumption to declare his intentions to me.'

'I –'

'Let me finish. He's not of our class, Delia, and that means he's neither suitable nor eligible to marry my daughter. And, you're right, I did trust him, but you must understand how all this makes me feel, well, betrayed somewhat.' He paused and considered again. 'You've put me in an impossible situation. I understand that you have, or think you have, feelings for him, but let me make it very clear: marriage to him is simply not an option now, nor at any stage. I'm surprised and disappointed in you, Delia. You've always been so solicitous of others, but now you seem to have only been thinking of yourself and haven't stopped to consider anyone else in this fiasco.'

'That's unfair and unreasonable, Papa. You're using different standards to judge me. You didn't know what Elizabeth was like when Clement announced he'd proposed to her, yet she was received with open arms, and you'd only met Desmond Hattersley less than a handful of times when he was welcomed into our family. You've met Hugh a few times and you even liked him, so why doesn't he deserve the same treatment?'

'Because he's not of our class and we know nothing of his family, his background or his connections. Have you thought this through?'

Of course she hadn't. She hadn't had time. She hadn't expected Hugh to suddenly reappear and ask her to run halfway across the world and become his wife.

'Continuing this liaison, never mind contemplating a marriage, would threaten both your siblings' future plans,' her father said quietly. 'The Stokeses would surely demand that Elizabeth finish with Clement and, in all probability, issue court proceedings for breach of promise, dragging our family name into the mire. I know his future mother-in-law is a difficult woman, but her husband is top rank in the army in the Raj, and that could have implications for Clement's career and his hopes of promotion. I imagine the Hattersleys would find a gentler way of disengaging themselves from any connection with Mona, but as you know, people believe that there's no smoke without fire, and her reputation would be sullied by association too. Her future prospects, if any at all, would be severely limited.' He paused to let this sink in. 'As I said, continuing this liaison, never mind contemplating a marriage, would threaten your future prospects too. I urge you to think about these things. People talk and news of this episode may get out and harm your reputation.'

'I didn't mean to cause so much upset, Papa. Maybe it would be better if I just eloped and got out of everyone's way.'

'My dear, you're being fanciful now. That sort of thing happens in penny dreadfuls, not in real life. Do you think you could just dash off, a young unaccompanied and penniless girl, and sail across the ocean for several weeks? What would you do then, arriving in a foreign country where you know not a soul? Your good name would be besmirched forever. And no money or deed can ever buy back a reputation. You have to think of the realities. Supposing this Mr Dunne turned out not to be what you think he is? You wouldn't be the first young lady to have been won over and duped by a charmer. Supposing he has a wife and a family over there in America. What would you do then? You certainly couldn't come back. How would you support yourself?'

She started to cry. Tears of frustration and helplessness. Her father took her in his arms and said, 'It's best for everyone that you put him out of your mind for good and all. We've all had our hearts broken, and the emotions of first love are powerful, but it gets better, I promise you. Clement was out of order and I'm sorry you were hurt today, but as your Mama said, by this time next year your whole world will have broadened and you'll look back and laugh at this situation.'

He was right about one thing, she thought. By this time next year, if not a whole lot sooner, her world would have broadened – not because she had gone to London to be presented, but because she would have 'taken the boat' to New York to be with Hugh Dunne.

Lord Peter stood up to leave. 'Think about what I said. We've all had a lucky escape. If that liaison had continued, you'd be cut off socially and financially. All the papers have been signed for Clement to have joint power of attorney and control of the estates on my sixtieth birthday in October. And, as you saw today, when he's crossed he's not easy to placate. He would make sure that you'd be left without a single penny, and I'd be powerless to oppose him. Put all this behind you and focus on the year ahead. I promise you it will be an exciting one for you, Delia – your presentation and Mona's wedding, new gowns, balls and all the things I'm told you young ladies enjoy. I think a trip to London might help. What do you say?' He patted her arm and smiled at her before leaving the room. 'Let's organise that.'

Clement stood behind his father's desk, a glass in his hand. His father waited a few seconds for him to step aside, but he didn't.

'Aren't you taking liberties, Clement? May I remind you this is my study and you are not yet master of this house. I would also like to remind you that we still have guests and you have taken enough drink.'

Defiantly, Clement swallowed the golden liquid and banged the glass down on the desk.

'You have to stop this madness right now, Papa. Delia has always had you wrapped around her finger. How can you trust her when she says that little runt has gone away? For all we know he could be waiting in Ballina for her, and she's so headstrong and gullible that she'd go to him.'

'She wouldn't do anything that foolish. She knows exactly what's at stake. And you, my son, would do well to curb that temper of yours.'

'And let a grubby little peasant destroy this family? Have you lost your mind?' he replied. 'Don't forget I have a say in this too, you know. It was your idea to give me the right to make decisions concerning family and estate matters.'

'Yes, but only if for any reason I should be incapable of doing so myself.'

'Well, Father, I happen to think this is one of those times. If my precious little sister continues to have contact with that nonentity, she's dead to me from here on. Cut off from any contact or support whatsoever. Do I make myself clear?'

'Perfectly. Now let me make it clear to you, dear son,' he said quietly, 'that while I can't condone your little sister's behaviour, I certainly don't condone your barbaric behaviour today either.'

'I'll show him. I'll get that land and cottages back from him, no matter what it takes.'

'Now, that you won't do. I'll not go back on a deal that I've shaken hands on. That's not how this family does business.'

There was a faint knock on the door and he went to open it.

Lady Leonora came in. 'You can be heard throughout the house, shouting like that, Clement, and at your father too. What has happened to you? Have you no respect? You're not on an army training ground now.'

He held his hands up in exasperation. 'How am I going to explain this situation to Elizabeth and her mother? They already think you've been shirking your responsibilities with the amount of freedom you've given Delia, and in the way you've flouted convention by allowing her to join adult activities before she's out in society, the way she's free to ride out with the grooms on her own and read anything she likes. It's no wonder she was able to have clandestine meetings with whomsoever she wanted. And now this. You too, Mama, have to accept some responsibility for this humiliation. God knows what they'll say about it, or what might have happened if we hadn't come across the two of them when we did.'

'Lady Constance's opinion is of little consequence here,' she replied. 'I'm more concerned about my daughter and her welfare, and by your brutal behaviour today. It's inexcusable.

You've probably left your sister scarred for life. Her heart may mend – that cut may not. That's a legacy from you that she won't be boasting about.'

'I've had enough of both of you namby-pambying her, even more so since she got ill.' He banged the desk with his fist. 'Am I to be the villain here? Can't you see what's going on? She could be with child for all we know, and I'm setting off for India in a few days to get married. This could jeopardise that and my career too. Elizabeth's father is my general.'

He was interrupted by more knocking on the door. This time it was Mona who entered. She had obviously been crying.

'Am I to be met with the news when I arrive back in India that my sister is expecting that scoundrel's bastard?' Clement continued. 'Do you think the Stokeses will still think of me as a suitable son-in-law then?'

'Delia is with child?' gasped Mona. 'I don't believe it! I warned her about her reputation and about being too familiar with that fellow. I assumed she'd listened to me and I never gave it another thought.'

'You knew about them?' her mother said. 'Why didn't you tell us, Mona?'

'I didn't think it was anything serious. I came upon them one day when Elizabeth and I were riding. They were both on horseback and were just talking. But with child? Does Elizabeth know that? How will I tell Desmond?' She burst into tears.

'Now, let's not run away with ourselves,' her father said. 'This is pure conjecture on your brother's part. We have no reason whatever to suspect that is the case at all.'

'And we won't know until it's too late, will we? Until our lives have been ruined,' Clement said. 'You saw the way they were today. He had his hands all over her. Are we going to pretend that this never happened? Can't we send her away somewhere until it all blows over and we're sure of no further complications?'

'You show a very callous streak, and I don't like that. It's your sister you're talking about,' his father said. 'She told me that man never laid a finger on her, and I believe her. She also told me that he's on his way back to America and I believe that too.'

'How could you not have noticed what was going on under your noses? And what if she's lying?'

'Then, son, I'll be as disappointed in her as I am in you right now. And that is all I'm prepared to say on the subject.'

'What will I tell Elizabeth and Lady Constance?'

'If you hadn't raised your voice so they might easily have accepted it was an accident and that Delia is understandably upset at being hurt. Now I'm sure they're wondering who Mr Hugh Dunne is, and, knowing that woman's penchant for sniffing out gossip and scandal, I'd say she won't be content to leave it until she knows all the facts.'

'And if Delia is with child and we find that out later on? What then?'

'Then, my son, we'll have a problem; a very big problem, and one we'll deal with should it arise, which I'm sure it won't.' He turned and held the door open for his wife to go ahead of him.

Mona stayed in the study, tears in her eyes. 'How could things take such a twist when everything was going so well?' she asked her brother.

'"There's nothing more to say on the subject." Did you hear that? The man is delusional. This is an awful mess. I could lose my commission. Did Elizabeth say anything to you?'

'No, she and her mother exchanged a lot of disapproving glances, which said a lot more than their words could have done. They're not dining with the family tonight – they're having supper in Lady Constance's room. I can't imagine they're very happy with the situation, or with you either,' she said.

'She could decide to forbid the marriage because of this.'

'She'll not do that, Clement. She won't want to lose face in front of all her friends and family at home in India. But what were you thinking of, raising your crop like that? Someone was bound to get hurt.'

'You're making a villain of me too. You didn't see them together on the bridle path, our sister wrapped around that peasant and he around her, pirouetting and shrieking like gypsies. I needn't tell you I saw red. All I could think of was what if Elizabeth or her mother had come upon them like that. And now I don't know what they're thinking about it all.

They've shut me out, but you know what sticklers they are for convention. You're lucky the Hattersleys have already left. At least you don't have to explain to them.'

'I know, and they're very fond of Delia, especially Desmond. He already looks on her as the sister he never had.'

'That's the trouble – everyone is fond of her. I just hope her comeuppance is not our undoing.'

'Do you really think she could be with child?' Mona asked.

'I don't know, but it's always a possibility. If she is, it'll ruin everything for you too. Could you ask her? We're leaving in two days and, assuming I'm still considered suitable, I need to know that we're not in for any more shocks when I arrive in India.'

'I don't know. She's very angry with me. She thinks I abandoned her once Elizabeth came on the scene and, you know, she's right. I did rather neglect her, but, still, that's no excuse. She ought to have known better.'

'See what you can do, will you? I'm sure you'll find a way.'

She promised she would.

'How's your face?' Mrs Murphy asked, when she brought some soup and buttered fingers of bread to Delia later on. She stood by her bed and watched her eat them.

'It stings a bit but it's not too bad.'

'You've really shaken the household up. There were ructions in the study earlier – you could hear Mr Clement sounding off from the top of the stairs. He's seems the most put-out. I actually think he's afraid of Lady Constance and her reaction.'

'I'm not surprised. She scares me too,' Delia said. 'I'm sorry I've upset everyone and I know it couldn't have come at a worse time, but I didn't plan for this to happen. I actually thought Hugh must have had feelings for Noreen when he told her he was going to help her find a placement in New York. He hadn't even left me an address and there she was expecting a letter from him. You have no idea how happy I felt when I saw him today.'

'It shows in your face, child, but you've got to put this behind you. Look at how it's upsetting everyone.'

'I can see that. Papa is proposing a trip to London to help me put it in the past once this wound heals.'

'I think that's a good idea. Distraction, that's what you need.'

After dinner, Mona poked her head around the door and said, 'Is it safe to come in?'

'Of course, silly,' Delia said.

'I'm sorry for earlier and for making you feel I've been neglecting you, although you're probably right. I was rather taken over by Elizabeth and her ideas. She'll be gone in a few days and it'll be like old times. I promise.' She hugged Delia. 'Does your cheek hurt? Clement is devastated by what happened. He didn't come up because he felt you might still be angry at some of the things he said.'

'I am, but I understand why he must be embarrassed in front of the Stokeses. I'll be on my best behaviour until he leaves with them, and I'll apologise to Lady Constance for my outburst.'

'I'm sure she'll appreciate that. Clement will too. Tell me, did you really say yes to that man?'

'His name is Hugh, and I did, although that doesn't make any difference now. He's gone and that's the end of it.'

'You got very close very quickly, probably closer than Desmond and me. Can I ask you something ... something a little delicate? Did you –?'

'How could you suggest such a thing, Mona? Mama and Papa have told me to put him out of my mind, but I can't do that if everyone keeps mentioning him.'

'I won't do it again,' Mona told her. 'And I'm glad we had this chat, Delia.'

'So am I. Mrs Murphy said she'd bring me some hot milk. Would you tell her I'll have it now?'

Mona went straight to the library, where Clement was pacing up and down. He had expected to talk to Elizabeth before dinner, to explain and clear things up, but that hadn't happened.

'Did you find out anything? Was she intimate with him?'

'No. I didn't. She was clearly shocked and disgusted at me

for asking her such a thing. She also said she can't put Hugh out of her mind if everyone keeps bringing him up.'

'I'm tearing my hair out here, Mona. I don't know what to do or what effect this nonsense will have on my future.'

'Listen to Papa and deal with the consequences, if and when they should occur. At least you'll be continents away. I'll be here in the middle of it. Perhaps I could come and visit.'

'Certainly, if this hasn't broken me and Elizabeth.'

Later, Mrs Murphy carried a tray and some fresh towels to Delia's room. Without uttering a word, she took Hugh's envelope from their folds and placed it between the pages of the book on the bedside table. Delia had a strong urge to hug her.

The housekeeper looked at her bandaged head and said, 'The bleeding seems to have stopped so I won't disturb that dressing. I'll have a closer look in the morning. Meanwhile, try to have a good sleep.'

'I will,' Delia answered, knowing that would be an impossibility, 'and thank you!'

She had a future to try to work out.

Chapter 19

She did feel much better in the morning, but only because she had spent half the night going over Hugh's instructions, formulating a plan. She wouldn't mention him again. She'd be the dutiful daughter she'd always been. It wouldn't harm her to be polite to their guests for the short remainder of their stay, and she'd go along with her parents' decision to take her to London.

Her mother had come in to check up on her, and while she was there they heard horses' hooves on the driveway.

'That's Clement and Elizabeth off for a gallop. At least they are talking again. I was worried they might not be.'

'I think I need to apologise to Lady Constance, Mama.'

'I think you do, although I do understand what made you speak to her like that. She can be *de trop* at times, but rudeness solves nothing, and you must try to think before talking. Candidness is not always attractive, especially in a young lady. Do you feel like coming downstairs for breakfast?'

'Yes, Mama. They'll all be gone tomorrow, so I'll make an effort to send them away with good memories.'

'Good girl. And we can plan our time in London.'

Initially, the atmosphere was frosty in the dining room. Delia apologised and explained that what had happened the previous day had been a horrible accident and that she was in shock, but thinking back on the incident, she had mistakenly blamed Clement. Lady Constance accepted her apology.

It took a greater effort to be civil to her brother, but she did and the equilibrium was restored somewhat. Elizabeth hardly spoke, even when Lord Peter tried to lighten the mood.

'I hope you'll be bringing home some good memories of your time in Ireland,' he said to Elizabeth.

'I will, but I'll be glad to get back to India and to see Papa and my friends.'

'Understandably, we have a much wider circle over there,' Lady Constance volunteered.

'I'm sure,' he replied and turned his attention to his scrambled eggs. As they were leaving the breakfast room, Lady Constance surprised Delia by asking, 'May I talk to you alone? Perhaps in the drawing room in half an hour?'

She was already seated when Delia arrived a few minutes early, having had her wound dressed by Mrs Murphy.

'Young lady, I have some things to say to you. Things that need to be said and it seems that no one in this household is prepared to say them. You may have fooled your family, but I've seen your sort before. You're a wilful child. By your brother marrying my daughter, you'll become part of our family and that makes you, and these issues, my concern also.'

Delia wanted to say that she thought her mother should be present but Lady Constance held her hand up to stop her speaking.

'I know about your unsavoury little trysts. Your brother filled me in when I interrogated him, and I want to tell you this, in no uncertain terms: if there are any unwelcome consequences from this liaison with your tradesman, you need never expect any contributions from Clement or from my family. We would never accept such scandalous behaviour, and I'd take a crop to you myself. If you have allowed that man to violate you, you can find a charitable organisation to take care of you.'

Delia stood up to leave. She was shaken by Lady Constance's directness and felt afraid of what she might say in turn.

'Sit down. I haven't finished yet,' she ordered. 'I will not have our families dragged down by some loose-moraled chit of a girl and some opportunistic money-grabber. Do I make myself clear?'

'You do, very clear. But, Your Ladyship, you are not my mother and I think she should be here for this conversation.'

'Don't come the innocent with me.'

'I doubt Mama would approve of what you are suggesting, especially as you are a guest in our home.'

'Perhaps that's her failing.'

Gathering strength from she didn't know where, Delia stood up again, defiantly this time, and, hiding her anger, she said, 'You may put your mind at rest, Lady Stokes, because if and when I need such help, you will certainly be the last person I would ever come to for it, never mind for kindness or sympathy. You have my word on that.'

'You may be smart, but you are insolent and *une mal élevée enfante.*'

'*On peut dire la même chose de vous, votre* ... Ladyship,' Delia replied. 'It's inappropriate for you to suggest such a thing to me and to judge everyone by your ridiculous standards.' With her head held high, she said, 'I wish you a speedy journey back to India,' and walked out the door.

Lady Stokes didn't reply.

Delia feigned a headache and stayed out of everyone's way for the rest of the day. She did feel violated – not by anything Hugh had done, but by that pretentious woman's far from subtle innuendos. Delia had no doubts that Clement had known about this exchange, had possibly even suggested it. It was also quite possible that he had sent Mona to quiz her the previous night.

She only had to hold her composure for another day and she could do that. She could do anything to be with Hugh again.

All day long there was a great movement of traffic on the corridor that passed Delia's bedroom. Noreen's older brother had been brought in to help Tommy as trunks and packing cases were hefted down the stairs and labels checked before being dispatched to the station. This required several return visits by the trap. She didn't go to dinner that night. She couldn't trust herself to behave in the presence of that odious woman and her haughty daughter.

Clement came to say goodbye to her on Wednesday morning, the first time she'd seen him since he'd attempted an apology in her bedroom in front of her parents. 'I missed you last night, but let's not part on bad terms, Delia. God knows when we'll see each other again. I could be injured, even killed, in the line of duty and I'd hate to leave things like this between us. You know I never meant to harm you. I only have, and always have had, your best interests at heart, and I didn't want to see you throwing your life away on someone who isn't worthy of you.'

'Well, there's no fear of that happening. You saw to that. I don't want to part on bad terms either, so I wish you and Elizabeth a safe journey and a happy marriage.'

'Will you tell her that?' he pleaded. 'I know you and her mother had words. I won't ask about that exchange because I know she can be a difficult and tactless woman. But it would mean a lot to me to know you and Elizabeth parted as friends.'

'Of course I will,' she replied.

He left and returned a few minutes later with his fiancée.

'I hope your face heals well,' Elizabeth said as she leaned forward to shake Delia's hand.

'I hope so too. And I wish you both a happy marriage.'

'Till we meet again, little sister,' Clement said and extended his hand too. They didn't embrace. Such a different parting to the joyous greetings on his arrival several months earlier.

Mona and her parents went to the station to see the Stokeses off. Lady Constance had made no contact at all. A relieved Delia wandered through the quiet rooms and sighed with contentment. She certainly wouldn't miss them. She went down to the kitchen, as she often did when the house was empty, but Mrs Murphy had gone out to deliver some surplus eggs to Mrs McCormack and the Widow Lynch. She could have given them to Noreen to take, but, delighted that the pressure was over, she just wanted to get out in the fresh air for a while. Noreen was in the scullery scrubbing silver with baking powder and vinegar, her hands red and raw looking. The draining board was stacked with tureens and platters, all waiting for the same treatment. The two baskets of cutlery sitting on the floor were next in line.

'Have you to clean all those like that?' Delia asked.

'Yes, Miss Delia.'

'That'll take you all day.'

'Oh no, miss, I have to have this lot finished by lunch. Then Cook is going to show me how to tackle the copper pots and pans. She says I'll need to know these things when I go to work in New York. And now that the guests have left, I won't be needed here any more, so she's giving me a few lessons before I finish. There's so much to learn. Look at all the different kinds of knives, forks and spoons there. I'll never be able to tell them apart or why there has to be so many. And I'm talking too much again. Ma would kill me if she heard me. Sorry, Miss Delia.'

'There's no need to be. Did you hear from Mr Dunne?'

'No, miss, I'm not sure if he's still at sea. Will I tell Mrs Murphy you were looking for her?'

'No, it wasn't important.' She hesitated. 'Noreen, I need to talk to you.'

'Have I done something wrong, miss?'

'No, you haven't, but I need your help.'

Part 2

Chapter 20

Mademoiselle's reign over the schoolroom was coming to an end. The Kensley-Balfes had decided that they no longer required her services now that Mona was to marry and Delia would be taken up with preparations for her season. She'd accompany the family to their London address and from there travel to her potential new family for a few days' trial, to see if the children liked her and she liked them

Delia hated the idea of saying goodbye to her. She had been part of her life for nine years and had been an inspiring element of her growing up. She had also been Mademoiselle's favourite, finding French and history less of a burden than Mona did, and she had enjoyed the discussions they frequently had about literature, both French and English.

Mona had been non-committal when she'd heard the news. She was too excited about the prospects of going to the Hattersley's Scottish castle for the famous October ball, meeting up with her newly found debutante friends and showing off her fiancé.

'I'm happy to say the wound is healing well,' Mrs Murphy told Delia's parents when she changed the dressings. A red line, about three inches long, ran from above her ear down to her jaw. 'That scar will fade in time, although there'll probably always be a little welt there,' she said as she gently patted some liniment on it.

'Mrs Murphy, you have the magic touch, with your mysterious lotions and potions. I've seen the results before – when the groom was kicked in the head by that angry mare and when that farmhand had an argument with his scythe. You're unflappable,' His Lordship said. 'I've seen soldiers crumble under less.'

'When you've seen some of the things I've seen in my time, you learn to stay calm – on the outside anyway.' She smiled, secretly delighted with His Lordship's praise.

'Now, girls, we need to decide on your London wardrobes. And Mona, we have to talk about what you'll need for our week in Scotland. We'll only be up there for seven nights, and you'll have Mademoiselle most of that time for company, Delia,' her mother said. 'before she moves on.'

It was a while since the whole family had travelled together, and the trunks were taken down from the attics in preparation. Underclothes and night attire were washed, starched, dried, pressed and checked for loose buttons, before being wrapped between layers of tissue paper and laid carefully in the travelling cases.

'If we keep them in different trunks, Mademoiselle, it will save us having to sort them out again before Mona goes on to Scotland.'

'How clever you are. I didn't think of that,' the governess said as she helped Mrs Mooney with the task.

Outfits were teamed with matching shoes, gloves, mufflers, purses, wraps and coats. Their riding habits, whose skirts were always a few inches longer than walking-out ones and often had lead weights in the hems to make them drape properly when sitting side-saddle, went to the bottoms of the trunks. On top of these their dresses were layered, individually folded and carefully arranged between soft cotton lawn.

A few days later the trunks were dispatched ahead of the family to be taken by train to Dublin, then on to the steam packet across the Irish Sea and from Liverpool to the house the Kensley-Balfes had leased. Mademoiselle, Lady Leonora's maid and Sir Peter's man would accompany the luggage a day ahead of the family.

In a well-stocked hamper, Cook and Mrs Murphy made sure they had enough supplies to keep them happy as they travelled.

It took well over two days to make the journey, and by the time they arrived they felt grimy, irritable and tired.

'A hot bath, a light supper and a comfortable bed – that's all I want,' announced Lady Leonora. 'Thank goodness we gave ourselves three days to recover before setting off for Scotland.'

'That'll be a tiring journey too, but the grouse shooting will make up for it,' her husband said. 'And I'm sure the Hattersleys will be excellent hosts.'

Tilsley, the butler, took their coats and hats and passed them to a house maid. He said he'd send Mrs Tilsley up immediately to attend to their needs.

The housekeeper arrived looking agitated. She kept wringing her hands. She was obviously upset by something. 'Your Lordship, Ladyship, I'm afraid there's a problem. Some of the trunks have not yet arrived.'

'What's happened to them? Have you reported this to anyone, Tilsley?'

'Not yet, Your Lordship. Mrs Tilsley only discovered it this afternoon when she and the maids were unpacking,' the butler said.

'I hope they haven't lost my new gown and slippers for the ball,' Mona said. 'I'll be devastated if they have. Or my riding habit and boots. Delia and I want to go riding along the Serpentine.'

Her father said, 'Perhaps they've simply been misdirected and they'll arrive tomorrow. Let's not panic. It's getting late and we're all tired. I'm sure they were all correctly labelled.'

'They were, sir. I checked them myself before they were taken to the station.' Mademoiselle said.

'See. I told you. There's nothing we can do tonight so let's turn in. I'll wager they'll be here before sunrise.'

'I hope so, Your Lordship. There have been a lot of stories of unscrupulous gangs in Liverpool stealing luggage from sea travellers and selling the contents or demanding big sums of money to hand them back to their owners.'

'So I've heard, but let's not let our imaginations run away with us.'

'Don't stay up too late talking, girls,' their mother said as they settled down with Mademoiselle for a chat.

'Are you anxious about meeting a new family?' Mona enquired.

'A little, but I will feel happier once I've spent a few days getting to know them. Hopefully they will approve of me and want me to stay.'

'Of course they will, but I'll miss you,' Delia told her. 'We both will.'

'I'll miss you too. I've seen you grow up before my eyes. You, Delia, from an inquisitive and sometimes precocious little girl to a determined single-minded young lady. That makes me very proud.'

Delia wondered how long that would last. She doubted that anyone, apart from herself, would be proud of her if her plans worked out.

'And me?'

'You, Mona, from being a serious little one, who resisted being taught anything she didn't consider useful, to being a poised and elegant young lady, who'll make a wonderful mark in society. Another success, I think you'll both agree.'

'It's almost exactly a year since I've been in London. Last time Mama took us to Liberty and to Harrods. Can we go there again?'

'You'll have plenty of time next week when I'm in Scotland,' her sister said.

'But, Mona, I want to do them with you, before you disappear out of my life again, and before Mademoiselle leaves too.'

'I'm getting married, not dying,' Mona replied.

'I know, but you'll be caught up in your social engagements after that and we'll be going back to Kensley. And I really want to go on the underground. Can we do that?'

Mademoiselle laughed again. 'You're still a little girl at heart. And, yes, we can. It'll be an education for you. In Paris it's called le metro.'

There was still no sign of the missing luggage the following day. It transpired that the delivery was two trunks shy and they both contained Delia's belongings.

Wires were sent back and forth to the rail and sea packet

companies. Tilsley was dispatched to the lost-property offices of London and North Western Railway Company, but none of these avenues yielded any results.

'I think I should postpone my visit up north,' Lady Leonora declared.

'You can't do that to me, Mama. You already missed lots of my engagements when Delia was ill, and this is more important. You have to meet the rest of Desmond's family. Tell her she must go, Delia.'

'Of course you must go, Mama. And by the time you return the luggage will probably have turned up. If it hasn't, I'm sure I can fit into some of Mona's clothes. It's not as if I had a wild calendar of events to attend while you're gone. Go and enjoy yourselves. You can worry about me after that.'

In between this upheaval, Lady Leonora dealt with the correspondence that had accumulated in her absence, and her husband frequented his club. The young women went shopping in Knightsbridge, and their father gave them ten shillings each in case they "saw something they couldn't live without".

'It's nice being together like this, Delia, and I'm sorry you felt excluded when Elizabeth was here. I suppose I just wanted to spend as much time with her as I could, knowing she'd be gone in a few months,' Mona told her.

'I do understand.' She hugged her sister.

With still no sign of her trunks, Delia and Mademoiselle

eventually waved the family off for their week in Scotland. Hugh's name had never been mentioned since the Stokeses' departure and Delia was determined to keep it that way.

Mademoiselle was leaving later that day to meet her trial family in Kent. The butler and Mrs Tilsley were charged with accompanying Delia should she need to go anywhere.

Delia went to her room and wrote several letters. She'd promised she'd write to Mrs Murphy, so that was the first one. When she'd finished, she sought Tilsley out and asked where the nearest postbox was.

'There's one just two streets away, on the corner, Miss Delia, but you can leave those with me and I'll have them posted for you.'

She declined, saying she'd enjoy the short walk.

'Your mother would not approve of you going out unaccompanied. You could easily get lost in a big city like this.'

'Hardly while going to the postbox and back again.' She laughed, and he agreed reluctantly. 'Still no sign of my luggage?'

'I'm afraid not.'

'Perhaps I'll meet someone walking around in my clothes,' she jested.

'Heaven forbid,' he said.

'Don't look so worried. I'll only be gone a few jiffies,' she said, and she was, back in plenty of time to lunch with her governess before hugging her and wishing her well as she set off to catch the train at three.

Next morning, Tilsley appeared with a letter that had just been delivered. Delia took it and went to her room. She ran the letter opener under the flap but didn't open it. She knew what it contained. Instead, she wrote a reply and told Tilsley she was off to post this and she'd be straight back. He insisted she take an umbrella as it was threatening to rain.

'See, less than ten minutes, and I didn't get wet or lost, Tilsley!'

He laughed as he opened the door on her return and took the brolly from her.

'I'm certain I could make it to Harrods and back too.'

'I can get someone to accompany you if you wish to go there.'

'I don't, but I'm sure I could if I needed to,' she said.

'I don't doubt it. I don't doubt it at all,' Tilsley said.

It rained all afternoon and she curled up at the fire with a book she'd taken from a shelf in the library.

The postman brought another letter for her the next day and she repeated the ritual. Without looking at the contents, she replied to it and set off to the postbox.

'At least the rain has stopped, Miss Delia, and I'm glad to see you've wrapped up warm. There's a chill wind out there today. Winter's on its way.'

'I could hear the windows rattling so I borrowed one of my sister's mufflers.' She waved the ends at him. The scarf camouflaged the bulkiness beneath her waisted overcoat.

Then, with Tilsley's blessing this time, she set off. There was a satisfying sound as she dropped the envelope through the slot, but she didn't turn around to go back. She kept walking. She walked until she reached the underground station. There she replicated everything Mademoiselle had shown them a few days previously and, counting the stops, she exited at Liverpool Street Station, followed directions to the ticket office and purchased a first-class seat on the next train to Liverpool. The station was a hub of activity, but she had the compartment to herself. A porter asked if she had any luggage and she replied, 'It's gone ahead.'

A little over five hours later, the train steamed into Liverpool Lime Street and she walked the short distance to the North Western Hotel. 'I have a reservation for two nights, Noreen McCormack is the name. I believe my maid may already be here.'

'Yes, ma'am. She arrived this morning,' the receptionist answered. 'Have you any luggage to be taken to your room?'

'I believe it should have arrived a few days ago, from Ireland.'

'And you'd be right. It's already up there.' He clicked his fingers and a bell boy appeared. 'Accompany this lady to her rooms.'

Noreen was sitting looking out the window. She jumped up when Delia entered and dismissed the boy.

'Oh, Miss Delia, you've no idea how glad I am to see you.

I was terrified you wouldn't show up, or that I'd give the wrong name, or that I'd be left alone in this strange place.'

'You needn't have worried. You've done really well. Was your journey all right?'

'Yes, Miss Delia. Mam's cousin met me off the train in Dublin and we went on a tram! She took me to the port to get the steamboat and she asked an older couple to make sure I was all right when we arrived in Liverpool. They looked after me and walked me to the Stella Maris Boarding House. It wasn't very far. I said goodbye to them there and went inside and, you were right. There was a long queue before me trying to get rooms. I waited for about ten minutes, then I left and came around the corner in here. I was shaking. I've never seen anything as big or as posh in my whole life. Or so many mirrors and lights. But I gave them your note and they brought me up here. I feel quite proud of myself.'

'And so you should. It was a lot to ask and I'm very proud of you too, Noreen. Everything is going as planned. We have to keep our heads down until we're on the boat. First thing tomorrow we'll go to the agents and make sure of our bookings. They may let us on board then, although it will probably be the day after. I've decided we're going to travel second class – that way there'll be less chance of us being recognised.'

'Miss Delia, I can't afford to do that. I only have nine pounds and a few pennies to my name. Oh, I almost forgot – Mam's cousin gave me half a crown.'

'And you hold on to that, Noreen, you'll need it all to set you up in New York.'

'But I can't do that, miss.'

'You can. Mr Dunne gave me more than we need to cover the hotel, our tickets and other expenses. Don't carry your money around with you, though, especially in this city. We'll put it in the hotel safe. There are gangs of pickpockets out there on the streets, runners they call them, who can spot an innocent traveller a mile away, and you don't want your money whipped away from you. You've done me an enormous service, one that no money could ever repay. Have you eaten anything since you arrived, Noreen?'

'No, I felt queasy on the crossing and Mam's cousin told me if I felt that way that it was better not to eat, so I decided to wait a while, but I'm fierce hungry now.'

'Then let's order something to be delivered to the room. I'm hungry too.'

Noreen helped her with her coat and Delia laughed when she saw her looking at the two chatelaine bags hanging from her waistband. 'This was the only way I could think of getting past the butler without arousing suspicion. I had to sew an extra button on for the second one and then I could scarcely fasten my coat up over them, but the scarf helped conceal the bulges too.'

Noreen laughed as she put the coat in the wardrobe.

'They told me downstairs that my trunks were sent up. Are they here?'

'Yes, they're in the other room, my room,' Noreen said with a smile, pointing to a door behind her. 'I didn't unpack anything. I didn't know if I should.'

'You did right. I'll just take out what I need and we'll see what happens then.'

'I never slept in a big room like that or in a hotel before. It's very posh. And the linen is snowy white.'

Delia laughed. 'I suppose it is, but this is just the start, Noreen. We're both going to be doing a lot of things we've never done before.'

'How did you learn so much, Miss Delia, about eating in your room, the runners, the hotel safes and things like that?' the young girl asked.

'Partly because Mr Dunne wrote it all down for me, as though he was working on a project, making this journey step by step and detailing every little thing I'd need to know and do. I'm not nearly as clever as you might think.'

'I doubt that, Miss Delia. There's so much I can learn from you.'

The wind was biting as they headed to the Cunard Steamship Company the next day. The streets around the shipping offices were thronged with people, obviously intent on travelling too, many with several children hanging out of them and juggling with umbrellas, suitcases and oversized parcels. Noreen was wearing the new coat that Delia had helped Mrs Mooney make, and Delia complimented her on how fashionable she looked. She saw the enthusiastic clerk give her an admiring look before checking their reservations on the RMS *Etruria* passenger list. Noreen was oblivious to it.

'She's one of our newest ships, five decks, two funnels and auxiliary sails. That's her there on the poster.' He pointed to a large shiny framed picture on the wall behind his desk. This was his moment and he was going to enjoy it. 'She's a fine-looking specimen, don't you think? I have your reservation listed here, in our first class?'

'Yes, but I wish to change that to second and to upgrade my maid to second class also, to be nearer to me. I'm not a very good traveller. She was originally booked in third class.'

'Our first class is really luxurious, the latest in Victorian chic. The rooms are located on the promenade, upper saloon and main decks, and there's a separate dining room for those passengers. It's our first vessel with refrigeration in the kitchens too. There's also a music room and a gentleman's smoking room, although I doubt that'll be of much interest.' He smiled.

She smiled back at him, wondering how many times a day he went through this patter. 'It does sound delightful, but I'd prefer if you could change us both to second class.' She said with more confidence than she felt.

'Very well, ma'am. Our second-class rooms are less opulent, but they are comfortable and quite spacious. You need to report for boarding tomorrow morning, and if the vessel is cleared for departure, we'll set sail at first tide on Saturday. You should arrive in New York in nine to eleven days, depending on weather conditions.'

She took their tickets, thanked him and left.

'That's another hurdle out of the way. Now I need to wire Mr Dunne and let him know what's happening. I think I can do that from the hotel. I'll ask them to book a hackney to take our luggage to the ship too. Have you everything you need for the journey?'

'Yes thank you. Mam made sure of that.'

'She'll miss you.'

'She will, but it won't be forever. I'll save up enough for them to come and join me. It may take a few years, but I'll do it.'

'I've no doubt about it.'

Two days later, shortly after dawn on 23 October 1886, on a soulless grey drizzly morning, the RMS *Etruria* set sail for New York. The rain continued and the skies stayed a sulky grey as they sailed across the choppy waters of St George's

Channel. The ship wasn't yet full, but it would be after it called at Queenstown, its last embarkation port.

On arrival there, Delia and Noreen watched from the deck as a huge crowd of steerage passengers surged forth, carrying suitcases and baggage of all descriptions, and crates of supplies were loaded on to the vessel for the journey. They spent the night docked in Queenstown. As they steamed out the following noon, the sun shone weakly and the giant funnels belched out smoke and ash and left a trail of grey behind them. From the deck they watched the people waving on the shore becoming smaller and smaller until they eventually disappeared.

'They say that cathedral was built with money the emigrants sent home from America. I hope I'll be making enough over there to build my own,' she heard one man say to another and they laughed. 'So do I!' the other said. The spire of St Colman's on the hill was the last thing they saw before heading out on the endless monochrome of uninviting water.

Delia was sure that by now news of her disappearance would have been conveyed to her parents in Scotland. She was not proud of the worry and trouble she was causing them, but she had spent the last few weeks agonising over her decision. She had no doubts whatever that she was doing what was right for her, following her heart, but she wasn't happy about how it would affect those that she cared about.

To optimise her chance of escaping, she had had to take

action while her parents were out of the way. Mademoiselle could have proven to be a stumbling block, but it was as though the fates had come together to orchestrate her absence from the scene too. That meant she didn't have to lie to her.

Fearful that they'd try to follow her and stop her if they knew where she'd gone, she had addressed and posted the newspaper advertisements that Hugh had supplied her with to herself. These showed dates and tariffs and other information on voyages leaving from Southampton, not Liverpool. She had left these in a book by her bed, knowing they'd be found.

She didn't know if her parents would have had warned the Tilseys that she could bolt, but she hadn't wanted to take the chance, so she'd set about winning the butler over by doing a few false runs to the postbox. That meant she didn't have to lie to him either.

She hadn't told Mrs Murphy of her plans. By not knowing, she could honestly deny all knowledge of Delia's flight, and her future at Kensley Park would be secure.

She knew that Mona would never forgive her for what she was doing, and she could understand that. The unfortunate timing of her disappearance, coinciding with Mona's first outing in British society as Desmond Hattersley's fiancée, could be disastrous. If he broke off the engagement, she'd be the butt of scandal, gossip and disgrace. And she'd most likely not get another offer until all that had died down, if at all.

And that, of course, would depend on whether the Stokeses rejected Clement as well.

That didn't upset her so much. She was still angry with him. When she thought of Clement and Elizabeth and her detestable mother, she was almost sorry that she wouldn't be able to see the looks on their faces when the news reached them. She'd never forget the hatred in his eyes the day he and her father had come across the two of them and the violent way he had struck out at Hugh. He had changed from the big brother she adored to someone she didn't know any more and didn't particularly like. She put her hand up to the side of her face. She might be able to put him out of her mind, but she'd always carry the scar as a reminder.

As for her parents, she knew they'd be hurt, sad, angry, let down, disappointed and everything in between. She had kept her part of the bargain and not mentioned Hugh's name since they had told her to forget all about him. But perhaps if they had allowed her to tell them a little more, they might have realised that she had not forgotten him that easily, and most likely never would.

One of the last letters she had written and posted had been to them, explaining. She had sent it to the London address so that she'd be well on her way before it caught up with them. In it, she told them she accepted the consequences of her actions, but she had made her choice and it was too late to try and prevent her leaving. She told them how sorry she was to be the cause of hurt and how she hoped they understand and forgive her some day.

Delia was walking out on everything, and there was no going back now. It had been made quite clear that she needn't expect charity when she came to her senses, when it all went horribly wrong. She knew what she was leaving behind, but she had no inkling of what lay ahead of her in the New World.

The only thing she knew was that Hugh would be there, and that was enough for her.

Chapter 21

New York, 1886

Delia's constitution proved to be much stronger than Noreen's as the ship rolled, pitched and heaved for several days before the winds dropped, the weather broke, the skies cleared and the seas took on a calmer mood. Each passing day brought them nearer to their destination and closer to the realisation that she'd probably never see her family again. She cried a little, but not in front of Noreen. She missed them so much that it hurt, yet part of her was angry that this was the way it had to be. When these bouts of melancholy threatened to overwhelm her, she went over her notes from Hugh in her mind, remembering his touch, his kiss on her lips, his warm embraces, his funny accent, and she'd try to visualise what her new life would be like.

Noreen's enthusiasm as she made discovery after discovery on board amused Delia and, if anything, made her realise what a life of privilege she had enjoyed. On the voyage, she taught the young girl the duties of a lady's maid and about the social mores involved in dressing for day and night: what to wear and what not to wear on different occasions. To pass the time together, they shortened and altered one of Delia's older dresses to fit Noreen, and when they had completed the task, Noreen asked if she could keep the strip of velvet they had cut from the hemline.

Two days later she presented Delia with a long draw-string purse that she had sewn from a patterned chintz, with bands of the blue velvet. 'It's specially for when you're travelling. I put a long strap on it, to put across your body and wear under your coat. That way, if it's too heavy, it won't pull on the button or your waistband.'

'That's beautiful, Noreen, and very astute of you. Thank you. Where did you get such an idea?'

'From you, Miss Delia, when you came to the hotel looking like you were wearing saddlebags. Because this is much longer than your other ones, the bulkiness won't show at your waistline and it'll keep your possessions safe.'

'I'll treasure this. You definitely have a gift and a bright future ahead of you.'

'I hope so, Miss Delia.'

'And I know so, Noreen.'

The sea days dragged; the sameness of the endless seascape was uninspiring. The excitement at seeing another vessel, no matter how far distant, was the highlight of some of them.

They agreed that time seemed to move slower the further they sailed away from home.

On day ten there was great excitement when their cabin steward knocked on Delia's door with some urgency. 'You can get your first glimpse of America if you want, but you'll need to go up on deck.'

They put their coats and hats on hastily and found the deck already crowded with people, some crying with relief that they'd really made it across the Atlantic Ocean. Others cried because they knew this step was one they'd never be able to reverse.

'See that – it's called the liberty statue. The captain told us President Cleveland himself dedicated it just a few days ago. Some fanfare that was, with a parade and fireworks that lit the sky up something magical,' the steward said. 'This is something you'll be able to tell your grandchildren. It didn't have a name when you left Queenstown. Now it's called Liberty –because there's a broken chain under one of the feet to symbolise the end of slavery.' He was so proud anyone would have thought he'd erected it himself.

'Is it a lighthouse?'

'Indeed it is, sir. Shines its light for twenty-five miles, it does, if conditions are right and not murky like today. I reckon it's the tallest lighthouse in the world. And you can climb up inside it too.

Some of his audience looked sceptical, but as they

approached, they could see it more clearly. As the ship steamed closer, the figure of a woman grew larger and larger and larger until it was towering over ships, big and small, many on excursions to see this colossus from the water.

'I'd love to have seen the fireworks,' Noreen said, but Delia's mind was on seeing Hugh again.

The city skyline slowly came into focus and the waters of New York harbour became busier and busier with vessels and freighters of all shapes and sizes keeping to their shipping lanes to avoid collisions. It would be a while yet before they reached their dock at Castle Garden Emigrant Depot, and despite the damp cold of the November day, the excitement all around them was palpable as the passengers stood transfixed.

Noreen's eyes were wide with anticipation, and she joined others waving enthusiastically at the people on a steamship that had obviously just departed from New York, heading in the direction whence they had just sailed.

'Everything looks very big,' she said, as the cavernous emigration sheds and the top of the old fort at Castle Garden reared up into view. 'You won't abandon me, Miss Delia, will you? I'd hate to get lost here.'

Delia placed her hand reassuringly on her arm. 'Of course not, Noreen. Now make sure you have your money safely attached to your belt. I have mine in my new purse.' She smiled. 'If we do get separated for any reason, don't go with anyone you don't know, no matter what they tell you. Just go to the one of the exits and wait there until we find you, and find you we will. But first, I have to locate Mr Dunne. You do have his address, don't you, as a last resort? Don't look so worried. It's the first time for most of these people too, including me, so we're all feeling a bit lost,' she said with much more confidence than she felt.

All five hundred first-class passengers were disembarked first. Delia and Noreen stood by the rail looking down on ladies in marvellous chapeaux and furs, wearing kidskin gloves and beaded or fringed velvet retinues, while their menfolk sported fur-trimmed greatcoats with bowlers or top hats. She could just imagine her parents being among the throng of people walking confidently down the gangplanks, before snaking their way inside the buildings for processing by the uniformed officials.

It was mostly a formality for the better-class passengers, while those in steerage were subjected to a much more rigorous vetting process that could see them standing in lines for several hours. Such vetting often involved medical examinations, which, if unsuccessful, saw the weak and infirm being deported from Castle Garden on the next available vessel going back east, their hopes and dreams shattered before they had a chance to find their new world.

The longer it took, the more anxious she became. She was beginning to panic inside. What if they were turned back? What if she gave the wrong answers? What if she couldn't find

Hugh? Supposing he had changed his mind? Had she done the right thing?

Eventually the signal was given. It was the turn of the second-class passengers to leave the ship. They joined a queue and waited their turn.

'Have you family here?' the official asked Delia as she handed over the papers Hugh had had prepared for them.

'Just my fiancé.'

'His name?'

'Hugh Dunne.'

'Occupation?'

'Draughtsman.'

'Does he live in New York?'

'Yes,' she said, offering his address. 'He was born here.'

'Where does he work?'

She handed over the paper Hugh had left with her. She could feel her heart thumping as he read through this, nodding.

'Have you travelled alone?'

'Noreen McCormack, my maid, is with me.'

He looked back at her papers and scribbled a signature on both sets, before putting a stamp on them.

'Pass through,' he said, and she let out a deep breath of relief.

They were in. They were in America. Two young girls, scarcely women yet, both from diametrically opposed backgrounds and with widely differing ambitions for their futures, but both sharing the determination to survive and embrace whatever lay ahead.

They found themselves surrounded by tearful and joyful reunions as people recognised long-unseen family members, younger siblings and sweethearts. Hats of all shapes and sizes blocked Delia's line of vision, and she felt the panic rise again. How would she ever find Hugh in this melee?

'Move along, folks, move along. Those behind can't get through,' shouted an official wearing a visor with an oversized badge on the front. They were being propelled along when she heard a voice call, 'Delia, Delia, over here! Noreen – here!'

Noreen saw him first and ran towards him. She hugged him with enthusiasm.

'Welcome to America,' he laughed. Then he spotted Delia making her way towards him. He stood there looking at her for a few seconds before stretching out his hands to her. 'You came. You really came,' he said. He folded her in his arms and held on to her as though he'd never let her go.

She inhaled the smell she remembered, his familiar smell, and any doubts she may have had about her decision vanished. She felt safe. 'I told you I would,' she said when she could breathe again.

'I can't believe you're both here. Did everything go as it should?'

'Yes, like clockwork, thanks to your careful planning and to Noreen. I couldn't have done it without her.'

'How was the crossing? It can be very rough,' he said.

'The first few days were awful. We just kept to our beds and wanted to die.' Delia laughed. 'Then we got what I believe is called our sea legs and things got easier.'

'It's odd, but I keep thinking the ground is moving and that I'm still on the ship,' Noreen said.

'That's not odd at all,' he reassured her. 'It's just your balance resetting itself to being on dry land again. It'll pass. Let's get out of this crowd. Your luggage will be delivered to your lodgings, but I'll tell you about those later. God, it's good to see you, Delia. I was terrified something would go wrong.'

'So was I,' she said, suddenly feeling shy.

'Hold on tightly to me,' he said, linking one girl on each side of him, and they set off through the bustle of porters with flat caps and hackney drivers touting for business. The steerage passengers had begun to disembark, many of the women and children shivering in unsuitably flimsy coats and shawls. Ill-fitting suits and greatcoats had taken the shape of their menfolk on the journey, many of whom had nothing else to wear.

'Let's find a place to have a sit down and I'll tell you the plans.'

'You sound different. I can't put my finger on what it is,' Delia told him.

'You mean I sound more American? When I came back from Ireland I was told I sounded more Irish.'

'That must be it. How is your work? Did you get into trouble for taking so long to get back?' she enquired.

'The chief was very accommodating, but one of the partners did take me aside for a quiet word. Luckily his family came over in the famine from County Mayo, and he said he understood what drew me back. I promised I'd make the time up and I've been working day and night since so that I could have a few days to get you settled.'

He steered them in the direction of a tea rooms and ordered for them. He answered their questions as they waited for their tea to arrive and explained the cents and dimes to them. Once the muffins were buttered, he proceeded to tell them what he'd been up to. 'First of all, you, Noreen. I've arranged for you to go and see about a position with a good family. The housekeeper, Mrs Bradley, knows me and she's expecting you on Saturday morning at 10.30. She's looking for a scullery maid.' He handed her a piece of paper with the details. 'Don't look so scared. We'll get you there safely,' he reassured her.

Delia suddenly remembered the day she had seen Noreen, up to her elbows, scrubbing and rubbing the silverware in Kensley Park, with her hands red and raw, and she felt strangely protective of the young girl. 'She's capable of much more than just scullery duties,' she told Hugh. 'I've been teaching her some upstairs skills and she can sew very proficiently.'

'They'll all stand to her,' he replied. 'I suspect she'll have to start at the bottom, but, Noreen, if you get the chance to tell Mrs Bradley any of those things, then do so. She will work you hard, but she's a fair woman. The family she works for is one of the city's oldest.'

'I don't mind hard work. I just hope their cook makes muffins like these,' she said. Hugh nudged the plate slowly in her direction and smiled at her. She didn't need any encouragement to help herself to a second one.

'You've thought of everything, Hugh, haven't you?' Delia said.

'I tried to.'

Delia longed to be alone with him. She had so much to say, to ask, to tell, but she felt she couldn't be so intimate in Noreen's presence.

'I've also booked you ladies into a modest hotel until you settle in. We can go there when we finish our tea. It's a tram journey away, but not very far.'

'I have money left over – we travelled second class – so that can cover the hotel.'

'But I had budgeted for first!' he said.

'I know, but I thought we'd have less chance of being spotted.'

'That was clever of you. At least you don't have to worry about that now you're here.'

Noreen stifled a yawn, and Delia realised how tired she was feeling too.

It was dark when they emerged, and Delia thought that to the young country girl this city must seem like fairyland with its streetlights and horse-drawn carriages, barouches and trams, pedal cyclists and wide footpaths filled with people, busily intent on reaching their destinations. Hugh escorted them to the tram, bought the tickets from the conductor, then stood aside for them to enter and take their seats first.

'The waiter and the conductor called you sir,' said Noreen.

'It's considered good manners to address everyone as sir or ma'am here. Funnily enough, I never thought that strange before,' he replied.

Delia said, 'Everything and everyone looks different, even from London.'

'I suppose it is. Here the different nationalities tend to live together in the same neighbourhoods, the Irish, the Poles, the Italians. It made sense when they first arrived because they spoke the same languages and ate the same foods. They felt safe among their own.'

'This is where we have to alight,' he said a few minutes later as the horses were reined in.

They walked back a little and turned down a less busy street. The entrance to the hotel was up a short flight of steps that led into a brightly lit hallway.

'We're expecting the luggage to be delivered this evening,' Hugh told the receptionist.

'We'll take care of that, sir. Dinner is served until seven thirty in the dining room on the first floor.'

'I don't think I could eat anything else,' said Noreen.

'You may go to your room if you'd prefer. I'll have something with Mr Hugh before I turn in, but I'll come up with you first.'

Hugh was seated at a table in the corner of the dining room when she came back down. He stood up and took her hands. He kissed her on the cheek and said, 'Darling Delia, I've been wanting to do that since I spotted you in Castle Garden. I thought I'd never get you alone. I missed you so much.'

'And I've missed you. You've no idea how I've longed for this moment.'

'How is your cheek? Did your wound heal well?' He reached over and lifted her hair back to inspect it. His fingers sent electrifying sensations through her body and she put her hand over his and held it there. 'I was so sorry to have to leave you to face your brother and father after they caught us together. I felt I was abandoning you.'

'It wouldn't have been safe to have stayed, not the way my brother was reacting. I was so proud of the way you stepped up and asked my father for my hand,' she said. 'That took some courage, and I honestly think he respected you for it.'

'I'd walk through fire for you, Delia. You're the love of my life.'

'And you mine. Can you really believe we're together?'

'I've spent the last weeks imagining this, and I was terrified something might happen and you wouldn't be on the ship.'

'And I was terrified that you wouldn't be there to meet us, or that I wouldn't be able to find you.'

'I'll always be here for you,' he said, looking into her eyes and taking her hand.

'I'm so happy. I can't find the words.'

'You have to meet my relations.'

'What do they think about me?'

'They don't know about you yet. I was afraid someone somewhere might leak our plans and try to put a stop to us. New York is like a village, and you know what the Irish are like – everyone is connected though marriage or they know someone whose second cousin met their third cousin, once removed, on the way to mass or church or whatever. I've learned that the only way to keep a secret is by not sharing it with anyone. But I know they'll love you as I do.'

'When are you going to introduce me?'

'I was thinking about that – how does Friday sound?'

'Perfect!'

'And if you still want me in your life after that, I was thinking a walk up the aisle could be the next step. What do you think of that? I can't have you swanning around New York without a chaperone. You never know who might take your fancy and snatch you away from me.'

'That's true.' She laughed.

'I was going to wait until you had become acclimatised to the place before telling you this, but now that you're here I don't see any point in holding it back. I've spoken to Fr O'Hara, he's the parish priest at St Jerome's, and he's agreed to marry us in the church on the Saturday before Advent.'

'But I'm not a Roman Catholic. Does he know that?'

'Of course he does, and he knows our family too. He's christened all of the Dunnes that were been born here in America and he was a good friend of Granda's. My aunts do the flowers for the altar and Uncle Dan is behind the fund-raising for the new church they're hoping to build on the site of the one we'll marry in.'

'And he agreed?'

'And he agreed – but only after I explained how you had no one here but me, and that I wanted to make an honest woman of you and take you as my wife before you were led astray by someone less concerned with your well-being. I also told him that if God wanted you to become a Catholic, he'd surely find a way to make it happen. He couldn't argue with that logic so he's agreed to bless our union.'

'I'm beginning to see what being Irish over here means.'

'We all look out for each other, especially when we're away from home. That's how we've survived no matter how hard times were.'

'That makes sense.' She nodded. 'I have so much to learn.'

'And I'm talking too much. What do you say about the

date? Would you rather wait? If so, it will have to be after Christmas, because there are no weddings during Advent and even I can't make Fr O'Hara bend that rule!'

She could scarcely believe what she was hearing. Life had been a whirlwind since she'd decided to run away – now, here she was on the threshold of marriage. Once she was Mrs Hugh Dunne she could really shed her old persona and become the person she wanted to be: the one she felt she was meant to be.

'Am I assuming too much too soon, Delia? I don't want to pressure you. You've already made so many sacrifices for me.'

'Don't ever let me hear you say that again, Hugh. I haven't made any sacrifices for you. I did and am doing exactly what I want to do. I can't wait to be your wife and, yes, I do believe I have no previous engagements for the last Saturday in November, so let's settle on the date.'

'That makes me the happiest man in New York.'

'And me the happiest woman. And you know, Noreen has played such an important role in all the subterfuge and in keeping our secrets, so I'd love her to be a witness, although she may have secured a place by then.'

'If she makes an impression on Mrs Bradley, I think I may be able to use my influence to get her a few hours off that day.'

'And just how do you come to have any influence with the housekeeper of one of the barons of New York?'

'It's a long story. I'll tell you tomorrow.'

'What if she doesn't get the placement? She's a dear and

devoted girl, and she's certainly not shy about saying what she's thinking. However ...'

'However?' He grinned at her.

'However – if she doesn't make an impression, I can't just leave her to her own devices.'

'Of course not. We'll take her on as our housemaid, although her prospects will be much better if she gains experience in one of the big houses here. Don't worry, it'll work out, you'll see. Now, I'm going to go and let you settle in. I hate more than anything to leave you, though it's such a relief to know you're so much closer to me now than when you were on the other side of the Atlantic Ocean.'

'I can hardly believe I'm here.'

'And I can't imagine how you must feel about getting married with none of your family here.'

'They'll never want to hear from or of me again. Clement told me I'd be considered dead to them if I continued to see you, never mind elope or, worse again, marry you.'

He reached over again and squeezed her hand.

'My family is in New York now.'

'I just hope I'm worthy of you – I've cost you so much already.'

'Don't talk like that, Hugh Dunne! Don't ever talk like that again!'

Chapter 22

Over the next few days Hugh took them to see some of the sights of New York. As they explored, the gusting winds caused flurries of newly turned russet, golden and brown leaves to fall. These skittered and swirled as they pursued each other along the pavements and swooshed around street corners, bathing the city in golden pools of colour.

Hugh pointed out several of the grand mansions of the seriously wealthy on Madison and Fifth Avenues. 'These are the people whose houses I hope to design some day. Their owners are in things like mining, furs, steel and banking. What do you think? These are their townhouses. They have others in the country or by the coast where they spend their summers, away from the noise, the dirt and the heat of the city.'

'They look very grandiose, almost ostentatious.'

'That sums them up very accurately. They are ostentatious, all right, and one of their rituals is to promenade up and down

Fifth Avenue every afternoon at five, showing off. We can come back then and you can see for yourselves!'

'Isn't it rude to gawp at them?' Noreen asked.

'No, they love it,' he replied. 'That's why the women get dressed up – to show off their finery and to see everyone else's.'

And later that day Hugh accompanied them to witness the practice. The streets were crowded. Barouches and carriages, often drawn by prancing matching pairs of horses, made a great spectacle. These
were punctuated by hackneys, buggies and cabriolets. Cyclists on messenger-boy bikes with enormous baskets on the front wove perilously in and out of the traffic, whistling tunelessly and miraculously avoiding disaster. Men in long coats and cravats raised their tall hats in recognition of acquaintances.

Before that, Hugh took them for a ride on the elevated railway that he had described to Delia in Ireland. He was as amused as Delia was at Noreen's childlike wonderment at what she was seeing. He pointed out the building where he was apprenticed to William Appleton Potter, one of New York's most prominent architects. 'I'll show you some of the buildings he's designed another time.'

They went window shopping and stepped inside the emporiums of R. H. Macy & Co. and Bloomingdale's. Noreen whispered to Delia, 'The assistants look like fashion plates in those ladies' magazines you have.' She agreed – they were beautifully groomed and coiffed.

They stopped to admire some lace collars and a countertop arranged with colourful gloves of all lengths, with the most intricate embroidery details and tiny buttons. The millinery department had a woodland backdrop and displays of fine hats, some with gravity-defying adornments. Even the most un-fashion-conscious could not ignore that birds and feathers were very much in vogue that winter.

'It's a wonderland,' Noreen said.

'It surely is,' Hugh agreed. 'My cousin Kate works here.'

'Here in Bloomingdale's or here in New York?' asked Delia.

'In Bloomingdale's. She's in the accounting office. You'll be meeting her later.'

'I could never imagine having the courage to come in here on my own,' Noreen said.

'At the rate the city is growing, in time, everyone will shop in places like this,' Hugh told her.

That night they met his family.

'Are you nervous, Delia?' he asked when he arrived to collect them.

'Terrified!' She laughed. 'I hope they'll like me and won't think me too uppity for them.'

'You're not uppity, Miss Delia,' Noreen said.

'I hope not,' she explained, 'but there are perceptions that people who live in the "big houses" in Ireland are standoffish, high and mighty and often not very nice. And sometimes it's not so easy to shake those impressions off.'

'I'd be more concerned that you might regret coming once you've met all of my clan. We're a loud and gregarious lot. They haven't enjoyed the social standing that you have, nor indeed the money, but they are genuine, decent people, who care about each other and they are respected among their peers. I'm sure they'll love you.'

'I'm sure I'll love them if you do,' she replied, and he took her hand and held on to it. After a short tram ride, they walked a few hundred yards and stopped outside a three-storey block.

'Welcome to my New York,' he said with a flourish.

They climbed one flight of stairs in the building where his aunt Peggy lived with her husband. Delia had never been in an apartment block, or indeed in an apartment, before, although she had found herself looking up at these buildings, wondering what they were like inside. How many apartments were in them? How many people lived in each one? Could you hear people talking in the next one to yours? Was there any privacy? This was truly alien territory for her, yet another experience to add to the things she'd have to tell Mrs Murphy about when she got around to writing to her.

Hugh told her that the newest ones being built had electrical lighting and were five floors high and sometimes took up a whole block. She couldn't imagine that. How would the size of a whole block compare with the house in Kensley Park? Whenever thoughts like that crept in to her mind, uninvited, she quickly banished them and concentrated on plans for her upcoming marriage. What would she wear? Where would they live? There was so much to do and so little time to do it. There was no time to assemble a bottom drawer. She had seen her mother accumulate the finest embroidered Irish linens, Carrickmacross lace and other items for both her girls, for when they had homes of their own. These were folded and wrapped in fine cotton, and placed in two deep drawers, with camphor to make sure the moths didn't enjoy them first. They'd never be hers now, and that didn't seem to matter any more either.

She could sense Hugh's excitement as he escorted his ladies to meet his family. The door was open, waiting to welcome them. Warm cooking smells emanated from behind a sea of grinning faces.

'These are the matriarchs of the family, my dad's sisters, Peggy and Gracie,' Hugh said, 'and Peggy's husband, Dan.'

Peggy's welcome was guarded. 'So you're the colleen who swept my nephew off his feet.'

'Now, Peggy, you promised you wouldn't embarrass me.' Hugh laughed. 'Dan, can't you keep her in check?'

'What do you think? She's your flesh and blood. I'm only married to the woman.' He laughed and said, 'And you're very welcome, miss, to our humble home.'

Delia saw his wife give him a disapproving look, before saying, 'It's all a bit overwhelming when you first arrive. I was only six, but I remember it only too well, how everyone sounded different. This is my sister, known to all as Aunty Gracie. She's a widow for – how many years is it now, Gracie? Nine or ten?'

Gracie answered, 'Ten, and I want you girls both to know you're never to feel lonely. Our doors will always be open to the two of you, and there'll always be a bite to eat – isn't that right, Hugh? No need to stand on ceremony.'

'You're very kind, thank you,' Delia said, feeling herself relax. Noreen smiled.

Grace continued, 'I have to tell you, there are a lot of disappointed mothers around here – disappointed that their daughters didn't get him first.'

'Now you're the one who's embarrassing me, Gracie.'

'Pay no heed to him.' She laughed. 'He can take it. He takes after our father. His granda and he were very close.'

'Yes, Hugh has told me a lot about him,' Delia said. 'He seems to have been a great man.'

'He was,' Grace agreed.

'As for this fellow ...' Peggy said, taking Hugh by the arm. 'He kept very quiet about you, but we had our suspicions that something was going on when he kept postponing his return from Ireland. He only sprang all this on us a few days ago.'

Hugh laughed. 'I was afraid meeting you lot might chase

her back on the return voyage, but I'm reliably informed that ship sailed this morning. You'll have plenty of time to hear all about how we met later – let's finish the introductions. These are all my first cousins. You can figure out who belongs to who as we go along. This is Nancy, after our grandmother, Timmy, Eoghan and Kate, the one I told you who works in Bloomingdale's, Gerard, Sean, Mary, Bridget and Jack, after Granda, and this is the baby of us all, Una.'

'I don't like being called a baby,' she protested. 'I told you that before and you promised when I was eleven you'd stop calling me that.'

'I know I did, but you're so easy to tease. I can't resist it.' He laughed.

'I'll never remember the names,' Delia said. 'But, Una, I will remember that you're the youngest and not the baby, because I am too. I'm very pleased to meet you,' she shook her hand, 'and thank you all for your warm welcome. And this is Noreen McCormack, who lived on our – who lived near us in Ireland and who has come to New York to seek her fortune.'

'There's many have done that before you, and there's plenty of opportunity, Noreen, especially if you can read and write, which I believe you can.'

'Sit down and make yourselves as comfortable as possible,' Gracie said. 'It's a bit crowded in here.'

'Well, they all wanted to meet you,' Peggy said defensively, turning to Delia. 'You'll have to take us as you find us.'

'I've put you to a lot of trouble,' Delia began, but Grace interrupted her.

'Whist, will you? It's no trouble at all. Tell us about yourself, before this lot bombard you with questions.'

'I may be the reason Hugh stayed too long over there, but he's the reason I've come over here. I'm sure he's told you that my family doesn't approve of us even being friends, never mind anything closer.' She noticed Peggy's lips tighten and sensed disapproval from that quarter too. 'My brother threatened to disown me, and that was before I ran away without telling anyone. No matter how long we'd wait, they'd never approve of a marriage between us.'

'Aren't you very young to be taking such big steps?' asked Dan, Peggy's husband. 'It's an enormous decision to walk away from your family, never mind to cross an ocean to get away from everything that's familiar to you.'

'Perhaps it is, but I didn't plan the timing of it. It happened and I know this is my destiny. It's what we want. We love each other.'

Hugh put his arm around her shoulder and said, 'We surely do. She's the one for me. I knew it the first time I laid eyes on her. I tried resisting but it was no use. I even got as far as Queenstown and had to turn back. I couldn't leave her behind.'

'I don't deny that you have feelings for each other, but I can't pretend to be happy about the situation,' Peggy said in a forthright way that Delia would come to accept. 'We're not out of the same drawer, and there's many an Irish person living here who'll not take kindly to you because of that. There's still a lot of bad blood between the gentry and peasant stock.'

'Now, Peggy, this isn't the time to bring politics up,' her husband said.

'He's right,' said Hugh, taking Delia's hand. 'We have chosen each other. She's given up a lot to be with me, and I'll do whatever it takes to make sure she doesn't regret it.'

'I hope when you get to know me you'll accept me for who I am and not where I came from,' she said. There was an awkward pause, which was broken by a curly haired freckled girl who Delia thought was the one called Bridget. She looked about the same age as Noreen.

'Did you really live in one of the big houses in Ireland?'

'I did, and our people, yours and mine, would have been neighbours before yours emigrated.'

'She's being modest,' Hugh said, filling some of his cousins in on her background. 'Delia lived in Kensley Park. It's a pretty big estate. Her parents are Lord and Lady Kensley-Balfe – our ancestors were tenants on the neighbouring estate. So were Noreen's. The Crosbies were our landlords.'

'Tenants and landlords, is it?' muttered Peggy, to no

one in particular, and Delia noticed her husband reach out a restraining hand. She knew from Mrs Murphy what connotations the term landlord carried with it, especially landlords during the devastating famine years. Somehow she hadn't been expecting it here, and she felt compelled to stand up for her family.

'Don't judge me from what you've heard. There were decent people around then, too, who didn't evict their tenants or let them starve. I understand mine were amongst those.'

'Aye, that's how the story goes over here,' Dan said and Gracie nodded. His wife didn't.

Kate, the one who worked in Bloomingdale's, asked, 'If your parents are Lord and Lady, does that mean you have a title too?'

'I would have if I chose to use it, but I won't be doing that!'

'What would it be? Would we have to curtsy when you came into a room?' Una asked.

'Absolutely not.' She laughed. 'And it would simply be Lady Delia.'

'Enough quizzing,' Gracie said. 'You must be famished with the hunger – let's sit down and eat. It's a bit of a tight squeeze, I'm afraid. We're not usually all here together.'

Eoghan, a few years younger than Hugh, asked him, 'So, how did you manage to win Delia over?'

'Modesty forbids and all that,' he started, but she interrupted.

'He literally made my horse bolt and then he came and rescued me. I couldn't fail to be impressed.'

'Well that's an original approach. Did it take you long to plan that manoeuvre?' he teased.

'No, I was too irresistible.' Hugh replied.

'You had your own horse?' Una asked with wide eyes.

'Yes, I had,' she told the little girl, realising that it was going to be harder to put her life of privilege in the background than she had thought.

'Did you?' Una asked Noreen.

'No!' She laughed. 'We had chickens.'

Everyone praised the meal, which Peggy and Grace had cooked, and the questions kept coming, from the younger family members in particular. They wanted to know all about the life Delia had in Ireland. And the more she told them, the more she realised how ill-prepared she was for the real world.

When they heard the date of the wedding, both aunts offered their help.

'Where are you going to live?' Gracie asked. 'You can't bring your bride to your apartment. That area isn't safe anymore. There are too many tenements around there now.'

'And what would she do all day while you're at work? She couldn't just go wandering about on her own down there,' Peggy said – Delia was getting the impression that whatever Peggy said was listened to.

'She won't have to. I've found a new place on Alexander Avenue.'

'Alexander Avenue – isn't that where those fancy brownstones were built? Where all the doctors have bought?' asked Dan.

'I hadn't heard that, although someone in the office referred to it as the Irish Fifth Avenue. The house actually was a physician's, but the poor old fellow, Doctor Parks, died. They had no family so it's a huge house for just his widow and the help. The chief in the office was great friends with him and it's through him that I've ended up renting the second floor and the attics for a very affordable sum. I still have to show it to Delia,' he said, smiling at her, 'but I'm sure you're going to like it. It's quiet and there are lots of trees around to remind you of home.'

'And it's not too far away from us either,' Grace said.

By the time they were ready to go back to the hotel, she felt she had known them all her life, and she liked the informality and warmth between them. She was a bit put-out by Peggy's hostility – she hadn't expected that. But the others didn't seem to mind when she told them that she didn't go to mass: they accepted her as she was. They said goodbye with hugs and little formality, and they reiterated the open invitation to 'call anytime', an invitation that would never have been uttered in her circles, where strict guidelines applied to such matters. Noreen was showered with good wishes for her interview.

'Will I fit in? Do you think they liked me?' she asked Hugh the following morning, while Noreen was away being interviewed by Mrs Bradley. It was the first chance they'd had together for a proper exchange of thoughts after meeting his family.

'I know they did. If they didn't you'd have known it by now, and the cousins wouldn't have been so interested in everything you had to say. You had them eating out of your hands. To them you're an exotic species. I doubt a real "Lady" ever visited any of their homes before.'

'Me? An exotic species?' She laughed. 'I wonder how long it will be before they find me out.'

'I'm sorry about Peggy. She still remembers how hard the first few years were for my parents when they got here, and I suppose she heard a lot of stories. But putting her aside, Soon-to-Be-Mrs-Dunne, are you still willing to marry me after the clan gathering?'

'Yes, of course I am. I can't wait. And I'll do my best to show her how wrong she is.'

'I'm sure that won't take much. Last evening was a bit of an assault, and for that I apologise, but you see how they are. If I'd left anyone out they'd never have forgiven me. And I wanted to give you a flavour of life, of my life, here in

America. Do you think you'll be able to adjust to living in an apartment? It won't be forever. I promise you that.'

'I'm looking forward to it.'

'I've been saving hard and that, along with Granda's patent dividends, mean that when I finish my apprenticeship at William Appleton Potter's, I will buy a house for us. It won't be a grandiose one, at first, anyway, but one with a front porch and a rear yard. That'll do us until I become famous like Richard Morris Hunt or Stanford White. Then I'll design and build one especially for us – one that's suitable for a lady of breeding and class, one where our children can play on the lawns and maybe even have a pony.'

'That all sounds very ambitious, but, Hugh, I could live anywhere, so long as you are there with me.'

'I'll never leave your side – I promise you that – now meanwhile, would you like to come and see where we'll be living?'

'I'd love to,' she said and he squeezed her hand, delighted not to have to share this moment with Noreen.

'Come on then.'

Ten minutes later they arrived at a tall narrow house that she now knew was called a brownstone because of the colour of the brick exterior. They took the short flight of steps leading to the hall door, and she was sure she saw the curtain twitch as they did so. They had to walk down the owner's hallway and up a flight of stairs to reach their quarters. First impressions were good. It was tastefully decorated and everything was gleaming. She felt excited when she saw 'their' apartment. It was large and bright and had a fair amount of furniture in it.

'Since she changed her living arrangements, Mrs Parks has no space to fit all her pieces and she asked if we'd like to have them. She did say that if you hate them, we can tell her and she won't be offended.'

'I think they're marvellous. They look very good where they are. Tell her we'd be delighted with them, yes, thank you.'

On one side of the hallway there was a large drawing room to the front with a bay window affording views of the suburban street below. Double doors led to a dining room and, beyond that, a kitchen with an anthracite stove. On the return, their bedroom had doors that opened on to the roof of the kitchen below. This had a railing around it. Beyond it was what Hugh referred to as 'the yard'. It was only after hearing him say this a few times that she realised he meant a garden. There was a bathroom and separate water closet and, upstairs, three smaller rooms in the attic.

'I love it, Hugh. It's perfect.'

'These can be a nursery, a study, a maid's room, who knows?'

'Time will tell,' she replied, smiling at the thoughts of making her life there. 'I'm going to have to learn to be a wife before a mother, otherwise you'll die of starvation.'

'I could live on your soda bread.'

'Thankfully, Mrs Murphy taught me a bit more than that.

I can make bread and butter pudding with egg custard. I can scramble eggs, make chicken and apple pies and possibly even blackberry jam.'

'That sounds like a great combination.'

'Don't tease,' she said. 'Your aunts have promised to show me some more.'

'They're both great cooks.'

'They even told me they'll take me to the market and teach me how to shop! Peggy made me realise that there's so much to learn – things I never thought of before, things a girl from the big house would never have learned. I hope she and you won't be disappointed in me.'

'Whatever happens, it won't be that. You could never disappoint me, Delia.'

'I hope not.'

He took her in his arms and hugged her, then, finding her lips, he kissed her for longer than propriety permitted and she didn't want him to stop.

'This is the first time we've really been alone since your brother and father found us together.' Just as he was about to kiss her again, they heard footsteps on the stairs. The owner's maid had been sent to see if they needed anything and to tell them that, if they had time, Mrs Parks would love them to join her for some coffee before they left. They accepted, and Hugh winked at her with a one-of-these-days-we'll-be-together look as the woman disappeared down the staircase before them.

Chapter 23

Grace and Peggy were as good as their word and devoted much of the next few weeks to helping Hugh prepare the apartment for his new bride. They also baked a cake and prepared the refreshments for a light meal there after the ceremony. Mesmerised as she was by New York and the familiarity of Hugh's family, Delia missed home, her sister, her parents, Mrs Murphy and Tommy.

Delia couldn't really believe it was her wedding day, and as she looked out her hotel room window, the first flurries of snow began to drift from a leaden sky. New York was much colder than she had imagined, and immediately unbidden memories of the previous winter sprang to mind. Memories of Mademoiselle teaching Mona and her about Napoleon's retreat from Moscow as it snowed outside the tall windows at Kensley Park. She wondered how Mademoiselle was getting on with her new family and if she would ever hear from her again.

Was that really only a year ago?

'*Il neigeait*,' she recited to herself.

'*Il neigeait, nei-ge-ait* – it's soft,' Mademoiselle Corneille had corrected, '*Nei-ge-ait*, like the sound of the snow itself falling. There's nothing sharp about it.' And there wasn't. When she was younger, she had thought that snow had the ability to soften everything, right before her eyes, and that when it melted all the hard edges would reappear.

Now she knew that not everything could be softened that easily. Here, almost three thousand miles away from her family, she was wondering if their attitudes to her would ever soften. She did have regrets about her decision to cross the ocean – not to be with Hugh, but because of what it might do to them. She loved them and had never intended hurting them, but she had seen no other way to follow her destiny.

She and Mona had always been close, and she harboured a hope that one day her sister might come to understand why she ran away. Her father might have listened, had she chosen to confide in him, but he would ultimately have sided with her mother. Undoubtedly, they would have found somebody suitable and married her off for her own protection. Clement was quite another matter. Delia didn't care for Elizabeth or her odious mother, with their pretensions and so-called standards. And after his behaviour, she told herself she didn't care what happened to him or with his relationship.

She would have given anything for her parents and her

sister to have been with her to witness her becoming Mrs Hugh Dunne. Hugh's aunt Grace had encouraged her to put pen to paper. 'That way you'll know you did everything you could to mend fences.'

She had listened to her and had written four separate letters, one to her parents, one to Mona and one to Clement, asking them to understand and forgive her. She had addressed the fourth to Dr Canavan, asking if he would pass the enclosure on to Mrs Murphy. She wanted to make sure she would receive it, and she felt she could reply on his integrity for that. Whatever about her family's reaction to her running away, it was important for her to know that Mrs Murphy knew she was safe and happy and that she was with Hugh. She wasn't sure exactly how long this correspondence would take to reach them, or indeed where it might catch up with them.

She peeped out from behind the curtains at the leaden day. The snow was getting heavier, but that didn't bother her. In a few hours, she'd have shed the shackles of being the daughter of a titled and entitled family and become one of the ordinary people. She was looking forward to learning about being the wife of Hugh Dunne, an apprenticed draughtsman, soon-to-be fully fledged architect in his own right.

A knock on her door announced the arrival of Noreen, who had come to help her get ready for the ceremony. She had started working in the Fifth Avenue house two days after meeting with the housekeeper. Kate, Hugh's cousin who worked in Bloomingdale's, had moved into the hotel, to Noreen's room, so that Delia would not be unaccompanied in the dining room, and the two women had formed an unexpected bond that made Delia feel right at home in her new circumstances. Kate was already helping her dress for this very special occasion by the time Noreen arrived to offer her services too.

'You look very stylish – quite the lady, in fact,' Kate told Noreen.

'I feel like a lady in this, thanks to Miss Delia and Mrs Murphy,' she replied. 'She was the housekeeper in Kensley Park. And this was Miss Mona's frock, but I retrimmed the sleeves with some shot-silk ruffled ribbon and added a belt to match. It brings the colour out.'

'I'd never have recognised it,' Delia said. 'And that pork-pie hat – it didn't have those feathers on it the last time I saw you wearing it?'

'No, Miss Delia, but I saw them on the hats in the windows in Bloomingdale's and one of the maids got them for me. It's not every day I'm asked to be a witness.' She smiled. 'It's a great honour and my mam would kill me if she thought I'd let you down.'

'Well, you certainly haven't done that, Noreen. She'd be very proud of you if she could see you now,' Delia said.

Noreen hummed as she laid Delia's clothes out on the bed in her room.

'You did that as well as any lady's maid, Noreen.'

'I had a good teacher.'

Delia replied, 'Mrs Murphy taught me a lot too.'

'I meant you, miss. Look at all the things you taught me on the voyage. Mrs Bradley was impressed when I told her.'

'That's good. I just wish we could have brought Mrs Murphy with us to New York,' Delia said. 'I'd love her to have been here today.'

'So do I. But I don't want to think about home or I'll get sad again.'

'No one is allowed to be sad today,' Kate said to the two of them.

She brushed, teased and coaxed Delia's hair until no traces of her scar were visible, before securing her hat with pearl-topped hat pins. She stood back to admire her handiwork and asked Noreen what she thought.

'She looks swell.'

'Swell?' asked Delia.

'Yes, swell, it means wonderful in American,' Noreen said.

'Well I never. Scarcely a few wet weekends here and you're picking up the dialect already.' They laughed. 'And truth to tell, I do feel – swell in this,' she said, twirling in front of the full-length mirror. 'You don't think the bustle is too high?'

'No. It's perfect. It's what the young ladies upstairs in my house are wearing,' Noreen said. 'They have a funny name for it – something like bell ... bell figora.' She giggled.

'*La bella figura*,' Kate corrected. 'It means a pleasing shape – the high bustle accentuates the waistline. And with those panels of lace and moiré satin trims, it's just like the patterns the seamstresses at Bloomingdale's are working on. You have an eye for fashion.'

'You flatter me, but I think Noreen does. I simply envy the skill and craftsmanship that go into making garments like this.'

'I want to know all about your work and the household – are they kind to you there?' Kate asked Noreen as she fixed her hair.

'Oh, yes, I don't know what Mr Hugh said to Mrs Bradley, but she's been really nice to me and so have the others. They left some periodicals beside my bed in case I was feeling homesick. And I was a bit, the first few nights, but now that I know my way around the house it's better and I can practise my reading looking at them too. The butler is frightening – he's English – but happily I'm too lowly for him to have noticed me, so I just make sure to keep out of his way.'

Powdered and dressed, they made their way downstairs, where the concierge wished her well. He held the umbrella over their heads as the three made their way between the piles of shovelled snow to the waiting carriage. Delia had butterflies in her stomach and wished again that her mother and sister could have been with her to see how happy she was.

Peggy's husband, Dan, was waiting in the church porch. In

contrast with the grey skies outside, flickering candles cast a warm glow over the inside of the building. Dan took her arm and walked her up the short aisle to where her groom was waiting. She hardly noticed anyone, her eyes focused straight ahead. Hugh's expression broke into a broad grin when he saw her, and her heart flipped as he came to greet her.

The ceremony was short, but personal. Canon law forbade Fr O'Hara from celebrating a nuptial mass for a non-Catholic, but they made their vows 'in the sight of God' and he blessed their union, wishing them 'a long and productive life together, whatever it offered them'. They signed the marriage register in the wood-panelled sacristy, where the faint aroma of incense lingered.

Dan was Hugh's witness and Noreen was Delia's. It was only when they emerged that she realised how many were in the church, some she recognised from the family get-together two weeks previously, and, although there were others she wasn't sure about, she smiled at them all as though she knew them. It was too cold to stand around talking, so Hugh invited them all back to their apartment to warm up.

It was there she discovered that three handsome and well-dressed young men she had spotted outside the church were Hugh's work colleagues. They were talking to a much older man with an impressive moustache that twirled up at the ends. He had an authoritative look about him that gave him an air of imperiousness, in spite of not being very tall, but there was a twinkle in his eye that made her warm to him.

'These are my fellow apprentices,' Hugh told her as he made the introductions. 'James Brown Lord, Mitch Belfield the Second and our office jester, Cornelius R. Shriver, and this is our esteemed mentor, none other than Mr William Appleton Potter, architect extraordinaire and our boss,' he said reverentially, bowing to him. 'It's really good of you to take the time to come along today, sir.'

It was clear to Delia, as she shook his hand, that there was mutual respect and affection between these men. Mr Potter had been talking earlier to Mrs Parks, who had conquered the stairs to wish her new tenants long life and happiness. Delia had forgotten it was through this contact that Hugh had found their apartment.

'Thank you. I had to come along and toast you both, then I'm going to leave you to celebrate with those closer to you. I hope you'll be happy living in America,' he said to Delia. 'It's a big change.'

She agreed and he turned back to Hugh.

'Now, young fellow, as you seem to think you are responsible and mature enough to take on the responsibilities of a married man, I think it's time I gave you your papers so you can have a shot at taking on the world too.' He drew a long envelope from an inside pocket and handed it to him.

'Congratulations, young fellow, you're fully fledged now. I'm sure you'll go far, and do our name proud on the way.'

'Sir, I wasn't expecting that.'

'

You've earned it and you show great promise. Come and talk to me on Monday. Congratulations on your marriage too.' He shook hands again with them both and, taking Mrs Parks by the arm, led her carefully back down to her quarters.

Although Hugh had taken Delia to see her new home briefly before, she hadn't taken it all in and could never have imagined what it would be like filled with so many people. Hugh's family had done him proud. They had prettied it up with flowers and greenery and produced a feast of delicacies for the guests. Delia also had her first taste of a real Irish-American hooley, where instruments were produced, traditional music played, and people sang, laughed and danced. Tactfully, everyone went home before it got too late. Noreen and the cousins had tidied everything away. She was enjoying herself so much she hadn't noticed them doing this. At last they left and she found herself alone with her new husband.

She felt shy. She thought she knew what to expect and had blushed with embarrassment when Peggy tried broaching the topic one evening the previous week. 'The wedding night can be ... Let's say it's not always as you imagined it would be at the beginning.'

Delia had quickly changed the subject, but now she

wondered should she have listened. In truth, she was a bit wary of Peggy still. Now she had to admit to herself that she was nervous. What if she was a disappointment to him: if she didn't know what to do or say or how to behave?

She needn't have worried. Hugh was all consideration and kindness. He led her by the hand up the half-flight of stairs to their room and left her to get ready. After a little while, he knocked and came in, just minutes after she had climbed into the bed they would share. She was waiting for him, her hair loosened from its clips, falling around her shoulders and forming a halo in the gaslight.

'You look beautiful, Delia. You don't know how I have longed for this moment,' he said nuzzling her neck.

Her pulse raced and her heart thumped as flames of desire emanated from her very core, coursing through her body in great waves. Was her touch doing the same wonderful things to him as his was to her? She had her answer as she felt his body respond.

'I don't want to hurt you,' he whispered as he undressed her. He entered her tentatively at first, then more urgently. Their movements developed a rhythm of their own and she experienced sensations of lust that she'd never known existed or could ever have contemplated feeling, never mind enjoying. She gave herself totally to him.

As they lay entwined in the afterglow, he told her, 'I loved you the first time I saw you and I'll love you with my dying breath. I promise you, Mrs Delia Dunne, that I will devote my life to making you happy.'

'And I loved you, Mr Hugh Dunne, from the moment you came out of your derelict cottage and scared me off my horse, even though my landing was not very elegant. I will love you forever too. Today, and tonight, were perfect. I never thought I could be so happy.'

'You looked wonderful. I felt so proud of you when I saw you arriving in the church. I couldn't really believe it was happening. And you charmed everyone.'

'I liked your friends too.'

'And they liked you. Mitch wanted to know if you have any sisters.'

As soon as he said this, she could see he regretted it: regretted reminding her of her family who should have been part of their perfect day.

'I'm sorry,' he said.

'Don't be. You're all I need, and I'm yours now.'

He wrapped his arms around her and they slept. They made love again in the early hours, long, leisurely, lustful love that left them both sated. When they had rested, she swung her legs out of bed and caught a glimpse of herself in the mirror and thought, *I'm a woman now. I look the very same – yet I feel so different. I feel complete.*

'I'm going to make us breakfast,' she said, pulling a

robe around her. The city was strangely quiet that Sunday morning, and as she drew the curtains back she saw why. It had continued to snow heavily during the night, deadening the sounds.

'Do you know how?' He laughed.

'It *is* my first time ever doing it, so I might need your help, but I'm a fast learner and I watched Cook and Mrs Murphy often enough. Wait until you see, I'll be a perfect wife in no time at all.'

'I don't doubt it,' he replied. 'I'll light the fires. And we can afford to get a girl to come in and help out now that I've got my papers, because it means I'll get paid a proper salary and we can start saving for our first real house. It may take years but I'll do it, I promise you.'

'I don't doubt that either. Is that what the chief wants to see you about tomorrow?' she asked, placing a plate of eggs in front of him.

'I'm not sure. I hope he doesn't want me to leave to make way for a new recruit. I need stability now. He believes passionately in the apprentice system, rather than going down the university route. He thinks hands-on experience is superior to book learning. That's how he learned.'

They heard a note being pushed under their drawing-room door and Hugh picked it up and read it. 'Will you excuse me for a few minutes? Mrs Parks want to see me about something.'

It was more than a few minutes before he came back. It was

half an hour, and he was beaming from ear to ear. 'Mrs Parks has agreed to allow us to share the services of her housekeeper. I spoke to her about it last week. She had been worried that Mena might wish to move on to a busier home since Dr Parks died. This way she'll get to hold on to her and we'll have help too. You won't have to worry about keeping the fires going or about the laundry.'

Delia felt both delighted to hear this, and a little disappointed too. 'I don't want to be a burden on you, Hugh. I want to learn to do everything normal wives do. I know I have a lot to learn, but I will. You'll see.'

'You've been used to having a whole household looking after you, beavering away in the background. Having a little help is the least I can provide for my lady wife. Mena's family is Irish too, or at least Irish American.'

They didn't venture out in the weather, but spent that day indoors in front of a roaring fire, eating food left over from the wedding feast and making love on the rug during the afternoon.

'I'm going to miss you when I go to work tomorrow,' he told her, covering her with a wrap.

'I'll miss you too, but I've a busy day planned. Aunt Peggy – she told me I could call her that – is taking me to the greengrocers, the general grocers and the butchers and she's going to help me set up accounts with them so I can arrange my weekly orders. I think it's a not-so-subtle way of letting me know what a useless existence I've lived up to now and how far short I fall in basic domestic skills.'

'She hasn't said anything like that, has she?' he asked.

'She doesn't have to. She's been perfectly nice to me, but I can sense that she doesn't exactly approve of "decorative" women. But I'll show her there is more substance to me than merely being ornamental.'

'Would you like me to talk to her?'

'Oh, please don't. That might make things awkward. My trunks are being delivered from the hotel after lunch too, so I can sort everything out and turn this place into our home.'

'I feel my home could be anywhere, so long as you are in it.'

'That's exactly how I feel,' she agreed. 'But it would be nice to know where my stockings are and where your studs and ties lived, instead of having to open every drawer looking for them.'

'Your enthusiasm is infectious.' He laughed. 'And I'm glad you've had a few weeks to get the feel of New York.'

'And so far I love what I've seen.'

'That's only been a smidgen of it. I want to show you Pearl Street Power Station, where the electric light is generated. In a few years all houses will be fitted with electricity and there'll be no more smoky fumes to contend with, just you wait and see. And I want to show you the Vanderbilt mansion on the corner of Fifth Avenue. It's built like a French palace. They're one of the richest families in America and feel entitled to showy displays of wealth.'

It was her turn to laugh. 'And you think I'm enthusiastic? There's a pair of us in it.'

They reached for each other and he said, 'Right now I'm only enthusiastic about one thing – pleasing my wife.'

'I'm delighted to hear that,' she said holding her arms out to him.

Chapter 24

'You should have woken me,' she told Hugh when he brought her a cup of tea. He had risen early, resurrected the embers in the kitchen stove and lit the fire in their drawing room before she had surfaced.

'You looked too cosy. Have a good day and keep warm,' he told her, kissing her lingeringly on the lips. 'I wish I could stay in there with you, but I must be off.' He blew her a kiss from the doorway and she heard him go down the stairs. Wrapping a shawl tightly around her shoulders, she went down to the drawing-room window and watched him set out for the office, his footsteps leaving their imprints in the fresh snow that had fallen during the night.

His colleagues teased him a little, saluting him as he arrived. James Brown Lord had made a nameplate for one of the drawing desks, a privilege afforded only to the fully fledged professionals. It stated: Mr Hugh Dunne, Architect. The rest of the staff congratulated him and he confided to James, 'I'm a little apprehensive. I hope the meeting this morning doesn't see me cut loose from the firm. Of course, I want to go out on my own one day, but not quite yet. I'd like the chance to make a name for myself first.'

'I doubt the chief will want to be rid of you that quickly. The office is working at capacity and there are no signs of that letting up.'

'Let's hope you're right,' Hugh said, sounding more assured then he felt. How could he go home to his new wife and tell her that he didn't have a job any more? It was torturous waiting and watching for the secretary's door to open. He'd never realised how much traffic went in and out of it in a short space of time. Eventually he was summoned. He tugged his waistcoat down and, fastening his jacket buttons, entered Mr William Appleton Potter's hallowed office. The chief was lost in contemplation as he studied some drawings.

He turned and began, 'I hate to do this to you, young man, but I have no choice. I realise the timing is awful, especially when you've just moved and got wed, but it's a sign of the times and I have to think of the future of the firm.'

Hugh couldn't believe it. His worst fears were about to be realised. He just stood there, at a loss for words.

'Sit down, will you?' The chief indicated a seat and went behind his desk. 'There's a lot to discuss.'

Discuss? What could there be to discuss, apart from the promise of a good letter of recommendation – surely he wouldn't be denied that, even though he had taken liberties with the length of time he'd spent in Ireland?

'You know this country is enjoying the fruits of its current industrial revolution and that we've been fortunate enough to benefit from some of the business that follows such a spike in investment. Several of our projects have been acclaimed, like the buildings at Princeton University and Admiral Charles Baldwin's house at Newport, although I can't take all the credit for that, as Robert H. Robertson and I were partners at that time. There's a growing demand for factories and offices as well as apartment blocks – the Astors have fairly well cornered that market for themselves. Land is changing hands quicker than the seasons, and the Wendels are buying up more and more of it. While I can see the need for quick solutions, I can't say I see any merit in erecting the monstrosities that are popping up everywhere to accommodate the waves of European immigrants arriving weekly. Mark my words, they'll end up turning these into ghettoes if no one calls halt.'

Hugh was still at a loss as to where this conversation was going, so he held his counsel.

'Thankfully, we've stayed out of that segment and, as a result, could probably term our clientele as being among the wealthy classes – and by that I mean they can afford to indulge their whims and fancies, not in providing for the masses, but in providing for themselves. I have here,' he reached across his desk to one of the stacks of paper spread out in an orderly fashion and retrieved what he was looking for, 'a commission to build a summer house in Newport, Rhode Island. It's not the one we had hoped to start earlier this year on Bellevue Avenue. This one is on Ocean Avenue, and if you're willing to uproot your new wife and move down there, I'd like you to undertake this project on behalf of the firm. We've already designed and built the family's Fifth Avenue mansion. Now they want a summer cottage. What say you, Mr Dunne?'

Hugh didn't know how to answer.

'If you don't feel you are ready for this or are averse to moving right now, I could pass it on to Mr Young Lord. You and he both show remarkable vision and talent, and I think you understand the trends for shingle and shingle gothic that seem to be in vogue.'

'I am at a loss for words, sir. I thought you were going to dismiss me, not offer me a promotion.'

'Is that a yes?' He laughed. 'Of course, you wouldn't have to move down there straight away. There'll be the usual surveys and plans that need drawing up first, but once they've been approved you'll need to be on site full-time. The blueprints of Admiral Baldwin's house and of John W. Ellis's Stoneacre are in the back studio. Take them out and peruse them. They'll give you an idea of the terrain.'

'Thank you for your faith in me, sir,' Hugh said, knowing the interview was over.

'There'll be a substantial increase in your salary, but I must warn you – you'll earn your money. Don't be lulled into thinking that you'll be working for the president of the Manhattan Stock and Trading Conglomerate – it'll be Mrs President who'll be pulling the strings and changing her mind every day, if not several times on the hour! Some of these "arrivisti" clients are not easy to please. They think their wealth entitles them to buy not just the services, but the professionals they hire too. I wish you good luck on your first solo assignment.'

'Thank you, sir. I think I'll probably need it.'

'I'm sure you'll make a great success of it and, in time, when everyone knows your name, I'll be able to tell everyone I gave you your start.' He shook Hugh's hand.

'That's a heavy burden – I hope I can live up to those lofty aspirations.'

As Hugh emerged from the inner sanctum, he saw the anxious faces of his peers wondering what his fate had been. James came over and enquired, 'Well?'

'Well,' he answered. 'It's as I suspected.' He paused. 'I'm being discharged,' and just as the commiserations were about to begin, he added, 'to Newport Rhode Island. I've been given my first project as an architect!'

There was great jollity in the office and he couldn't wait to get home to tell Delia his news.

Delia's day had been eventful too. She still hadn't posted her letters home, and now that Hugh was fully qualified, she felt the need to amend them and add the good news. She did this while waiting for Peggy to arrive. When she did, she brought dinner in two casserole dishes and put them in the tiny pantry. Instead of feeing grateful, this made Delia feel even more inadequate. 'You just have to heat them up,' Peggy told her before they set off to visit the local shopkeepers.

Holding their skirts up out of the snow, they walked a short distance to the clutch of shops. Peggy had it all planned out, and, in sequence, they visited the dry goods store, the greengrocer, the bakery, the victualler and the hardware/ironmongery store. Before they left each one, Mrs Hugh Dunne's name had been entered in their ledgers as a new account holder.

And, although she had stood mesmerised at the variety of goods in the grocery shop, while assistants in brown shop coats scurried about filling orders for other customers, she told Peggy, 'I feel very important now.'

'We're all important in our own way,' Peggy said pointedly and as though regretting the sharpness with which she said it it, added, 'We all had to start somewhere.'

'I'd never have done this without you.'

'That's what families are for,' she replied. She had already drawn up a list of staples that Delia must always keep in her store cupboard – things like flour, rice, spices. She had another of perishable items and another for the butchers. They left these for delivery and headed back to the house.

At the top of the flight of steps, they scraped the compacted snow off their boots before going into the hallway. Even though the house felt welcoming, Delia knew it would take a while before she considered it home.

She was telling Peggy, 'So much has been happening in my life over the past two months that it's only now I'm beginning to feel I can relax and get used to it all,' when Mrs Parks opened her drawing-room door.

'I must confess I've been looking out for you,' she said. 'You must be frozen venturing out on a day like this. Will you join me for a cup of tea while you thaw out?'

They accepted gratefully.

'I've never felt cold like this or seen so much snow before,' Delia said as Mena took their coats.

'It gets colder than this and the snow heavier too,' Mrs Parks replied, ushering them inside.

The drawing room was elegant, like Mrs Parks herself. An enormous fire roared up the chimney and the grand piano stood open in the corner.

'I find playing passes the time very pleasantly. I hope it won't bother you.'

'Oh no, It's one thing that I do miss,' Delia said.

'You play?'

'I do – I did, but I'm very out of practice. I haven't touched the keys since leaving Ireland.'

'Then you must come down and practise whenever you feel like it.'

Delia thanked her, feeling sure it was an offer that wasn't really meant to be accepted. There were books everywhere, stacked on occasional tables and on shelves. The old lady said, 'Unfortunately, my old eyes are not what they used to be, and on dark days like this, no matter how many gas lamps are lighting, I find it difficult to see the print. It's so frustrating.'

Delia found herself saying, 'I would be very happy to read to you sometimes if you liked, if you don't think I'm being too forward.'

'Of course not. Are you familiar with any of our American authors – Henry James, Louisa May Alcott, Harriet Beecher Stowe?'

'I'm afraid not. My reading was confined mostly to English and French novelists.'

'French writers like Dumas and Maupassant?'

'Yes, I've read them both. We always had a French governess and she was a great devotee of Maupassant's short stories, using them to enlarge our vocabulary.' She had let that slip before realising and saw the look of puzzlement on Mrs Park's face.

'You read French?'

'I do.'

Aunt Peggy changed the subject. She knew Delia didn't want her past being discussed. 'Mrs Parks, have you read Mark Twain?'

'Indeed, I have. Everyone is talking about him.'

Peggy nodded in agreement and took Delia by surprise when she replied, 'They are and you could do worse by way of introduction to American writers than starting with him.'

'Well, my dear, it would be a pleasure to have you read to me sometimes. There are so many books I'd love to go back to and, truth to tell, I'd enjoy the company too. I find some days are long and lonely now, since my dear husband died, and I've heard all my friends' stories – too many times in a lot of cases.' She smiled. 'That's one of the penalties of getting old. You must feel free to borrow and read any of the books that appeal to you. They are no use to anybody sitting unopened on the shelves.'

'That's so kind of you, Mrs Parks. I'm afraid we've overstayed our welcome. We mustn't tire you out.'

They took their leave and went upstairs to find a fire glowing in the drawing-room grate and the stove crackling away in the kitchen. Delia could hear footsteps above on the floorboards and realised that Mena was busy upstairs. On investigation, she found the housekeeper unpacking the trunks that had been delivered while they were out.

'I can do that, Mrs ...' Delia realised she didn't know her full name.

'I answer to Mena. Everyone calls me that. It's short for Philomena.'

'It's very thoughtful of you to start on this, Mena, but I can do the rest. It'll be good for me to have things to do.'

'Very well, but if you need anything, those bells by the fireplaces are still connected to the kitchen. Just ring. I'd be delighted to be of service.'

Peggy left shortly after being showered with gratitude by Delia.

'It's all a bit befuddling at first, but, mark my words, you'll soon adjust. I promise you.'

'Perhaps, but I'd never have managed any of what we did today without your guidance.'

'I know that,' she replied matter of factly. 'Either Grace or I will call by tomorrow morning and check in on you.'

'You've done so much for me already. I don't want to be any more of a nuisance.'

'Hugh has given us our orders,' she replied. 'To be honest, Grace is happy to have something to do now that hers are all grown up and out at work. She never got over losing her husband,' Peggy said. 'Now I must be off.'

Delia walked down the stairs behind her, helped her with her coat, and let her out into the darkening street, more determined than ever to show her, and everyone else who doubted her, that she could handle the transition. Not for the first time had she reason to be thankful for Mrs Murphy's practical approach to life, which had exposed her to a few of the necessary skills for survival without the support systems of maids and servants. They may not be much in Peggy's eyes, but without those and Noreen's common sense around all the subterfuge in duping the Kensley-Balfes, she'd really have been lost.

After she had gone, Delia set about shaking her coats and dresses before putting them on padded hangers, as she had seen the maids do in Kensley Park and Grosvenor Square. She folded and layered her lingerie before placing it carefully in the drawers that she had first lined with tissue paper. Her shoes and boots went into one side of the bottom of the cavernous wardrobe. She placed her hats in their boxes on the shelf on top. Her ribbons, clips and the bits of jewellery her grandmother had left her found their home in one of the shallow drawers. She was very pleased with the progress and was admiring her afternoon's work when she heard the hall door closing. Her heart jumping with excitement, she waited until she was sure it was Hugh's footsteps that she heard.

He bounded up the stairs and saw her standing on the landing. 'You've no idea how wonderful it is to see you there waiting for me!'

As he hugged her, she remembered the dishes Peggy had brought. They were still in the chilly pantry. What sort of wife did that make her? Her husband's first day back at the office and no dinner ready on his return. Her eyes filled with tears.

'What is it?' he asked.

'I forgot about the dinner,' were her first words of greeting. 'I forgot to put the dishes in the stove to heat. That's all I had to do and I forgot.'

'There's no need to be upset. We can put them in now.' He led her down to the kitchen and she placed them in the oven.

'I'm so sorry.' She sobbed. 'They'll take forever to heat up and you must be starving.'

He wiped the tears from her cheeks with his handkerchief and said, 'I know how we can pass the time while we wait.' He kissed her gently and led her back upstairs.

Chapter 25

About an hour later they were sitting at the little table in the kitchen, surrounded by the warm aroma of beef stew and apple dumplings.

'What are you thinking about? You seem to be miles away.'

'I'm just thinking how smells and aromas can evoke memories. For a moment, I was right back in the kitchen in Kensley Park while Cook prepared her stew.'

'It's funny that, because I was right back in my early childhood when my mother was still alive and she used to make her Irish stew. Later my granddad took over the task, and I suppose, as this is Peggy's, it's officially the family recipe. Chopped, mixed, seasoned and cooked with memories and love.'

'Is that a subtle way of telling me that I'd better learn how to make it so that I can pass it on to the next generation?' she asked.

He laughed and said, 'The thought never entered my head.'

'You're not very good at telling lies, are you?' She laughed back at him. 'And you haven't told me about your day.'

'That's because I was enjoying hearing about yours, but I do have some news, some pretty big news that will affect both our lives – I've been given my first solo assignment as an architect and I'm very excited about it.'

'Oh, Hugh, that makes me feel an even greater failure as a wife – I was so taken up with my day that I never even asked you how your meeting went.'

'

You've only been a wife, and I a husband, for two and a half days – I think it takes a bit longer to learn the roles.'

'I'm sure you're right, but tell me now. I want to know everything about the assignment.'

'I've been given a summer house to design for the president of the Manhattan Stock and Trading Conglomerate – in Newport, Rhode Island.'

'Is that far away?'

'It's not quite two hundred miles north of here. The next state is Connecticut and then you have Rhode Island, the smallest one, where everyone with money wants to spend their summers. Don't look so worried – I won't have to go there straight away, or at least only for a few days at first to survey the terrain and the site. As the clients live in New York, all the initial plans and discussions can be done here, but I will have to move there for a time when the building works start.'

'You will?'

'Yes, we will, the two of us. You didn't think I was going to leave you, did you? I know it's hard to imagine when there's a blizzard out there right now, but New York gets very hot and smelly in the summer, and anyone who can gets as far away as possible. You'll love it there: the air in Newport is fresh and invigorating, and you'll have deduced from its name it's on the sea. It's on a river too!'

'You've been there before.'

'I have, a few times. The chief has already designed several houses there and I went with him when one of them, Stoneacre, was nearing completion.'

She didn't want to contemplate the idea of moving on again, and so soon. She wanted to settle and put down her own roots, but sensing Hugh's exhilaration, she knew she couldn't dampen it, so she didn't ask if the move was to be permanent. Following him was just another part of being married and being a good wife, and she promised herself in bed that night that she'd embrace the challenges and not complain about them.

Chapter 26

Delia couldn't believe four months had passed since she'd taken the boat from Liverpool, or how since she'd been married routines had become established so easily. Hugh's family had turned out to be more than she could ever have hoped. They were thoughtful and devoted, noisy and opinionated and, apart from the odd comment or look from Peggy, they had accepted her as though she had always been one of them.

Hugh's aunts had taught her the rudimentary elements of cooking, and she was becoming quite adept with the ingredients available, some of which seemed strange to her, especially those in the Italian grocery store further down the street from her usual one. Now when she went into her regular shop, she was addressed by her name and greeted like a valued customer. Once the man in the greengrocers had learned that she had recently come over from Ireland, he occasionally slipped an additional bloom or two into the flowers she bought.

Noreen often visited on her half-day, and sometimes Delia took her to Bloomingdale's. Noreen still didn't have the confidence to venture in on her own, but she delighted in window shopping and in buying ribbons and trims to update her small wardrobe.

Hugh's cousin Una hung on Delia's every word, still incredulous that she had had her own pony and that she had grown up with grooms, a piano teacher and a governess. Una had wheedled all this information from their 'private' chats together, and Delia made sure she always had time for her. She took her shopping with her sometimes too.

Delia's pattern frequently involved her spending an afternoon with Mrs Parks. She became genuinely fond of the older woman and respected that she never quizzed her about her background, while knowing that she must be curious about it. Often when she'd hear the strains of a Chopin nocturne or some Debussy wafting up from the drawing room below, she'd find herself fingering the imaginary keys as she played along, the silent half of a piano duet. It was at times like that she missed home most. She missed being able to go for a ride or a walk in the grounds of Kensley Park with her sketch pad. The slushy pavements were no substitute for the leafy paths there, but then she'd think of Hugh and that always brought a smile back to her face.

Occasionally Mrs Parks entertained, and Mr William Appleton Potter was usually included on the guest list, along with two other couples, one of whom lived in a similar brownstone further down Alexander Avenue. Both men had been colleagues of the late Dr Parks.

'It's refreshing to have some new blood among us, and such attractive company,' one of the women said. 'It makes such a change from having to listen to interminable gossip about the Nobs and the Swells.'

'I'm not familiar with either of those, I'm afraid,' Delia said, feeling completely out of her depth.

'Isn't she charming?' The woman laughed, touching Hugh on the arm. 'Keep her like that.'

One of the wives explained to her that some of the society columnists had begun referring to those with 'old money' as the Nobs and those who had more recently joined the ranks as Swells.

'You'll see a lot of that in Newport, believe you me,' the older physician said.

His wife said, 'Of course, we have no royalty here so we've created our own.' She laughed. 'Were you presented?'

'No, my sister was earlier this year. It would have been my turn next season had I not decided to come to America and marry Hugh.'

When she had asked Hugh not to tell people about being from the gentry back home, she had done it as much to protect herself as to prevent them from being talked about. But she found it was too easy to be lured into divulging snippets like those she had just revealed, and she knew they'd cause speculation when she wasn't present.

Mrs Parks prevented any further discussion by telling them that Delia highly recommended Thomas Hardy's novel *The Mayor of Casterbridge*. 'Have any of you read it yet?'

Delia felt very much alone when Hugh went to Rhode Island to survey the site. She cried with loneliness for him and her family. She yearned for some contact from Ireland and had given up on hearing from her sister or parents. The letters she had sent after her wedding had remained unanswered, apart from a short note from Dr Canavan.

> *I did as you asked, Miss Delia. I passed on your letter to Mrs Murphy.*
>
> *Although I can't say your conduct has my approval, I have seen enough of life to know pure love can be a powerful driving force, and it really can overcome many obstacles.*
>
> *I wish you and Mr Dunne well in your new life, and hope that some day you and your family will be reconciled.*
> *Yours respectfully,*
> *Kevin Canavan MD.*

She had shed a few tears when she received this. Dear

Doctor Canavan. He understood. She put the note between the pages of her diary and read it from time to time.

Delia looked forward to Noreen's visits. They always came with the hope of some news from Ireland. Noreen's leisure time was a moveable feast and completely at the housekeeper's discretion or whim. Depending on her mood, this half-day entitlement could be given as a morning, afternoon or evening. But today she was expecting her and as soon as she had arrived she announced.

'I have something for you, Mrs Delia,' she said, producing an envelope from the purse she carried under her coat. 'It's from Mrs Murphy and it came in a letter from home the other day.'

Delia felt a lump in her throat as she slit the paper and some folded pages flittered out on to the table.

'Will I make us a cup of tea while you're reading?'

'That would be lovely, thank you, Noreen.'

Dear Miss Delia,

I got your letter and am happy to know that Mr Hugh was waiting for you when you reached America and that he married you. I was so worried that you'd find yourself in that strange place, amid strangers, and that he wouldn't be there for you. I never thought you'd include Noreen in your plans, but thanks to the good Lord you did, as you could both look after each other. It made Kevin and Mary McCormack very happy, when Noreen's letter arrived, to know their daughter was safe with you too. I heard about her brother switching the labels on the luggage on the way to the station. That was very cunning. And don't worry — I know these are secrets and that they will go to their grave with them and to my grave with me. I'm also sending you back the letters I was hiding for you in case they get discovered by anyone here. Your mother and father's hearts are hard right now and I don't know if they'll ever soften. We're forbidden to mention your name in the house any more. Her Ladyship was in a fluster and we all thought Miss Mona's engagement would be called off, but the danger of that passed and they've set a date for her wedding. It will be during the summer here in Kensley Park. Needless to say, Her Ladyship is very happy about that now. I don't know how Mr Clement took the news. There was a lot of discussion that stopped when any of us went into the rooms upstairs. I'm not rightly sure what's going on, but I do know I don't like to think of what it will be like in two years' time when he'll come back here with Lady Elizabeth to take over running the estate. I'm sure that will mean big changes for us all. Miss Corneille asked after you in her last letter to your mother, and I know Miss Mona refused to reply to hers. She told your mother that she thinks she helped you run away. She said you couldn't have planned it on your own. I pretended I wasn't listening. I hope you are happy where you are. I really do. I miss you pestering me all the time. This place is not the same without you. The joy has gone out of it. May the good God bless you and Mr Hugh and keep you and Noreen safe and well.

Yours respectfully,
Mrs Murphy

It was a lot to take in. For a woman who said she could only write grocery and laundry lists, she had managed to conjure up all sorts of images in Delia's mind. And as for Mademoiselle, she felt sorry that her good name should have been inadvertently tinged with suspicion when she was completely innocent.

She felt her eyes well up and knew Noreen was watching her, but she couldn't trust herself to speak.

'I've poured you some tea,' Noreen said, passing over a delicate china teacup and saucer, which she took gratefully. Mrs Parks had insisted on giving Hugh and Delia a dinner and tea service and a canteen of silver cutlery, as well as matching hand-cut crystal glasses.

When Delia protested that she couldn't take them, that it was far too much, Mrs Parks said, 'You'd be doing me a favour. When my husband was alive, grateful patients often gifted us things like these. If we'd had children we could have put them away for their bottom drawers, but as we hadn't, they're just taking up storage space. I would love you to have them, my dear, with my blessing. I suspect had you married at home you'd have been given lots of such items.'

Consequently, the sideboard, another gift, was filling up with things Delia could grow to treasure and cherish. Her linen cupboard also.

'I don't know what I'll do when you've gone to Newport. It'll be the first time I've really been on my own,' Noreen said.

'You'll be fine. If you can get your time off together you can spend it exploring with your friend Tilly. She sounds very nice and I'm glad you've someone of your own age to mix with in the house. And there's Bridget and Kate and Hugh's other cousins too, so there's no need to be lonesome. You all get along very well, don't you?'

She agreed and asked, 'Do you need any help packing?'

'I would be very grateful, Noreen. I'm afraid I'm not very good at that yet.'

'Practice makes perfect,' she said matter-of-factly, and Delia could hear the echo of Mrs Murphy's voice in her reply.

Dr Canavan had ridden up to the kitchen door and asked to see Mrs Murphy. His visit didn't arouse suspicion in anyone but her, as he often procured rat poison from the apothecary for Tommy to use in the barns and stables. Making sure there was no one to witness the transaction, he had passed on Delia's letter.

'I was entrusted to deliver this into your hands. It's from America, but it must stay between us. You understand?'

'I do, doctor, I do. It's a sad business.'

'It is indeed,' he agreed.

When Tommy had come back later that day from Ballina he had the other two letters Delia had written after her marriage – one to Mona and one to her parents. Mrs Murphy had taken them from him and placed them with other letters on the salver. They had sat there for two days now, and she wondered how their arrival would be received. Lord Kensley-Balfe was on business in Dublin and his wife and daughter had accompanied him to the city to do some shopping.

On their return, His Lordship picked the letters up and, realising what they were, told his wife and daughter to come into the drawing room. 'Mrs Murphy, we'll take some tea right away, thank you.'

'What is it, Peter? What's the urgency? Is there bad news? Clement's not been injured has he?' his wife asked anxiously.

'No, my dear, nothing like that. But there's news from Delia. There's a letter for you too, Mona,' he said, handing it over.

'You can burn it. I don't want to read it,' she said. 'I don't want to hear anything she has to say. She almost destroyed my life with Desmond and do you know what hurts even more? It's that she didn't care. She just swanned off regardless of how we'd feel. You've no idea how I felt in Scotland when I heard she was missing. I imagined she'd been abducted or worse, and then to discover she'd eloped with that – that low life. I can't explain the shame and embarrassment I felt, and just as I was getting to know his family. I wanted to run away and never come back.'

'I know it was hard on you, Mona, but you might regret not reading it later,' her father said.

'I won't,' she answered defiantly. 'I don't care if I never see or hear from her again. She's destroyed my friendship with Elizabeth too.'

'Well, my dear,' he said, turning his attention to Lady Leonora. 'How do you feel about ours? Would you like me to read it to you?'

'I don't know. I'm angry and hurt and I do understand how you feel, Mona, but she is my daughter too, and disappointed as I am in her behaviour, I can't help worrying about what's happened to her.'

'I'm sure she's not worrying about us,' Mona said.

'She's scarcely more than a child and we don't know if that man has taken advantage of her, or abandoned her wherever she is once he realised she wouldn't be coming to him with a fine dowry.'

'I'll read it then,' he said.

'Well, I don't have to sit here and listen to it,' Mona said. She stood up, snatched the envelope addressed to her and flung it unopened on to the dancing flames in the grate. She flounced out of the room just as Mrs Murphy came through with the tea tray. Not a word was uttered until the housekeeper had left the room.

'We're very fortunate that the Hattersleys had some distant scandal that made them so forgiving and liberal-minded or we might have been shipping Mona off to India with the fishing fleet to try and find a match for her. And we still don't know what impact all this business will have on Clement's life.'

'He'll survive. He'll be back here running the estates in no time at all. He vows he'll have retribution and the first thing he'll do is try to get those cottages back,' he said as he opened the letter and read it through to himself first.

'She's married.' he announced.

'How are we supposed to receive such news? Is that supposed to make us happy?' his wife asked.

'She says she is safe and very happy and she's living in New York. She asks for our understanding and forgiveness, which she hopes in time we will grant her.'

'I don't think I can forgive her, Peter, no matter what she has to say – I don't think I ever will. She's brought shame and ignominy on the good names of both our families.'

He nodded, then said, 'The fellow is qualified now as a professional architect. with prospects, as she puts it.'

'Prospects? Prospects! What does she know about prospects? What prospects can she have with a nobody?'

'He may not always be a nobody.'

'Don't try to defend him to me, dear. I'm sure now – I'll never have anything to do with him or them again, and that is my final word on the subject.'

'Won't you read what she has to say?' He proffered the letter.

She took it. 'I know what I need to know,' she replied and, without glancing at it, she squeezed it into a ball and threw it into the fire and watched it burn.

Chapter 27

Newport 1887

One morning, over a breakfast of pancakes and jelly, which Delia had mastered the art of making, Hugh suggested taking Grace along with them to Newport until they got themselves established. Delia felt as though he were reading her mind. She was looking forward to the move with anticipation and trepidation in equal measure.

'I think that's a wonderful idea. Do you think she'll agree?' she asked.

'I don't think she'll hesitate for a moment. She's become very fond of you.'

'And I of her. She's such a kind lady.'

'She never really got over losing her husband. Now that her young ones are making their own lives she's a bit of a lost soul. You see how excited she gets when anyone talks about places they've been. Going away will give her years of stories to tell when she comes back.'

'I'll ask her this afternoon when she comes around,' Delia said.

'It wouldn't have to be forever, maybe just for a few months. Now I really must go and show the chief that I'm worthy of his faith in me.' He kissed her as she held his coat for him.

Suddenly the future seemed more manageable. She didn't know what she would do all day in a place where she knew not one other person and where there would be no cousins for diversion or aunties to go out and about with.

Secretly, she hoped that wouldn't be for too long, as she imagined them starting a family soon.

That afternoon when Grace called on Delia she found her sitting by the window sewing. She picked up her handiwork, examined it and exclaimed, 'This is beautiful. Where did you learn to sew like that?'

'Mrs Murphy, our housekeeper. She showed me how to cut patterns and use materials from clothes we'd finished with. Together we made garments for some of the poorer children in the parish.' As she spoke, she remembered those 'poorer children of the parish' were actually Noreen and her siblings, but Grace didn't need to know that.

'I don't know if I told you this already, but before I married I worked as a seamstress for one of the wealthy New York families.'

'You always look so stylish,' Delia said.

'Thank you. It's easy when you make your own clothes,'

she said with pride. 'The secret is to vary the trims. Even the lah-di-dah ladies have that done. I went back to it after my husband died. I turned my front room into a workroom. I'd much prefer to be doing that than toadying to someone's every whim. There's something satisfying about creating something from scratch.'

'I always thought I'd love to own and run a haberdashers,' Delia said.

'Really?'

She told Grace about their visit to Liberty in London and how entranced she had been by the selection of exotic goods there and the colourful slub silk and notions they had bought that day for Mona's coming-out dresses.

'When I worked for the New York family they had a house-keeper who was a right battleaxe, but she was fond of a bit of style and was always remarking on my Sunday dresses. Once, I offered to redo the bodice of one of hers, to refashion it and make it more modern. After that, I had her in the palm of my hand. The woman had been so delighted with the result that, in return, she recommended me and now I have a few regulars that I make for, mostly ladies from the Church.'

'Do you still make for that housekeeper?'

'No. She actually lives in Newport these days. The family kept her on a retainer at their summer cottage, although she's not really able for the stairs there. She's more of a caretaker now, opening it and closing it down at the end of the season. She looks after hiring additional staff too.'

'In Ireland cottages don't have stairs.'

'In Newport they have, several flights of them, and upwards of twenty rooms, stable blocks and carriage houses, armies of gardeners and servants.'

Delia was sceptical – surely Grace was exaggerating. She would ask Hugh later, but first she wanted to ask Grace how she'd feel about accompanying them to Rhode Island. As Hugh had predicted, she needn't have had any worries about her refusing.

'You can look up your old housekeeper friend while we're there too.'

"Well, if that isn't a bit of serendipity, I don't know what is.' Grace laughed.

Over her next few visits Grace made lists that covered every eventuality and some they had never conceived. She helped them organise their packing and told them they'd be expected to have a hooley before they left. Noreen and her friend Tilly were invited too. This was very different to the first shindig Delia had enjoyed with Hugh's family. Now she knew all the names, and the fact that she was from a titled family no longer intimidated them. Even Peggy seemed to have come around a bit.

Apart from that one letter from Mrs Murphy, there had been no communication from any of the Kensley-Balfes, and although Delia told herself she didn't mind, she did. Very much. She couldn't understand how a mother and father could shut the door on their child as though she had never existed. There was more laughter and kindness between Hugh's people than she had seen between the likes of Lady Constance and Lady Elizabeth, and she was genuinely fond of them.

On their last morning in Alexandra Avenue they called to say goodbye to Mrs Parks. When she heard that they were taking the ferry direct from New York, she exclaimed, 'Oh, how grand. I'm told that has revolutionised the journey. In my day, you had to take the train to Providence and then the ferry from there, with all the stops and changes. It seemed to take forever and it wasn't the most comfortable journey, I can tell you.'

'Nowadays it takes only eight and a half hours, but there are restaurants, a concert hall and comfortable cabins, so when we wake up we'll be there,' Hugh told her.

'It's wonderful the way the world is moving so fast,' the silver-haired lady said, turning to Delia and taking her hands. 'I have so enjoyed your company. With your reading and piano playing, you've given me a new zest for life. Don't ever lose that sense of wonderment you have. It's infectious. And you, young man, look after her. She's very precious. Mind her well.'

'I know that, Mrs Parks. I most certainly do. We can't ever

thank you enough for everything you have done for us and for your wonderful generosity and welcome.'

'Shhh. I declare it gave me more pleasure knowing you appreciate it. I'm sure you'll be happy in Newport, and I hope you'll be blessed with children. It wasn't in the great plan for Dr Parks and me, but I pray it will be for you both.'

Delia had to stop herself from shedding a tear as she promised to write often. Then they went back upstairs to their apartment. It looked sad and forlorn with their belongings crated and packed, and although it had only been home for a little over four months, it was where they had consummated their love for each other and began their married life together, a life she wouldn't swap for anyone else's. Yes, she thought, this place would always hold a special place in her heart.

The sailing wasn't until five that afternoon. Hugh had organised two hackneys: one to collect Grace and take her to the ferry dock station; the other to fetch them and some of their personal belongings – the rest would follow later in the day. After meeting Grace by the ticket desk, they boarded

It wasn't very full, and the continuous sound of water lapping against the hull lulled Grace to sleep in no time at all. Hugh and Delia sat close together, holding hands and talking quietly as the coastline altered in the distance. They changed their clothes and dined in a surprisingly elegant dining room. Afterwards, they listened to an orchestra for a while before going to bed. Grace's stateroom was next to theirs, and Hugh put his finger to his lips after he released Delia from a long embrace. They laughed as they got ready for bed. Their lovemaking was tender and quiet and she said, 'Have I told you how much I love you, Mr Dunne, and how amazing you are?'

'You have, Mrs Dunne, but don't ever stop, because I'll never get tired of hearing it.'

They fell asleep in each other's arms to the rhythm of the waves. She wasn't seasick on this journey.

It was still dark when they arrived at Long Wharf, which was already a hive of bustling noise and activity. Grace was ready, eager to get her first glimpse of Newport. A carriage waited to take them the short distance from the jetty to Clarke Cooke House at Bannister's Wharf. They'd be staying there for a little bit until their effects arrived and until they'd found suitable accommodation. They settled in and after lunch went for a walk to explore their new surroundings. Delia liked it from the very beginning, with its views across the harbour to the fort and the islands.

'The sea looks bluer and more inviting than the way I remember it from the steampacket crossings between Ireland and England and from the endless trans-Atlantic voyage.' she told him. 'I'm beginning to understand why people would want to spend their summers here.'

He squeezed her hand and said 'I'm so happy to hear that.

I always trust my first impressions and look where that got me with you.' He laughed.

On his previous visit he'd sourced a few prospective houses for them to view. 'If I'd left it any later it would be much more difficult. In another month there won't be a room or property to be had here, with the influx of the gentry and their armies of servants. We'll look at them tomorrow.'

The houses were very different to European ones. They had wooden facades painted in pastel colours. By comparison with the grandiose and often austere-looking properties she had grown up frequenting, they were tiny, but they looked cosy and inviting. She found herself wondering what her sister would think of them, when she was presiding over the Hattersley estates that would come her husband's way one day.

'Here we are,' he said, stopping, with a flourish of his hand. 'Let me know what you think of this.' It was one he had looked at on his last visit and had thought very suitable, but he had held off making a decision, hoping for Delia's nod of approval first. Grace had decided to let them make these inspections without her 'tagging along'.

Delia loved the look of it from the outside. It was a two-storey with double windows on either side of the wooden porch. There were five windows on the next level and two attic rooms in the gables.

'I'm intrigued by that railing around the roof,' Delia asked. 'Wouldn't it be very dangerous to go up there?'

'It's said, but I don't know if there's any truth in it, that the mariners' wives used to go up on the roofs to keep lookout for their menfolk returning from their fishing and whaling expeditions. Both were very dangerous occupations, and the death toll was so high that they became known as widows' walks.'

'Oh, how sad,' she said.

'I'm not even sure how much of the sea you can see from many of them, but they've become a feature of the architecture in these coastal states. A lot of Portuguese were involved in seafaring, much like the Irish were and still are the builders here, and I imagine they might have brought that tradition of these lookouts from Portugal with them.'

'How did you get to be so knowledgeable?' she asked her husband, taking his hand.

'I guess I'm just a curious sort of fellow.' He grinned. 'That and from keeping my eyes open and my ears always on the alert. It's surprising how much you can glean that way.'

'I'll have to try that,' she said. 'My mother was forever telling me I asked too many questions.' He took her hand and she found comfort in that. Thoughts of home and her family often came to her mind at the most unexpected moments.

'See that house over there,' he said, pointing to a much larger one, surrounded by a white picket fence. 'That one has a cupola on the roof too. These were allegedly where the captains lived and from where they kept watch for the traders returning with the treasures that were going to make them rich! Sometimes they were at sea for months, even years, at a time.'

'I'd never have made a mariner's wife. I was so lonely when you were away for a few days at a time.'

The house they were viewing had a wooden exterior painted light blue with white windows and shutters. Like many of the others they had passed in the neighbourhood, it had a small garden to either aide, and this stretched a reasonable distance out behind. It promised lots of greenery, despite the long winter having denuded it of its foliage. A gully in the cobblestones ran the length of the street to allow rainwater to drain away quickly.

She liked it straight away.

'It may be a little roomy for us right now, but we could change all that.' She blushed. 'When the chief comes to Newport he'll expect to stay with us. And as he's paying for its rental, I don't feel we can complain too much.'

'I'm not complaining at all. I love it. I really do,' Delia said. 'And I like him as well, so his being here is no hardship.'

'And he's a big admirer of yours. He wouldn't have entrusted this project to me if you hadn't met with his approval.'

Hugh remembered the conversation the chief had had with him about his hopes of opening a permanent office in Newport, depending on the outcome of this project.

William Appleton Potter had said, 'Undoubtedly more work will follow. We got this project as a result of Snug Harbor, Admiral Charles Baldwin's house on Bellevue Avenue.' He chuckled. 'That caused a bit of a flutter, the wooden staircases, the elaborate wainscoting and that cathedral roof. Truthfully, I find them all a bit *de trop*, but I'm just the piper. If my clients want golden cherubs, imported from Italy, dangling from the ceiling, supporting the bathtubs and water closets and sitting on the mantel shelves – they can have gold cherubs on the ceiling, supporting the bathtubs and water closets and sitting on the mantel shelves, wouldn't you agree, Dunne?'

'Assuredly.' Hugh had laughed.

'It was on the back of all that ostentation that John W. Ellis. commissioned us to design Stoneacre, right between Ruggles and Victoria Avenues. It seems his friends were impressed with his dome and shingle-style piazza. They were written about in several journals here and in Europe. And now we come to you! It's your turn to make your mark on the landscape for William Appleton Potter Architects.'

'Those are pretty big shoes to fill,' Hugh had replied.

'And that's why I've chosen your feet to fill them. Having someone on hand to deal with everything will be key. These clients are demanding, very demanding. They have more money than they'll ever spend, but they don't waste it either. They expect value for every cent and that includes your time and attention too.'

'I'm willing to give them that,' Hugh replied.

'Do it well and we'll all benefit. Do it badly and the firm will suffer a damaged reputation, from which it will recover, but you'll sink without a trace.'

'As I said, pretty big shoes to fill,' Hugh answered.

When Hugh told Delia what was at stake, she proudly told him she had no objections to having a discreet brass plaque on the wall beside their hall door or to having an office in her house.

A week after arriving in Newport, they had moved into the pretty wooden house on Division, just off Touro Street. Hugh had contacted an employment agency on Thames Street before they'd arrived, and it was as a result of this that Delia found herself waiting to interview the candidates the agency had recommended. The prospect terrified her. Grace had offered to help, but Delia was determined to do it on her own, even though she knew she could get it all wrong. What if she hired someone who wasn't properly experienced, or that she didn't like, or who was dishonest? She didn't share those worries with Hugh. He had his own duties to occupy his thoughts. It was clear that her role now was as the woman of the house and running it was her concern, like a mature adult with grown-up responsibilities.

She knew from the articles she'd read in *Ladies Home Journal* that there were some questions she must ask if she were to come across as competent in this regard. Domestics needed to have good references and to be flexible. It wasn't like hiring someone for a large home like Kensley Park, where tasks were performed by various staff of different, but very clearly defined, roles. What she needed was someone to cook simple meals and look after the household, the laundry, the ordering of their provisions and general duties.

She had seen how her mother treated the domestic staff; always with respect and good manners, and how Clément's prospective mother-in-law managed to do the exact opposite, always making them feel unworthy and insignificant. She also knew the staff at Kensley Park would do anything for her parents, and for their offspring in turn, and that was the kind of working relationship she aimed to achieve in her own modest home. She had been adamant that she would not employ Grace or any of Hugh's family.

'Even though some of them could do with the income?' Hugh asked.

'Yes, despite that. They are my family now, and having any of them work for me would drive a wedge socially between us, and I'd hate that to happen just when they've accepted me.'

'You think of everything, don't you?' Hugh had said, hugging her as he left for the site. 'That's what I love about you. Good luck with your interviews.'

Grace had tactfully decided to absent herself. She had made

arrangements to visit the housekeeper she had sewn for in the past in New York, leaving Delia, the lady of the house, in charge.

'So tell me. How did your day go?' Hugh asked when he returned unexpectedly mid-afternoon.

'I'm not falling into that trap again!' She laughed after kissing him. 'Tell me about your day first and why you are at home at this time.'

'I could lie to you and say I had figured that no one would have started working here today so we'd have the house to ourselves, but that's not why. The builders have arrived on site and several deliveries of timber and brick came today. If I want the foreman to have authority over his men when I'm not around, I have to allow him some autonomy and not let them think I am watching his every move. It's called strategy.' He laughed.

'There's that wisdom again. Will I ever learn it?'

'It doesn't happen overnight, and I had two good teachers, both two wise men – my granda and the chief. Now, tell me how you got on?'

'The first candidate was a rotund lady, a very, very rotund lady, with a large bosom, a very, very large bosom, and she was out of breath when she arrived. Two of her front teeth were missing and I was sure I smelt alcohol. Her hair was, well, not exactly dishevelled, but it was not as I would want it to be. She certainly would not have made the right first impression on opening any hall door. And I was worried in case she'd have a strong weakness going up and down the stairs, never mind before she left, so I told her I didn't think she quite fitted my needs.'

'A strong weakness – I like that,' Hugh said. 'I think that was probably a good decision.'

'The second one was a timid woman who answered everything in monosyllables, and I was at a loss about what to ask her after a few minutes. I thought she'd been here for hours, but when I glanced at the clock it had scarcely been ten minutes. I don't know what it was, but I just felt uncomfortable in her presence. Is that awful of me?'

'Not at all. That was your instincts clicking in. We should always listen to them. They seldom let us down. And just remember, the successful candidate doesn't have to live with us, especially as Grace is here. I'd be more comfortable having someone around when I'm not here, but we can discuss that again.'

She nodded, acknowledging the logic in that.

'Were there any others?' he asked.

'Yes, one more. A Mrs Mary Flynn, and she was on a mission!'

'I can't wait to hear this.' He laughed.

'It's not funny, really. Before I could ask her anything,

she gushed, "I need the work. My husband is poorly after a railroad accident, and while he's off there's no money coming in. It was their fault, and they won't admit it. The unions are involved, but I can't wait around for them to sort themselves out, I have five little ones to feed."

'I felt very sorry for her and was trying to think of how to reply when off she went again, at a gallop. "I'm from a family of ten myself and I'm used to working hard. I make decent brown bread and a good Irish stew, and, if those bushes out there keep their promise, your cupboards will have enough jams, chutneys and preserves to last you though the winter," she said, pointing out the window.'

'She had me won over at the brown bread and Irish stew,' he said, 'but what did you think?'

Delia grinned. 'Me too. I liked her, despite her speed, and she's starting tomorrow morning – on a two-week trial.'

'I'm very proud of you, Mrs Dunne. And on a trial too.'

'I thought it was better to give myself a way out if she's hopeless. They're Irish, as you probably guessed from the brown bread and the stew. Both their families were part of a large group of copper miners from somewhere in West Cork. She said they all came over together to work in the mines here. Then when they shut down, the younger ones took work on the railroads. That's how her husband had his accident.'

'Life isn't always as we wish,' he replied.

'I felt sorry for her.'

'You can't be too soft, Delia. You're the employer so it's important you keep a little distance.'

'I'll try to remember that.'

'I've learned it's easier to give instructions if you do. Now might I make a suggestion?'

'You want to finish setting up your office?'

'I do, but that's not what I was thinking. For the moment we have no interruptions and a few ideas come to mind ... What would you think, Mrs Dunne ...?' He took her hand and led her up the stairs. She followed laughing.

They made very fulfilling love, greedy for each other and happy to be able to satisfy each other's needs. Gone was the shyness she had felt in the beginning of their intimacy. Gone too were the fears she had had that she wouldn't be enough for Hugh.

She was and she knew it, and he was enough for her, and that knowledge added to their pleasure in each other's bodies.

Chapter 28

Later Hugh showed her his designs for Gull Haven. It was the first time she'd seen them, spread out and anchored on the drawing desk that had been delivered a few days earlier.

He'd spent almost every waking minute he was at home in there, and she'd wondered what he had been doing, hammering and sawing away. And now it was revealed – his office, fitted and kitted as a proper working environment. In the alcoves on either side of the fireplace he had slotted in deep shelves that now housed rolls of drawing paper and of blueprints, tied with navy ribbons. Rows of geometrical instruments, inks, pens and pencils had all been allocated their own places too.

'Having this set up here means that I'll be able to spend more time working at home,' he told her.

'Do you really understand what that maze of lines and graphs means?' she asked, trying to make sense of the plans spread out on the high desk.

'I hope so – I drew them.' He laughed. 'They're not complicated once you know how to read them. See, these arrows are for elevation – the distance from ground level to the windows, tops of the doors, roofs, chimneys, etc. These markings show the thickness of the walls, which way the doors open and so on. There are others for the plumbing and pipes. Then there are separate projections that specify materials, types of fittings and fixtures, sanitary wear, fireplaces, tiles, floorboards. It goes on and on, right down to nails and shingles.'

'Now I understand why the apprenticeship takes so long. There's much more to it than making a sketch of a pretty house.'

'I believe there is,' he said, smiling at her. 'But that's part of it too. It has to appeal to whoever it's intended for.'

'I can't wait to see it being built.'

'We'll go out on Sunday and I'll take you along Bellevue Avenue and the Cliff Walk and you can see some of the other cottages that have gone up here.'

'Why do they call them cottages?'

'Affectation, I suspect,' he answered. 'And to make their neighbours envious. They're mansions in reality and, as their owners can afford to buy anything they want, they see no reason why they shouldn't show it off to the world.'

'How strange,' she said.

'It is, I suppose. They certainly don't believe in hiding their lights under a bushel.'

They heard Grace returning from visiting her old house-mate. She was full of news and gossip. 'I couldn't get away from the creature. The family have gone to Europe to buy the latest fashions and she has nothing to do rattling around in that empty house.'

'That seems a very long away to go. Surely they could procure everything they'd need here in America.' Delia said.

'Of course they could, but it wouldn't be the same as being able to tell their friends that they bought their gowns from Worth or their lingerie from Jacques Doucet of Paris. Just fancy, a man selling ladies' lingerie! But I suppose it is France, and they have a reputation for being – saucy, don't they?'

'You are funny,' Delia said. 'I'm sure he doesn't actually sell it himself.'

'You wouldn't know with French people. That Mr Worth dresses all his mannequins in black and he has them walking round and round his salon showing them off. If madam likes something, she can decide on what colour and materials she wants them made up in and only then will they be measured up.'

'That does sound unusual, all right,' Delia said, 'but I'd love to see Paris one day.'

'And you will, my love. We'll go there one day so long as

you don't expect me to visit salons and the like,' Hugh said. 'It'll be a while before I could afford that.'

Grace kept them amused with more tales as they ate their supper. 'Mrs O'Shaughnessy eventually got around to asking me to make her a day dress. She has cousins working in the mills at Fall River and they are allowed buy the flawed fabrics at a fraction of what they would cost to buy in the stores. Anyhow, that's what she was like today – next time I see her she could have changed her mind. She's fallen out with all the seamstresses she's used in the past and, to be honest, I'd say that's why I'm back in favour. I told you she's a curmudgeonly one, but for some reason she seems to trust me.'

Delia suggested she could use the attic room beside where she slept as a sewing room. 'I might even come up and join you sometimes. I think I'd better smarten myself up before these fashion plates start appearing in Newport.'

'And that goes for me too!' Hugh's aunt said.

The following Sunday afternoon Hugh took them for a walk along tree-lined avenues. Many of the cottages were still closed up, but there were signs of life about others. Delia admired mostly the classical ones. As they passed other promenaders, people smiled at them.

Grace asked, 'Do the owners really only use these mansions in the summer time?'

'A few are used all year around,' said Hugh. 'but mostly they're only occupied for seven or eight weeks. Some of their owners have several other homes, in New York and Boston or Philadelphia.'

'I can't imagine the amount of moving that's involved in packing and transporting all those clothes just for a few months,' said Grace. 'I suppose that's why they have armies of servants who accompany them. And why the agencies have people on their books to go in and open windows and keep the houses heated and aired during the other seasons.'

'Always thinking of the practicalities, Grace.' Hugh laughed.

'I am, because I would be the one doing the packing and unpacking, that's for sure. As for the ironing ...'

'I know you told me that these people are amongst the richest in America, but I'm coming to think that doesn't necessarily mean they have style,' Delia said. 'Most of these cottages look beautifully elegant to me, but others, I think, are really brash and not in very good taste.'

'And you'd be right,' Hugh said, 'but don't let anyone hear you saying that.'

'I hope your clients don't fall into that category.'

'I'm very happy to say they don't. They have travelled extensively in Europe but they don't want a hotchpotch of bits of this and bits of the other.' He told her he was going to show her one on the corner of Stevens Street, to see what she thought.

'It's been described in an architectural journal as "steamboat gothic".'

'Who lives in it?'

'It was built for a wealthy New York Hotelier, Parian Stevens, and his socially ambitious wife, now his widow.'

'I can't wait to get a look at these people when they start arriving. Do they leave their ivory towers and go walking about, mixing with ordinary people?'

'No. They mainly mix with each other, and even then they are selective. Those who have "old money" look down on those who are "in trade".'

'I'm glad we'll be too insignificant for anyone to notice us,' said Delia.

'If they knew you had a title, you'd be on the top of their society guest lists,' Hugh said.

'Then we must make sure they never find out,' she said emphatically. She had had enough experience of class divisions and she didn't like what it could do to people.

'Having an unproven architect by your side could be considered a drawback and a definite social no-no.'

'That'll be their loss, on both counts,' she replied, 'although I still want to see them in all their finery.'

'That won't be a problem – they love to be seen. Every afternoon at five they go on parade along here in their carriages, and the locals and visitors alike go promenading just to see them. There's even a hierarchy about that too. Those of lesser social standing daren't overtake anyone of higher social rank!'

'What a load of poppycock!' Delia said and they laughed at her. 'Well, it is. Don't they realise how silly all that nonsense is?'

'These people live and breathe by their self-imposed conventions.'

'Look where convention got us! I assure you both I'll never be one of them,' Delia retorted.

'I think you've already shown us that,' Grace replied.

'I agree,' said Hugh. 'My little runaway bride.'

'Let's not tell them that either,' she suggested.

He took them by a large empty plot and announced proudly, 'Ladies, it may take a little imagination, but you stand before what will be Gull Haven.'

They could see from the road that the foundations were in process. Along one side, stacks of sand-coloured bricks were arranged, and on another, what seemed like the contents of a timber yard were piled high. A watchman sat in the doorway of a small wooden hut, embers from a half-full brazier keeping the water in his billy-can hot. He greeted Hugh with respect and stood up as he approached.

'Good afternoon to you, Pat. I just want to show these good ladies the views this house will have when it's finished.'

'Very good, sir,' the man answered, lifting his cap to

Delia and Grace. 'Mind where you step – it's quite uneven in places.'

'Thank you, we will,' Hugh replied, leading them to the far side of the plot, where it began sloping gently towards the sea. 'Where you're standing right now is what is going to make my name. This cottage – or mansion, whichever you prefer – is going to have one of the finest views in the state. Over there there'll be a gazebo, big enough for a tea party or a small orchestra. All along that side of the house there'll be an orangery that will capture the evening sun and lead out onto a grand terrace. That'll be where we're standing now.'

'I can see how you get excited by the prospect of creating something from absolutely nothing. You have me excited just thinking about it,' Delia told him. 'You must bring me up here every week so that I can see it growing.'

'You are a marvel, Delia. Another woman would have no more interest in such things, but you really do. Am I a lucky man or what?' he said to them both and Grace nodded.

He pointed out The Breakers. 'That grandiose specimen is the summer home of the railway heir and mogul Cornelius Vanderbilt. His wife is the queen of Newport society and her balls are legendary. He's supposed to have paid the previous owner, Pierre Lorrilard IV, a staggering $450,000 for it.'

'I wonder why he sold it?' Delia said.

'Because he wanted more space for his horses.'

'Of course he did.' She laughed

They ambled on and he pointed out the palazzos of bankers and industrialists, and told her that the fantastical edifices with candle-snuffer towers and ivy-covered loggias were beloved of the textile and mining millionaires. Grace was incredulous.

'These make the New York houses look like tenements,' she exclaimed.

'Well, I'd hardly put it like that,' he laughed, 'but these are hard to ignore.'

'At least we can find each other in ours. You could be lost for days in some of those. I think I'd prefer our modest one.'

'It will do for the present,' Hugh said

'It's perfect, and now that our pieces of furniture and china have finally arrived, it really feels like our home,' said Delia.

'I hope you told Mrs Flynn to be careful with them,' Grace said.

'She was there when I was unpacking and she certainly seemed to know how to handle such delicate ware.'

'You chose wisely there,' Hugh said.

'I'm trying to keep a little distance, like you told me to, but it's difficult as she talks so much and I feel it's impolite not to answer her.'

Grace agreed. 'She does go on a bit about her family.'

'I never realised what a balancing act having help is. Mrs

Murphy seemed to run Kensley Park without anyone knowing how she did it. Next to my family I miss her most of all.'

Mrs Parks had added another chest to the ones they had left for the freighting company to send after them. It contained beautifully embroidered table and bed linen, runners, napkins and face towels.

'That woman took a great shine to you,' Grace said. 'I don't think any of these have ever been used. They look spank new.'

Their house was already pleasingly if sparsely furnished when they signed the two-year lease, but as Delia arranged her things, it began to take on a real sense of home for her – her and Hugh's first real home together. Heavy lace curtains allowed her to peep out on the street whenever she heard footsteps, and she could see if they belonged to Hugh or one of their neighbours.

She was becoming familiar with her surroundings and the different neighbourhoods. At first, she loved to walk with Grace along the little roads, lined with neat wooden houses, their shutters smartly painted and their window boxes showing off their early summer blooms. It only took a few weeks for her to venture out on her own sometimes, and when she did she made her way along Thames Street towards the waterfront, past the sail makers, the ships' chandlers, the hardware, dry goods and general stores. She could see herself living quite happily there in the future.

One morning she left Hugh engrossed in his drawings. Grace was upstairs in her sewing room, busily finishing Mrs O'Shaughnessy's day dress. Mrs Flynn had two flat irons on the stove and was working her way through the pile in the laundry basket. Closing the door behind her, Delia headed down the hill. She felt she'd never tire of being so close to the sea. Everything about it thrilled her and gave her pleasure – the early morning sunrises over the water to the east and the wonderful sunsets from the Cliff Walk on the other side of the island, the lighthouses spreading silvery pathways of light across the night sea and over the changing moods of the waves. She even liked the raucous screeching of the gulls, the way the winds seem to whip up in the afternoons and the taste of salt in the air.

She loved observing the activity along the wharfs, to watch the fishing boats coming and going, the constant traffic of vessels of all shapes and sizes plying their trades. She studied the fishermen as they offloaded crates of still-wriggling fish, recently plucked from their watery habitat. She marvelled at the colours of their scales as the sun caught them and reflected blues, greens, pinks, greys and silvers. She even liked the pungent smell as she passed the gutting sheds, where some hawkers sat outside, cleaning and filleting the contents of their creels, while they exchanged banter with some of the older fishermen. These no longer took to the sea but they still made a contribution to the age-old business by repairing nets for those who did. The sea was in their veins.

She had a spring in her step as she walked along the waterfront. She longed to be able to tell her mother and sister about this place and how happy she was with Hugh. Would they even care? She couldn't believe her parents, or her sister, could erase her that easily from their consciousness, no matter what she had done. No doubt they'd be preoccupied now with preparations for Mona's wedding. She wanted so badly for her to know that she wished her happiness in her marriage. Perhaps she'd try writing to her one more time.

She felt her eyes fill up with tears. What had brought that on? she asked herself. She kept walking but began to feel decidedly out of sorts. A bout of sadness swept over her and she needed to feel Hugh's reassuring arms around her. She turned to face home and felt she was going to pass out. She put her hand to her head and leaned against a doorpost of one of the seafarers' cabins. Two young women spotted her. They came over and asked if she was all right. One knocked on the cottage door and asked the owner for a drink of water. The woman insisted she go in and sit down a bit.

'I'm so sorry. I didn't mean to intrude,' she said as the room came back into focus and her eyes adjusted to the darkness from the sunlight outside.

'It's no bother at all,' the woman said. 'You're not from around these parts.'

'No, I'm from Ireland,' she said

'Aye, you and half of Newport are Irish if you ask me.' She chuckled.

'It seems so,' Delia agreed. 'I don't know what came over me just then. That's never happened before. I was fine when I set out. It was when I was passing the gutting sheds – I just felt funny, weak and wobbly.' She noticed the woman glance at her hand and smile.

'You're probably in the family way. It took me like that each time I was. And that was six times altogether. I couldn't bear the smell of fish or coffee and I couldn't keep a thing down for months each time.'

'In the family way?' Delia repeated.

'Yes, that's what happens when you're married.' She chuckled again, then turned serious. 'You are married, aren't you? You look barely more than a child yourself. How old are you?'

'I'm seventeen and I got married in November.' She told her about Hugh's work and how it had brought them to Newport.

'An architect – you'll be hobnobbing with the high society in no time at all.'

'I doubt that,' Delia replied, wondering could she really be expecting a baby. Of course she could, she told herself. She was almost five months married. 'I must get home.'

'I'll walk with you if you like.'

'Thank you for your kindness, but I feel much better now. I'm sure I'll be fine.'

'You'll be happy here. It's a nice place to live, and if you'll be looking for work in one of the summer cottages, now is the perfect time to put your name down with a few of them. The owners are starting to open them up.'

'That's good to know,' Delia replied and thanked her again. She took some deep breaths and headed home.

Hugh greeted her with, 'I was getting concerned you were gone so long, then I thought, this is Delia. She's not going to get lost on me. I actually thought you may have gone to the library to see if they'd allow you to borrow books in your own name.'

'No. I went down by the wharfs.'

'You look pale. Are you feeling unwell?'

'I'm all right now.' She explained what had happened. 'I thought I'd never get away from that kindly woman. Every time I got a step closer to the door, she came up with something else she thought I should know.'

'And did you learn anything from her?'

'Apart from the fact that I am possibly with child, no!' She stopped and watched as her news impacted.

'What? You mean – you – me? We're starting a family of our own?'

'I'm not sure yet, but we could be.'

He scooped her in his arms and twirled her around. 'That's

the best news ever. We have to tell Grace.' He went to go into the hall to call his aunt, but she held on to him.

'No, Hugh. We mustn't, not until I'm sure, and even then, let's just keep it our secret for a little while longer?'

'Of course,' he agreed. 'We'll have to get you to a doctor.'

'There'll be plenty of time for that. You know, Hugh, it's strange, but earlier today I decided I'd write to Mona to wish her happiness in her marriage to Desmond. I think I'll wait until I know that I can give her our good news as well. Perhaps hearing they are going to have a grandchild will even soften my parents a little.'

She knew by the look on his face he didn't really believe it would change things, but he put his arm around her again and said, 'I think that's a good idea so long as you don't pin your hopes too high. I don't want you getting upset.'

'I won't and it can't do any harm to try. I thought they might be missing me by now.'

'I'm sure they are, but pride can make people behave in the strangest ways. Would you like me to try?'

'Let's see what happens first.'

'Don't you think you should rest now?'

'No! Hugh Dunne, the fact that I've been unwell once does not mean I have suddenly become an invalid,' she said and he laughed out loud.

'I should have known better than to suggest that!'

'You should.'

Chapter 29

Delia was sick the next morning, and the morning after that. She didn't need any more confirmation. She took her time over the letter to her sister. She spent a few more days mulling over what she'd say. She wanted it to strike the right note. It was important to her to try to mend the broken fences with her original family before starting her own new one. If it didn't work, then she'd put that part of her life behind her forever more.

> *My dearest sister,*
> *I hope this letter finds you well. I miss you so much and I long to share so much with you. I understand why you haven't written, but that doesn't prevent me from hoping that perhaps by now you will have had time to reconsider and may feel more like forgiving me for following my heart. I would so love to hear from you.*
>
> *I had to write because I know your marriage is imminent*

and I hope you and Desmond will find the happiness that Hugh and I have found in each other.

Since Hugh got his qualifications he's been given a challenging assignment. He's designing a summer mansion in Newport, Rhode Island, for the president of the Manhattan Stock and Trading Conglomerate. We're living in Newport now and will be for the foreseeable future. His widowed aunt is living with us too. We may move back to New York, but that will become clearer as time goes on. I think I'd like to remain here.

It's an interesting place and we are renting our first home – a typical wooden New England house. It's by the sea and very pretty. I am very happy and delighted to tell you that we are looking forward to being joined by a new member of our family in a few months' time. We have only recently found out and are still getting used to the idea.

Please give my fondest love to Mama and Papa. Tell them my news and please ask them to write to me. Tell them that Mademoiselle Corneille knew nothing of my intentions to sail to America, nor did anyone at Kensley Park. It was all planned by Hugh and me and I take full responsibility for it.

I miss you, dearest sister, and our chats and riding out together. I wish you love and happiness in your marriage to Desmond.

I cannot say the same for Clement, as I am sure you

will appreciate when you remember the circumstances of that last meeting. I bear both the physical and emotional scars of our last encounters. Perhaps time may heal those too.

Send my special love to Mrs Murphy. I miss her and her wonderful soda bread. Although my housekeeper makes a good attempt at it, it's not the same. And give my best to Tommy and the rest of the staff.

Your own loving sister,

Delia xxx

She walked to the post office and sent the letter, unsure if she would ever get a reply, but it felt good to say those things. She also sent a letter to Mrs Parks and to Noreen, telling them their good news. Mrs Parks wrote weekly, in a feeble spidery hand, telling them how much they had enriched her life just when she thought it had no more surprises to offer her. She replied to Delia's news with genuine delight.

Being a parent and a grandparent are both pleasures that life denied Doctor Parks and myself. In a peculiar way, I assume it was the Lord's way of telling us we should spread our caring to a wider circle than an immediate family, and my husband certainly did that. I like to think I may have been some little help too. I wish you had met him. I know he would have embraced you as a daughter. Having you in

*my home made me realise how lovely it would have been
to have had my own family too.*

*Does that make me sound like a bitter old woman? I
hope not.*

*I've had a wonderful life, but if there is just one thing
that I could change about it, it would be that. I hope I
may get to see your precious baby whenever he or she comes
along.*

*Make sure you eat well and get plenty of fresh air and
rest.*

With much affection,
Mrs Georgina Parks.

Mrs Flynn was proving to be a bit trying. She kept the
house in robust good order and her cooking was surprisingly
creative and tasty, but Delia found her familiarity a bit too
much at times, although at others, when she was feeling
homesick, she was glad of her company. She found it difficult
to keep the balance just right.

Delia took Hugh's advice and watched and listened
everywhere she went, whether to the stores with Grace or Mrs
Flynn, or when in the kitchen, as the housekeeper rolled pastry
or trimmed meat for a pie. From this contact she was getting
used to hearing the unfamiliar words and expressions she
had found so foreign when she'd first arrived in this country,
words like faucet and sidewalk, blocks and skillets.

She spent hours watching Grace sew, fascinated by her eye for detail and envying her skill. Hers and Noreen's. Their stitches were almost invisible to the naked eye.

'Do you think I could ever make my own clothes?' she asked Grace one morning.

'I see no reason in the whole world why you couldn't,' she replied. 'In fact, I did consider suggesting it to you several times but thought I might sound like Peggy, so I didn't.' She laughed.

'Poor Aunt Peggy. She still hasn't forgiven me for coming from the big house, has she?'

'It's not you she objects to – it's what you stand for in her mind. She doesn't mean any harm behind it all.'

Mrs Flynn often brought one of her brood to work with her, to give her injured husband a rest. She set them tasks like peeling or chopping, dusting and polishing alongside her.

She reminded Delia of Noreen's mother, Mary McCormack, back in Mayo and of how she managed to keep her children spotless and happy on very little, in their tiny thatched shack, and of her joy when she and Mrs Murphy had given them the pinafores and shirts they had sewn for the boys. She was working her way around to offering to use some of the discounted fabrics that Grace could get her hands on to make some garments for the Flynn children, but wasn't sure if she might insult the housekeeper by doing so. Hadn't

Hugh told her more than once that pride made people act in peculiar ways?

They still hadn't shared their good news with anyone in Newport, but Delia knew she couldn't hide it much longer. She found it harder and harder to keep the food that Mrs Flynn set before her down. Her waist was thickening and she couldn't walk as far as the cottages by the processing sheds any more without feeling nauseous. When she told Hugh this, he said, 'I'm not sorry to hear that. That area and particularly those cottages have a bad reputation.'

Delia didn't understand. The woman who took her in that day and gave her water was perfectly kind.

'Dearest, you've had a very sheltered upbringing. But this is a port and a port with a military base across the water at Fort Adams. That means there will always be plenty of unsavoury characters, who show their worst traits when they've had too much rum or bourbon.' She had a flashback to her own brother when he had drink taken and she didn't like the imagery. 'They don't always keep good company. A lot more goes on in those cabins than you'd imagine. I'd prefer if you stayed away from that area when you're on your own. Don't you think the Cliff Walk is preferable? And you can admire the mansions all along it.'

'I'll do that,' she promised. 'And they're even more interesting now that they're beginning to come to life again.'

As the days went by she had to stop herself from continually going into Hugh's studio when he was working from home. Her curiosity about his project increased each time they visited the site and she saw Gull Haven embed its footprint on the landscape. She wanted to know what each stage was and what would happen next. He told her about the marble ordered from Treviso for the hallway and grand staircase and how the decorative blue and white tiles for the orangery would be sourced from Lisbon. The chandeliers had already been commissioned for the ballroom and would come from Murano in Italy.

He showed her the sketches for the large stained-glass cupola, which had also been handed over to an atelier, this one in Bordeaux, with instructions from the client's wife that she 'liked the colours in peacocks' tails' and wanted the panels to reflect these.

'She wants to have silk made for the walls to carry on this theme, but that will have to wait until the atelier has come up with a few design options. Then they'll send them to us for our client's approval, or rather, as the chief had warned me, for the client's wife's approval. She's the overlord in this case, and what she wants she gets. The French craftsmen who'll make these will come over when they're finished and they'll assemble them in situ.'

'Won't that take forever?'

'It'll certainly be a full year before we get to the installation stage. If they'd let us use American craftsmen it could be done much faster, but that wouldn't impress their friends nearly as much.'

'Don't you think that's very sad, having to go to such lengths to outdo your friends?' Delia asked Grace and Mrs Flynn the next day in the kitchen as they discussed it.

'I know it seems wasteful and decadent, but at least their flights of fancy mean they're giving employment to a lot of people, and that can't be bad – can it?' Grace said.

'I hadn't looked at it that way,' Delia replied. 'I suppose you're right.'

'They've more money than sense, those people. They don't live in the real world,' Mrs Flynn said. 'They only see their children for a brief time every day and they even leave their schooling to governesses, who are often foreign and who have no regard for them at all. How can they know or love their children living like that?'

Delia's thoughts flew instantly back to the years spent with Mademoiselle Corneille in the schoolroom in the attics at Kensley Park. 'My governess was French, but she was kind and caring,' she said out loud. It was only when she saw the look of surprise on Mrs Flynn's face that she realised she had let her guard down. 'I mean, the governess where I grew up – the children upstairs loved her. She often lent me books to read. I'm sure their parents did love them too,' she said, hoping Grace wouldn't give her away. She didn't.

'So that's where you got your lovely manners from,' Mrs Flynn said. 'You have the air of a lady about you, a real air of refinement, if you don't think I'm being too familiar.'

The conversation had gone far enough. If it continued, she was in danger of becoming more personal. Hadn't Hugh advised her to keep a little distance, that it was easier to give instructions and for them to be carried out when he did? She had fully intended sharing her news with the two of them that morning, but now decided to tell Grace on her own first. After all, she was family. Mrs Flynn wasn't.

Grace was almost as excited as Hugh had been. 'That's all you need now to make you feel at home,' she said. 'A little one to keep you occupied.'

'But I do feel at home. Well, I do most of the time.'

'Don't you miss your family?'

'Of course I do, all the time, and especially so now. I'd love to be near them. I think my parents may have been kinder if it hadn't been for my brother. And Clement's fiancée is the worst kind of snob you could ever meet. Now, Peggy would definitely not approve of her!'

'Did your father not stand up to him?'

'Unfortunately, no. Traditionally, the estate should pass on to the heir when my father reaches sixty, which he will be later this year. Because Clement is serving in India, Papa wanted to put his affairs in order in case anything should happen to him before Clement returns, so effectively he has given him much more power than he should really have.'

'That's unfortunate.'

'It is. And he didn't approve of father selling the derelict cottages outside Kensley to Hugh in the first place, but at least that was done before he had any control. He can't do anything about that except make life unpleasant for any of your relatives who might want to go back to Ireland to live in the old homestead.'

'We'd better not tell Peggy that!' Grace said.

'Oh Lord, no.'

'Time is a great healer, Delia. Your family might come around yet, especially Mona.'

'I don't think it's going to be that simple. Clement told me if I ever even talked to Hugh again I'd be dead to him: dead to all the family.' She stroked her cheek where the raised scar was a constant reminder of that awful day in Kensley Park. 'I can't imagine how he feels about me now, especially as I bested them by running away. He would never have imagined me doing that.'

'But your sister must miss you.'

'I would like to think so.'

'There's a very strong bond between sisters. I know, and although Peggy and I don't always agree, we'd kill for each other if anyone tried to come between us. Wait and see – it'll all change when you both have babies of your own. From what you've told me, you two seem to have been close.'

'We were, or so I thought, but things had changed that winter. Once she and my brother's fiancée met they became inseparable. It was during her coming-out season and they were engrossed in their society whirl. Her family are insufferable, pompous snobs. In their eyes, I've brought shame and disgrace on all our families. I'm no longer considered worthy to grace their drawing rooms. And do you know what saddens me most of all? The fact that Papa met and liked Hugh before Clement came back on leave. He told us at dinner one night that he admired his ambition and determination, but that was before he realised they were focused on his daughter.'

'That knowledge must be difficult to bear, child, but you mustn't let these thoughts upset you now. You have to consider yourself and the little one growing inside you.'

'I'll be lost without you, Grace, when you go back to New York. You've been so kind and caring since we first met.'

'You don't have to worry about that. I'll stay as long as you need me. That's one of the few advantages of being a widow – there's no one waiting for me to return, and I like it here.'

The following Sunday they went for their weekly promenade along Bellevue Avenue. A knot of people stood outside the entrance to the Casino Theatre and Lawn Tennis Club, and Delia was curious to know what was happening.

'Oh, James Gordon Bennet Jnr is probably in town,' Hugh remarked.

'Who is he?' asked Grace.

'His father started the *New York Herald*, and he inherited that at a very young age. He's a perfect example of a spoiled young brat. He made a name for himself by winning the first transatlantic race from here to the Isle of Wight in England before he was twenty, but I think the bit of fame want to his head.'

'Why do you say that?'

'He's a notorious maverick who craves attention,' said Hugh. 'He was barred from the conservative men's club for ungentlemanly conduct, so he built the Casino complex to show the world that he didn't need them.'

'It sounds like he's a bit of a rogue all right,' said Grace.

'He certainly is that.'

'Is he married?' asked Delia.

'Not yet. He was engaged, very briefly, to a socialite from New York, but he turned up late to their engagement party. He was inebriated and urinated into the fireplace in the drawing room, in front of all the guests.'

'Is that true?' Grace asked.

'Absolutely. Then he went off to Europe for a few years.'

'And why was he barred from the gentlemen's club? Did he do the same things there?'

'No. He dared a friend to ride his horse into the Reading Room Club, but it was thanks to that escapade that he commissioned this club, the biggest and best in the land'

'From the outside it looks impressive,' Delia remarked.

'It is inside too. It's the place to be seen. If you like,' Hugh said, 'we could get tickets for a lawn tennis tournament some time. Everyone here is tennis mad.'

'I'd like that,' she said, and taking his arm, they walked on.

The mailman delivered a letter from Noreen McCormack the next day. In it, she told Delia that 'her' family was preparing for their annual vacation in Newport and that they would be arriving within the following week. 'I'll have no official day off the first week, because we'll all be too busy getting the house in order before the family arrives, but Mrs Bradley has promised me that I can visit you any day once my work is done.'

'I am so excited at the prospect of seeing her again,' she told Grace.

Noreen was her only contact with her former life, and she hoped she'd have some snippets of news from Ireland for her.

Chapter 30

'I brought a basket of roses and preserves for you from Wind Gates, ma'am,' Noreen said when Mrs Flynn had shown her in. Delia was amused at how she had changed from being Miss Delia to ma'am, but she made no comment. She was thinking it was quite like the old times, only then it was she who had been the one bearing the goodies.

'The roses are from the gardens. And I also have an invitation for you, ma'am, for Mr Hugh and yourself and Mrs Grace too from Mrs Bradley. She wants to know if you'd like to come to tea on Wednesday, before the family arrives, and she'll give you the grand tour of the summer cottage.'

'Is that permitted?' Delia asked, wondering if the staff at Kensley Park invited their friends in when her family was away in London.

'Oh yes, everyone does it. I've seen inside the Astors' and the Sterns' houses so far and they are swell. I think I've died and gone to heaven. I can't believe I'm spending my summer here,' she told them as Mrs Flynn served them tea in the drawing room.

'I hope it stays fine for you!' Grace laughed at her enthusiasm. 'Come back when the entertaining starts and tell us you feel the same way. Your family's reputation for hospitality is legendary.'

'I know we'll be run off our feet, but I can't wait to see the gowns and the finery on the ladies. You know how I love looking at the fashions.' She held out her skirt to show it off. 'I made this all my myself,' she said proudly.

'It's very beautiful,' Delia said. 'But I fear you'll not have much time for sewing or admiring the modes below stairs.'

'Some of the trunks have already arrived and I've seen the contents of those. There's a whole room off the kitchens just to store them once they're emptied. There are silks, laces and taffetas with so many ruffles and frills – I declare, I've never seen the likes before. Lots of the cottages have dumb waiters built in especially to haul the dresses upstairs after they've been pressed, so that they don't get tossed on the way up.'

'Well, I never,' said Grace.

'Some of them are so heavy I can hardly carry them. I don't know how the ladies can walk around in them, never mind dance.'

It transpired that Mrs Bradley also allowed Noreen help an under-lady's-maid when an extra pair of hands was needed upstairs, and she was allowed to lay out the garments for special occasions.

'I'm proud of you. You've done very well for yourself, Noreen,' Delia said.

'I have Mr Hugh to thank for that, for introducing me to Mrs Bradley.'

'It sounds as though you have had no bother settling in to your new life over here,' Delia remarked. 'Do you see much of Mr Hugh's cousins or have you been too busy to stay in touch with them?'

'Oh no, Miss Delia. I see them regular, when I've free time, and Mrs Peggy has been real good to me.'

'Aye, that's my sister for you. She's kindness to the core,' Grace said.

When Mrs Flynn left the room, Delia asked, 'So tell me, have you any news from home?'

'A little.'

'Mona's wedding?'

'That's going ahead at Kensley Park as planned, and everyone is in a tizzy getting things organised for the guests. All the gentry are arriving from England for it and there's going to be a hunt ball too. It's the talk of the parish.'

'You never told me how you got to be so tight with Mrs Bradley,' Delia said to Hugh in bed that night, as she lay curled up in his arms.

'They used to live near us in New York, but they were right

in the middle of a bad area with gangs trying to establish their territorial boundaries. I helped her son when he was in a spot of bother and put him in the way of a job. He got it and managed to hold it down, which I had had my doubts about. She never forgot that.'

'That's understandable,' she said sleepily. His voice always soothed her.

'Her family left Ireland during the famine and came over here on the same boat as my grandparents. Her husband didn't survive the journey, but the womenfolk kept in touch. Granda instilled into us that we must always look after our own, and that's what he did. When my grandma died, Mrs Bradley looked out for him. There's history between our families, and I knew when Noreen wanted work she'd give her a start. I also knew that Noreen wouldn't let us down. And I'd say Mrs Bradley's more than half-curious to meet you and see who I married from the old sod! And I'm more than half-curious to see the interior of that colonial-style cottage!'

She didn't answer and he saw she had fallen asleep already. He smiled and, carefully pulling his arm out from under her, covered her up. Since she was with child she could sleep anywhere, anytime. He studied her for a bit, kissed her on the cheek and turned over.

Not for the first time, he wondered about the upper classes and their attitudes to life. He had liked Lord Kensley-Balfe and considered him a gentleman in every sense. He may have just been starting out in his profession, but Hugh was determined to show her family how wrong they were about him. He wasn't a fortune-hunter. He wanted nothing from them for himself. But he did want something for his wife and their unborn child, and that was for them to apologise for their treatment of her and tell her they forgave her for loving him.

He also wanted to see the smug smile wiped off Clement's face as he acknowledged that he had done her an injustice. Although, in hindsight, Clement had done them both a service. He had pushed them into taking their fate into their own hands and, even if it meant he'd never be welcome in his own Mayo cottages again, they had given him a much more valuable legacy – his beloved wife and soon a child too. If Clement hadn't reacted so violently, Delia may well have been persuaded to follow the path her parents had chosen for her and, instead of being here with him now, she'd be doing her season, socialising with the titled upper classes in Ireland and Great Britain.

He sighed. He loved her more than life itself and couldn't believe his luck. He had talent, and one day her family, all of them, would have to acknowledge both those facts. He just hoped they'd all still be around to see it.

A few days later he accompanied his wife and aunt to Wind Gates. Mrs Bradley greeted them as though it was her own mansion. She gave them the grand tour, pointing out tapestries from Italy, china from Sèvres, furnishings from England.

'Is that the lady of the house?' Delia asked, admiring a beautiful full-length portrait of a woman clothed in evening attire. 'Just look at the lace and the pile on the velvet – you can almost feel the texture. Is it a good likeness?'

'Yes, he captured her perfectly. She was quite taken by him, I believe. He's the toast of London – that's where she sat for him,' Mrs Bradley said. 'She hasn't seen it hanging yet – it was only completed last month. The artist is coming over for the opening ball of the summer, for the reveal. We've instructions that he's to be given the best room in the house. He's already arrived in New York, I believe.'

'How I'd love to be able to paint like that,' Delia said to Hugh, who was studying it more closely. The signature read John S. Sargent.

'I thought so. He's a genius. I'll warrant that'll get him enough commissions to keep him busy for years.'

Outside the roses were blooming, the sky blue and the fringe of a gaily striped awning fluttered over part of the large patio. Mrs Bradley had arranged for them to have tea there, and a manservant poured. A maid in a dark blue dress with white cuffs, white collar and frilly apron served them delicacies and dainties. Noreen was allowed to join them briefly.

Mrs Bradley didn't ask any questions of Delia, other than those dictated by convention, but Delia got the distinct impression that she was aware of her history. Then she and Grace caught up on their family news while Hugh and Delia walked around the grounds, looking at Wind Gates from all angles.

'These are the sort of houses I want to build.'

'And you will too, Hugh, I know that.'

'You know the large one that's under construction on Annandale Road? The Taylor house? He was a guest here a few years ago and decided he wanted a summer place like this and engaged the same architects. That's why Gull Haven is so important to me. I want others to see it and be inspired like that.'

'They will, Hugh. It's going to be spectacular.'

The afternoon was over too quickly, and once they got home she wrote a thank-you letter to the housekeeper. It had been a revelation, coming, as she did, from where ostentatious displays of wealth and one-upmanship were looked upon as a lack of breeding. In America, it seemed to some to be not only acceptable but almost desirable.

As the weeks progressed, Newport became crowded with the arrival of the holidaymakers and their entourages.

Delia wrote to Mrs Parks:

Newport has come alive in the last few weeks and I have to say I do enjoy watching the spectacle of the 5 p.m. carriage procession along Bellevue Avenue.

Yesterday Mr William Vanderbilt's yacht, Alva, *after his wife, sailed into the harbour and caused quite a few admiring glances. It's the biggest and most expensive private yacht ever built.*

Delia would love to have been able to share these snippets of her life with Mona, to tell her about the beautiful people, dressed in their beautiful creations, being driven in their beautiful carriages by beautifully paired horses. She had heard it cost half a million dollars, but it seemed crass to mention that, so she didn't.

When the post had been delivered the next day, Hugh came out of his studio to tell Delia that the chief was going to be visiting them the following week. 'He'll be here for about seven days and will be attending a ball at Stoneacre – that's the cottage he designed a few years ago. He says if you are not up to having a houseguest he'll stay at a hotel.'

'Of course I am up to a houseguest, particularly him. I really enjoy his company, and I know you do too.'

'That's good. I'm glad you said that, because he says we are invited along with him too.'

'Oh, Hugh, can I really go to a ball in my condition?'

'Why, you're not that noticeable,' he said.

She looked down at her growing belly and smiled. 'Not that noticeable – really? Perhaps if I walk around backwards no one will notice.'

They both laughed.

'It's a fancy dress ball, so you'll get away with anything. The theme for the evening is Rural and Rustic Reality. I'm sure Grace will help you create something suitable for both of us. I'm not too bothered about what we'll wear, anyway – rather, I'm relishing the first-hand opportunity to see just how these people use their houses when they entertain,' he said.

'Don't you ever rest?' she asked him.

'Just being with you is enough,' he said. 'You're my balm and my calm.'

'And you're full of baloney.' She laughed. 'I hope I don't let you down on my first society outing.'

'You'll not do that. You were born into it. Socialising comes naturally to you. Look at how you fitted in so easily with Mrs Parks's friends. If anything, I hope I won't let you down.'

'You could never do that. What we have is real – we have real love, Hugh, and I think that's what a lot of these people lack. That's why they give themselves airs and graces and surround themselves with anything and everything that they think will elevate their status. They really believe that will make them happy, but it won't. Whereas I already have everything I want. Just being here with you is more than enough for me.'

'Have you really no regrets about not being presented in court?'

'None whatever. It's an important milestone in many girls' lives, but I think my experiences have been much richer and broader than getting to curtsey before a queen. I wouldn't swap any of them. I wish my family knew that.'

'How grown up and wise you've become since I first met you, Delia,' he said.

'I don't feel grown up and wise. I still have so much to learn. In fact, I don't feel any different, apart from what's happening to my body.'

'Oh, you are, believe me. You're changing, growing up in front of my eyes, from a shy – well, maybe not so shy – young girl into a voluptuous young woman, commanding her staff, albeit a very tiny staff, and running a home. I love you all the more for it.'

'Thank you, kind sir,' she teased. 'I'm glad you came halfway across the world to find me.'

'And I'm glad you came halfway across it to follow me.'

Chapter 31

William A. Potter's first words as Hugh met him from the ferry were, 'It's great to be back, to breathe in fresh air and to get away from the city smells.'

'You'll get plenty of fresh air here, sir,' Hugh replied, taking his portmanteau.

'It's good of you to put me up in the circumstances. I trust it's not too much of an inconvenience for Mrs Dunne at this time.'

'Absolutely not. That was always the plan and she wouldn't hear of you staying in a hotel. Besides, I doubt you'd have found a room anywhere here after the beginning of June. You could see the population growing day by day.'

The question 'How's the building coming along?' sparked off a lengthy discussion between them, of progress in some areas and not in others.

'I have all the drawings in the studio at home so we can go through them there when you've had a chance to freshen up.'

After greetings were made, he said, 'I come bearing gifts for my gracious hostess – not from me, I regret to say, but from Mrs Parks.' He handed over a box and in it was a delicately crocheted blanket and matching layette. Delia felt tears spring to her eyes. Seeing those tiny garments made motherhood much more of a reality, and she realised how little she knew about babies. Until then, she had tried to imagine what it would be like; now that she had something tangible to hold onto, it suddenly felt very different.

'Are you from a large family, Mr Potter?' Grace asked.

'By Irish standards, probably not,' he laughed, 'but by American ones, I suppose I am. I am one of nine brothers.'

'Oh, your poor mother,' Grace said. 'She'll have plenty of jewels in her crown up there in heaven.' He looked puzzled and she explained. 'You know, one jewel for every child you bore – that's what they used to say back home.' This was news to Delia too, but then things like childbirth were not openly discussed back home either.

William A. Potter was very easy company and, despite the age difference between the two professionals, it was obvious to Delia that they shared a mutual regard for each other. Grace fell under his spell too, and he told her if he'd been permitted to bring a partner to Stoneacre to the costume ball, he'd have chosen her to accompany him.

'Oh, you are a flatterer,' she said, and Delia was sure Grace actually blushed.

'I assure you, I'd much prefer your company to that of some of the predatory mamas on the hunt for prospective husbands for their unmarried daughters.'

'So you'd have me be a decoy for you?' Grace asked with a grin.

'I didn't mean it to sound as thoughtless as that. My apologies.' He sounded embarrassed. 'I just meant –'

'I know that.' She laughed. 'And frankly, Mr Potter, if I had been in a position to agree to accompany you, I'd only have been using you to get inside and have a good look around that mansion.'

'So that makes us quits.' It was his turn to laugh.

'But a costume party? I'm not sure how I'd feel about that – a widow woman of a certain age. Would I really have got away with dressing up as a shepherdess or a milkmaid?'

'Of course you would. And a very charming one you'd make too. Last year the theme was the Ancient Roman Empire and, let me tell you, there were many vestal virgins misrepresenting themselves! I don't think even one of them would have been qualified. Rural and Rustic Reality is much less challenging.'

They laughed at the thought.

For the following few days Delia sat in the attic chamber

that Grace used as a sewing room. Together they chatted as Grace remodelled one of the frocks that Delia had had made for her aborted London trip and which no longer fitted her. She added side panniers in blue satin to the skirt and made a new white pin-tucked front for the bodice on her smock. She finished it all off dramatically with bows and floral details to match the hairband she'd already completed. The new style ensured that Delia's delicate state was virtually hidden.

While Grace was doing this, she also instructed Delia in how to modify one of Hugh's shirts, and together they made him satin pantaloons and a waistcoat to match his wife's costume. They'd be venturing out into Newport society as Little Bo Peep and Little Boy Blue.

'I hope these don't look too simple,' Grace said.

'Anything but – they look very good. I do believe some of the guests' outfits will have been made by theatrical costumiers in New York and Boston. That's why these society hostesses fix their themes the previous season, to give their guests a chance to be innovative,' Delia said.

'It must be a wonderful luxury to have nothing else to worry them through the winter months but what they'll wear next summer at a fancy dress ball!' said Grace.

'Has Mr Potter said what he was doing about his costume?' Delia asked.

'He has, but I think he wants it to be surprise.' Grace replied.

'So he's sharing secrets with you now!' Delia teased. 'I'll have to keep an eye on you two.'

'Will you whist?' she replied.

Mr Potter went to Gull Haven each morning with Hugh and expressed how pleased he was at how the cottage was progressing. The owners had arrived in Newport to summer there and had rented an imposing property about six mansions further along Bellevue Avenue from their plot of land. Consequently, most weekends when his client arrived from New York he came to the site. He too seemed to be happy with the headway they were making and occasionally brought his friends along on the pretext of inspecting it, but in reality it was to show off the size and majestic scope of their project and to let them know that they hoped to be ensconced by the following summer.

As the weeks passed Delia's morning sickness lessened, and by noon each day she began to feel normal again. The doctor had told her that the baby was due towards the end of September. On the day of the ball, at everyone's insistence, she went to bed for the afternoon and, despite being both excited and apprehensive at the prospects of her first real foray into the local gentry, she managed to sleep.

Refreshed and eager, she dressed for the do. She and Hugh laughed when they saw each other in their costumes. 'I doubt any shepherd ever tended his sheep looking as dandified as this,' he said, offering his arm.

'Or as impractically shod as this,' she said, pointing a satin-slippered foot in his direction. Mr Potter was waiting in the hallway – dressed as a scarecrow, with baggy patched trousers tied with string around the ankles and waist, a checked shirt with patches too and a hat with straggly woollen red hair and straw protruding from beneath it. Bits of straw had been sewn into other seams creating the impression that he was stuffed with it.

'You look really authentic. Did you bring that with you from New York?' Delia asked.

'No, it's a Newport original, created by your clever Madam Grace. Isn't she a genius?'

'Whist, will you?' she said. 'You're embarrassing me.'

'You're a dark horse. You never said a word,' Delia said, grinning at Grace.

'I was sworn to secrecy,' she replied, looking towards Mr Potter.

'That she was,' he confirmed. 'I wanted there to be an element of surprise, and from the expression on both your faces, I think I can conclude that the outfit is a success.'

'Now go on, off with you all and have a great night,' Grace said, ushering them out of the hall.

'Oh, I know we will,' Delia said. 'It will be unforgettable – I just know it will.'

The carriage Mr Potter had ordered took them the short distance to the vast shingle-style cottage, with its creeper-clad piazza. The exotic cupola, illuminated from within, stood out like a colourful cathedral dome against the sky, welcoming everyone.

'It's very beautiful. You must feel very proud when you see your designs turn out like this,' Delia said to Mr Potter. The driveway and gardens were illuminated with myriads of flaming torches.

'I confess I do, and I do have a soft spot for this house and the grounds.'

Hugh helped her from the carriage and Mr Potter said, 'Let's go and mingle with the other rustic bumpkins and yokels.'

The house was aglow with hundreds of candles. A string quartet played in the hallway as they queued to be presented to their hosts.

'We are so happy to meet you,' John Ellis said as he raised Delia's hand to his lips, 'and all the way from Ireland too.' He turned to the couple beside him and said, 'May I present you to our house guests – they've come even further, all the way from Paris. His Excellency Monsieur Patrice and Madame Monique Duchene.'

'*Enchanté,*' the man said, bowing from the waist, his wife shaking hands.

Delia replied, '*C'est un plaisir de vous rencontrer. J'espère que vous appréciez votre séjour à Newport.*'

'*Vous parlez fráncais?*' Madame Duchene asked.

'*Oui, bien sur.*'

'*Oh, mon dieu!*' she said taking Delia's hand again. '*Je suis tellement fatigué d'essayer de fair comprendre a mon anglais et a son francais!*' she said, raising her eyes to heaven. They laughed, and as they progressed out on to the patio, Delia found herself still in the same company.

Staff circulated with champagne and cordials as the guests admired each other's costumes. His Excellency was kitted out as a county curate, with a long black cassock tied with a thick rope and topped off with a flat circular hat. His wife was done up as a gypsy girl, wearing a deep-fringed shawl over a low-cut white blouse with puffy sleeves and a draw-string neckline. Coloured petticoats peeped out from below a black skirt with ribboned bands of yellow, red and white around the hemline. A colourful bandana held her dark hair back, revealing two large gold hoops hanging from her ears. She carried a basket full of trinkets and posies that she handed out to those passing by.

Their hostess, Mrs Ellis, insisted that no one should be seated beside the person they had arrived with, so Hugh and Mr Potter were at other tables. By the time they were halfway through the eight-course meal in the glittering dining room, Delia felt she had known Madame Duchene all her life, and she mentally thanked Mademoiselle Corneille for all those French lessons. She was really enjoying herself. In all probability their paths would never cross again, and there was a certain freedom in that. Consequently, she found herself talking freely about her upbringing in Ireland and the family's periods spent in London.

'But you must visit us when you are there next. That's where Pierre is stationed for the foreseeable future.'

'Unfortunately, I don't envisage being there any time soon. You see, my family have disowned me.' There, she had said it. It was the first time she'd admitted the truth to anyone outside Hugh's family, and she felt a weight lift off her shoulders. 'I ran away to marry Hugh before I was presented and my parents didn't and don't approve.'

'Oh, how ridiculous. If I had met him before Pierre, I'd have run away to be with him too.' She laughed.

'*Vous êtes si gentil de dire que,*' Delia said.

'Of course, he's years younger than me, but that is so *romantique*. He is perfectly charming and he's a perfect gentleman. And he has a perfectly respectable profession. How could they disapprove?' Madame Duchene asked.

'I agree with you on all counts,' Delia said, 'but they didn't even give themselves a chance to get to know him.'

'Then that is their misfortune. You are always welcome at our home, both of you. Would you like me to visit your family in London and tell them how well you are?'

'No, I don't think that would be wise, but it's kind of you to offer.'

After the dinner was finished, they were instructed to gather on the lawn outside for a fireworks display. Delia was glad she'd taken a rest that afternoon. She was beginning to realise that these balls actually did go on until dawn in some cases, and she was glad she'd not had too much champagne already.

'I'm like a child about fireworks,' Delia told Madame Duchene, as Hugh joined them with Monique's husband. 'I can never get enough of them, and invariably when they stop I feel let down. I always hope that there'll be one stray one to illuminate the sky one more time, and there never is!'

Hugh laughed.

'Isn't she delightful, Pierre?' Madam Duchene said to her husband. 'I've told her they both must come and visit us in London or Paris. They absolutely must. I feel we are soulmates.'

'You must think I'm very naïve, but I never saw fireworks before coming to America. The first time I ever witnessed them was when Hugh took me up onto the widow's walk on our rooftop here in Newport. He teases me for my enthusiasm, but I can't help it. I love every magical twinkle of them. They make me feel happy inside – the way they fizz, pop, make explosive noises and draw fairy-like patterns in the sky.'

'I can see why you love this lady,' the Frenchman said.

'So can I,' Hugh agreed, putting his arm around her waist. Music started up again from inside the summer cottage and everyone made their way towards it. Delia's dance card already had several slots booked. An octet replaced the musicians who had played earlier and, as the music began again, Madam Duchene's husband led her onto the dance floor. He was a very accomplished dancer and twirled and led her gracefully to the music. He had made Delia promise him a gavotte. Mr Potter booked a dance with both the ladies, and their host, Mr Ellis, had secured a Viennese waltz with Delia.

'Are you enjoying yourself?' Hugh asked, taking her in his arms. 'You're not too tired, are you?'

'Oh, Hugh, I'm too excited and happy to be tired. It's wonderful. I'll never forget this evening as long as I live. Everything about it is absolutely perfect. The costumes, the food, the music, the surroundings. Are you enjoying yourself?'

'How could I not, with you by my side? And speaking French with such facility too. I'm mightily impressed at the ease with which you've blended in with the swanks!'

'And much as I hate to admit it, I like the people I've met and I love the house too.' She lowered her voice. 'It's not too flamboyant at all. In fact, although very grand, it's very tastefully done.'

'That's partly due to the chief's restraint. That's his style. Just wait until Gull Haven is finished. It will be even more beautiful and, dare I say it, even a little less showy.'

'I don't doubt it.' She smiled.

'In time, I think I could quite happily leave New York

behind and settle here in Newport. How would you feel about that?'

'I think I could be very happy here. I feel at home and I like being by the sea.'

'So do I. When I've made my mark we'll build here. Not like this,' he waved his arms about, 'but a fine house nonetheless.'

'I don't think I'd really miss not having a ballroom,' she said.

'I'm glad, as I wasn't factoring one of those into the plans.'

The music stopped and he took her arm, saying, 'Come and meet my clients – that's them over there. They were asking about you earlier and insisting on meeting you.'

'I'd love to meet them too.'

He steered her in their direction, but before they left the dance floor, someone dressed as a butler came running in to their midst shouting, 'Fire! Fire!'

It took everyone a few seconds to realise this fellow was not in costume – he was the butler from the mansion next door.

'Fire! Fire! Cliff Tops is on fire. Where are Mr and Mrs Mulroney? They should be here somewhere.'

Chapter 32

Everyone rushed outside, through the patio and conservatory doors, to see for themselves. Flames licked along the gutter line of the upper floor of the neighbouring mansion, a large plume of smoke rising above it. It was hard to deduce how bad it was because the house had been designed so that the top floor, the servants' quarters, was hidden from view from below.

For a few seconds no one moved, then pandemonium ensued as all the men began to run out across the lawn after the Mulroneys and their butler. So many clambered over the picket fence that one section collapsed, making a natural gateway for others to follow.

'Stay here,' Hugh ordered Delia. 'Remember your condition. Don't go anywhere. We'll be back.'

'I will. Be careful,' she said. And he was gone. She saw him grab hold of the Ellis's butler's arm and issue instructions.

'Tell the staff here to fetch all the large containers they can carry and bring them next door. We'll form a chain and use the water from the pumps and the fountains out the front and back of the house to damp down the lower floors.'

Some of the women ran to assist, but with Hugh's words ringing in her ears, she followed at a distance and stood by the fence, staring incredulously. The house was a good distance back from the road and she heard Mr Potter shout, 'Are the family safe? And the servants? Get someone to account for everybody. Once that's done we'll start damping down and rescuing what we can before the flames spread.'

Hugh and some of the other men had taken control, organising everyone and looking totally out of place in their ridiculous rustic costumes. The church bell began to peal, a sound only heard at night when a fishing boat went missing or a fire was raging somewhere. Someone had obviously been dispatched to ring it. Within no time at all, they were joined by more staff and families from the neighbouring houses who had been alerted by the bell or by runners who had gone from house to house spreading word of the fire.

Human chains were organised to pass receptacles full of water towards the house, from both the back and front. Everything from saucepans and buckets, hip baths to chamber pots, was pressed into use. Hugh directed those out the front who were not involved in the chains to 'Remove anything you can from the first floor and downstairs – furniture, paintings, the piano, clocks, anything you can carry, and put them on the front lawn over there to the right, as the wind is blowing in the other direction.'

'What about the top floor?' Mr Mulroney asked Mr Potter.

'I'm afraid you can forget about that, sir. I doubt we can do much to salvage anything up there. It's blazing too fiercely to risk anyone's life,' he replied.

'I'll tell them out the back to concentrate on the lower levels,' Hugh volunteered. 'It's really caught hold.'

'It has and I doubt we'll be able to contain it up there for too long. In my experience, with older houses like this, the chances of dousing it sufficiently and preventing it spreading are very small. The timbers will have dried out over the years. They can go up like tinder and this wind isn't helping. It's fanning the flames,' Mr Potter said.

Hugh ran through the house and out the garden room at the back to pass on instructions.

'Save what you can, but don't put yourselves at risk,' he shouted. 'Most things can be replaced with money, but that can't replace you.'

The acrid smell of smoke began to fill the air, and smuts rained down on the rescuers, irritating their eyes and making it difficult to breathe. Sporadic columns of sparks erupted as beams or rafters shifted, surrendering to the heat, adding more fuel to the spreading flames. These could be seen rising higher and higher into the sky. Unlike the fireworks, this sight didn't thrill Delia or any of the others witnessing it.

As though reading her mind, a rotund milkmaid who was watching from the fence too asked of no one in particular, 'Do you think the fire could have been started by sparks from the fireworks?'

'Oh, I never thought of that,' Delia replied. 'I assumed it was started by someone being careless with a candle or gas lamp.'

An older man said, 'I believe there are those who think that fireworks shouldn't be allowed near dwellings for this very reason.'

'Do you think they can save the house?' the milkmaid asked.

'Probably not, at the rate it's taken hold,' the man replied. 'But at least they've managed to salvage a great deal of the contents, and that's something to be thankful for.'

Delia didn't say anything, but she had been thinking exactly the same thing. The drapes on the second floor were now alight and the sound of shattering glass could be heard as armies of servants, not just those from Cliff Tops and Stoneacre, scurried back and forth, pulling tables and chairs, chaises and sofas, paintings and ornaments, out to safety on the lawns. The grand piano had been saved, too, by a scarecrow, some shepherds and a handful of stable boys. It was impossible, in some cases, to distinguish the guests who had been merrymaking only a while before at the ball from the real domestics trying to save their home and livelihood. All were dirtied, grubby and damp.

'Come inside,' their host told those watching by the fence. 'Breathing that smoky air is not good for you.' With a glance backwards, Delia prayed that everyone would get out safely. It was a tragedy to see everything being destroyed like this, but she knew the way these people spent money they could afford to have the house replaced with a bigger and even grander version in jig time. That was not the issue, but it was a sad sight to witness nonetheless.

Hugh and Mr Potter were inside looking up at the atrium. The mezzanine walk that overlooked the grand hall was now alight as the flames engulfed the drapes on the floor-to-ceiling windows along both sides of the open space. The heat was too great for the dousing to have any effect. There was nothing more they could do.

'Get out, everyone. Get out, the ceiling's about to collapse,' Mr Potter roared as they heard a cracking sound above them. 'Leave it. Leave everything and get out. Run, *now*.' Hugh followed him, after a last glance to make sure no one was left behind.

As he crossed the wide hallway towards the porticoed porch, a shower of masonry dropped from a height, its supporting beam weakened by the flames. This was followed by several marble blocks. One of these felled Hugh like a cannon. William A. Potter, running from the sound, was oblivious to what had just happened and only became aware of it as others standing outside the front door began roaring at him.

He turned and saw Hugh firmly pinned to the ground and surrounded by debris.

'Water! We need water before his clothes catch fire. I need help to shift the masonry. Be quick about it or we'll all be caught!' Mr Potter shouted orders. Someone emptied a bucket over Hugh while several others tried to lift the masonry from him. It took several minutes, and sparks and embers continued to rain down on them. Finally, they managed to drag him free and carry him on to the grass.

'Stand back – give him some space!' someone shouted.

Delia was back inside Stoneacre and suddenly felt exhausted. Apart from the excitement of the evening, the fireworks, the dancing and speaking French all night, she realised that she had been standing by the fence watching the house burn for over two hours, and her feet and ankles were protesting.

'They are all going to need refreshments when their work is finished,' she said to Mrs Ellis. 'I think we should go and see if we can boil some water for tea and put cups and things out for them – after all, most of the servants are already next door.'

'How kind of you to think of that,' she replied. 'I'd much rather be doing something than sitting here worrying.'

'So would I,' Delia agreed.

She led a group of women and a few older men into the

kitchens and they went foraging in the pantries. There they found plenty of food. They spread butter on the various breads; they arranged fish and meats that had not been consumed at the dinner earlier on plates and salvers. They sorted platters of pastries and desserts, cheeses, chutneys and pâtés, and set about laying these on the long tables and on trays.

'I'm not sure how you'd like us to put these out,' Madam Duchene said to Mrs Ellis.

'Bring everything to the reception rooms. Everyone is out there working equally hard together. It's no time for pulling rank. Let them have their refreshments together too.'

Delia smiled at the woman, whose plans for hosting a perfect costume ball had been well and truly scuppered. This night would be remembered for a very long time, if only for all the wrong reasons.

'My dear, you look exhausted. I've only just noticed your condition. You've done more than enough – you must sit down at once, and I'll fetch you a cup of tea.' Mrs Ellis wouldn't hear Delia's protestations as she led her to an alcove off the music room. 'It's quieter in here.'

'I'll find you a footstool,' Madame Duchene offered, and as soon as Delia took the weight off her feet she fell asleep.

Minutes later, across the lawns at White Cliffs, the roof collapsed inwards and there was nothing anyone could do anymore. Weary servants and ball guests stood watching the silhouette become engulfed. The helpers dispersed. By morning, only the smouldering shell of the grandiose mansion would remain, its marble staircase leading nowhere and standing proud of the debris, its pillared entrance redundant and foreboding.

The family whose home it had been were now with their neighbours, and the domestics would be given refuge in other houses until decisions could be made about their status. Several of them had suffered minor burns, sore eyes and breathing difficulties.

Hugh Dunne was the only fatality.

Chapter 33

The marriage between Lady Mona Roseanne Kensley-Balfe and the Honourable Desmond Clive Philip Hattersley was due to take place at noon in the little chapel in the village close to Kensley Park. Mrs Murphy, Cook and a few women from the village had been busy preparing everything. The house had been turned over from top to bottom and the upstairs maids had been given new uniforms. The paintwork on the carriages and traps had been refreshed and the horse brasses polished till faces could be seen in them. The grooms had all received new boots, caps and jackets, and Noreen's brother had been brought in to help Tommy with the trunks.

'That's the flowers finished, Your Ladyship.'

'And lovely they look too, Mrs Murphy,' Lady Leonora said.

'Thank you, Your Ladyship. Isn't it just a pity that Miss Delia isn't here to see it?'

Lady Leonora wasn't sure she had heard correctly. The staff had been given very definite instructions not to mention that name in the house ever again. And no one had since she'd run away.

'What was that you said, Mrs Murphy?'

'I said isn't it just a pity that Miss Delia is missing out on the celebrations? I'm sure she'd love to have been here as her sister's maid for her wedding, but instead she's so far away. And with Mr Clement away out foreign too. It would have been nice to have all the family together for such a happy occasion.'

Later Lady Kensley-Balfe told her husband, 'I didn't know how to react. She knows she's forbidden to ever utter her name. It was almost like a reprimand. I had the strongest urge to tell her she was dismissed, but we need her this week, above all others. Then she mentioned Clement being so far away too, and, honestly, it all sounded so innocent. If it had been anyone other than Mrs Murphy, I'd have thought she was playing games with me.'

'My dear, perhaps it was innocent. Perhaps it wasn't. You know that she was always very close to Delia and perhaps she was just speaking her mind.'

'Should I bring it up again, when the wedding guests have gone?'

'No. I'd say it's best to pretend you didn't notice it. She was just saying what I'm sure we've all been thinking too.'

'I can't allow myself to think like that. This is Mona's day, and I'm determined to make it a memorable one for her and not let any sadness tinge it.'

'I appreciate that, but don't you sometimes think Delia paid a very high price for her happiness?'

'You know I do, but she also knew what running away would cost her. She chose to do it, and now she has to live with the consequences. Mona, on the other hand, has done as was expected of her and today is her reward. I'm going to check on her, to see if she's ready to leave for the church.' She gathered her skirts and left the drawing room.

Sir Peter sighed a sigh of resignation and sank back into his armchair. His youngest child wasn't the only one paying a high price for following her heart. He missed her vivacity and chatter, and today's celebrations only emphasised how a big a void Delia had left in his life. He had hoped he'd be able to get around his wife to soften her attitude in time, but that was now looking even more unlikely than ever.

He hadn't told her that Clement had recently been in touch with the family solicitors, instructing them to delve into the purchase deal he had done with Hugh Dunne to see if there was any way the land and the cottages could be reinstated as part of Kensley Park estate. He had also instructed that if anything should happen to his father while he was serving in India, not one penny in land, valuables or assets was to be passed on to Delia and Hugh.

Chapter 34

Delia had no idea how long she had been there in the alcove or how long she'd been asleep. It was the increased volume of voices close by that brought her back to consciousness. Mr William Appleton Potter was kneeling by her chair, his scarecrow wig missing, his face and hands sooty and grimed.

'Is the fire out?' she asked.

'Not yet, but we did our best – we rescued what we could.'

'Leave them alone,' someone whispered, too loudly.

'She has to be told, sooner or later,' came the riposte. 'And there's a child on the way. Their first.'

'They can't keep it from her forever.'

'There's never a right time, or even a right way.'

'Let's leave him to it. They worked together.'

Her chest tightened as the import of what was being implied filtered through. Fully awake now, she looked at the faces around her and she knew something dreadful had happened. But what? Was it her they were talking about?

'What is it? Has Hugh been injured?' she asked the chief, but even as she did so some primeval sense told her that Hugh was gone. She became engulfed in a great, wide, endless emptiness. She physically felt the loss of his energy in the world.

'I'm afraid it's worse than that,' he said, taking her hand in his.

'How did it happen?' she asked. 'He wasn't burned. Please tell me he didn't perish in the flames.'

'No, he didn't, Delia. He wasn't burned at all.' There was no way he could soften the facts. 'It was instantaneous. He was struck by falling masonry and would have felt nothing.'

'Where is he? I want to go to him.'

'We've taken him to one of the bedrooms upstairs.'

'Here?'

'Yes here.' He let this sit for a few seconds before adding, 'I've sent for Grace. She should be here presently.'

'That's very kind of you, but I'd like to be with him.'

'Why not wait until Grace arrives?' he urged.

'I'd prefer to do it now. Please,' she implored.

'Then may I accompany you, Delia?' he offered.

She nodded. 'Please do.'

Her head held high, she took his arm, while shepherdesses, gypsies, huntsmen, the butler and footmen, housekeeper, upstairs maids, servants, farmhands and milkmaids paused from taking the refreshments she had helped prepare and stood in silence as he led her up the grand staircase to be with her husband.

She let out a cry when she saw him. The body lying on the snowy sheets wasn't her Hugh. It looked just like him, but his essence had evaporated. Her valiant, vibrant Hugh, who had made her fall in love with him, had vanished. His spirit was no more. She felt her heart break.

'Oh Hugh, what have you done?' she asked him. 'You promised you'd never leave me.' Unconsciously, she spread her hands over her tummy as their baby moved, perhaps sensing their loss. 'You promised, Hugh. You promised.' She leaned over him, her tears falling on his face.

'I'll never forget you,' she told his lifeless form, as she wiped them away. She brushed his damp hair off his forehead, She touched his hands, which were still warm, and held them for a few moments in hers. She bent down and kissed him. Although someone had washed him and removed the Little Boy Blue shirt she had worked on, replacing it with a white nightshirt, he still smelt of smoke and smouldering timber.

'I have no idea what will become of us or where our lives will take us, but you'll always be there in them, Hugh. Always. And this little one will know everything about you: how wonderful you were, and how happy we were, and all the plans we had made for our future together. I promise you that. He or she will always know how much I loved you and how loveable you were.'

Chapter 35

She had forgotten the chief was in the room, standing there. She turned to him and he held his arms out to her.

'I'm so sorry. Delia,' he said. 'Words are inadequate to express how I feel.'

They hugged each other and she said, 'He's too young to be dead. He'll never get to hold his baby, and his baby won't ever know him. I don't know what I'll do without him. Why did this happen?' She wiped her eyes.

'I can't answer that, Delia. The ways of the world are strange and they don't follow any patterns. Just know, if there's anything I can do, you only have to ask.'

She couldn't think straight – the pain inside her was too deep. There were so many questions that needed answers but, instinctively, she knew there would be plenty of time for those – she had her whole lifetime ahead of her without him.

'You were very good to him,' she told the chief.

'I had great respect and affection for him, both personally

and professionally. He's been my apprentice for several years. and during that time he showed real talent and vision. I looked on him almost as a son.'

'He saw Gull Haven as his calling card, his gateway to success.'

'And so it would have been, Delia. I don't doubt that, and I give you my word that we'll finish it exactly as he planned it should be. That's the least we can do to honour him.'

A knock on the door announced Grace's arrival. 'My dear sweet Jesus, how could you let this happen?' she said, making the sign of the cross as she walked by Delia and directly to the bed. 'What did they do to deserve any of this?' She didn't touch Hugh, just stood looking incredulously, as though waiting for him to waken up and answer her. 'Holy Mother of God, I'm finding it very hard to find your mercy in any of this. Felling a young man when he's helping his neighbours, and leaving a young widow and an unborn babe. How can that fit in to your divine plans? I don't understand any of it.' She sobbed and Mr Potter led her to a chair and held his hand on her shoulder.

'Sometimes there are no explanations, leastways none that we can fathom,' he said.

'What do we do now?' she asked him. 'When I lost my husband, my sister's husband took care of all ... of all the arrangements.'

'Can I suggest you ladies try to get some rest, if you're able?

Our hosts have put some rooms at your disposal and a maid too. Everything else can wait until later in the day to be discussed. It's all a bit chaotic in the household, as you can imagine. Try not to concern yourself with anything else just now. It'll all be taken care of. I'll see to that.'

Delia went back to the bed and looked down at Hugh, remembering the first time she'd seen him as she sat in an ungainly fashion where her horse had thrown her. They had come so far in such a short space of time and had known great passion and happiness. Was this the price that had to be paid for that?

She leaned over and whispered, 'Goodbye, my darling, wherever you've gone. Thank you for everything you've given me.' She kissed him on the lips, stroked his tousled hair again and took one last look at him before leaving the room.

Mrs Ellis was waiting outside the door when she emerged with Grace, and she led them to the rooms they'd been assigned. Delia caught sight of herself in a mirror. Seeing herself in fancy dress just added to the unreality of the past night. For a second, she thought it was all a bad dream, but on a visceral level she knew it wasn't. There would be no waking up to find that none of this had happened. There would be no way to erase the memory either. Earlier she had told him she'd never forget this night. Little had she known then how prophetic those words would turn out to be.

Grace helped her undress and put her to bed.

She did manage to go to sleep, her arms across her tummy, protecting her precious cargo, not wanting to wake up ever again.

When she did, she was surprised to find some of her clothes already laid out on the chaise longue. Grace must have organised it. A maidservant filled a hip bath for her. She undressed, knowing there was no way she could avoid what was ahead. She couldn't cry. To do so would be to acknowledge her new reality. By not doing so, she was holding back the inevitable acceptance that her beloved husband was gone and that she was now a widow.

Mrs Ellis came to her room. She had tears in her eyes as she talked to her. 'Mr Potter has promised to take charge of everything, and when you feel up to it, he needs to talk to you about some of the arrangements.'

'You're all so kind. Thank you. Should I come downstairs?'

'Of course, whenever you feel up to it.'

The chief was drinking tea with the Ellises when she arrived down with Grace.

Mrs Ellis and her husband stood up. 'Please be seated.' He said. My wife and I want you to know that you are welcome to stay as long as you like with us, and if there is anything we can do, anything at all, then please ask.'

'I don't know how to thank you. You've been so kind already. I can never repay you for bringing Hugh here.' her voice broke.

'There is nothing to repay,' Mrs Ellis said and her husband added, 'Come dear, we'll leave the ladies to their business with Mr Potter. We'll be in the library should you need us for anything.'

'I'm so sorry to disturb you at this stage, Delia, Did you sleep?' the chief asked,

She nodded. 'A little.'

Mr Potter began, 'I apologise, Delia, for addressing such matters. This is a very delicate and awkward conversation to have but there is no way to avoid it. I'm sure you never considered such matters, but decisions have to be made as soon as possible as to whether you want Hugh's final resting place to be in New York or here in Newport.'

'You're right. We never had that conversation. I suppose we never thought we'd need to for a long time yet, for a lifetime even,' she answered, and as she did she remembered something. 'When we were dancing that night, just minutes before we heard about the fire, Hugh told me that he'd love to eventually settle down in Newport and he talked of building a house for us here. And I agreed. That was the last conversation we had. Isn't that strange? Do you think he had a premonition?'

'I couldn't answer that, Delia. Do you?'

'No. But it seems odd somehow, almost as though he was telling me something, that he wanted to stay in Newport. He has to stay here.'

'I think that's what he'd have wanted.' Grace said. 'He was very happy here.'

'What about you, Delia – what will you do?' he asked. 'Do you think you might go back to Ireland?'

'That's not an option. I'll have to find work to keep my baby and me,' she replied.

'You could come back to New York with me,' Grace said, 'until the baby is born, before making any big decisions.'

'I can't think properly. It's all happened too quickly and I don't think I'm ready to accept that I'll never see Hugh again. I can't really believe that he's dead,' she said.

The chief said, 'That's perfectly understandable and there's no need to rush into making any of those decisions just yet. The house is rented until next year and you're welcome to stay on there as long as you like.'

'I can't impose. I'll find a way of making money and paying you back for your kindness. I can become a tutor and teach piano or take in sewing. I'm not afraid of hard work,' she said.

'Let's not worry about things like that for the moment,' Mr Potter said. 'I was thinking of asking James Brown Lord to step in and supervise the work on Gull Haven. He's just about to finish his apprenticeship at the firm, and he and Hugh worked closely together on several projects. I'll personally oversee it all, to make sure that everything is done as Hugh wanted it,' the chief said.

'I remember him, and Hugh often talked about him. I think he would approve.'

'I think he would too,' Mr Potter replied.

'I know they've been really kind, but do you think the Ellises would be offended if we went back home? I feel the need to be in familiar surroundings,' she said.

'I'm sure they'll understand.'

'Have you contacted the rest of the family?' she asked Grace.

'Yes, Mr Potter sent wires off to them earlier today for me.'

'I notified Mrs Parks too,' he said. 'I was sure she'd like to be informed. But what about your family in Ireland? Is there anyone you'd like me to notify?'

She hesitated and, remembering the altercation with her parents and Clement, unconsciously pushed her hair back and felt her scar and said, 'No, thank you. I'll do that and I'd like to tell Noreen myself. Hugh was very fond of her and she of him.'

'I think she may already have heard by now. A tragedy like that is big news in a small place, especially among the Irish community,' Grace replied. 'But I'll send a note to Mrs Bradley and ask if she'll let her come to the house to see you later today. And, Delia, you need to think of yourself and your confinement. Let's get you home and into bed.'

The next few weeks passed in a blur, with Delia unaware of anything going on around her. Her sadness was almost overwhelming at times. She got through the days following

Hugh's death and burial, only because the baby growing inside her gave her regular reminders of his or her presence.

She told Grace, 'I feel with every kick it's telling me not to feel sorry for myself, but rather to think about us and what we are going to do.'

'And what will that be? I don't mean to be indelicate, but have you any money, from Hugh or from your family? You can't stay on here on your own after the child is born.'

'There's the income from your father's patent, the one he left Hugh, and that will see me through for the immediate future.'

'And have you decided where you'll live?'

'I honestly don't know yet, Grace. I've been avoiding making decisions. I would like to have stayed on here, although that's not practical right now unless I find a means of support. I can manage to eke things out until after the baby arrives. Mr Potter insists that I'm welcome to remain in the house indefinitely, but I know it's needed for Hugh's replacement. He can't be expected to live with a widow and a new baby.'

'You have all my support, and I still think you should consider coming back to New York with me,' she said.

'I can't monopolise your life, Grace. You've given me so much already. I don't know what I would have done without you.'

'Well, I'm not going to abandon you now. As you know my apartment is small and cramped and it's not what you've had here. It's not even in a very good neighbourhood any more. But it's where the family, your family now, is, and we'll be able to help until you've decided what's best for the future. You'll have Peggy, Kate, the other cousins and Noreen around you for support and that's important. Here you'll have no one.'

'It does seem to be the best solution, but it will only be temporary. I promise you that.'

'Then I'll start making arrangements.' Grace paused, then said, 'Would you consider selling the little cottages in Ireland?'

'No. They are Hugh's legacy to his child. Unless I'm destitute, I won't sell those.'

'You could always try writing to your parents again, asking them to help in the circumstances. I'm sure when they hear what's happened they'd be willing to help you. Or, if you like, I could do it for you?'

'Never. Grace. I won't do that. That would be the ultimate betrayal of Hugh.'

Later, when she was lying down that afternoon, taking the weight off her swollen feet and ankles, she contemplated her future. It wasn't going to be easy. Something triggered a distant memory, a memory of the time her father had summoned both Mona and her to his study to sign papers in the presence of two solicitors at law. Something to do with her grandma's legacy to the girls. She recalled it would only be payable on their twenty first birthdays, and only if they had been unmarried.

No, it was not going to be easy making her own way as a single mother in a foreign country, but she'd do it. She owed it to Hugh and herself to do so.

She had a few pieces of jewellery from both her grandmothers. They might be worth something. Hugh had left a small sum of money in the bank and the Mulroneys had insisted on lodging a tidy sum towards the baby, as a goodwill gesture for Hugh's help on the night their house had burnt down. Yes, she'd manage until after the baby was born. Then there would be decisions to be made.

Chapter 36

Delia didn't go out much over the next few weeks, but supervised the packing of her personal possessions with Grace and Mrs Flynn's help. Knowing there would be no space at Garce's apartment, she asked Mr Potter if she could leave some trunks in one of the attic rooms.

She was finding it difficult to get around and the heat wasn't helping. She felt constantly drained and tired and her back hurt. She still took her tea into Hugh's studio each morning and sat where she used to sit when he was working. It was here she felt closest to him, and she wasn't looking forward to leaving this behind, because in doing so she was consciously and deliberately letting go of something she'd never get back again. As she sat, she realised she had done a lot of that in the past year, and he would want her to keep going forward.

She'd let go of convention, and in doing so she'd let go of her family, swapped them for Hugh's, and now here she was again, letting go of the idyllic months they had shared in this house and this place, which they both had loved.

James Brown Lord arrived in Newport and Mr Potter brought him to Touro Street to see Hugh's plans.

She offered him Hugh's key. 'You must come and go as necessary. Everything you need to know about Gull Haven is in there.'

'You seem very knowledgeable about it all. I should take you on as my apprentice,' he remarked.

'That's what Hugh used to say.' She smiled at the memory. 'He talked a lot to me about the processes and taught me how to read the plans. Oh, and you might need to know that the final drawings for the stained-glass dome, which is being manufactured in France, are all there in that alcove.'

James looked at the chief and said, 'Definitely, I need this woman on my team.'

He laughed. 'I'm inclined to agree, but I'm about to escort her back to New York, so you'll have to soldier on your own.'

Three days later they were back in the bustling, noisy, hot city. Hugh had been right – the air was rank and she felt she was suffocating after the clear sea air of Newport. Noreen had promised to visit as soon as her family returned to their Fifth Avenue mansion.

Grace did everything she could to make Delia comfortable, and if it were not for her warm and loving care, Delia would have despaired of bringing a new baby into such circumstances. The apartment was cramped, and the bedroom she would share with her infant scarcely had enough room for more than the chest of drawers, the wardrobe, the single bed, a chair and a bassinet. She couldn't help remembering her bedroom in Kensley Park and the nursery she shared with Mona.

'This is where I do – did most of my sewing,' Grace said.

'I'm sorry to be such a nuisance. I'm really disrupting your life.'

'Don't talk like that, child. You're the most important thing right now.'

Peggy was one of the first among a constant stream of visitors from Hugh's family, all calling to offer their sympathy. 'Forgive me for asking, but I speak my mind,' she said. 'How will you be able to manage?'

'I have enough to carry me through until after the baby arrives. I thought perhaps then that I could become a governess or a tutor to one of the New York families. I could teach French and the piano too.'

'She could also teach drawing – I've seen her sketches and she has a real talent, Peggy. And she can sew too.'

Peggy smiled. 'Maybe I was wrong about you. I think I might have judged you too quickly.'

'Or perhaps I've come out of my cocoon. I'm not as helpless as you first thought, Peggy, and I still have a lot to learn, but you'll see that I'm willing to work hard to prove it.'

'Well, Hugh would certainly be proud of you,' Peggy replied.

'He *was* proud of her,' Grace said. 'I have to admit, Delia, that my sister was not alone in forming those opinions. I was just as critical when we met you, I might have hidden it better though,' she laughed, 'Because you were so young and had led such a sheltered life I never thought you'd be such a survivor. Now look at you, about to become a mother, widowed and not yet eighteen.'

Mrs Parks couldn't come to the apartment. The stairs were too much for her. Instead she invited Delia and Grace for afternoon tea. She welcomed them warmly and was visibly sad when talking about Hugh and his untimely end.

'It's hard to believe that it's not even a year since William Potter brought him here to view the apartment. He and my husband were great friends, and he knew I was struggling with loneliness in this big house after he died. It was he who suggested that I take someone in. I rejected the idea out of hand at first, and then he arrived with Hugh one day, on the pretext of being in the neighbourhood visiting some site or other. But I knew him better than that, and when he told me that the young man was about to get married, that his bride was on her way from Ireland and that they'd be needing an apartment, I saw the sense in it. And that was even before

I met you! And I have to confess I liked him instantly.' She reached her hand over and covered Delia's.

'So did I,' Delia said and smiled at the memory. 'I think I fell in love with him the moment I set eyes on him.'

'I can understand that. He was a very fine young man,' Mrs Parks said. 'You must be heartbroken.'

'I am,' Delia said. 'I can't believe our baby will never know its father, but I'm trying not to allow myself to think like that. I don't want it being born feeling sad and forlorn.'

'Oh, how brave you are.'

'I'm not brave, Mrs Parks. I'm just trying to be a realist to survive this. I keep telling myself that everyone loses people they love as they go through life, some sooner than others. You lost your husband. Mrs Murphy, our old housekeeper, was the only one left in her family after the great famine and she ended up in the workhouse. Hugh spoke about watching his parents die slowly, as the result of bad health brought on by the hunger and conditions in the forties and fifties. And I know he never stopped missing his grandfather. I survived the smallpox epidemic on and around our estates, and I honestly feel there must be a reason somewhere as to why I did, while Noreen's mother buried two of her little children at that time. Like Hugh, they were healthy, vibrant and young one minute and the next they were taken away.'

'You *are* brave, Delia. If the little one has half the spirit of either of you, you'll have no worries at all,' Mrs Parks remarked.

'And may I say that, despite the awful circumstances, I'm so pleased to have you back in New York. I missed hearing you play and I missed you reading to me.'

'I'll have to make that up to you before motherhood makes more demands on me,' she said, and Grace interrupted, 'But not now, Mrs Parks, if you can excuse us. She needs her rest.'

'Will you both please come again soon? Would Friday be an imposition?'

'No, it certainly wouldn't be,' Delia assured her before leaving.

Later she sat sketching, sitting on the squashy sofa that had seen better days. Grace said, 'I never heard you talk so freely about your life in Ireland. Have you changed your mind about people knowing who you are?'

'Who am I?'

'Well, your title and all that ...'

'That doesn't mean a thing to me. I'm Mrs Hugh Dunne, a widow, that's who I am, and whoever I was before merely contributed to making me that. And do you know, Grace, for all that I cannot imagine a future without Hugh in it, I wouldn't trade any one of those short months I spent with him for anything or anyone.'

'He really loved you.'

'He did. I know that in here,' she said, touching her breast.

'What are you sketching?'

'My memories. I can't let them fade. Every time I think of him lying lifeless in the bed in Stoneacre, I immediately try to visualise him dressed as Little Boy Blue, in the outfit he thought was too dandified, and of the two of us dancing around that enormous ballroom enjoying ourselves, making plans for our future in Newport. Although it fills me with sadness and longing, it also makes me smile. Then I move on to other memories. There are so many, yet so few. Don't you see why I can't let any of them fade away?'

'I do.'

She went into labour a few weeks before she was expected to, and Grace sent for the midwife, a big Irish woman who came with the recommendation that she had 'delivered all the babies for everyone for miles around, even a priest's child one time, God save us and bless us'.

'I think this little one is in a hurry to meet its mother,' the woman said after examining Delia. 'I don't think she should be here for another few weeks, but that can be a blessing in itself as it sometimes makes the birthing easier.'

If this was the easier version, Delia was pleased she didn't have to experience the difficult one. Grace and Peggy were on hand throughout the whole procedure. Grace had sent a note to Mrs Bradley asking if, in the circumstances, Noreen could be allowed some time off to be there too. 'She's the only person Delia has in America, and they came from Ireland together. Noreen was also a witness at the young people's wedding last November.'

Mrs Bradley agreed at once. She too would miss Hugh and never forget how he had helped her son from straying off the right path.

Eventually the contractions became stronger and more frequent, and Delia bit her lip to prevent her from crying out in pain, frustration and desperation.

'I can't do this. I don't want to do it on my own. I want Hugh. I need Hugh,' she called as the baby crowned and Noreen held one hand, Grace the other.

'It'll be all right. You'll see.' Grace muttered. 'We'll all be here for you.'

'Just another big push and you'll never be alone again,' the midwife said, and then, 'There, you have a fine healthy baby boy, a little son.'

As the midwife wrapped the squirming baby in a linen cloth, a tiny hand fought the air as though in a victory salute, and Delia cried as she had never cried before.

She cried for herself, for Hugh, for her son and the father he'd never meet, for the family she had who didn't even care to know about his arrival. She only stopped when the midwife put her baby to her breast.

'Try to relax – babies can sense unhappiness, and you don't want this little mite to think he's not loved or wanted, do you?'

Shocked by this Delia sat upright in the bed. 'Of course he's loved and wanted, more than anything in the world.'

'Then let him know that. Nurse him. The bond between a mother and her baby is stronger than any other.'

All around her people came and went, cleaning up and bathing both her and the newborn and putting the world to rights again. Eventually she fell asleep.

Delia decided that Fr O'Hara, the parish priest of St Jerome's, who had married them, should baptise their son too. It was her first time to leave the house since the birth and she watched as the holy water was poured over the baby's head, held by both his godparents, Grace and William Appleton Potter.

Afterwards they all congregated in Peggy and Dan's apartment for refreshments, and Delia held the sleeping babe in her arms as everyone chatted and laughed. Much to everyone's amazement she had decided not to call him Hugh, after his father. For her there would ever only be one Hugh, in her heart and in her life. Instead he was to be called Peter, after her father and Jack after Hugh's beloved granda. She had chosen Peter as an act of faith, that they might meet each other some day.

The sound of a glass being clinked got everyone's attention, and when they were hushed, Mr Potter spoke.

'As I'm now an honorary member of this family, I'd like to propose a toast, not only to this young man, Peter Jack Dunne, but to his courageous and gracious mother, and to tell her how much we admire and support her on this special day. It's memorable to be sure, for being his naming day, but also for another very special reason ..."

Delia was confused. What was he talking about?

He continued, 'Fr O'Hara told me earlier, this is also the day his mother, Delia, comes of age and I'd like to be the first to wish you a happy birthday.'

Dates hadn't meant much to her since Hugh died, and with the new demands on her, hours, days and nights just seemed to run into each other. It was the baby's christening. Then she realised it was her birthday. Her actual birthday. Her eighteenth birthday and that she had indeed come of age.

She wasn't where she wanted to be after all that had happened in her short life, but she knew where she wanted to go. There was a place for her in the world. She had no doubts about that. Now she just had to find it. She would go back to Newport and build the future Hugh had planned for them.

The baby opened his eyes as if to see what all the commotion was about. She looked into his blue eyes, his father's eyes, and said 'We'll do it together. You'll see. We'll do it together.'

Acknowledgements

As always, no book arrives on the shelves without enormous backup and I'd like to give a big shout out to all at Hachette Ireland, on this my eighth novel with them, and my first foray into historical fiction.

Top of the list comes my editorial director, Ciara Doorley, for, as always, allowing me the freedom to let my novels wander in the direction they want to go.

I have to mention Joanna Smyth, Editorial & Marketing Manager, for always being cheerfully efficient no matter how trivial or annoying my queries are.

For my copy editor Emma Dunne, for her wonderful hawk eye for missing commas, glaring mistakes and attention to detail.

Then there are the design and marketing teams who get my books noticed and out onto the bookshelves. Thank you all.

I must also include Kathryn Farrington, Vice-president of Discover Newport, Newport, Rhode Island and her associates, who facilitated me and afforded me access, above and below stairs, in the grandiose mansions of the Gilded Age.

I must also mention Mr Michael Slein, President of the Museum of Irish History there too, for sharing his knowledge and for his wonderful tour of the environs.

Some of this book was written in the Tyrone Guthrie Centre in Monaghan, where inspiration, laughter, creativity and friendship feed the soul and the mind. You know who you are – miss you all.

I mustn't forget my readers – without you there'd be no reason to write. I love getting your feedback and comments and appreciate your support.

I hope you enjoyed *A Suitable Marriage*.

Author's Notes

A Suitable Marriage is set in 1886, when class distinction, rank and knowing your place were very important elements in society. The Home Rule Bill was being debated in Gladstone's parliament and my fictitious family, the Kensley-Balfes, were preparing for their elder daughter's presentation to Queen Victoria, and Lord Kensley-Balfe 'did something' in Dublin Castle.

Whilst this story is purely fictional, some characters, places and establishments did exist at the time. Other factual historical events are alluded to in the text and these helped me set the story in the correct time line.

Liberty of London had opened eleven years earlier and had recently expanded, introducing exciting new exotic goods and *objets d'art* from the Orient. They brought forty-two villagers from India to stage a living village of artisans and suddenly their imported jewel-coloured tussore Indian silks were all in demand by high society.

Lord Frederick Temple Hamilton-Temple-Blackwood was Viceroy of India at this time. He was married to an Irish woman from Killyleagh Castle in County Down, Hariot Georgina Rowan-Hamilton. When he became viceroy she joined him in India and, at Queen Victoria's behest, she initiated a plan to improve the situation 'for women in illness and in child-bearing'. She raised enormous amounts of money from donors such as the Maharajahs of Kashmir and Durbungha. Thus the Countess of Dufferin Fund was established. Some of these hospitals and clinics still exist under her name.

Major Dennis Mahon of Strokestown, Co Roscommon was assassinated by some of his tenants during the famine. In the summer of 1847, he is reputed to have paid £4,000 for the emigration of 1,432 of his tenants to Canada. A quarter of these died at sea. Understandably, when this news reached Ireland, many others refused to leave. His response was to evict 600 families from his estates, numbering about 3,000 people. He had their cabins and shacks burned so they couldn't return.

J.L. Mott Iron Works, where Hugh's grandfather worked, did exist in New York, and was run by four successive Mott family members. It gave its name to Mott Street and Mott Haven on the Harlem River and made the first stoves for burning anthracite coal.

My fictitious and, not very charismatic, Lady Constance was a stickler for convention and protocol. Whilst you may think she was exaggerating when she told them that they had over sixty-six categories on this – she wasn't. There was an actual official government list that one could consult so that people didn't make faux pas. And that was apart from ceremonial customs and rituals that had to be observed too.

The 'fishing fleet' was a rather deprecating term given to young ladies who had failed to make a match during their debutante and immediate subsequent years. To broaden their chances of escaping spinsterhood, many of them headed across the sea to India to try their luck with the eligible men who were working in administration and in the services.

Ellen Terry and Henry Irving were the talk of London town and dominated the stage at the Lyceum Theatre for many years. They were playing in Shakespeare's *Merchant of Venice* when my characters were there.

The Dublin Horse Show, in conjunction with the Royal Agricultural Society of Ireland, held one of the earliest 'horse-leaping' competitions. The Horse Show continues as an annual event to this day.

The Shelbourne Hotel was the hotel of preference for the gentry visiting the city. St Stephen's Park Temperance Hotel, located on the corner with Harcourt Street, also commanded splendid views of St Stephen's Green, which had been handed over to the people of Dublin by Lord Ardilaun of the Guinness brewing family in 1860.

Clery's was the best shopping emporium and was right across from Nelson's Pillar, Eason and the General Post

Office on Dublin's main thoroughfare, Sackville Street, now O'Connell Street. The Spire now stands where the Pillar once did.

Variety shows were a popular form of entertainment. Dan Lowrey's Music Hall was one of the venues for such amusement and visiting acts. It's now the Olympia Theatre. And the lights are still on in the Gaiety Theatre in South King Street.

Society hostesses in Ireland at the time often included pieces from William Vincent Wallace's *Maritana* and from Michael William Balfe's *The Bohemian Girl* operas in their soirées, as well as melodies from Thomas Moore.

In Liverpool the Stella Maris Boarding House was well known to those emigrating to seek their fortunes in America, whichever line they choose to travel with. My characters used the Cunard Steamship Line and boarded the RMS *Etruria*, bound for New York on 23 October 1886. Queenstown, now called Cobh, in County Cork was its last embarkation port.

When writing this book, I hadn't known that was exactly the time the Statue of Liberty had been unveiled, that the designers had intended it to be a lighthouse, or that it features a broken chain under one of the Liberty's feet to symbolise the end of slavery. I just knew it had been gifted to America by France.

My characters arrived in the new world via the Castle Garden Emigrant Depot, which predated Ellis Island, where most Irish immigrants touch landfall in the following years.

St Jerome's Roman Catholic Church has long since since been replaced by a larger one and Alexander Ave, where Mrs Parks lived, was indeed known as Doctor's Row, and later as the Irish Fifth Avenue.

I have Hugh apprenticed with James Brown Lord to Mr William Appleton Potter, who was one of New York's most prominent architects at the time. He is still remembered for his buildings at Princeton University and for Admiral Charles Baldwin's house and the Ellises' Stoneacre cottage at Newport. Salve Regina University now owns an existing part of this estate. Their main professional rivals Morris Hunt and Stanford White, are also mentioned and all of have left their mark on the edifices of the Gilded Age.

Among the New York sights to beguile Delia and Noreen when they arrived in America were R. H. Macy & Co. and Bloomingdales – some of the first department stores in the world – and Pearl Street Power Station. This was illuminated with so many electric lights it dazzled with the promise of a brightly lit future for everyone.

The Irish are credited with building much of Newport, Rhode Island. In the early years of 1800s many miners left the Allahies in Cork and settled to work the mines there. When these closed down they gravitated towards work on the railroads. The Irish who came from Kerry were mainly the stonemasons, who worked on the impressive Fort Adams, a national landmark today. They settled close to each other and are reputed with building the fifth ward in the rapidly growing town.

The majority of domestic servants in the mansions were Irish too. On their days off they congregated at the top of the 40 Steps on the Cliff Walk to dance and sing songs from home. Many met their future spouses at such gatherings.

I found The Museum of Irish History a great source of interesting snippets of the rich heritage

One of my characters has a relative working in the cotton mills at Fall River. At this time over one sixth of cotton in New England was produced there, hence its moniker 'Spindle City'.

Of the thousands who worked in that industry, most were Irish and French Canadians. The mill owners had thousands of wooden-framed multi-family buildings made to accommodate them. These were usually three-floors and were known as triple-deckers. The mills themselves were enormous and, since the demise of the cotton industry, several have been repurposed for other uses today.

The proximity of the hoi polloi didn't please the upper classes in Newport. They objected to the influx of these workers to their beaches on their half days off. The gentry had had Easton's Beach. Or at least they had until the new trolley service brought the mill workers over from Fall River. Not wishing to associate with those who 'ate their lunch from buckets,' they relocated to Bailey's Beach and formed their own exclusive club. Today it's still private, with a waiting list where new members are added only when old ones die.

Bannister's Wharf is now the centre point of social and commercial life of the waterfront, full of interesting shops and wonderful restaurants, as well as the centre of festivals, water events and the place to watch firework displays.

In the Gilded Age being a member of the New York Yacht Club was *de rigeur* and a sign that you were accepted. While the women made social calls, the gentlemen spent their time on the waves, in a vain attempt to compete with William Vanderbilt, owner of the world's biggest yacht, called Alva after his wife. It cost a half a million dollars and had a permanent crew of twenty-seven. Another name to be reckoned with then was the notorious rake James Gordon Bennett Junior. The New York Herald had been started by his father and he inherited this at a very young age. Before he was twenty he had won the first trans-Atlantic yacht race from Newport to the Isle of Wight, and this is reputed to have been the start of the Americas Cup. Gordon Bennett Junior also built the Casino, introduced polo to the US, and built the Tennis Hall of Fame, all across the road from his mansion.

He also allegedly urinated into a fireplace at his engagement party, in his future in law's home, in front of their guests. That didn't go down very well, so he self-exiled in Paris for several years after. The Vanderbilt brothers' houses, the Breakers and the Marble House, were greatly responsible for the coining of the term, The Gilded Age. They are two of the most spectacular 'cottages' which still remain and which part of the ten surviving mansions from that period that are open to the public. These imitation French chateaux, Italian palazzos, Gothic and Shingle style homes are now all owned by The Preservation Society of Newport County and are the venues for food festivals and musical events.

As for the rest of my characters – they lived only in my imagination.

murielbolger@gmail.com